Unicorn on a Roll

Another Phoebe and Her Unicorn Adventure

Complete Your Phoebe and Her Unicorn Collection

Phoebe and Her Unicorn
Dana Simpson

Unicorn vs. Goblins
Another Phoebe and Her Unicorn Adventure
Dana Simpson

Razzle Dazzle Unicorn
Another Phoebe and Her Unicorn Adventure
Dana Simpson

Unicorn Crossing
Another Phoebe and Her Unicorn Adventure
Dana Simpson

Phoebe and Her Unicorn in
The Magic Storm
Dana Simpson

Unicorn of Many Hats
Another Phoebe and Her Unicorn Adventure
Dana Simpson

Phoebe and Her Unicorn in
Unicorn Theater
Dana Simpson

Unicorn Bowling
Another Phoebe and Her Unicorn Adventure
Dana Simpson

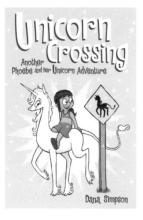

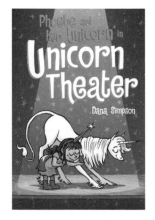

Unicorn on a Roll

Another Phoebe and Her Unicorn Adventure

Dana Simpson

Andrews McMeel
PUBLISHING®

INTRODUCTION

It was not long ago that if I suggested you should check out a clever, funny, sweet daily comic about a girl and her unicorn, I would have had to endure some eye rolls and serious questions about my maturity level.

But the times, they are a-changin' Dana Simpson's *Phoebe and Her Unicorn* has arrived at just the right time to perpetuate an unprecedented shift in opinion and openness to the genuine thoughts, feelings, experiences—and humor—in the lives of authentic girls.

In modern media, women and girls are finally starting to be seen as regular plain old human beings. Fifty years ago—heck, fif*teen* years ago—almost any depiction of a young girl would be some sort of hyperidealized version of childhood femininity. Girls in comics and cartoons were either precocious little sprites; bossy, irritating nags; or ethereal, fragile beauties, even at their tender ages. They were characters created by observers and idealizers, and because of this vantage, the audience watched them from a distance. But the characterization of Phoebe is indicative of a very recent, very new, very refreshing change of perspective of who girls really are. Though she is a girl who has many interests that are the usual girlish things, she is relatable to all regardless of gender or age. We don't watch her from the cheap seats; we are right up there with her on the stage, flaws and all. She's not a little Kewpie doll to be protected or admired; rather, we see ourselves reflected back in her. She is not just every girl; she is every child. She is US.

Now let's talk Marigold Heavenly Nostrils. Vanity, the supposedly "feminine" personality flaw usually assigned to antagonists and villains, is turned on its head. Yes, Marigold is vain, but she is caring and attentive, she keeps her promises, and though she reminds us all that every creature is basically beneath her magical majesty, she certainly doesn't treat anyone that way. She is riddled with self-love and is utterly unapologetic. And couldn't we all stand to feel a little more free to love ourselves? Her vanity is not portrayed as a trait worthy of revile, but as something that makes her funny, fun to be around, and utterly endearing. Some would say these are some pretty essential qualities in a BFF.

And when paired together, these two very modern depictions of female archetypes not only demonstrate for us a heartwarming, true friendship—they show us a little of ourselves; a little of what we aspire to be; and, perhaps most important of all, they make us laugh.

So hopefully soon the days of rolling our eyes at little girls and their dreams of magic and unicorns will be gone. It's about time that all of us, like Dana, realized that little girls are onto something. That bringing a little magic into our world is all it takes to help us through the trials and tribulations of life. So sit back and enjoy—girl, boy, child, adult—*Phoebe and Her Unicorn* is for YOU.

— Lauren Faust
January 2015

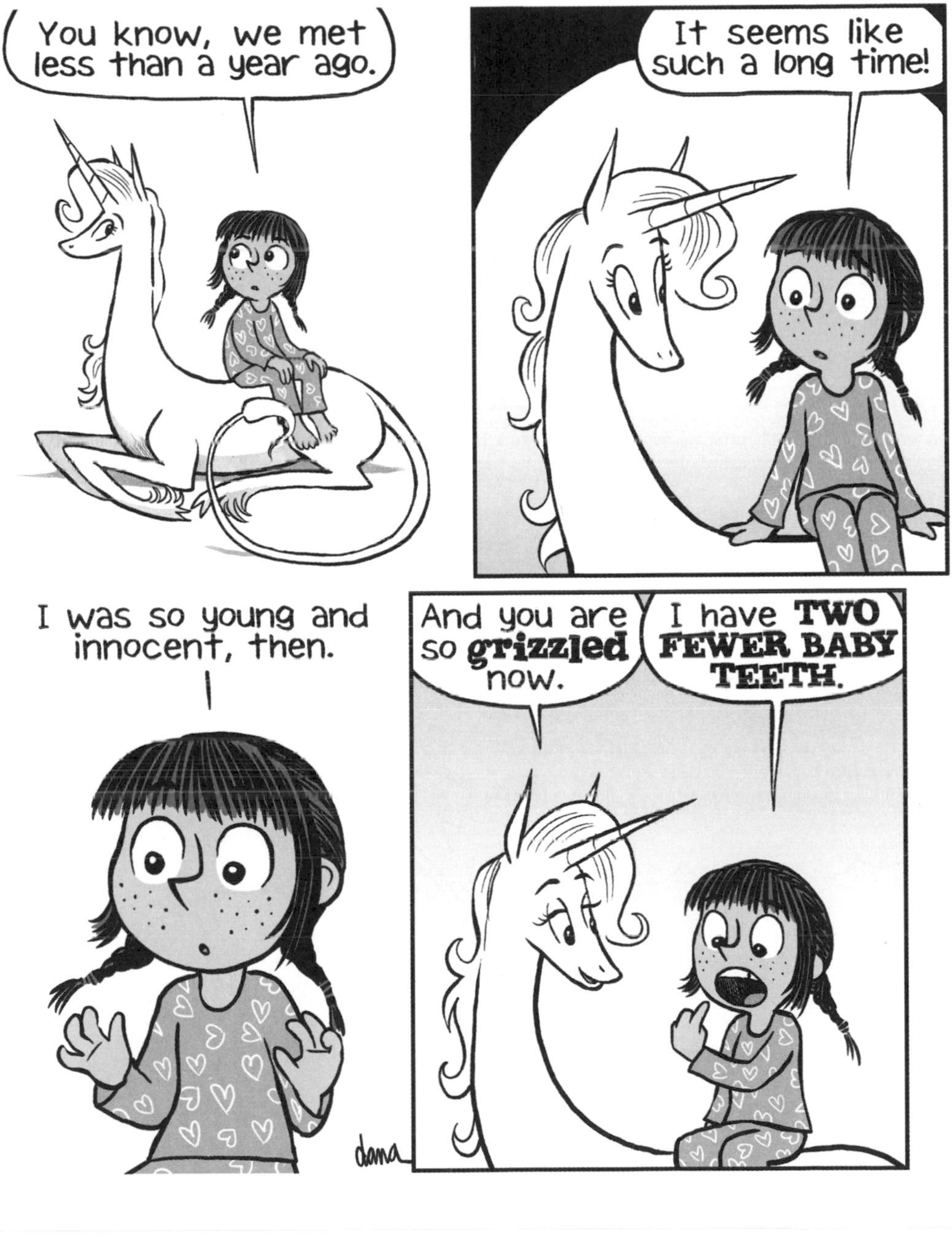
You know, we met less than a year ago.
It seems like such a long time!
I was so young and innocent, then.
And you are so **grizzled** now.
I have **TWO FEWER BABY TEETH**.
dana

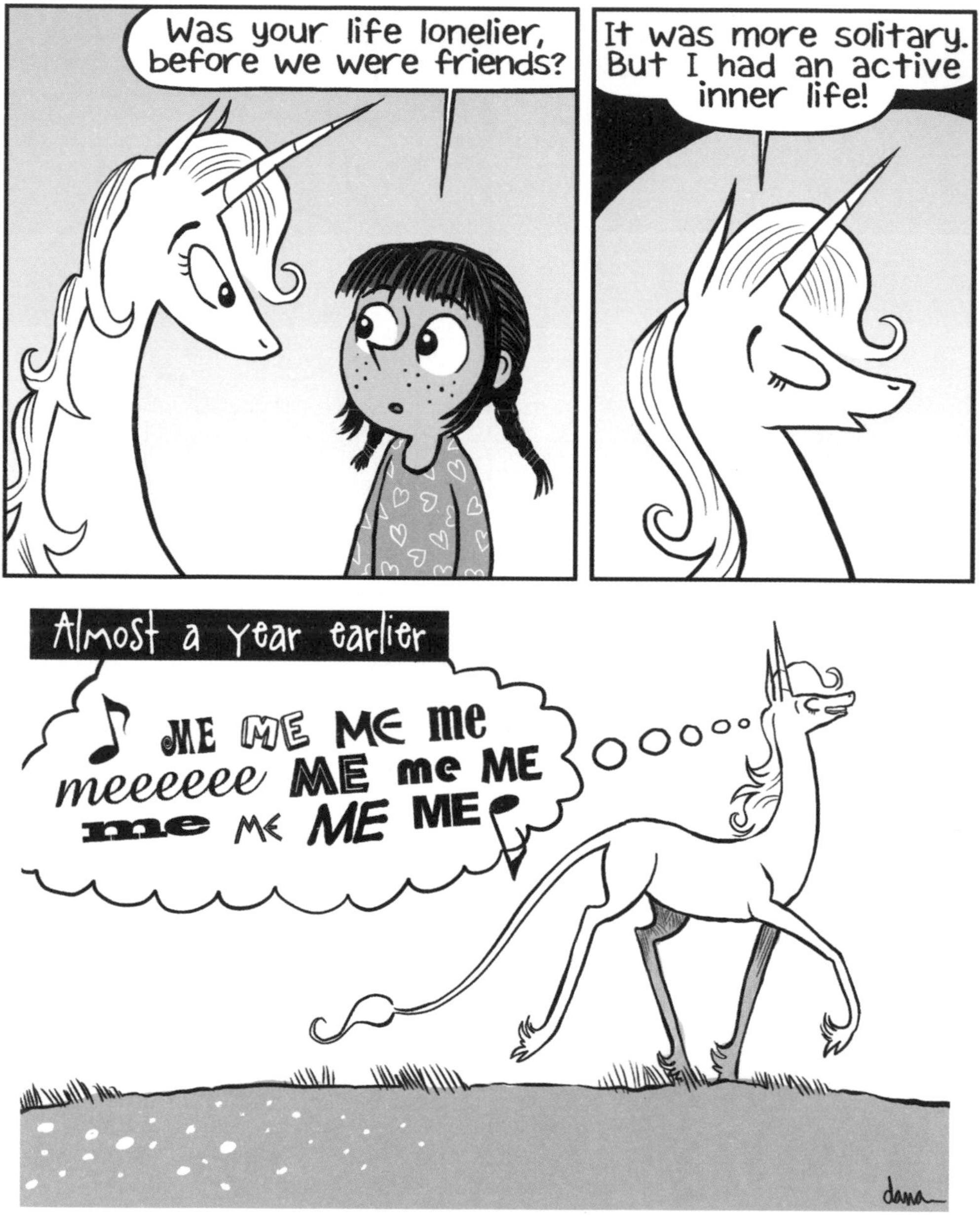
Was your life lonelier, before we were friends?
It was more solitary. But I had an active inner life!
Almost a year earlier
ME ME ME me meeeeee ME me ME me ME ME ME
dana

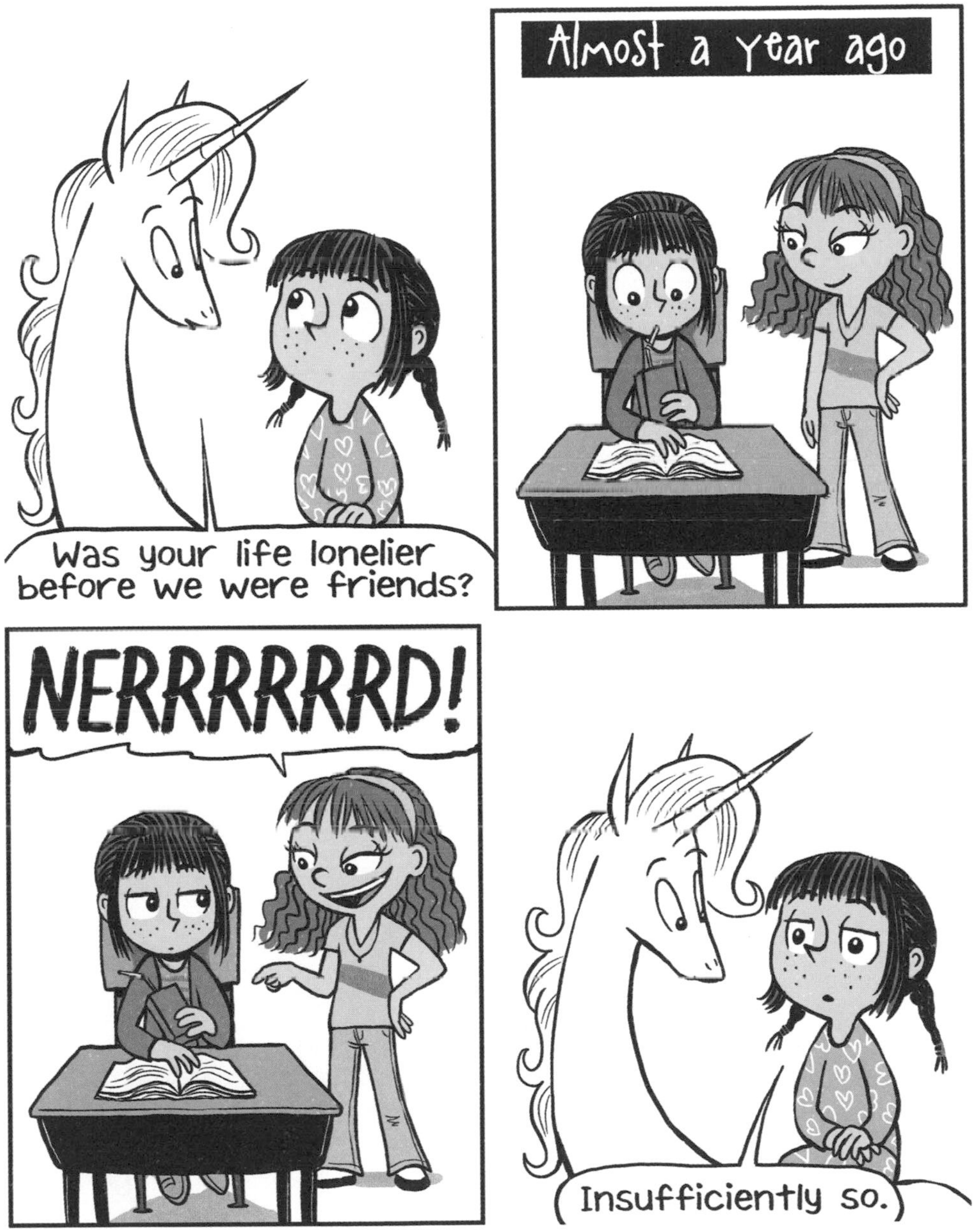
Was your life lonelier before we were friends?
Almost a year ago
NERRRRRRRD!
Insufficiently so.

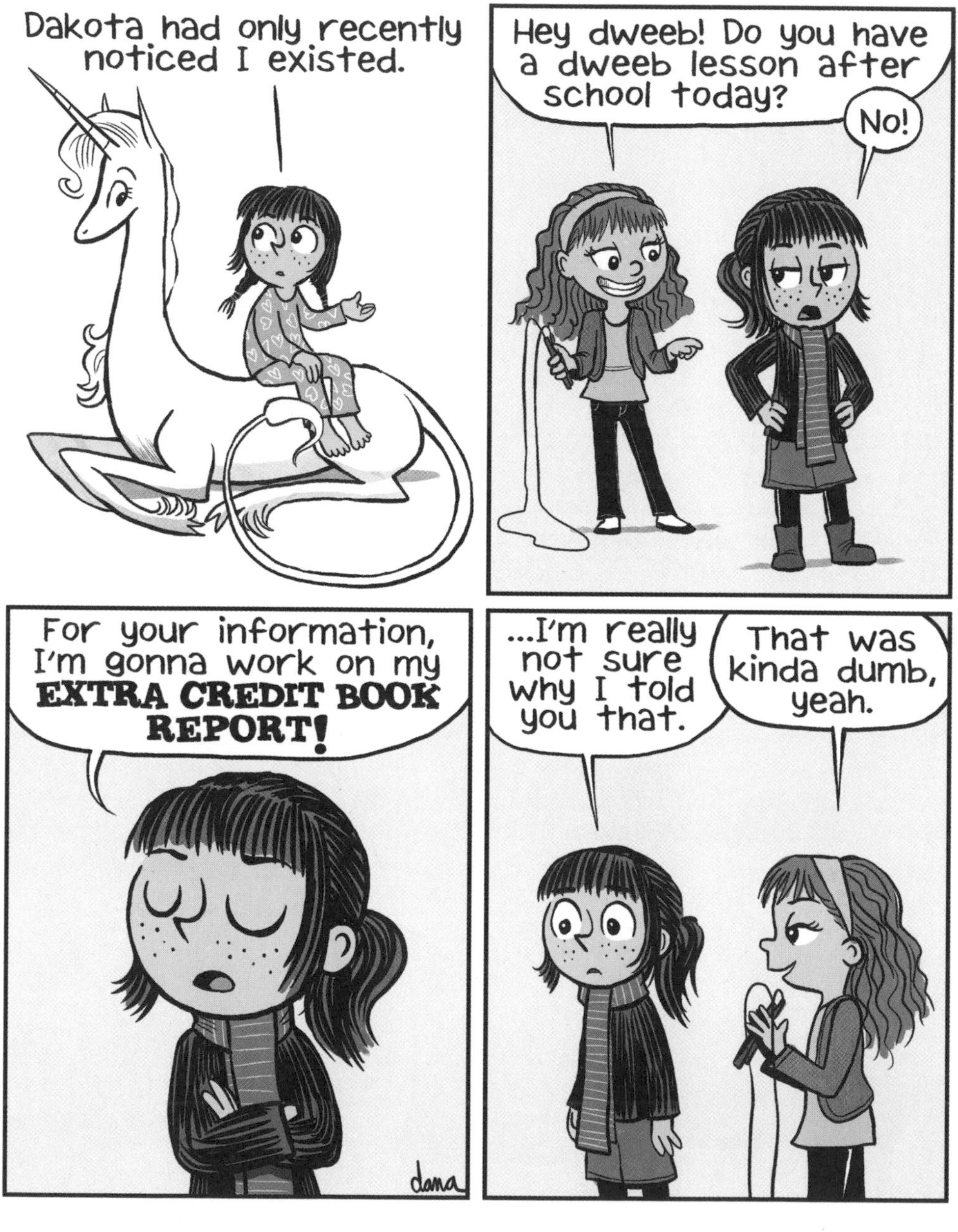
Dakota had only recently noticed I existed.
Hey dweeb! Do you have a dweeb lesson after school today?
No!
For your information, I'm gonna work on my EXTRA CREDIT BOOK REPORT!
dana
...I'm really not sure why I told you that.
That was kinda dumb, yeah.

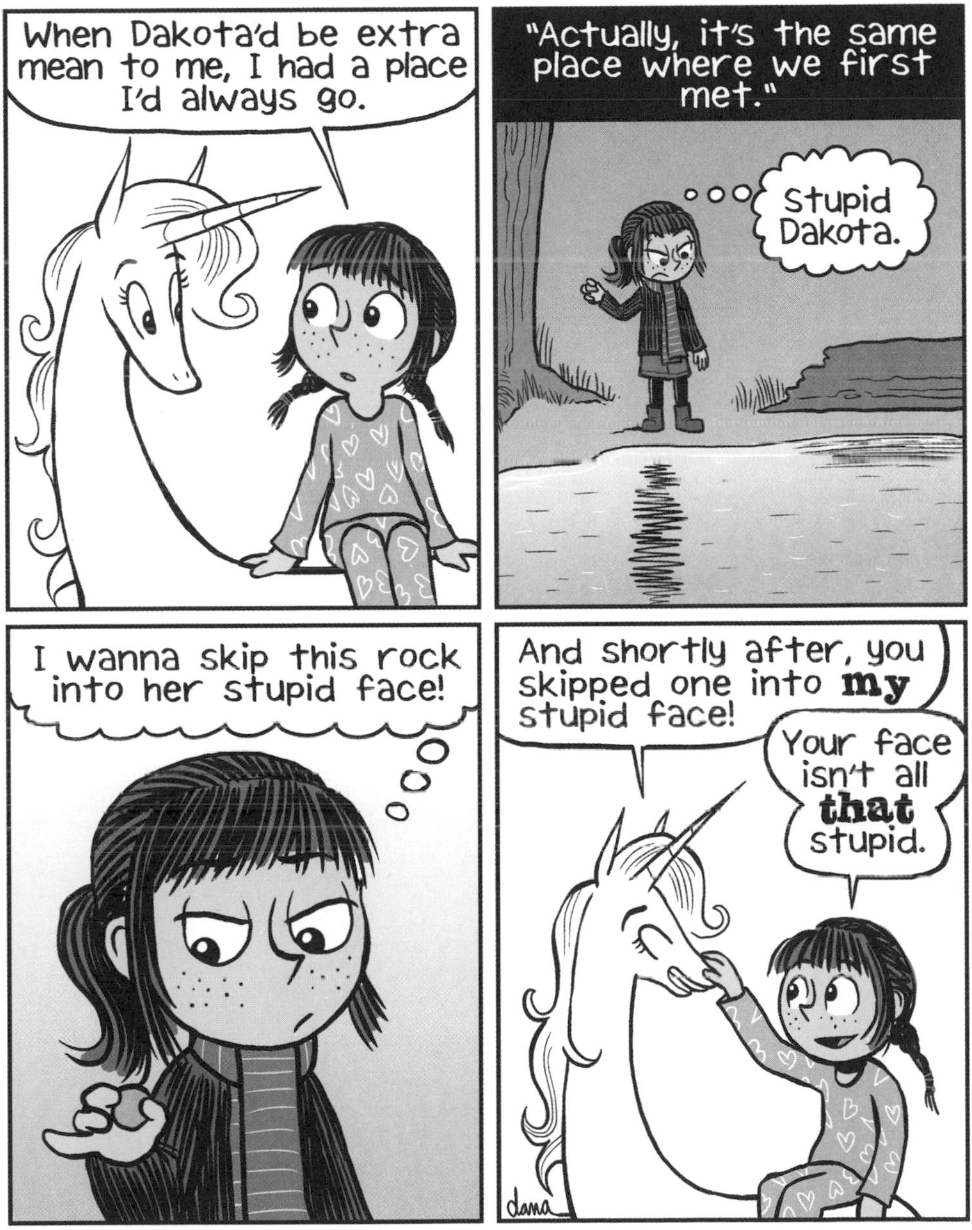
When Dakota'd be extra mean to me, I had a place I'd always go.
"Actually, it's the same place where we first met."
Stupid Dakota.
I wanna skip this rock into her stupid face!
And shortly after, you skipped one into **my** stupid face!
Your face isn't all **that** stupid.
dana

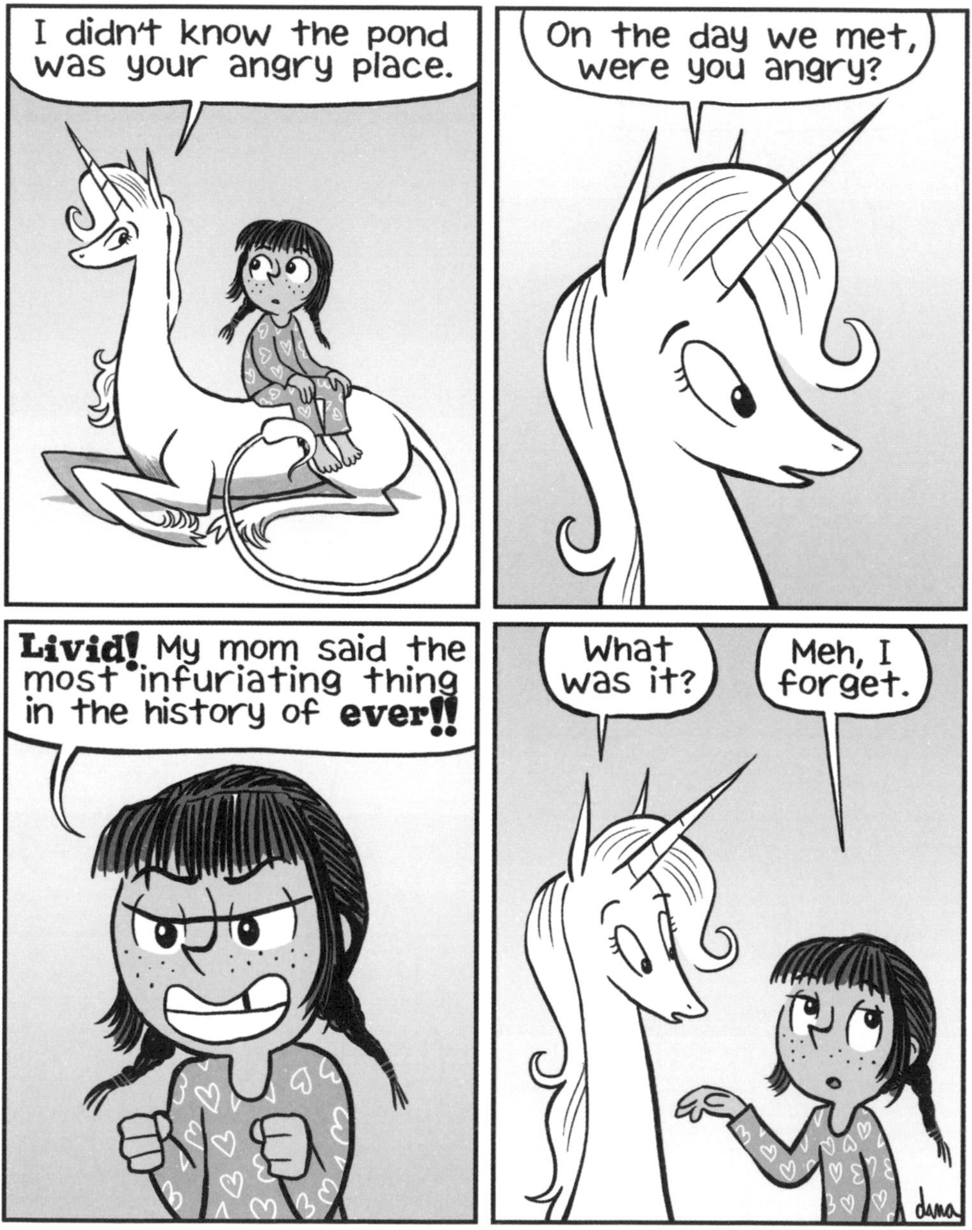
I didn't know the pond was your angry place.
On the day we met, were you angry?
Livid! My mom said the most infuriating thing in the history of ever!!
What was it?
Meh, I forget.
dana

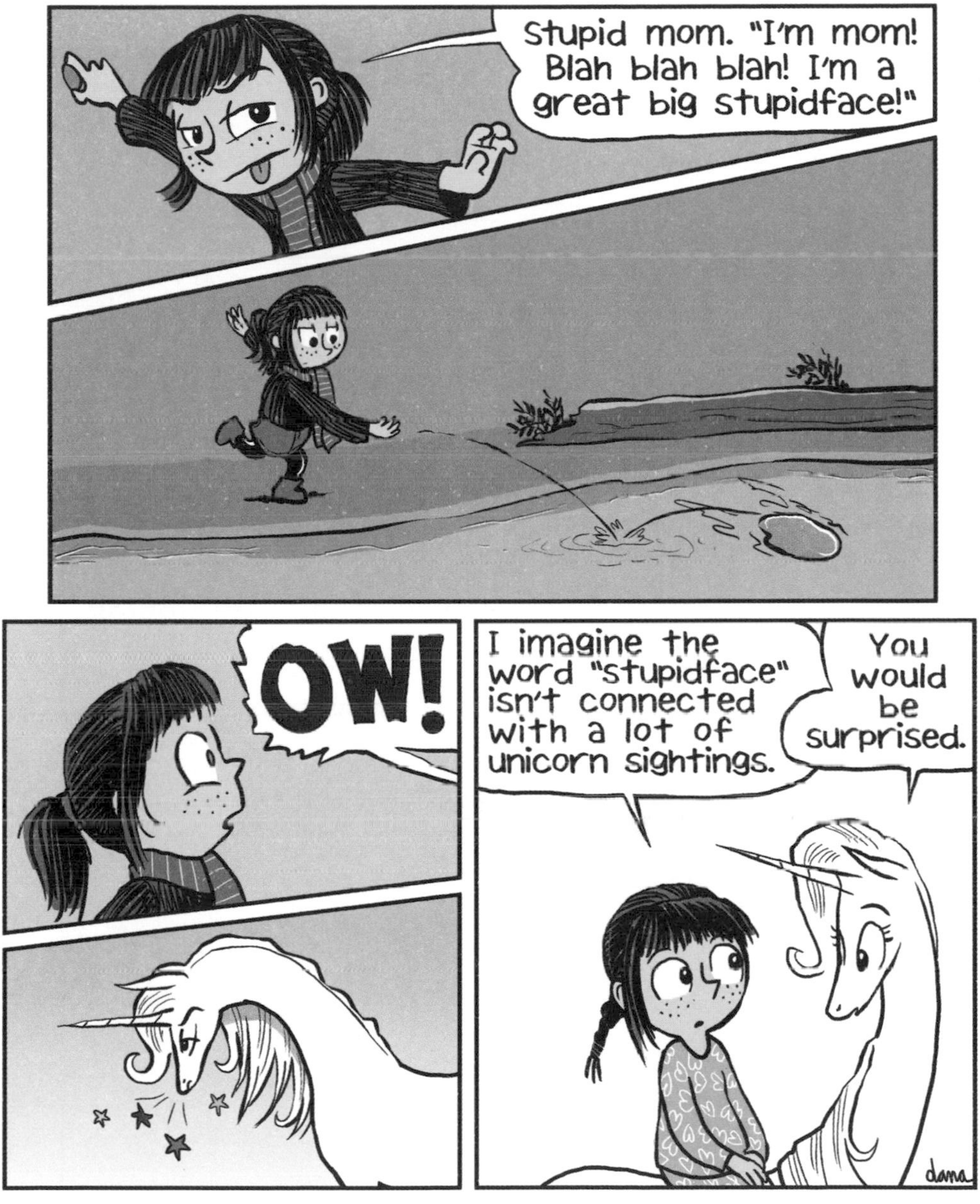
Stupid mom. "I'm mom! Blah blah blah! I'm a great big stupidface!"
OW!
I imagine the word "stupidface" isn't connected with a lot of unicorn sightings.
You would be surprised.
dana

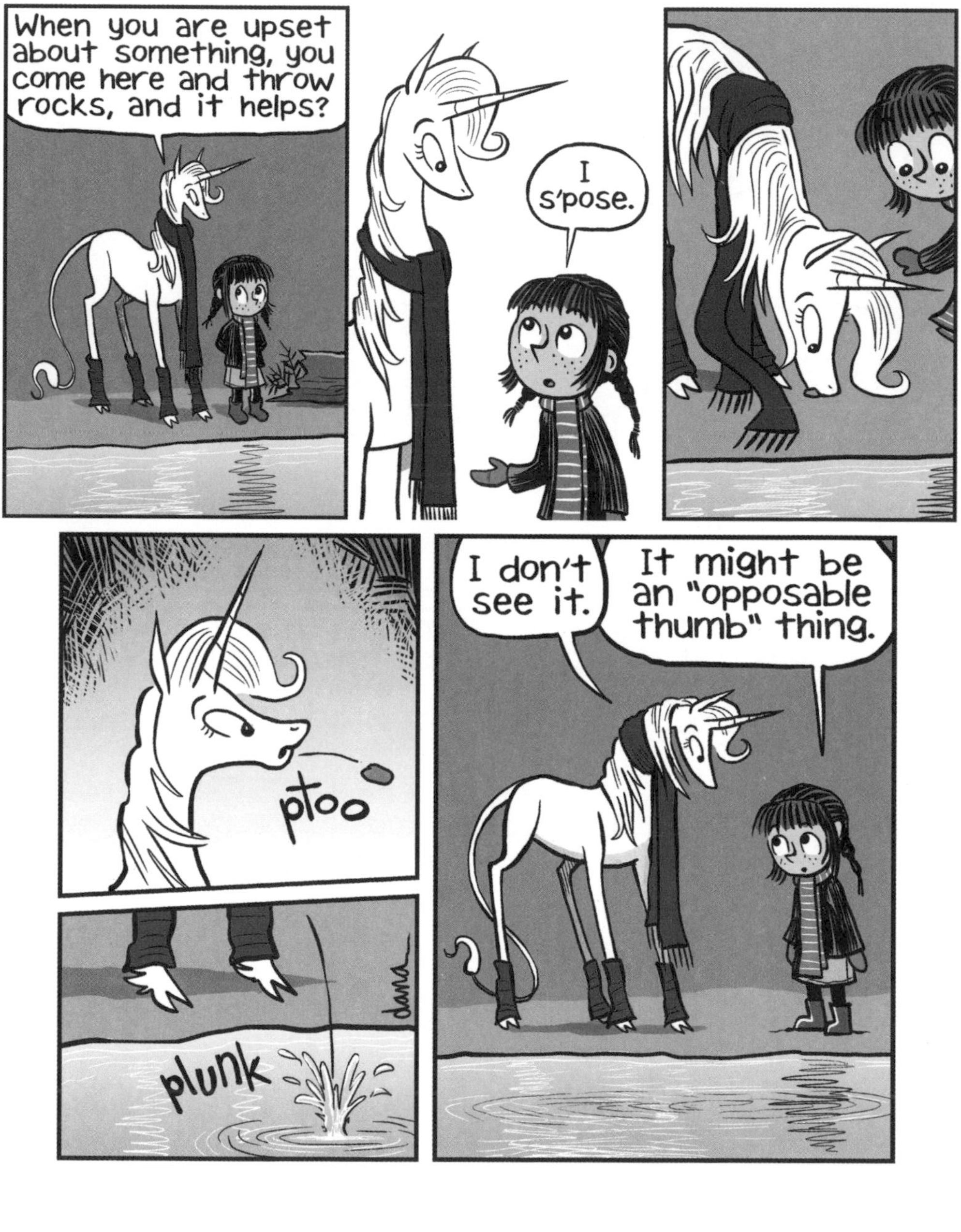
When you are upset about something, you come here and throw rocks, and it helps?
I s'pose.
ptoo
plunk
dana
I don't see it.
It might be an "opposable thumb" thing.

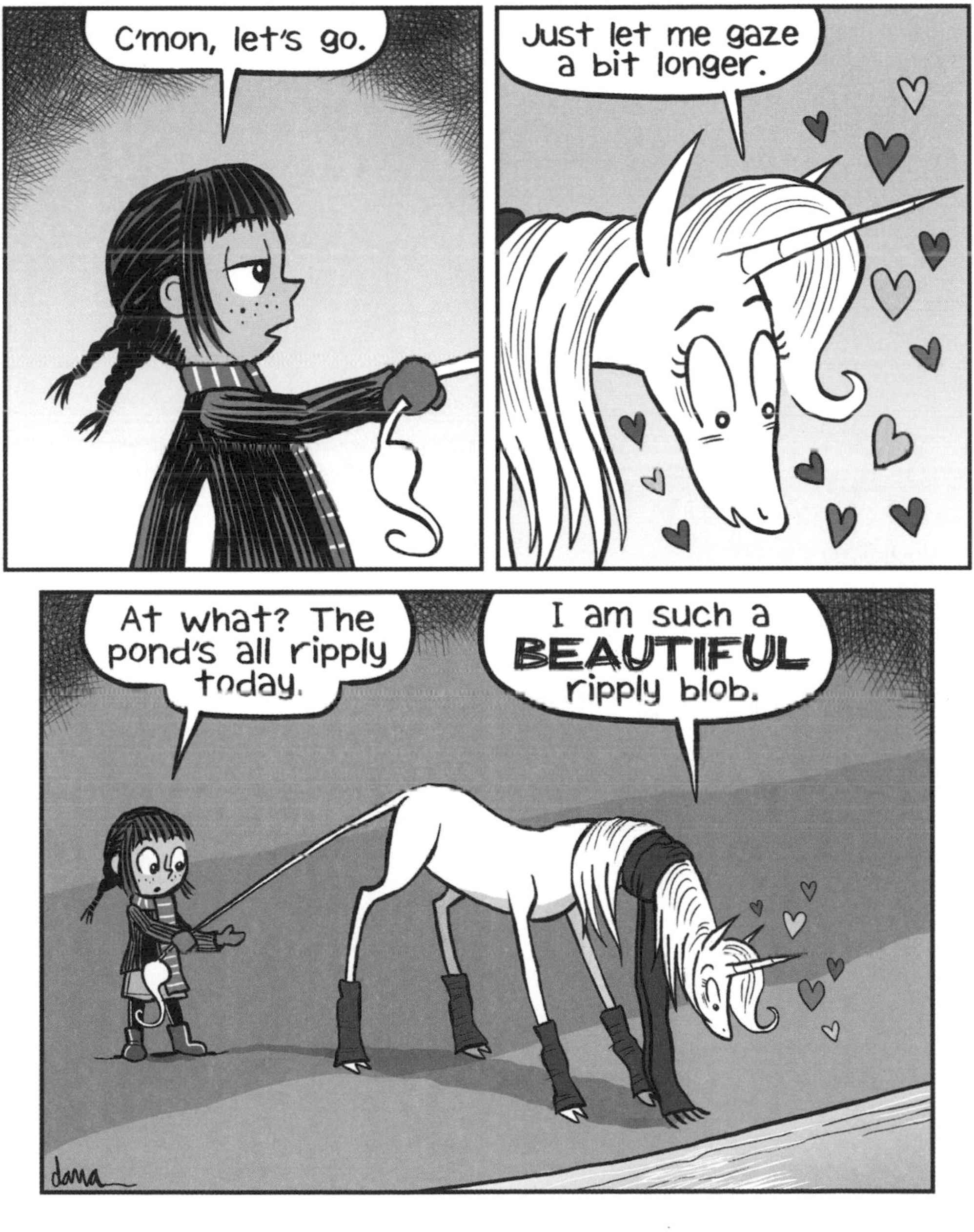
C'mon, let's go.
Just let me gaze a bit longer.
At what? The pond's all ripply today.
I am such a **BEAUTIFUL** ripply blob.
dana

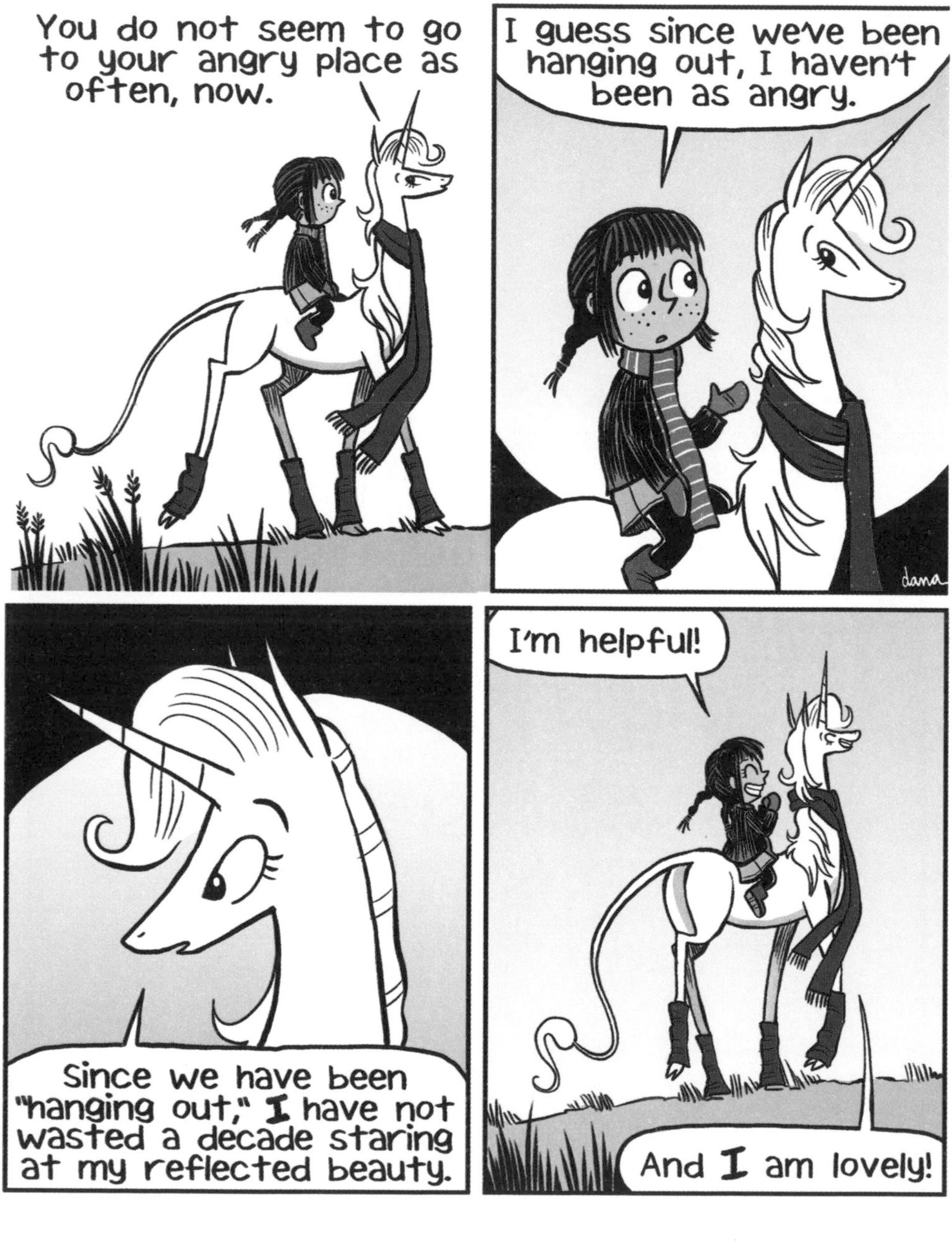
You do not seem to go to your angry place as often, now.
I guess since we've been hanging out, I haven't been as angry.
dana
Since we have been "hanging out," I have not wasted a decade staring at my reflected beauty.
I'm helpful!
And I am lovely!

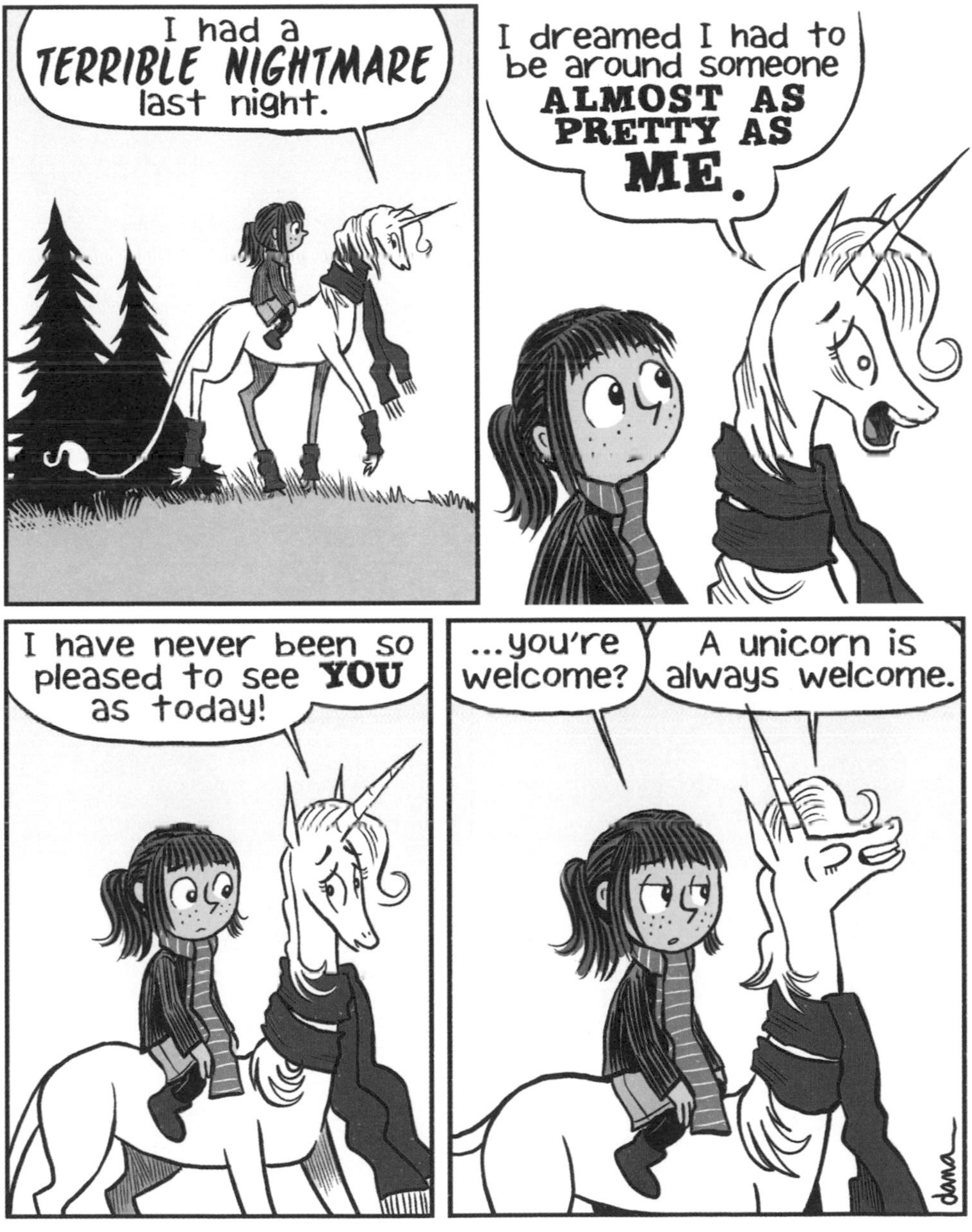
I had a TERRIBLE NIGHTMARE last night.
I dreamed I had to be around someone ALMOST AS PRETTY AS ME.
I have never been so pleased to see YOU as today!
...you're welcome?
A unicorn is always welcome.
dana

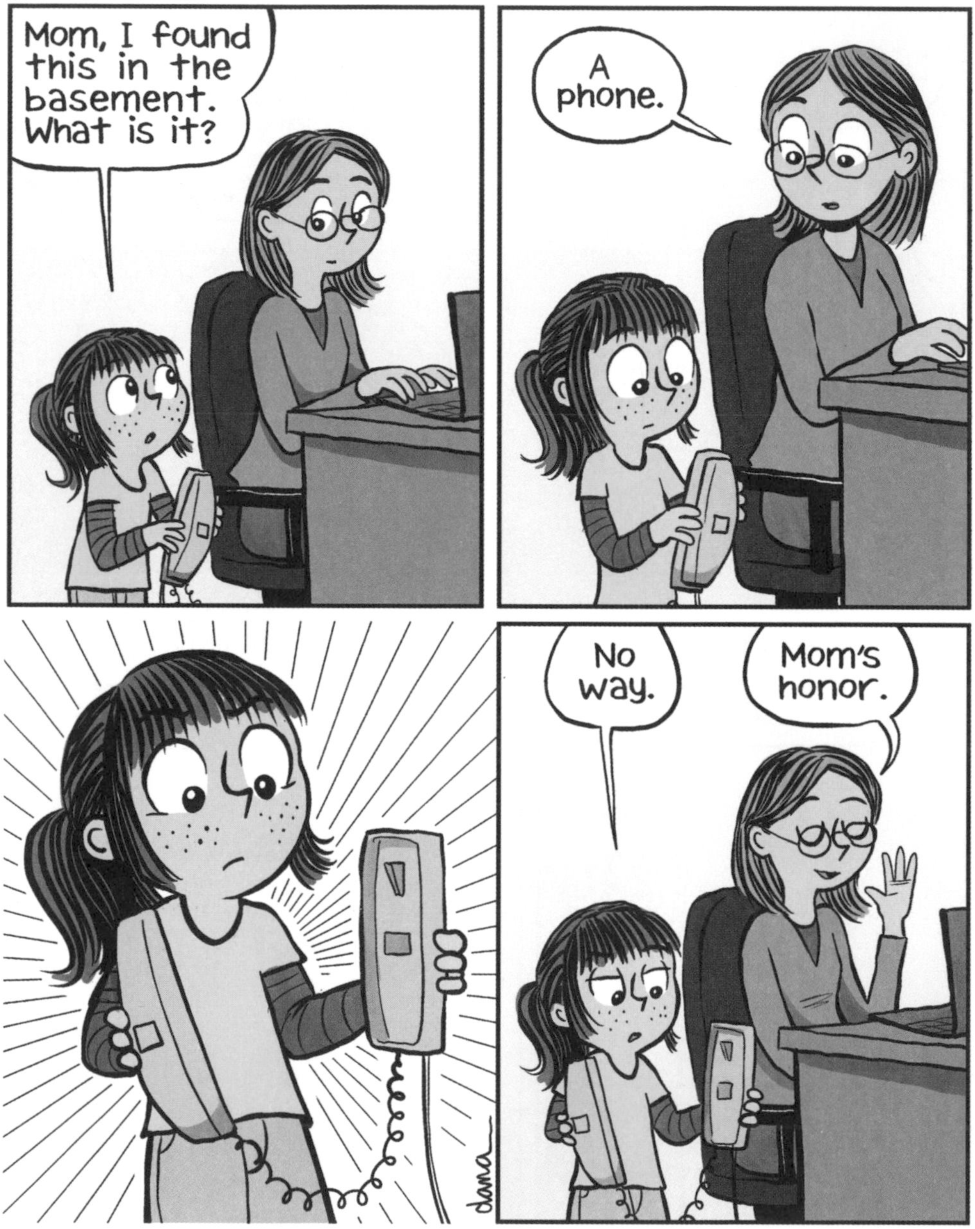
Mom, I found this in the basement. What is it?
A phone.
No way.
Mom's honor.
dana

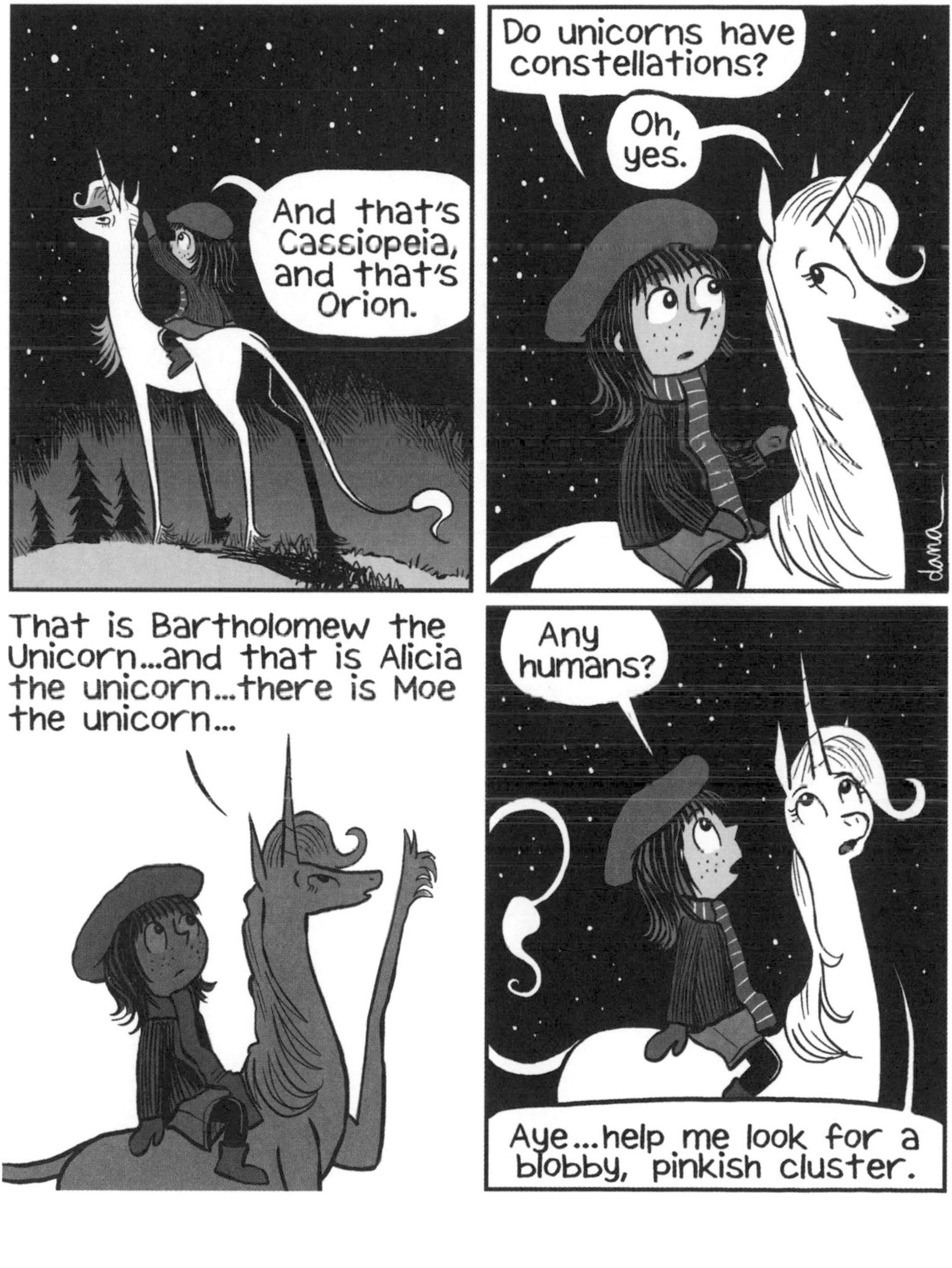
And that's Cassiopeia, and that's Orion.
Do unicorns have constellations?
Oh, yes.
dana
That is Bartholomew the Unicorn...and that is Alicia the unicorn...there is Moe the unicorn...
Any humans?
Aye...help me look for a blobby, pinkish cluster.

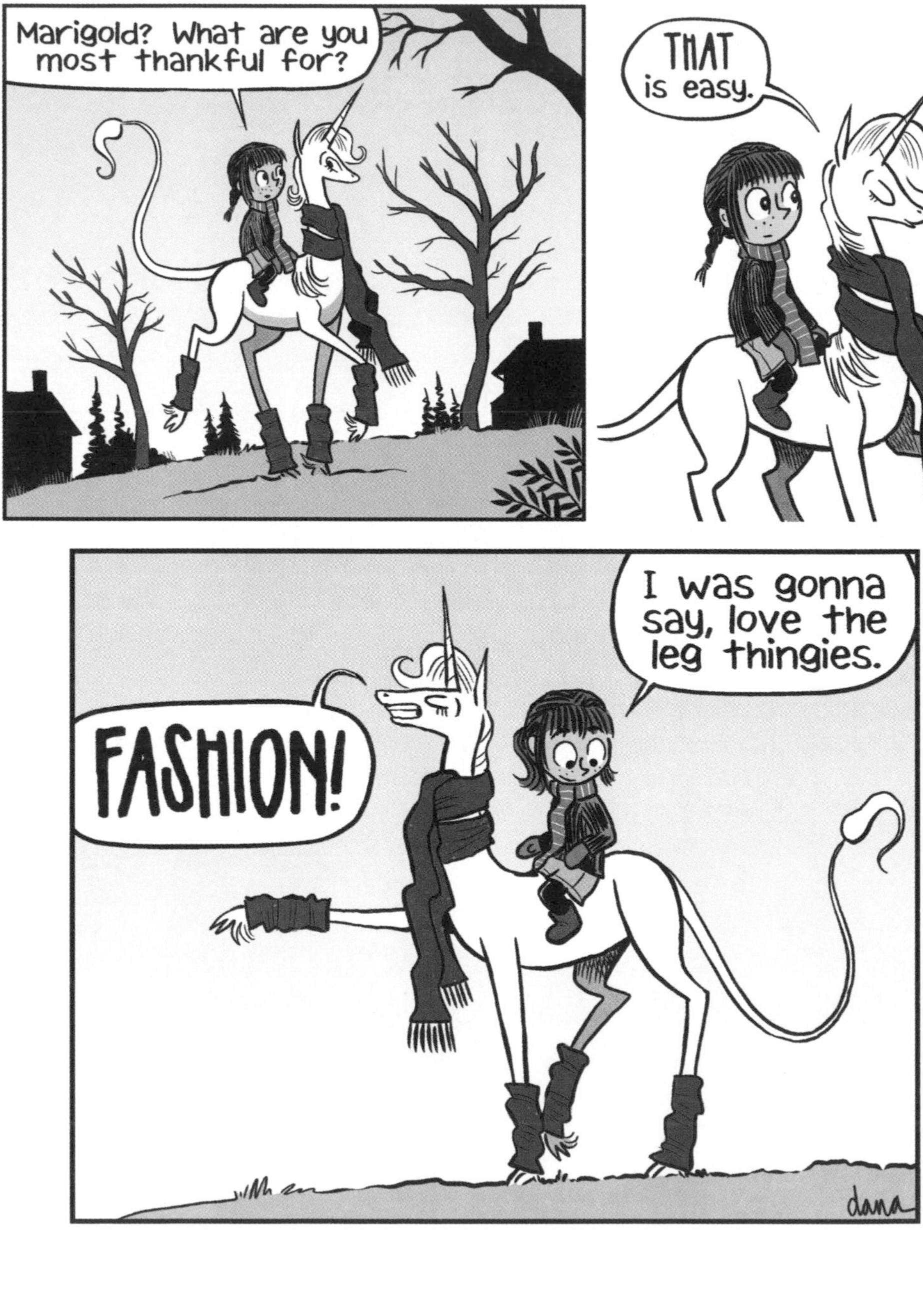
Marigold? What are you most thankful for?
THAT is easy.
I was gonna say, love the leg thingies.
FASHION!
dana

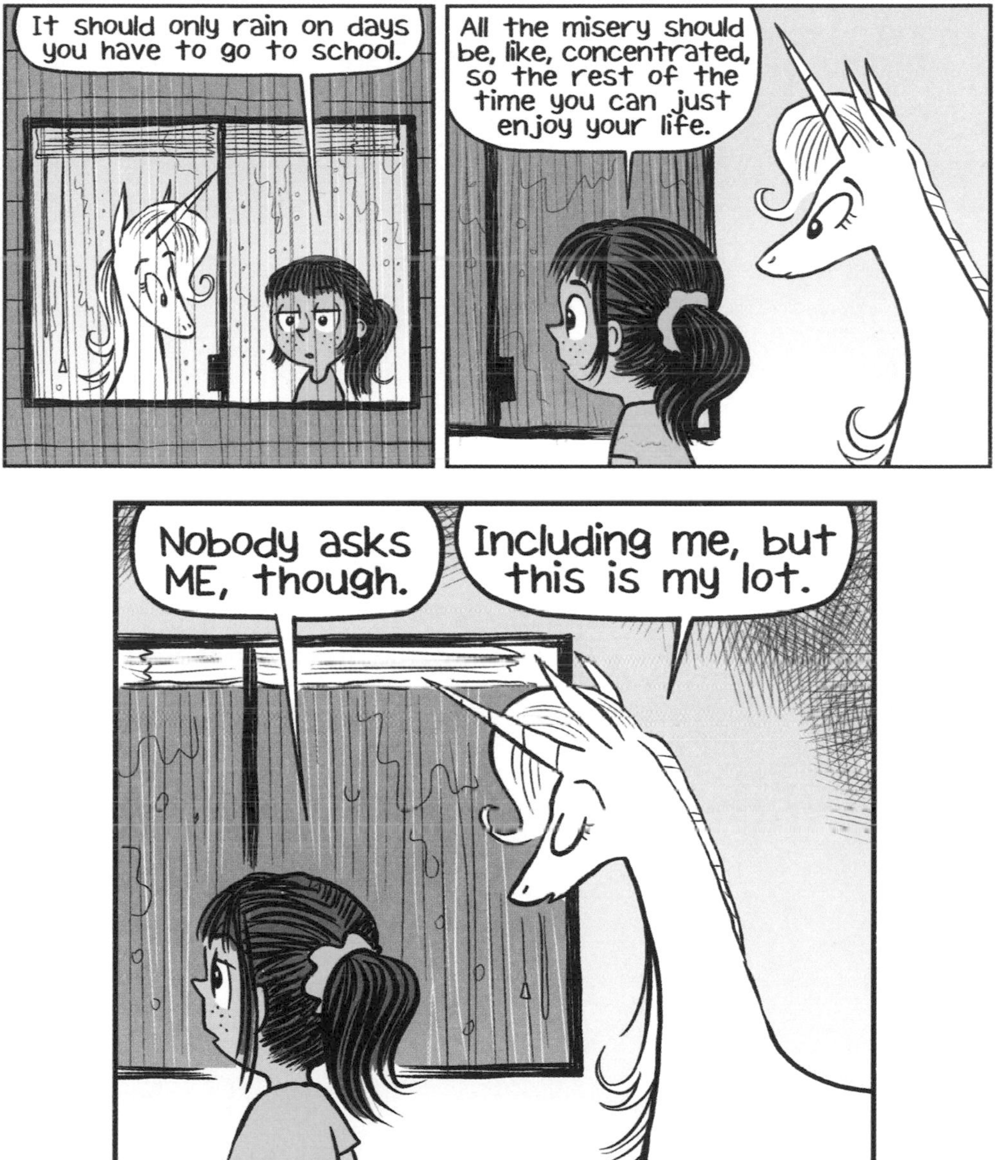
It should only rain on days you have to go to school.
All the misery should be, like, concentrated, so the rest of the time you can just enjoy your life.
Nobody asks ME, though.
Including me, but this is my lot.
dana

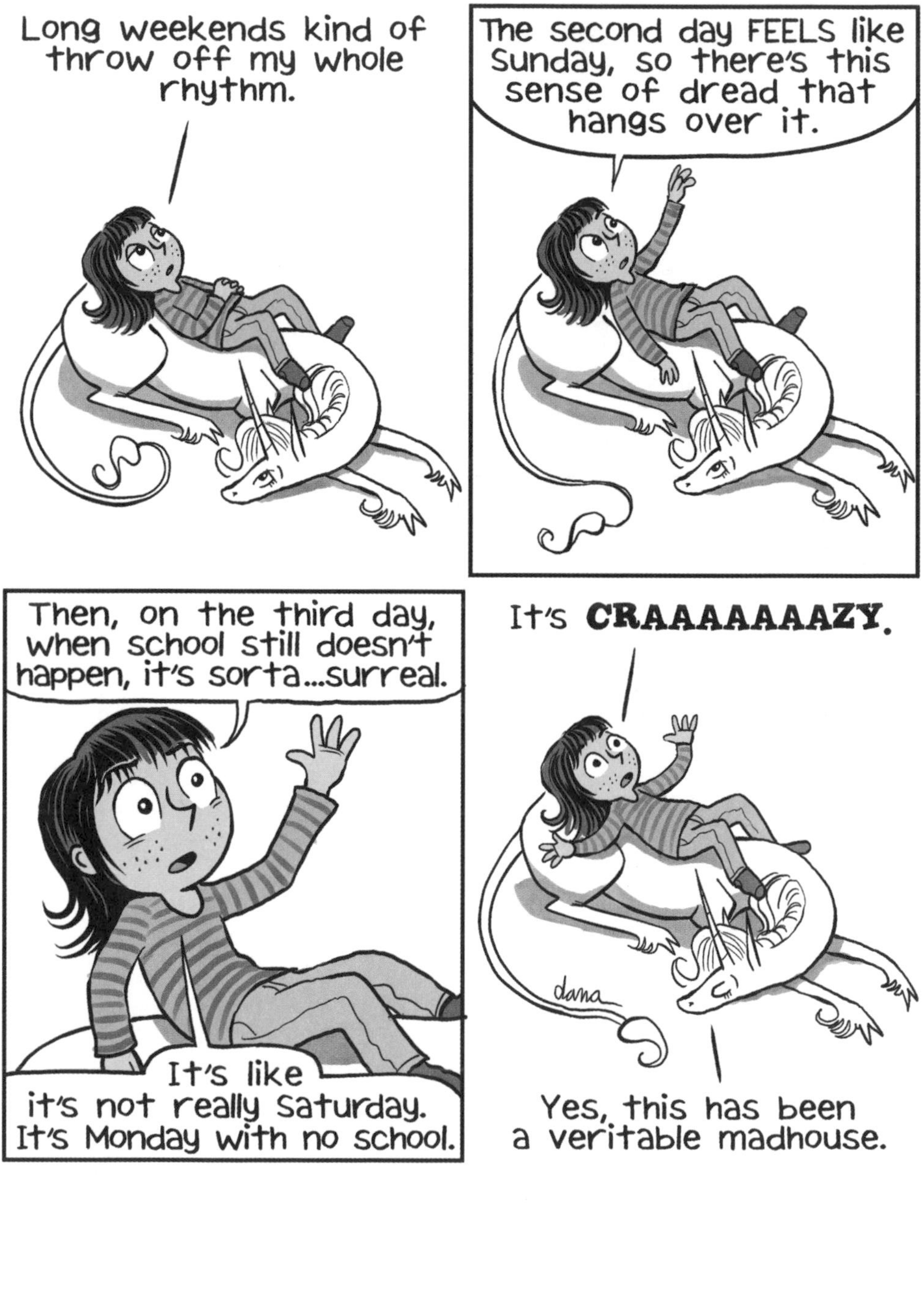

Long weekends kind of throw off my whole rhythm.
The second day FEELS like Sunday, so there's this sense of dread that hangs over it.
Then, on the third day, when school still doesn't happen, it's sorta...surreal.
It's like it's not really Saturday. It's Monday with no school.
It's **CRAAAAAAAAZY**.
dana
Yes, this has been a veritable madhouse.

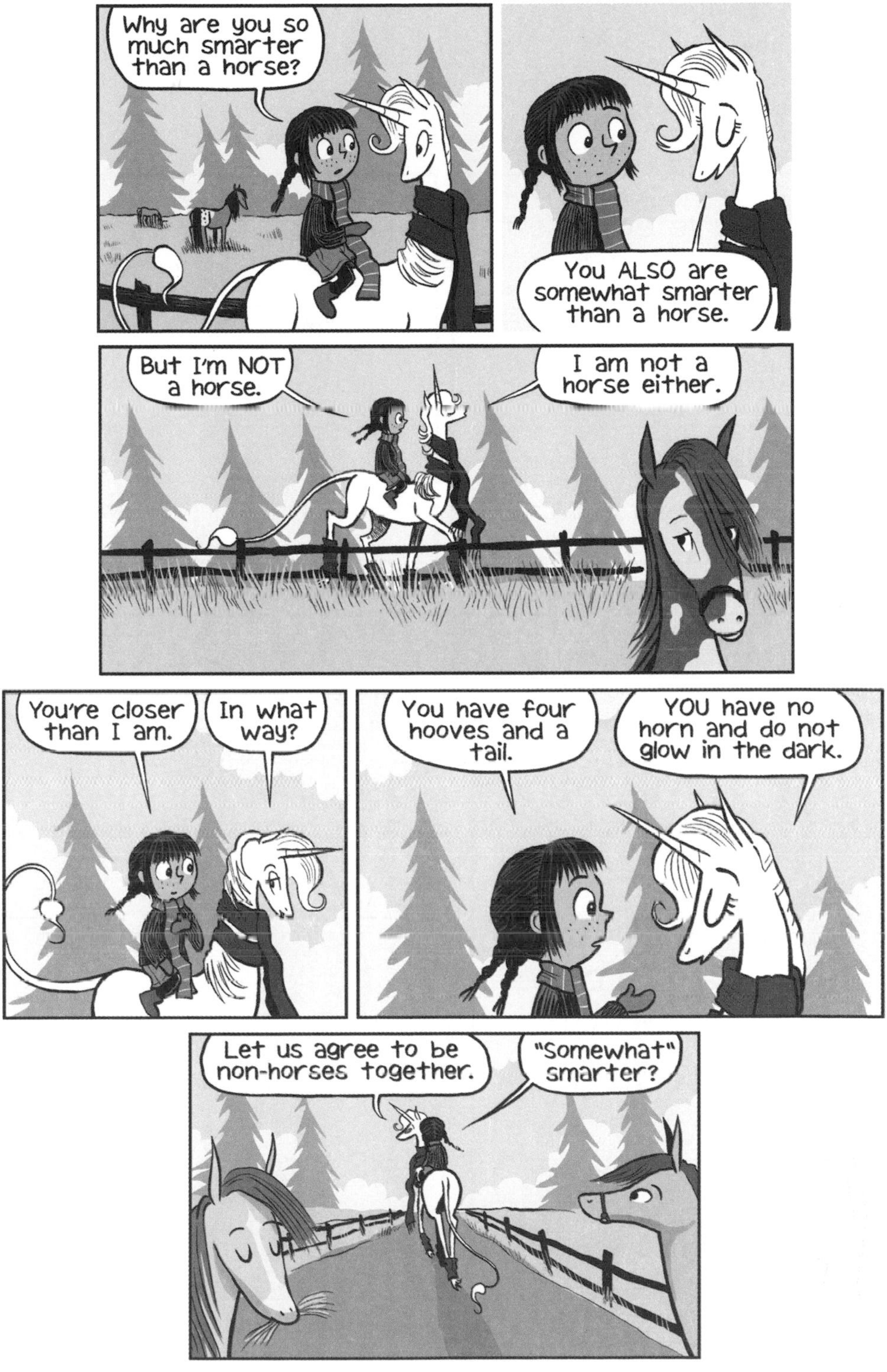
Why are you so much smarter than a horse?
You ALSO are somewhat smarter than a horse.
But I'm NOT a horse.
I am not a horse either.
You're closer than I am.
In what way?
You have four hooves and a tail.
YOU have no horn and do not glow in the dark.
Let us agree to be non-horses together.
"Somewhat" smarter?

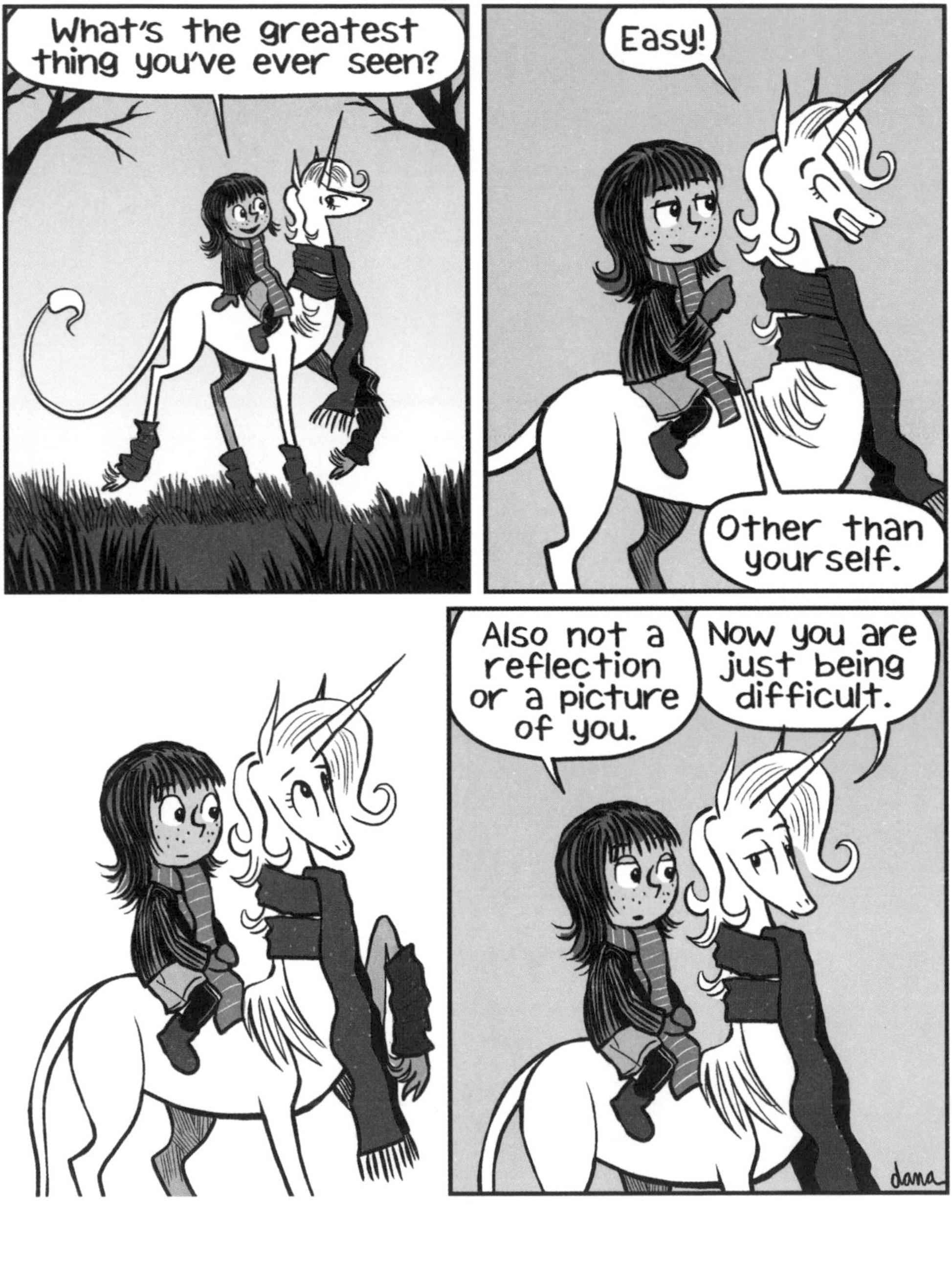
What's the greatest thing you've ever seen?
Easy!
Other than yourself.
Also not a reflection or a picture of you.
Now you are just being difficult.
dana

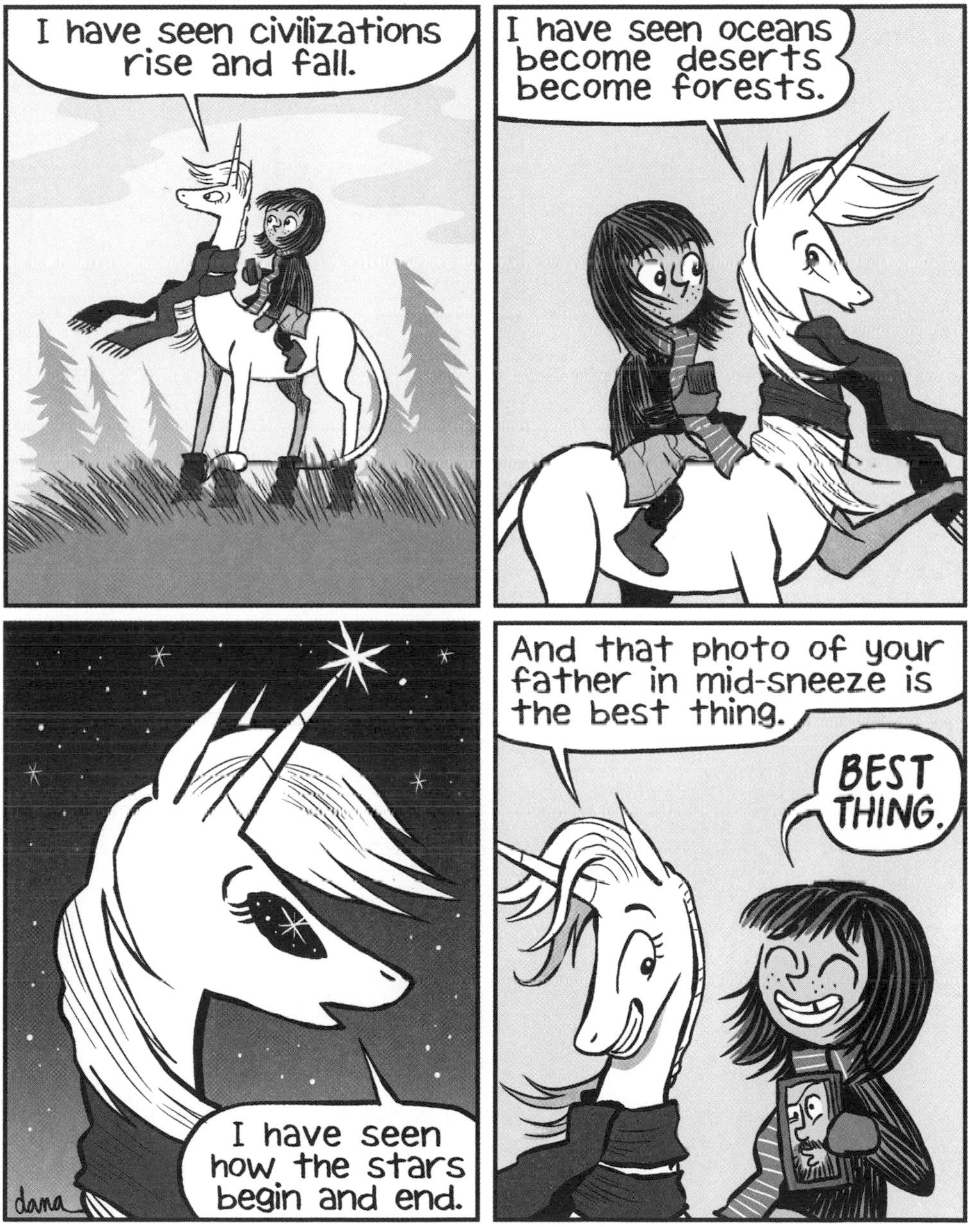
I have seen civilizations rise and fall.
I have seen oceans become deserts become forests.
I have seen how the stars begin and end.
And that photo of your father in mid-sneeze is the best thing.
BEST THING.
dana

One day at recess...

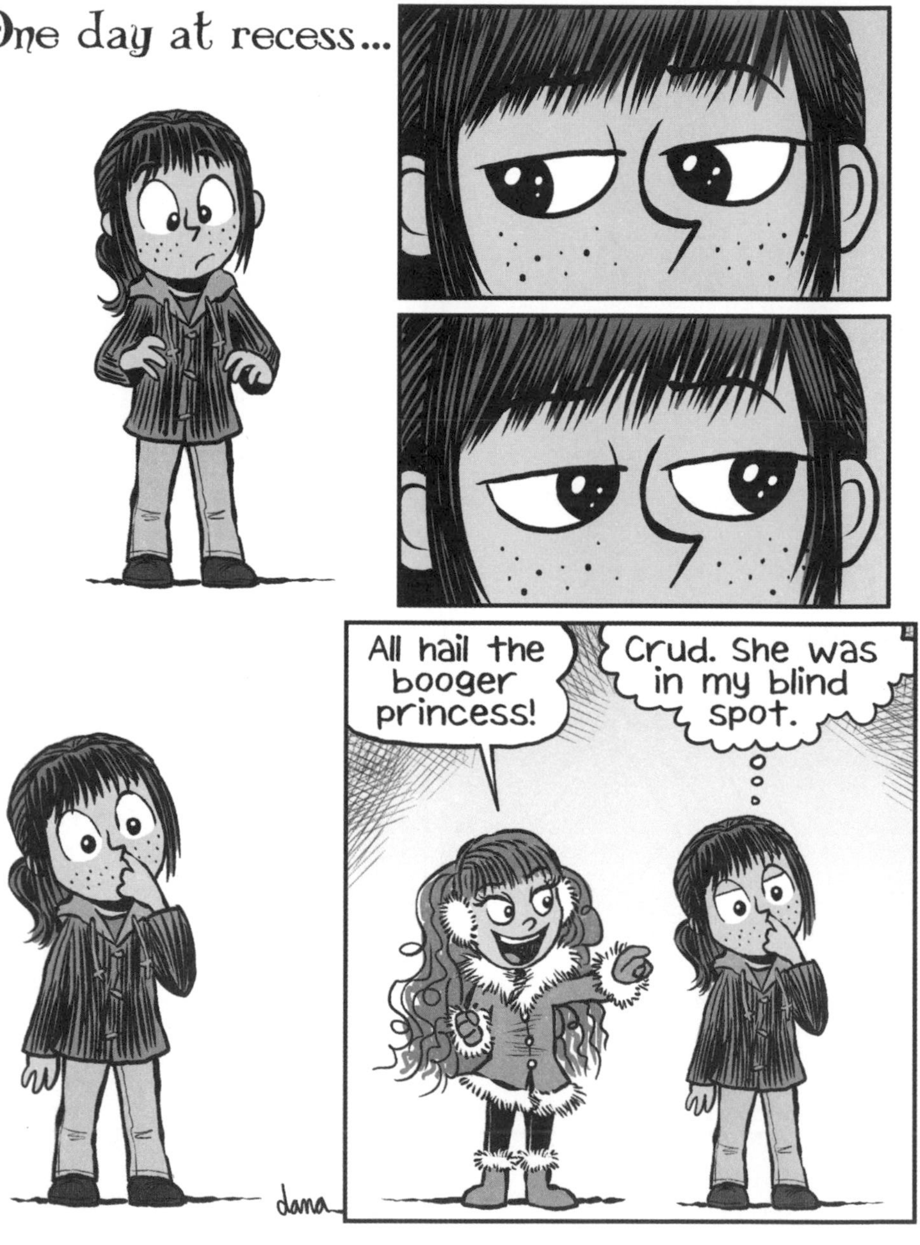
All hail the booger princess!
Crud. She was in my blind spot.
dana

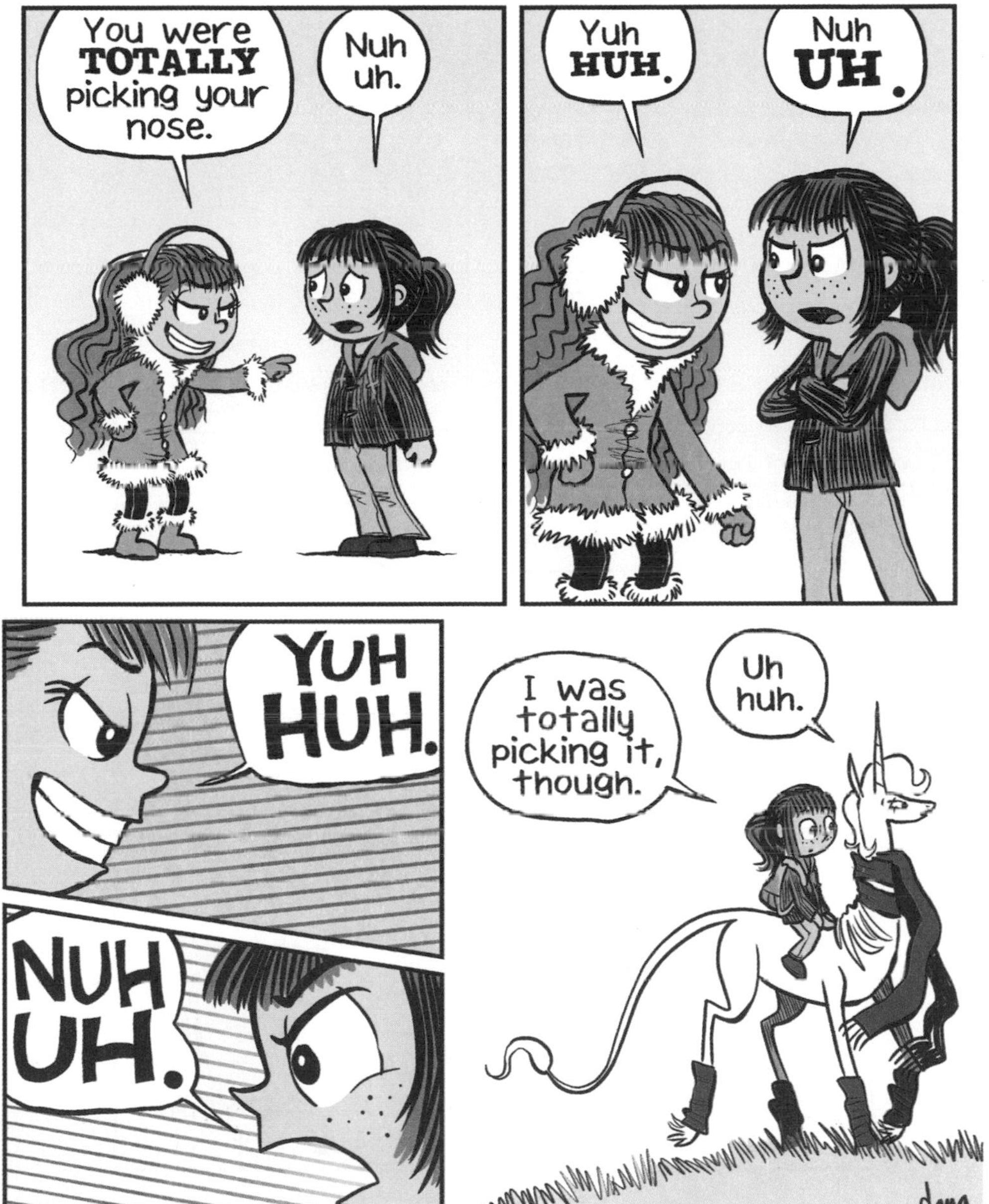
You were TOTALLY picking your nose.
Nuh uh.
Yuh HUH.
Nuh UH.
YUH HUH.
NUH UH.
I was totally picking it, though.
Uh huh.
dana

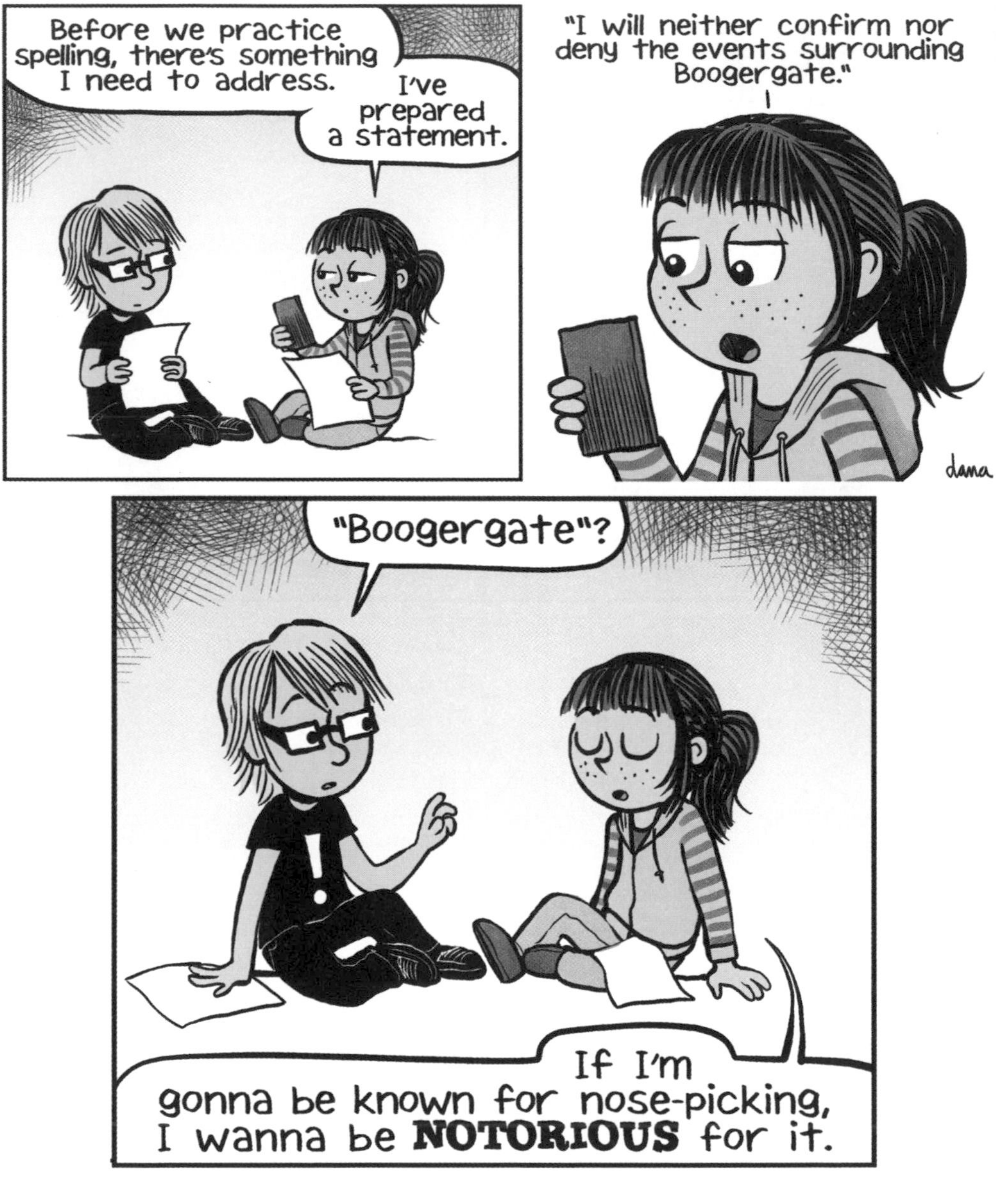
Before we practice spelling, there's something I need to address.
I've prepared a statement.
"I will neither confirm nor deny the events surrounding Boogergate."
dana
"Boogergate"?
If I'm gonna be known for nose-picking, I wanna be **NOTORIOUS** for it.

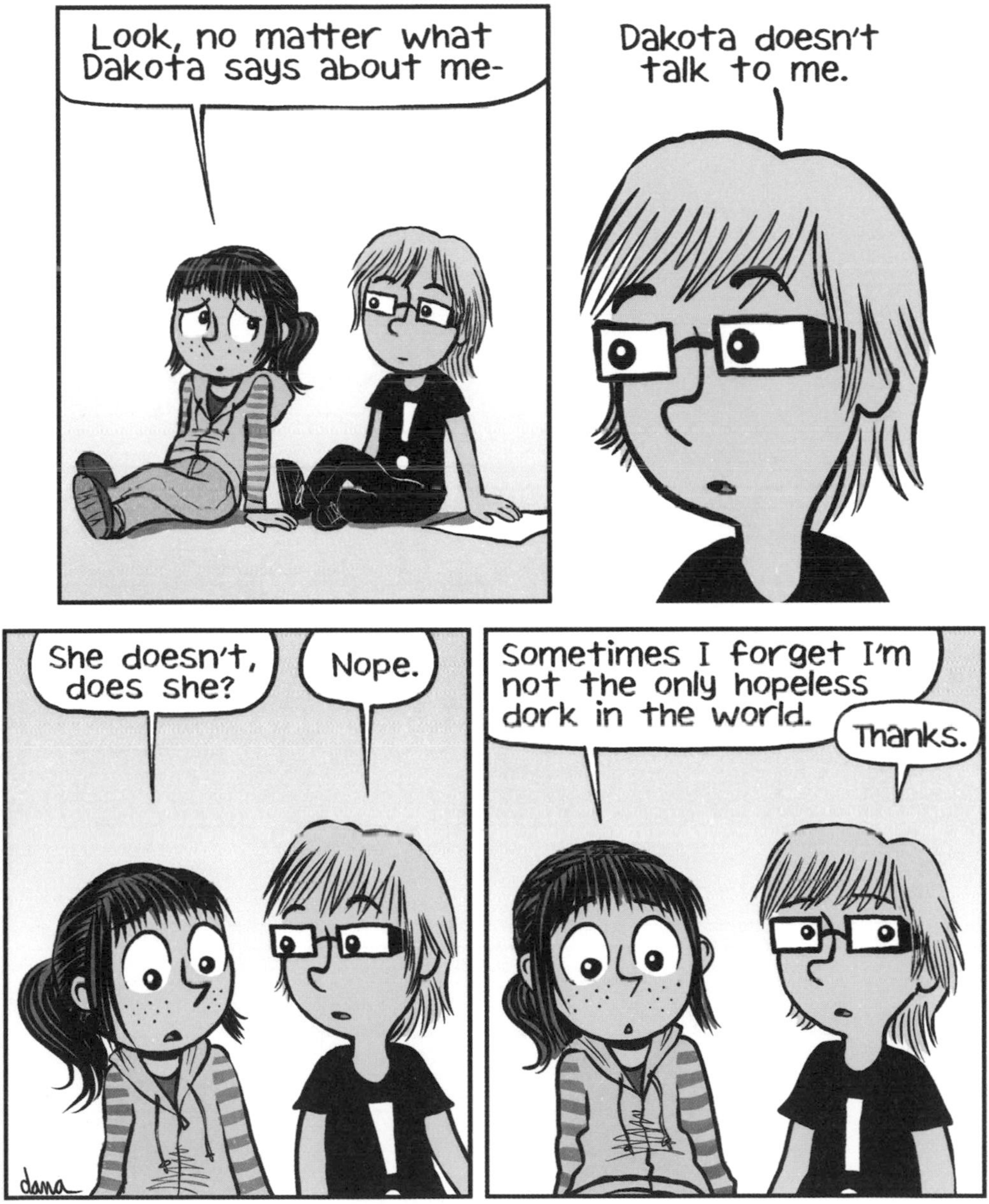

Look, no matter what Dakota says about me-
Dakota doesn't talk to me.
She doesn't, does she?
Nope.
Sometimes I forget I'm not the only hopeless dork in the world.
Thanks.
dana

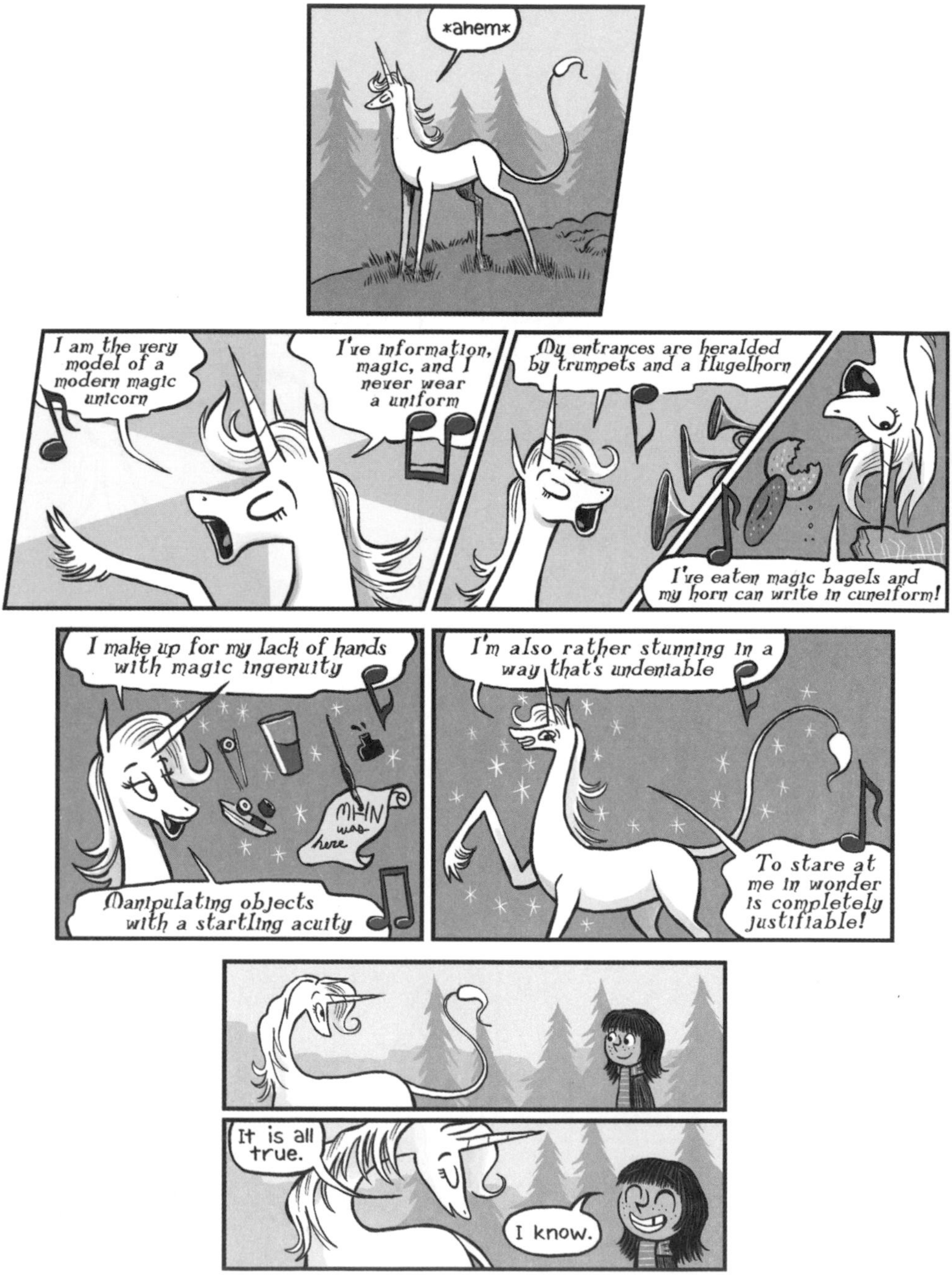
ahem
I am the very model of a modern magic unicorn
I've information, magic, and I never wear a uniform
My entrances are heralded by trumpets and a flugelhorn
I've eaten magic bagels and my horn can write in cuneiform!
I make up for my lack of hands with magic ingenuity
MAHN was here
Manipulating objects with a startling acuity
I'm also rather stunning in a way that's undeniable
To stare at me in wonder is completely justifiable!
It is all true.
I know.

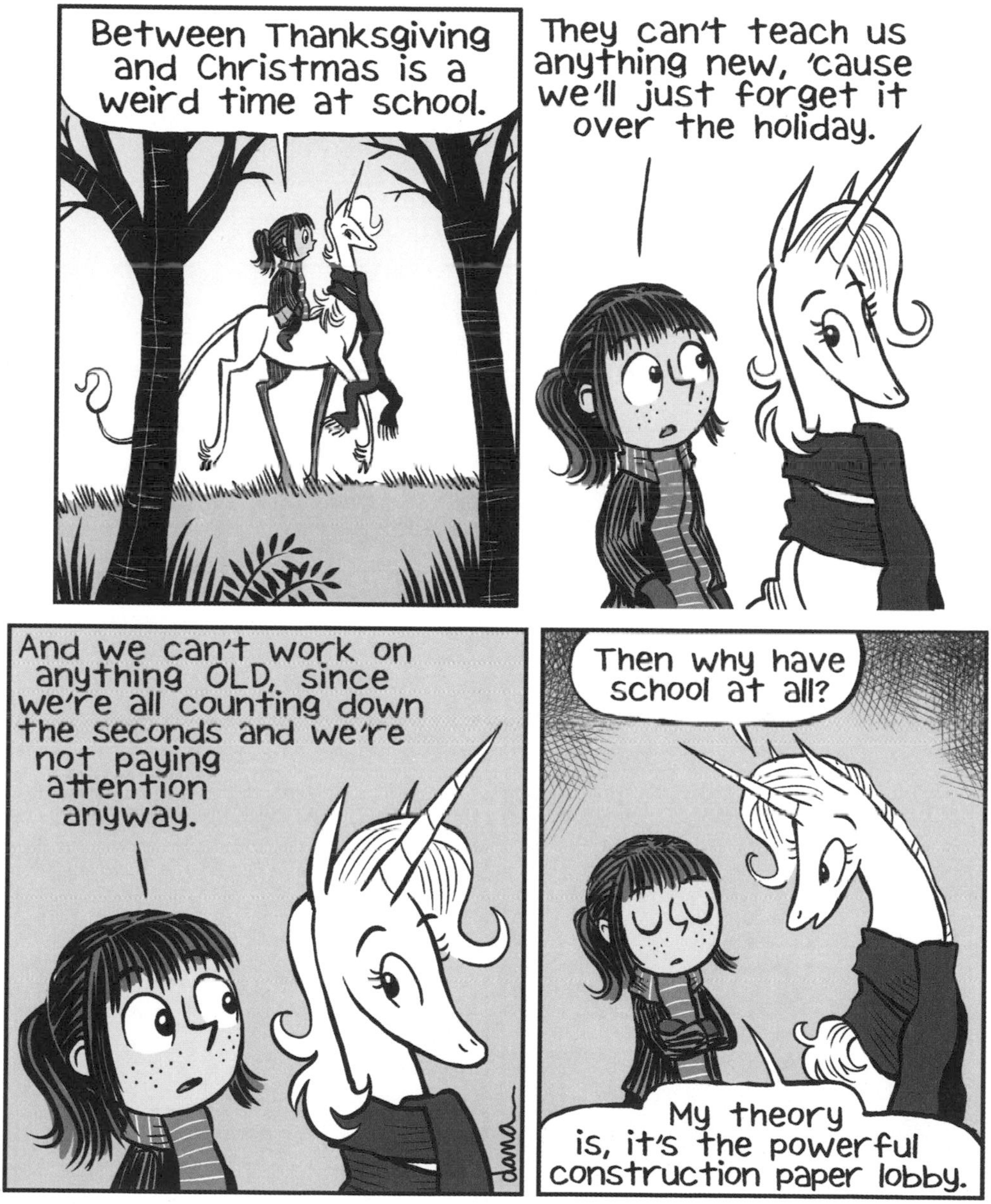

Between Thanksgiving and Christmas is a weird time at school.
They can't teach us anything new, 'cause we'll just forget it over the holiday.
And we can't work on anything OLD, since we're all counting down the seconds and we're not paying attention anyway.
dana
Then why have school at all?
My theory is, it's the powerful construction paper lobby.

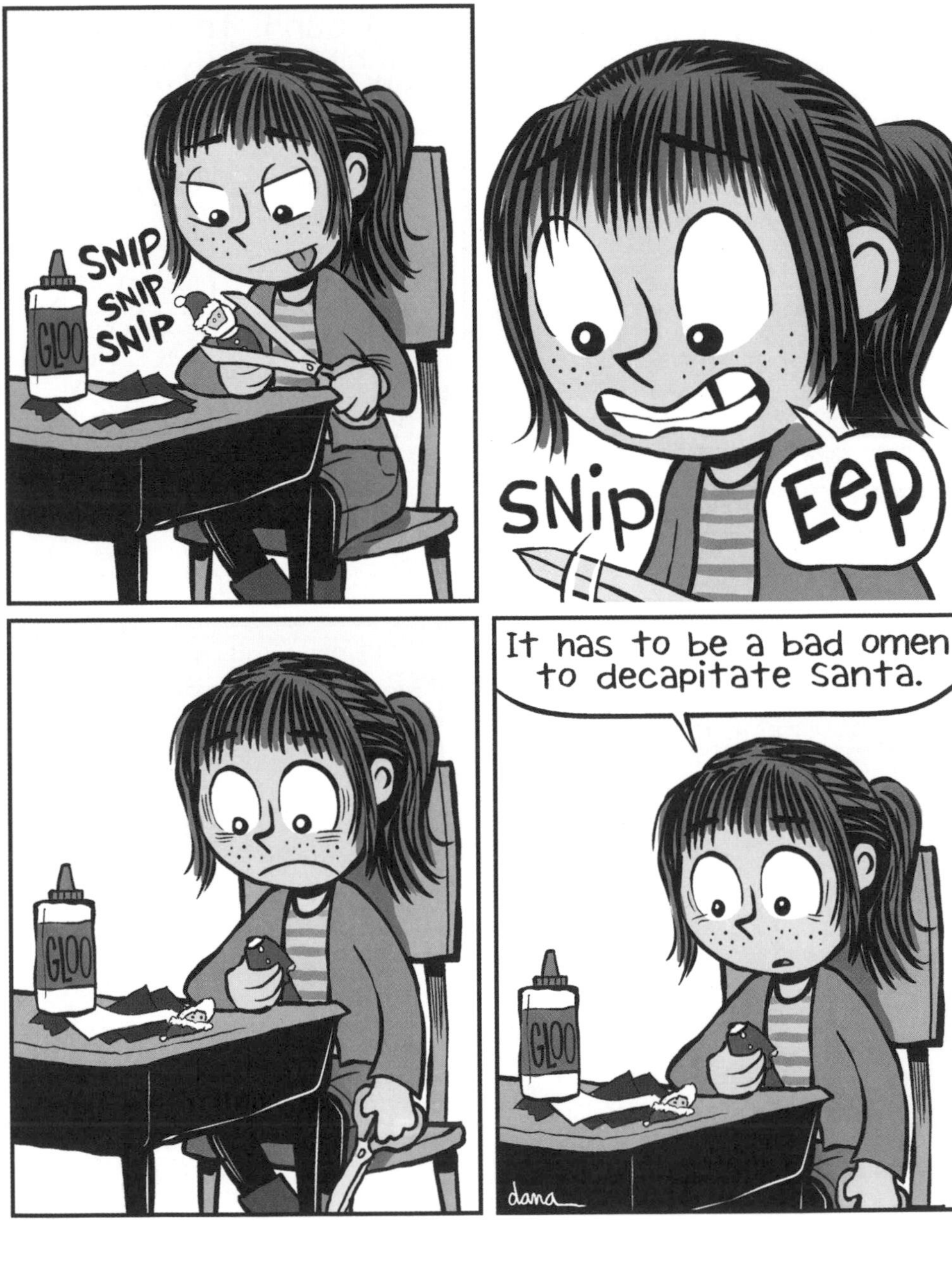
SNIP
SNIP
SNIP
GLOO
SNIP
EEP
GLOO
It has to be a bad omen to decapitate Santa.
GLOO
dana

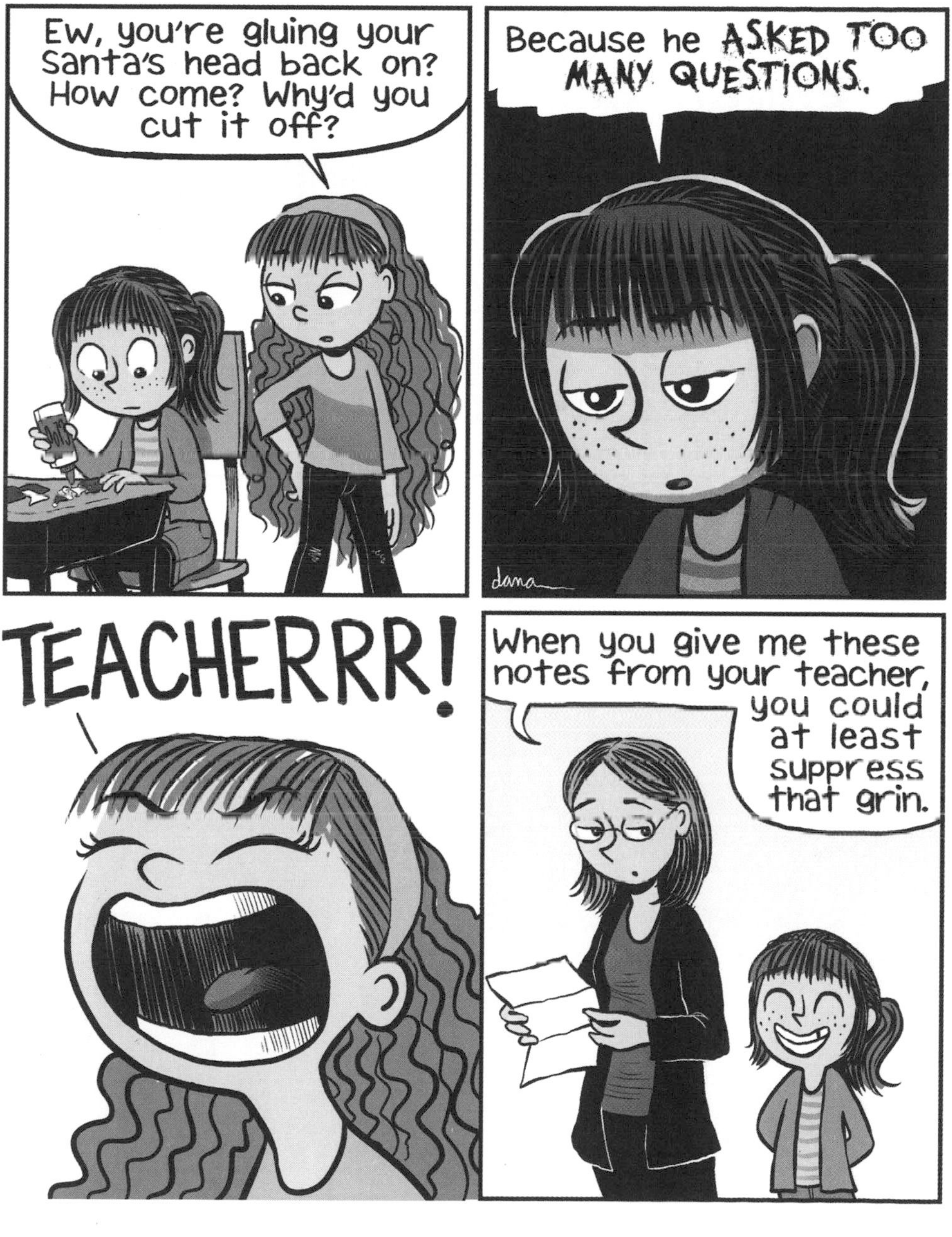
Ew, you're gluing your Santa's head back on? How come? Why'd you cut it off?
Because he ASKED TOO MANY QUESTIONS.
dana
TEACHERRR!
When you give me these notes from your teacher, you could at least suppress that grin.

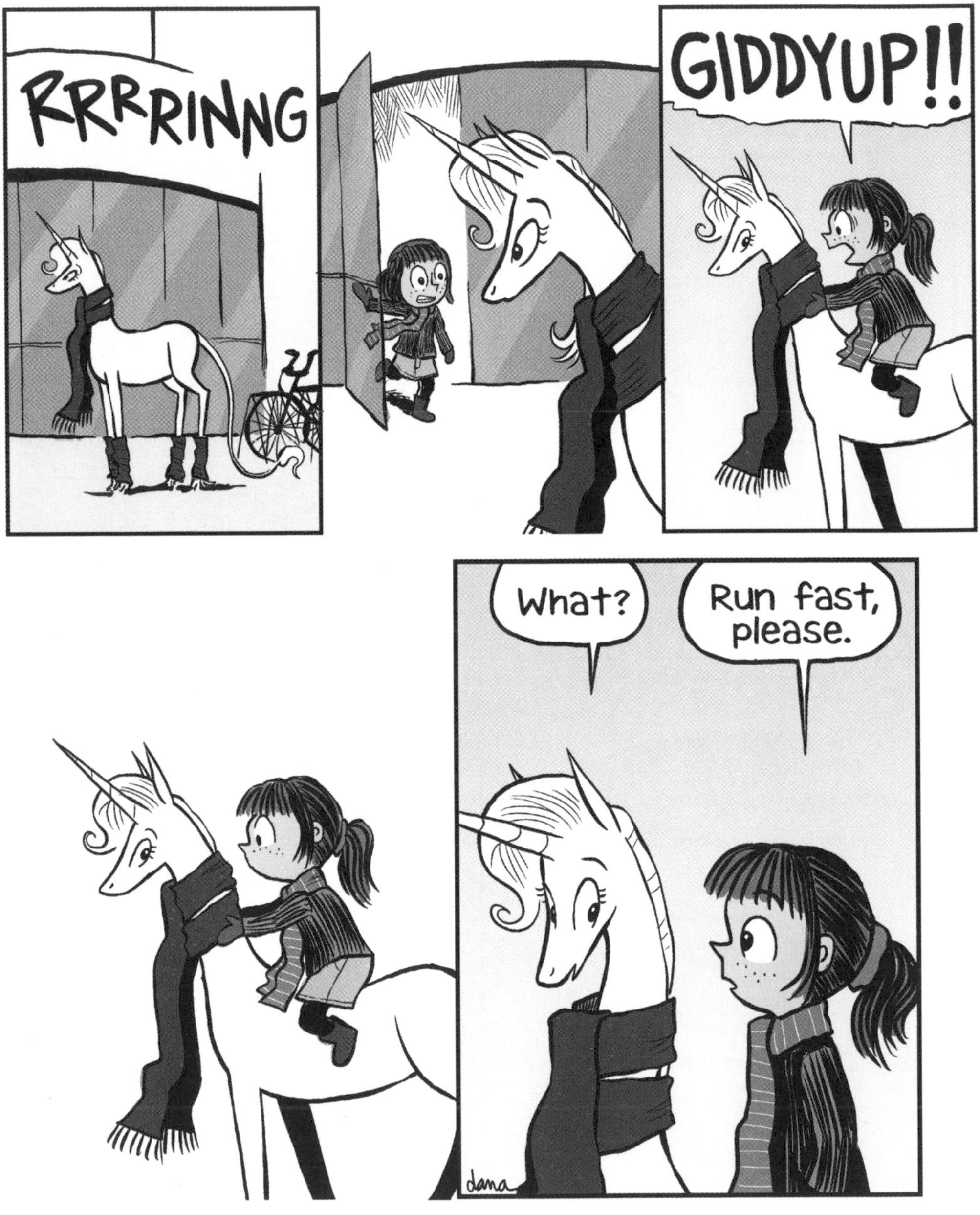
RRRRINNG
GIDDYUP!!
What?
Run fast, please.
dana

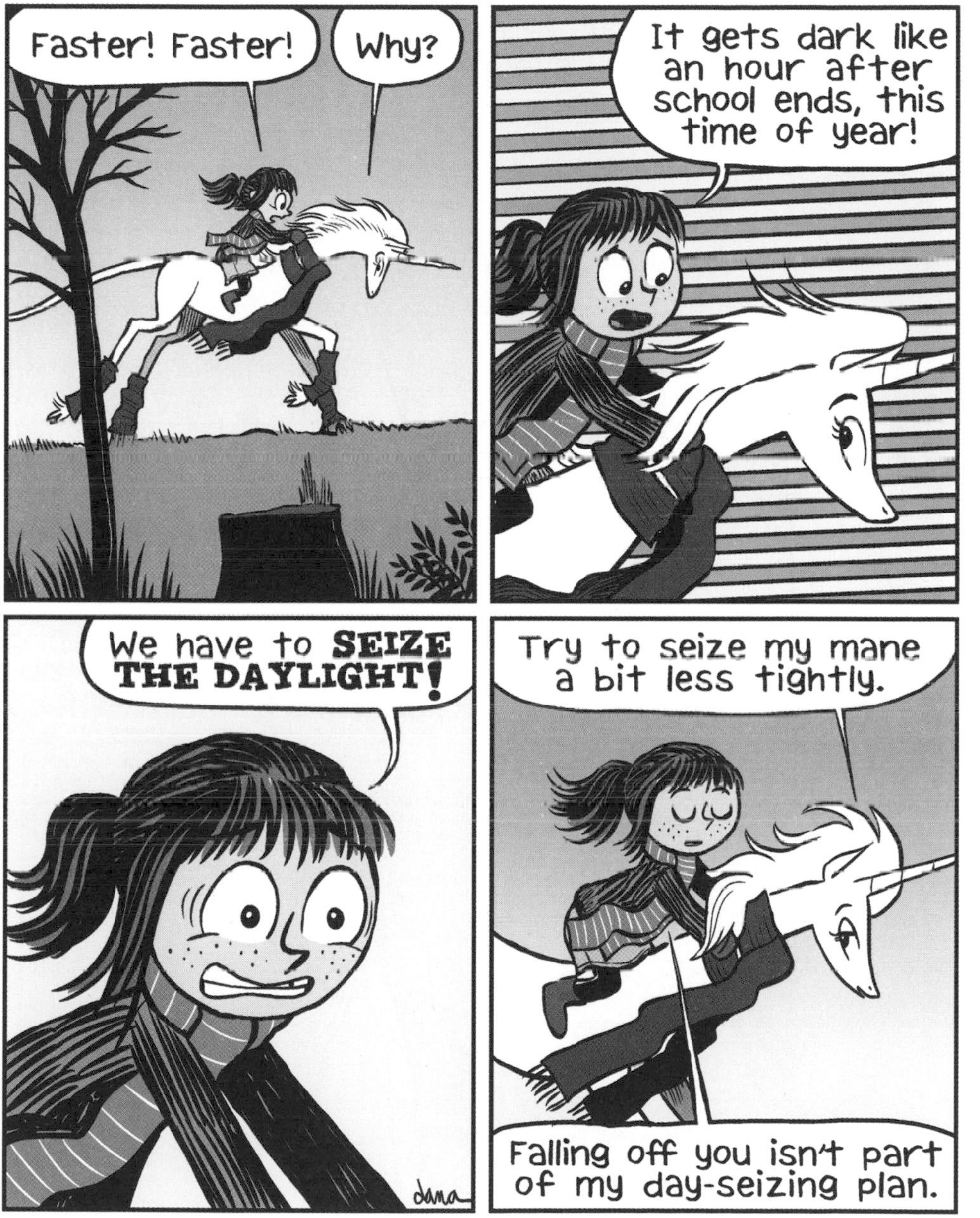
Faster! Faster!
Why?
It gets dark like an hour after school ends, this time of year!
We have to **SEIZE THE DAYLIGHT!**
dana
Try to seize my mane a bit less tightly.
Falling off you isn't part of my day-seizing plan.

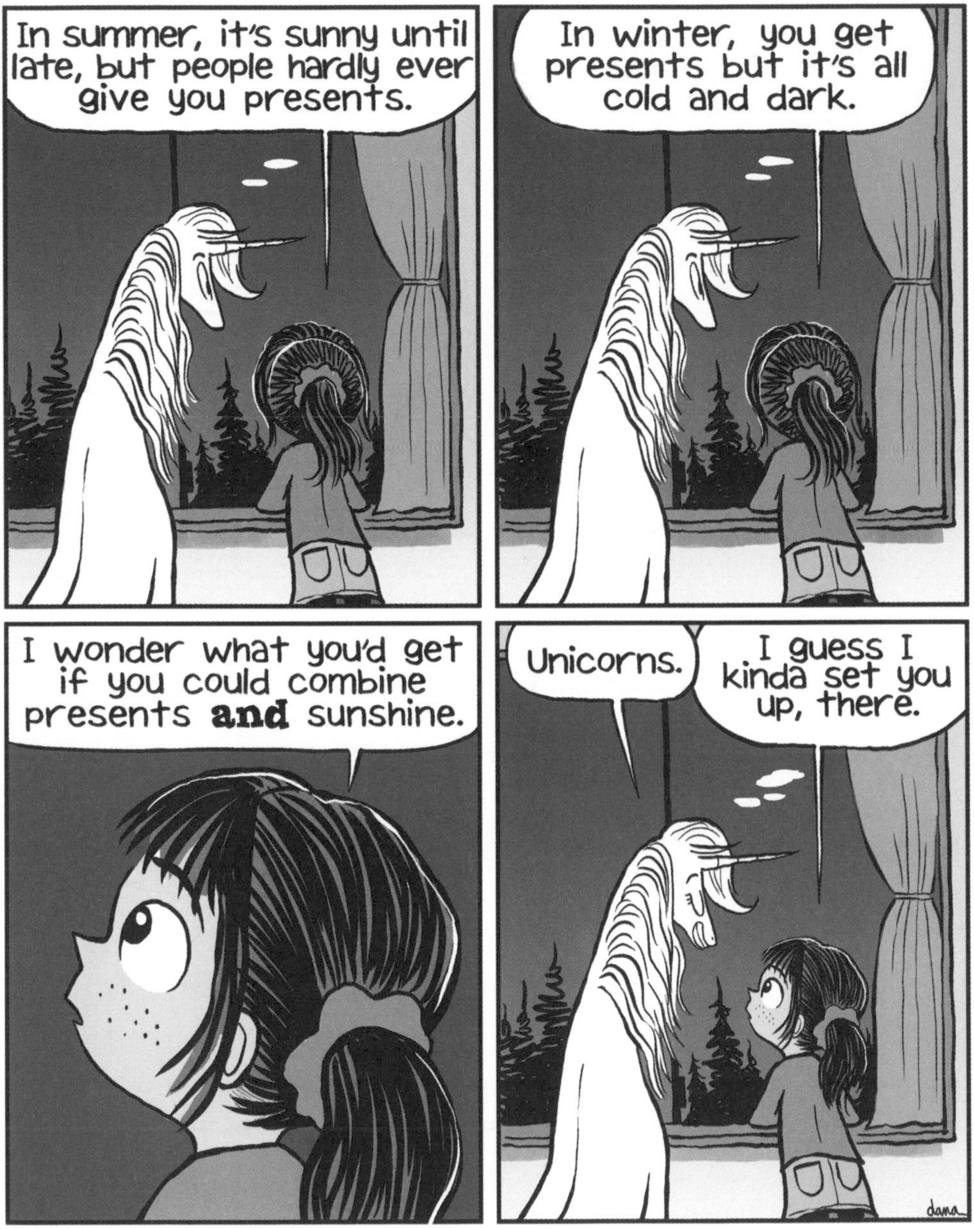
In summer, it's sunny until late, but people hardly ever give you presents.
In winter, you get presents but it's all cold and dark.
I wonder what you'd get if you could combine presents **and** sunshine.
Unicorns.
I guess I kinda set you up, there.
dana

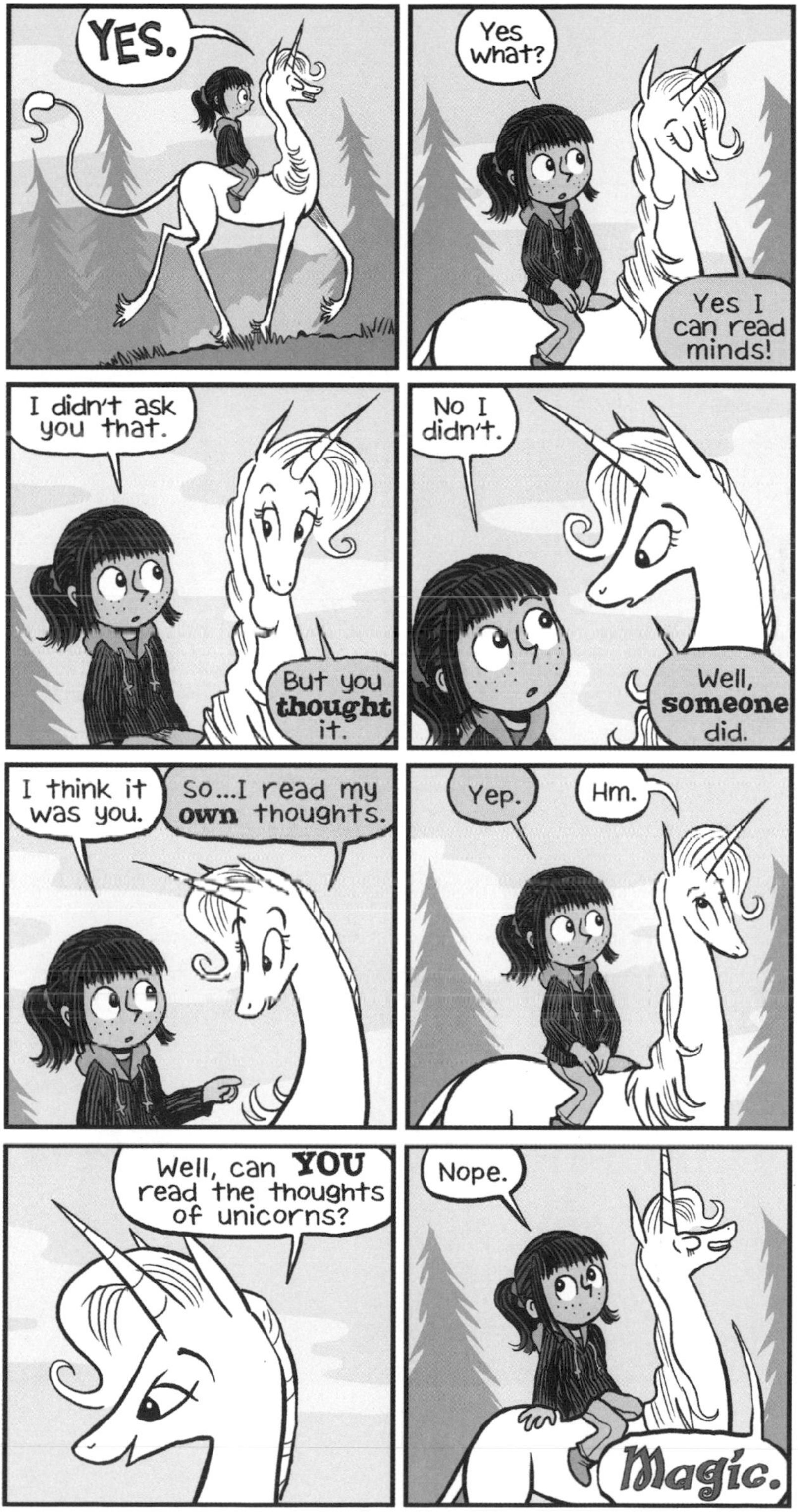
YES.
Yes what?
Yes I can read minds!
I didn't ask you that.
But you **thought** it.
No I didn't.
Well, **someone** did.
I think it was you.
So...I read my **own** thoughts.
Yep.
Hm.
Well, can **YOU** read the thoughts of unicorns?
Nope.
Magic.

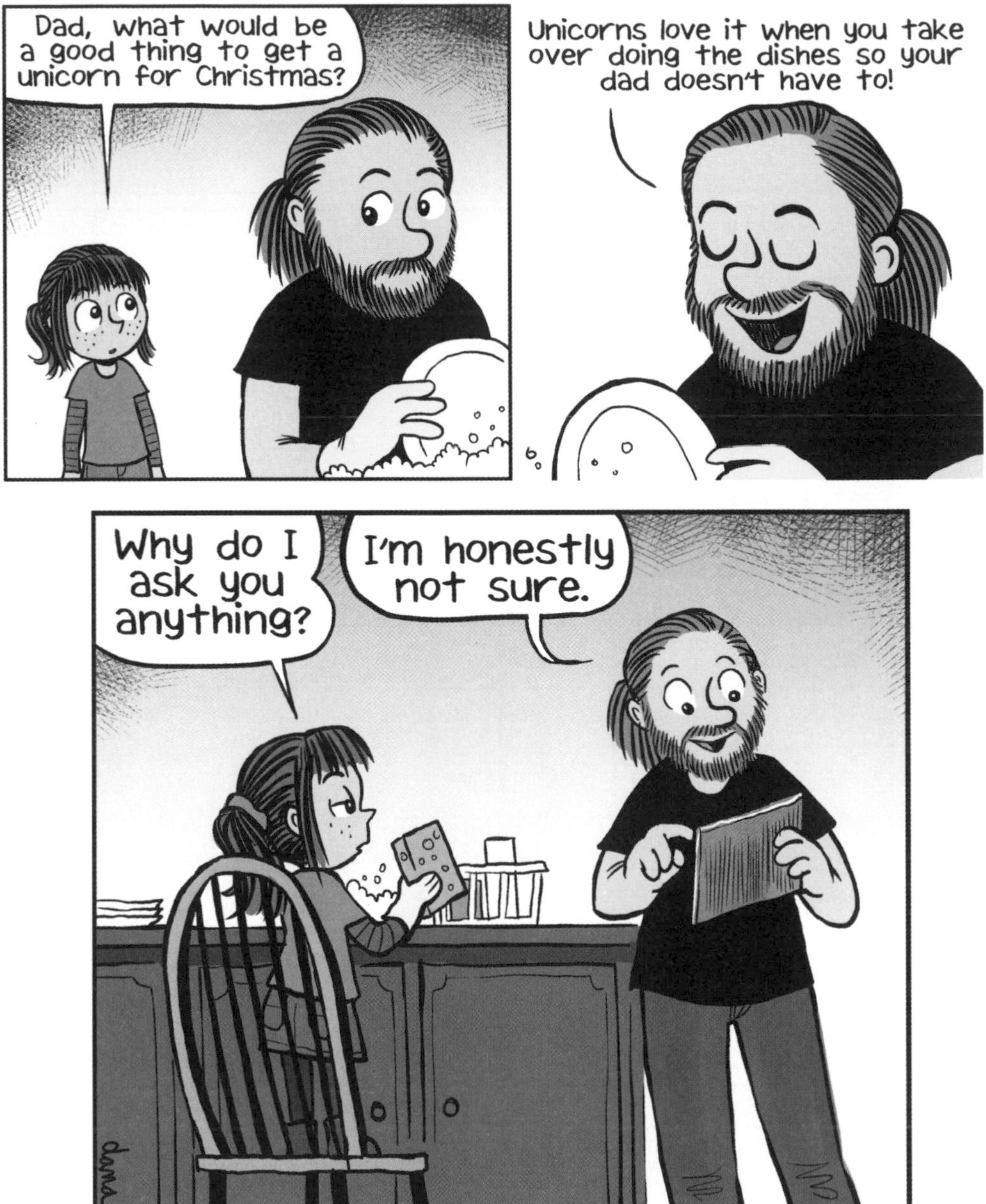
Dad, what would be a good thing to get a unicorn for Christmas?
Unicorns love it when you take over doing the dishes so your dad doesn't have to!
Why do I ask you anything?
I'm honestly not sure.
dana

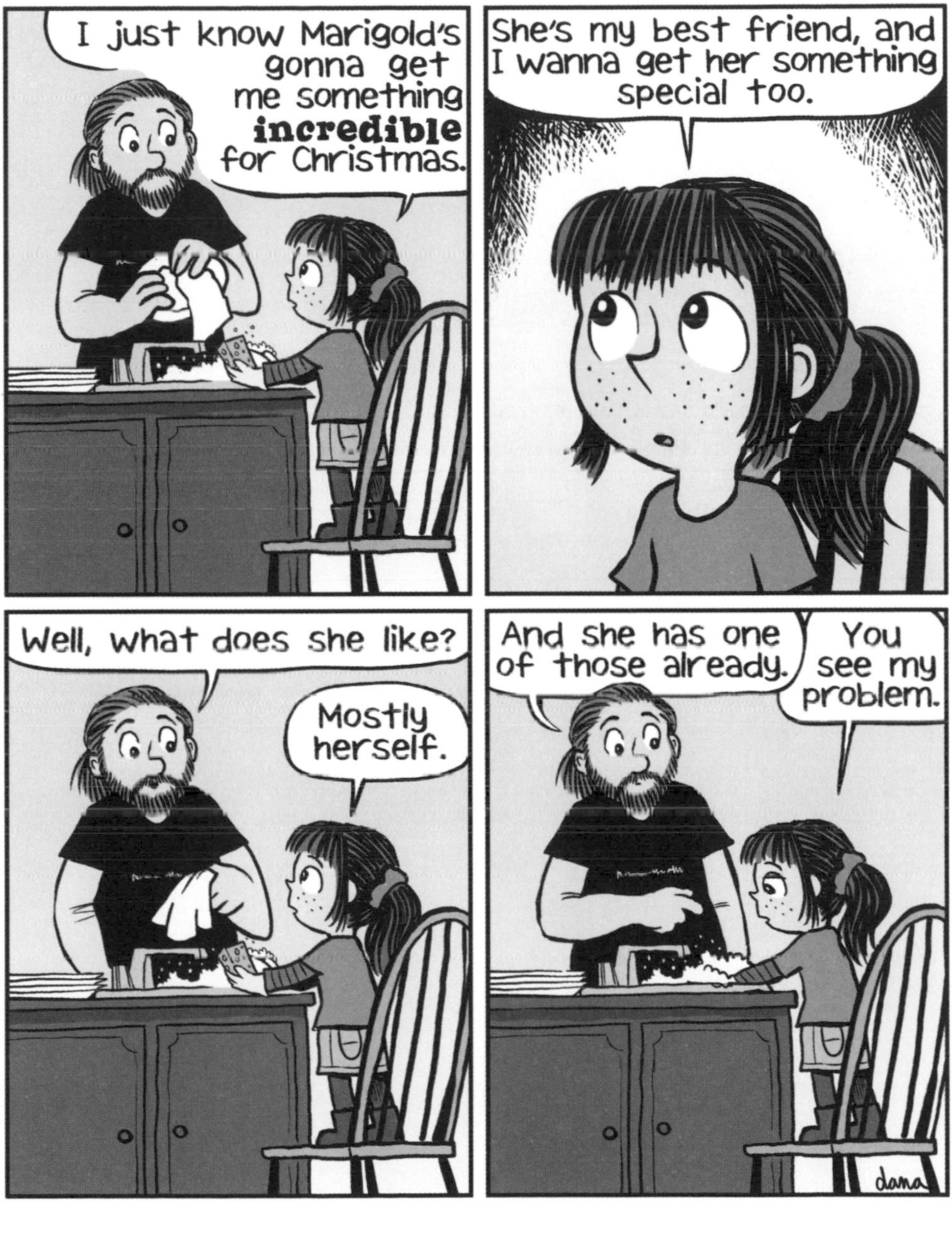
I just know Marigold's gonna get me something **incredible** for Christmas.
She's my best friend, and I wanna get her something special too.
Well, what does she like?
Mostly herself.
And she has one of those already.
You see my problem.
dana

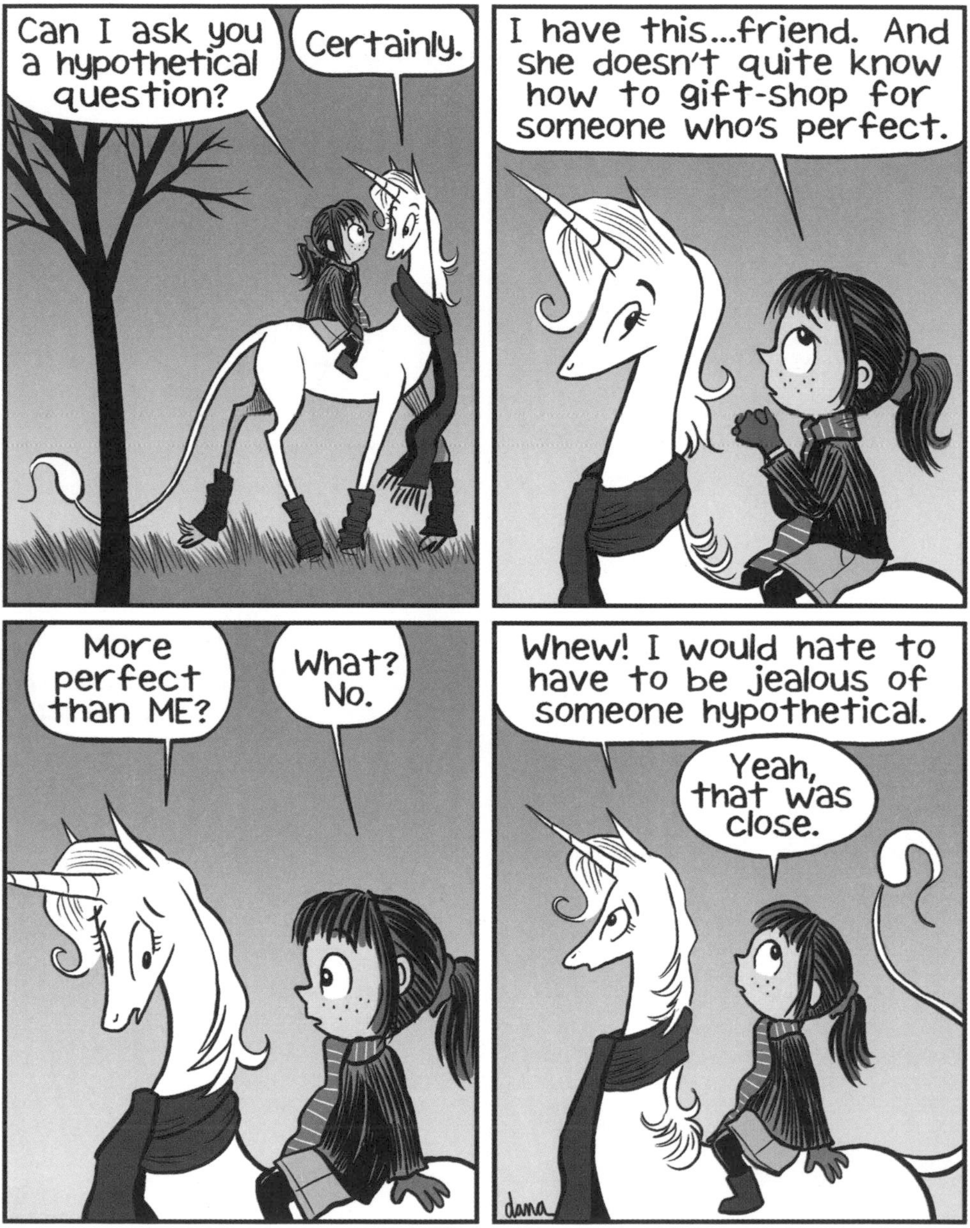
Can I ask you a hypothetical question?
Certainly.
I have this...friend. And she doesn't quite know how to gift-shop for someone who's perfect.
More perfect than ME?
What? No.
Whew! I would hate to have to be jealous of someone hypothetical.
Yeah, that was close.
dana

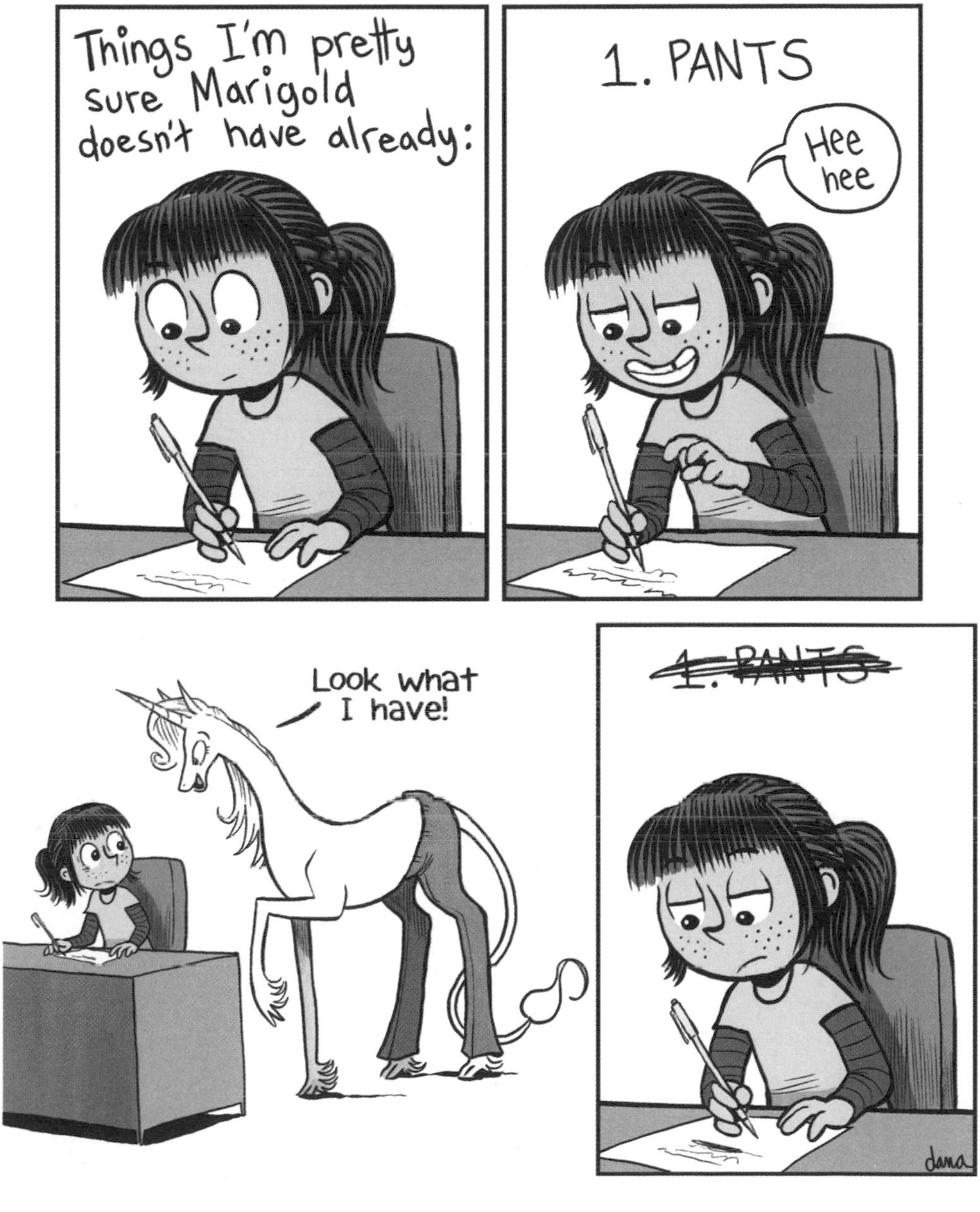
Things I'm pretty sure Marigold doesn't have already:
1. PANTS
Hee hee
Look what I have!
1. PANTS
dana

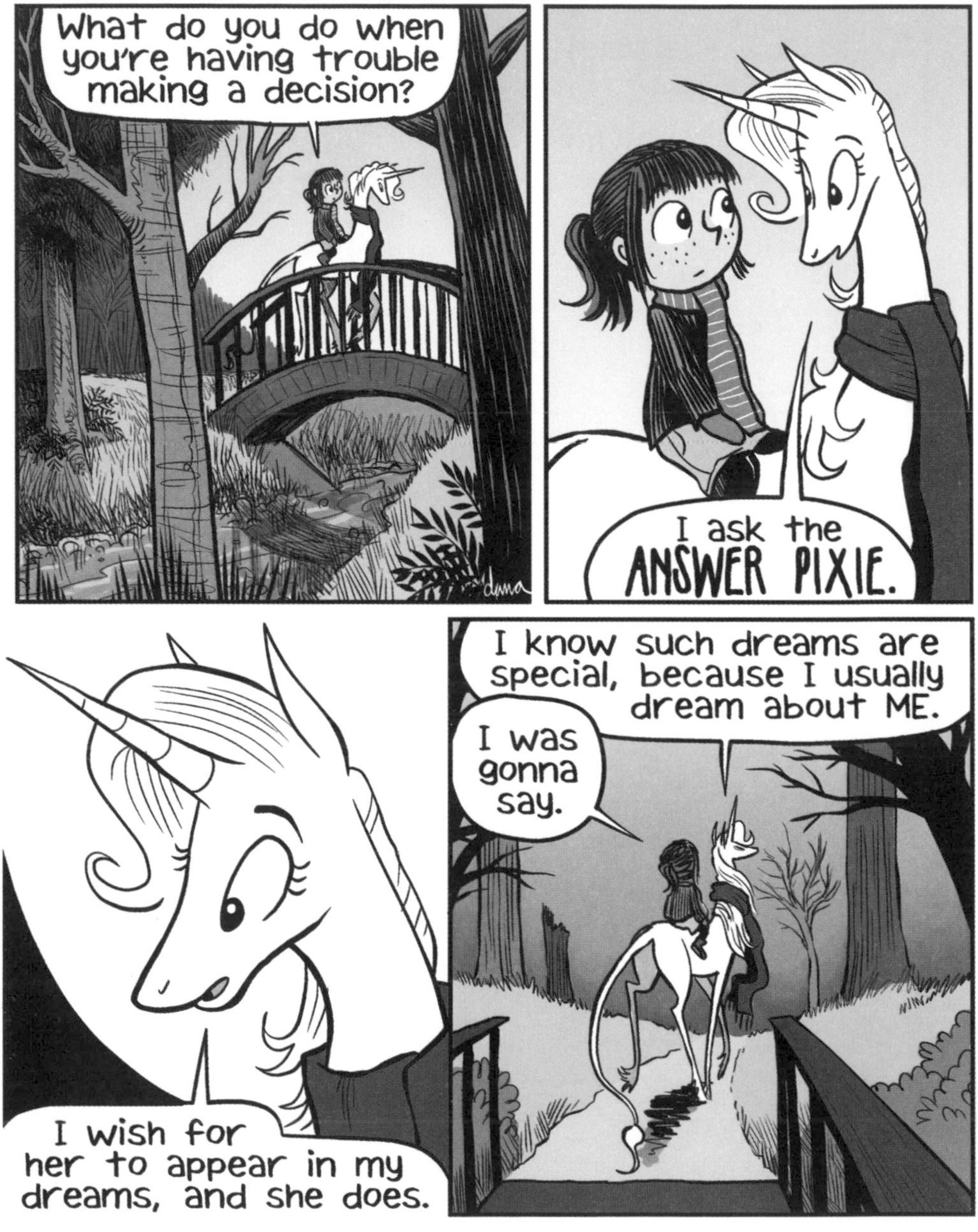
What do you do when you're having trouble making a decision?
I ask the ANSWER PIXIE.
I wish for her to appear in my dreams, and she does.
I know such dreams are special, because I usually dream about ME.
I was gonna say.

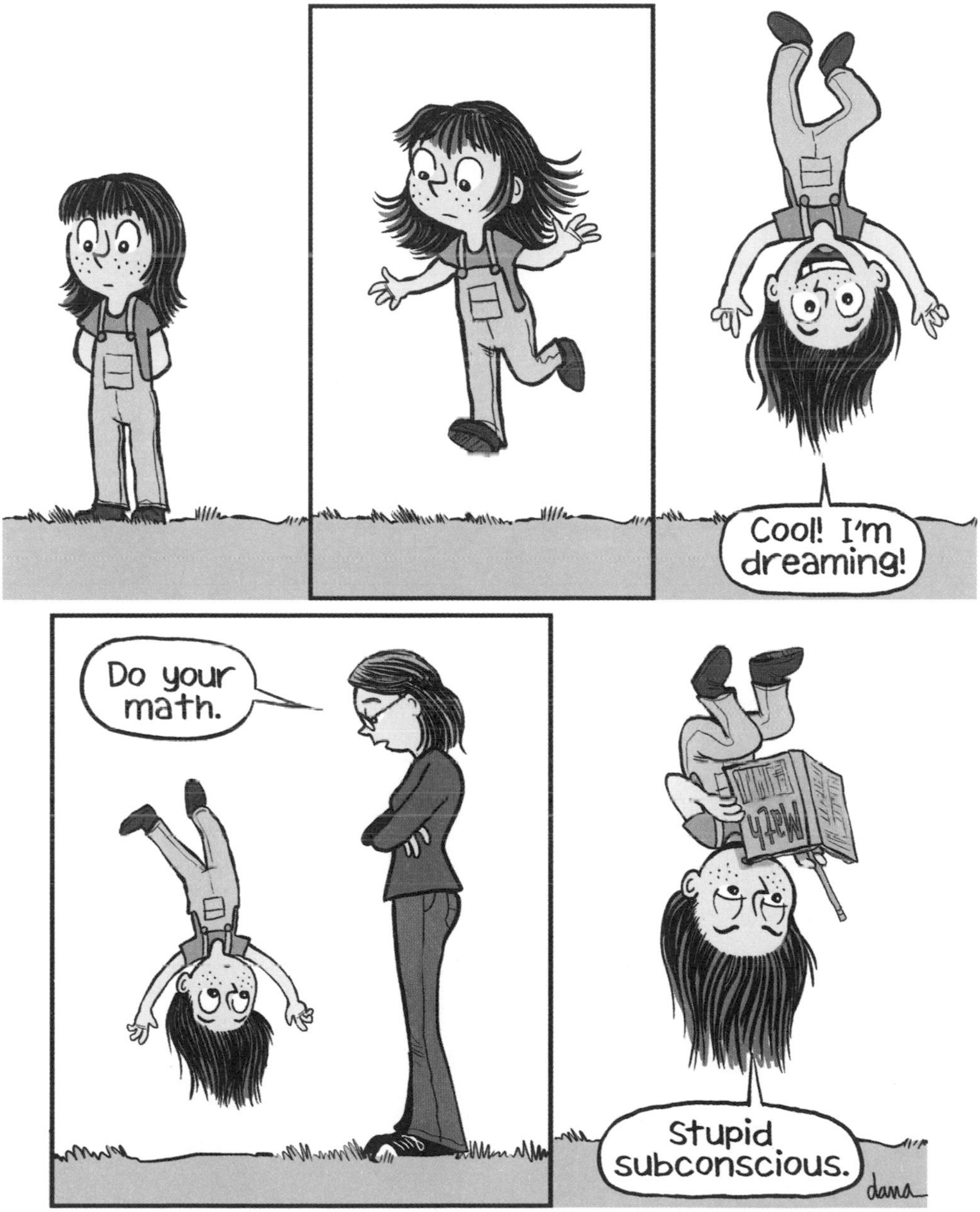
Cool! I'm dreaming!
Do your math.
Stupid subconscious.
dana

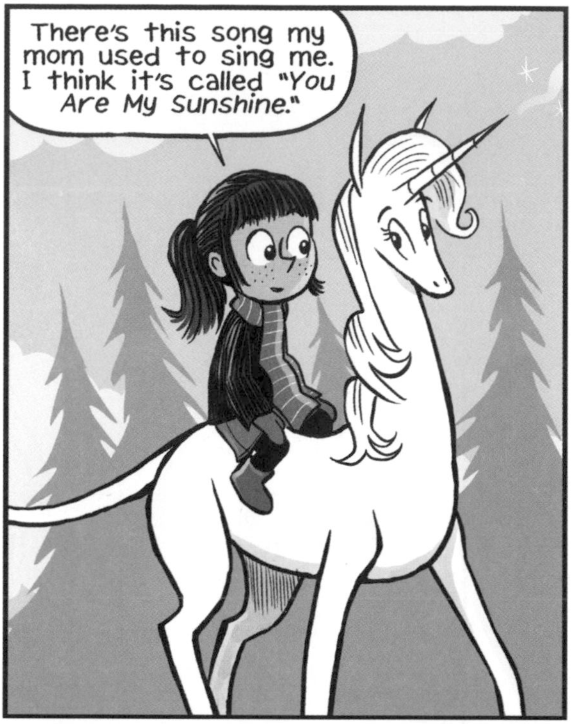
There's this song my mom used to sing me. I think it's called "You Are My Sunshine."

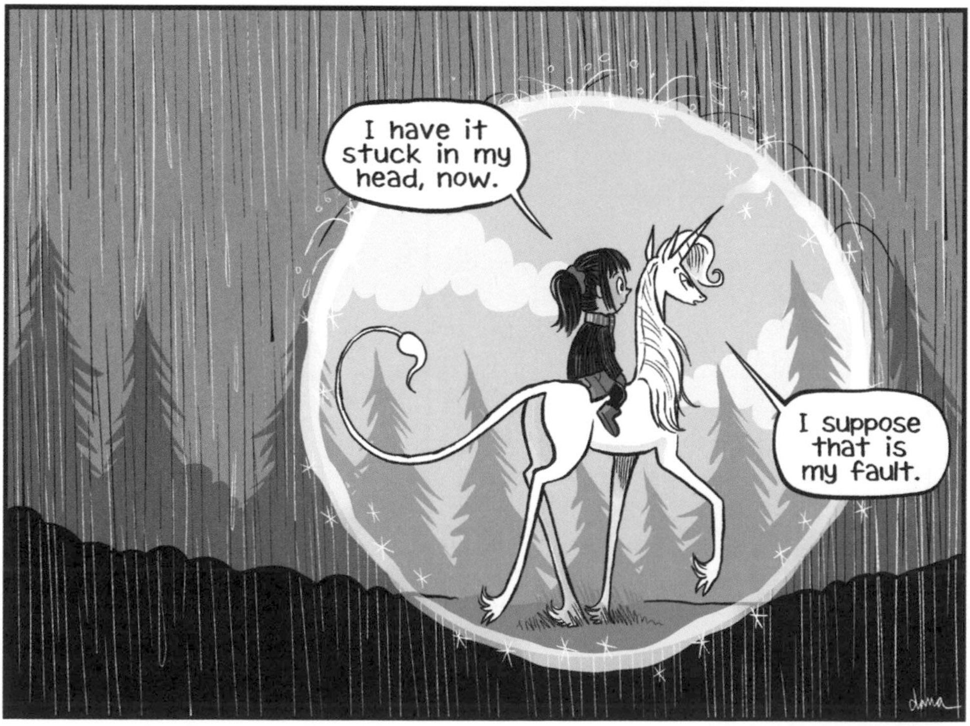
I have it stuck in my head, now.
I suppose that is my fault.

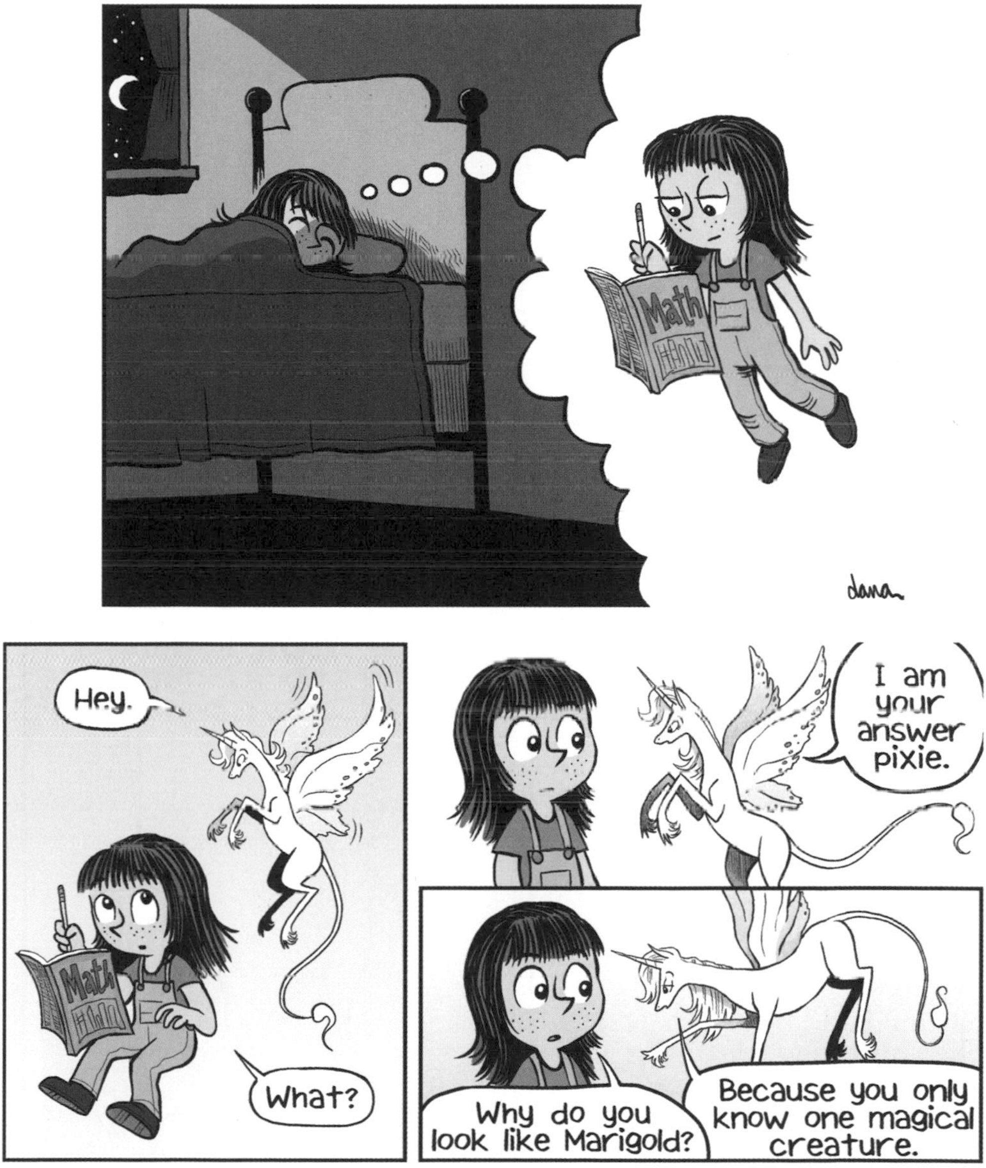
dana
Hey.
What?
I am your answer pixie.
Why do you look like Marigold?
Because you only know one magical creature.

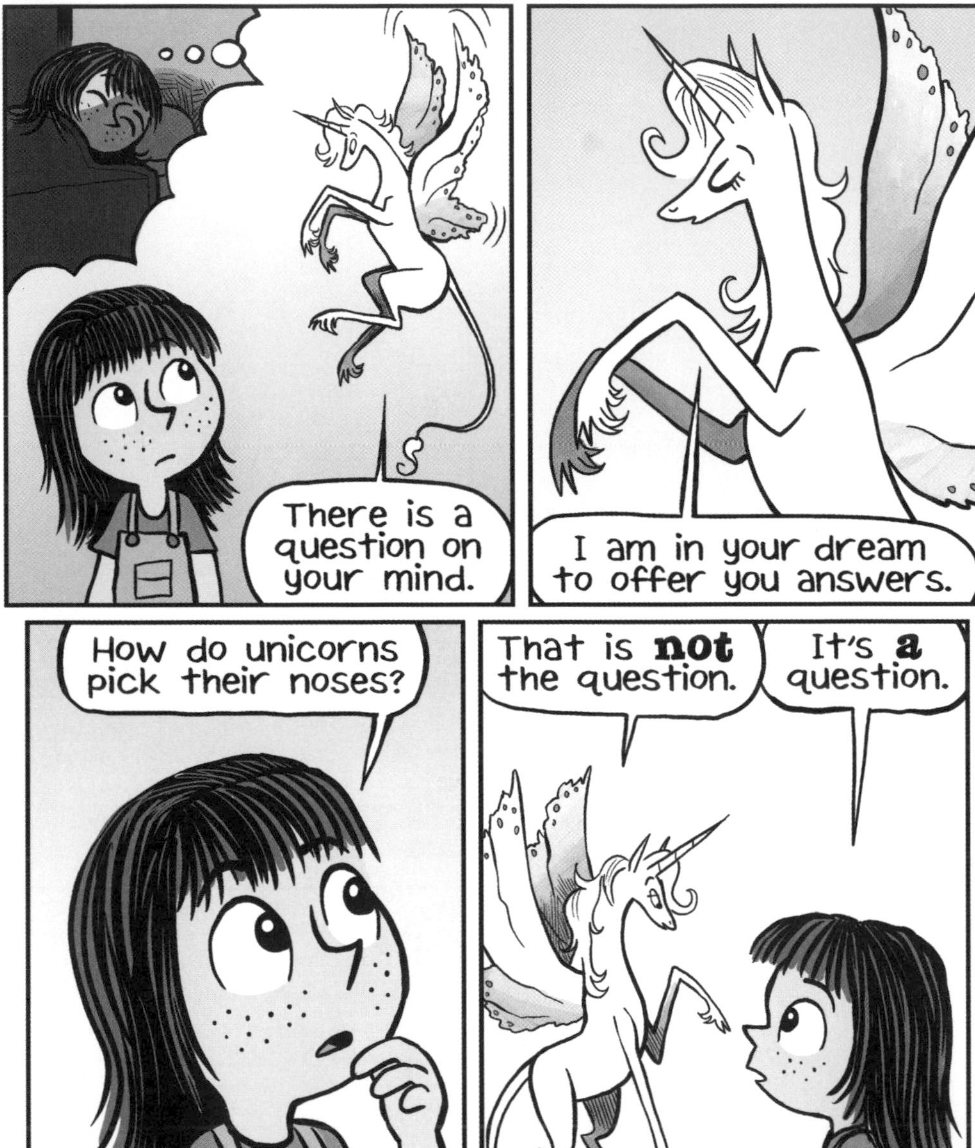
There is a question on your mind.
I am in your dream to offer you answers.
How do unicorns pick their noses?
That is **not** the question.
It's **a** question.
dana

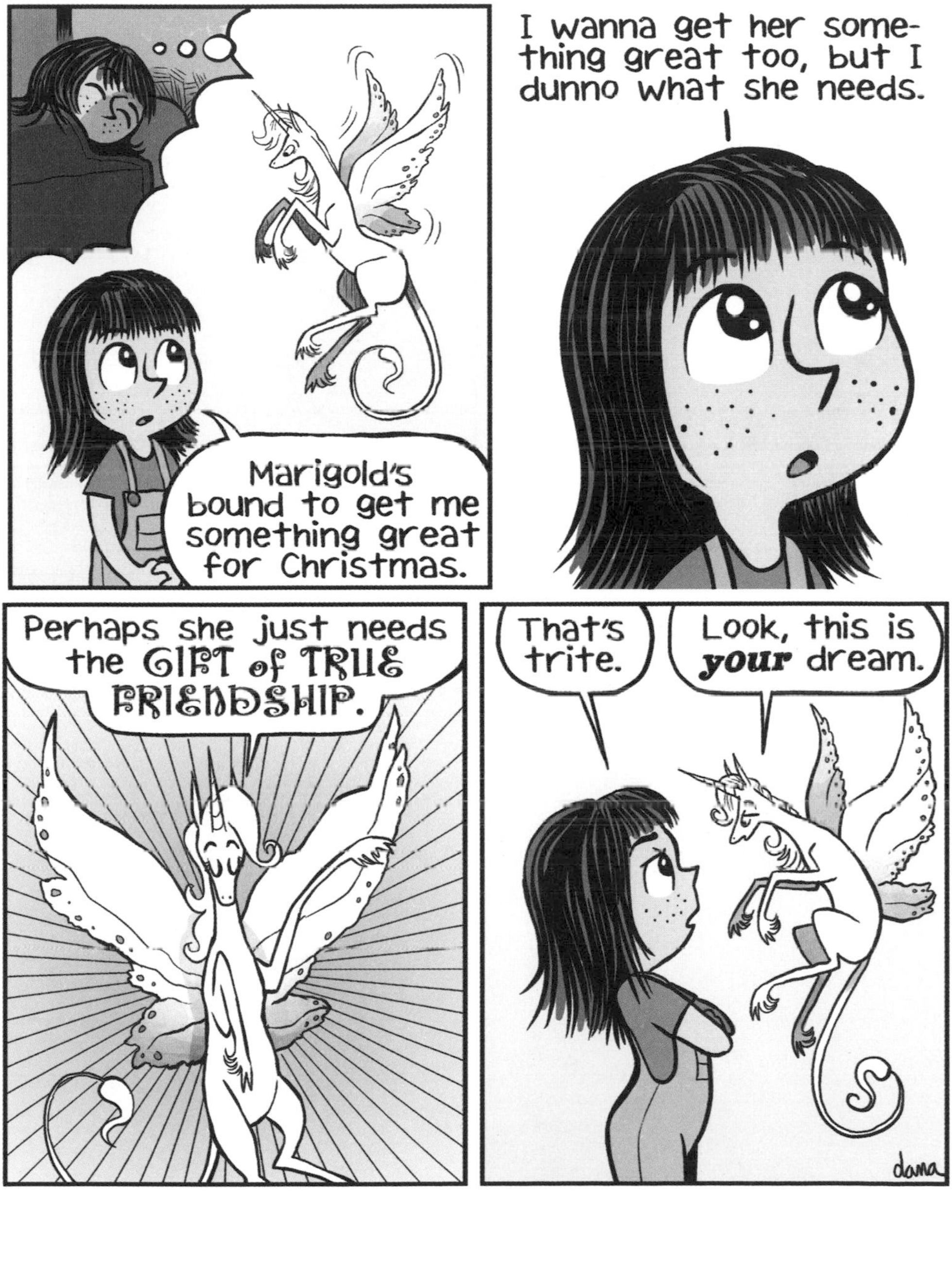

Marigold's bound to get me something great for Christmas.
I wanna get her something great too, but I dunno what she needs.
Perhaps she just needs the GIFT of TRUE FRIENDSHIP.
That's trite.
Look, this is *your* dream.
dana

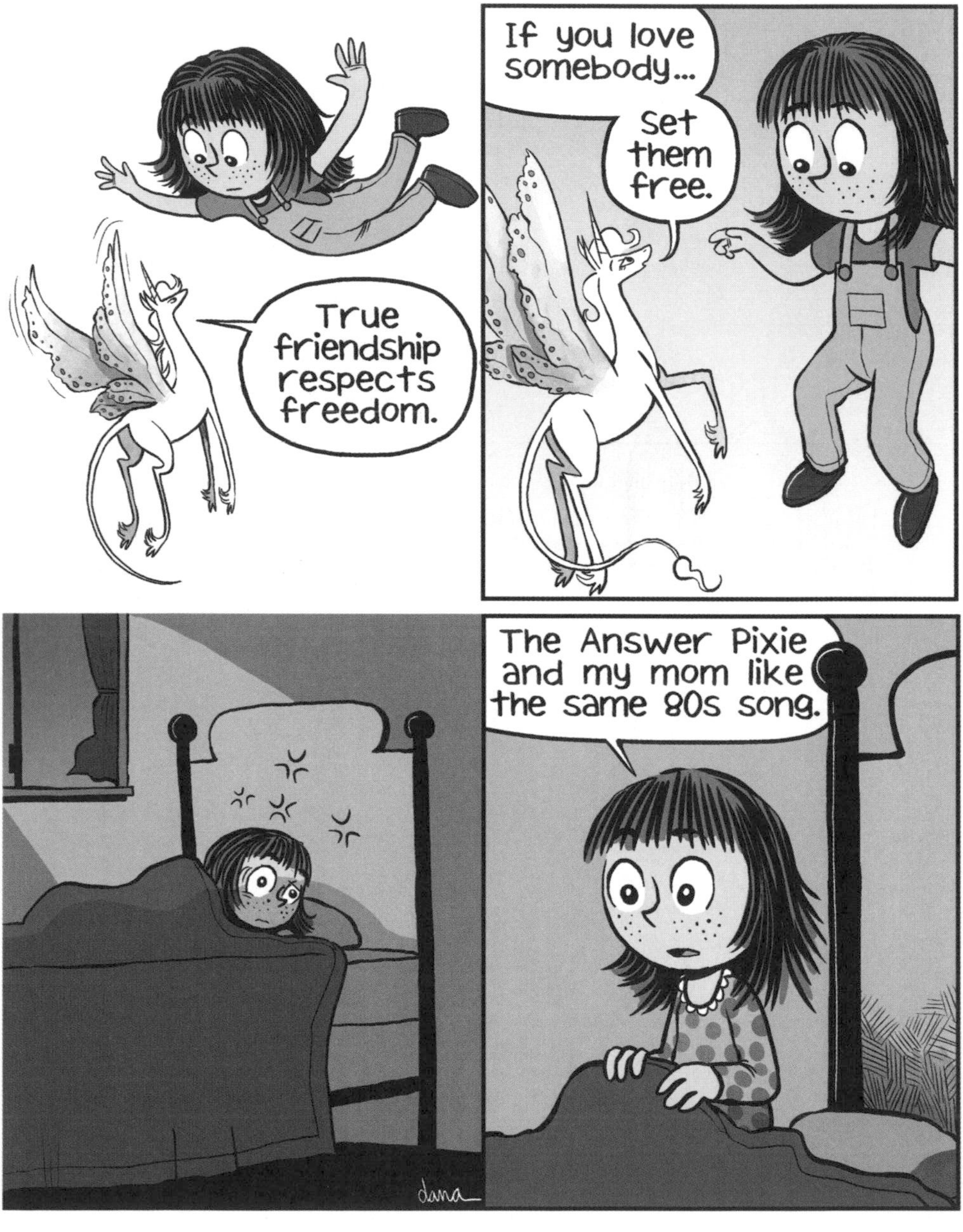
True friendship respects freedom.
If you love somebody...
Set them free.
The Answer Pixie and my mom like the same 80s song.
dana

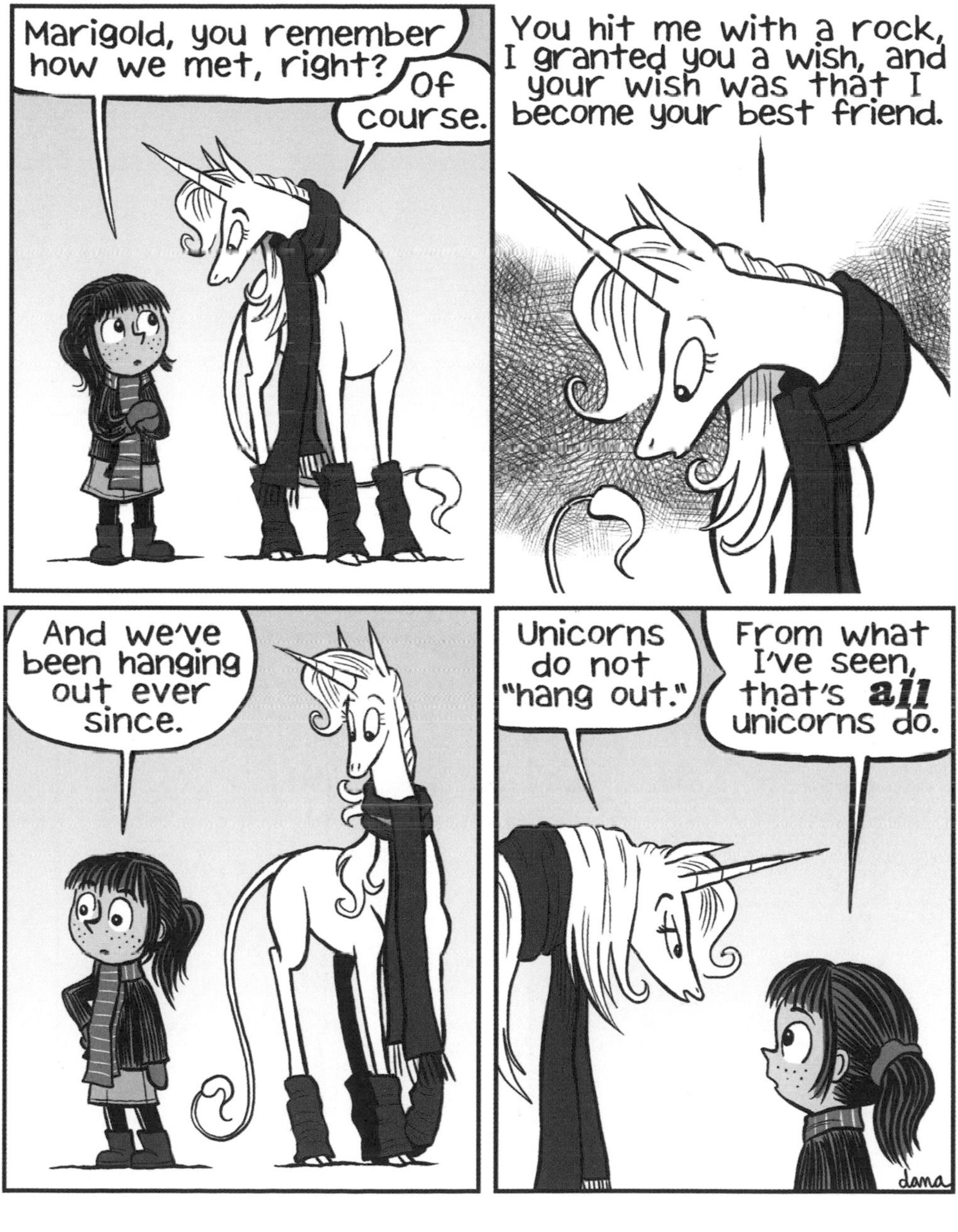
Marigold, you remember how we met, right?
Of course.
You hit me with a rock, I granted you a wish, and your wish was that I become your best friend.
And we've been hanging out ever since.
Unicorns do not "hang out."
From what I've seen, that's **all** unicorns do.
dana

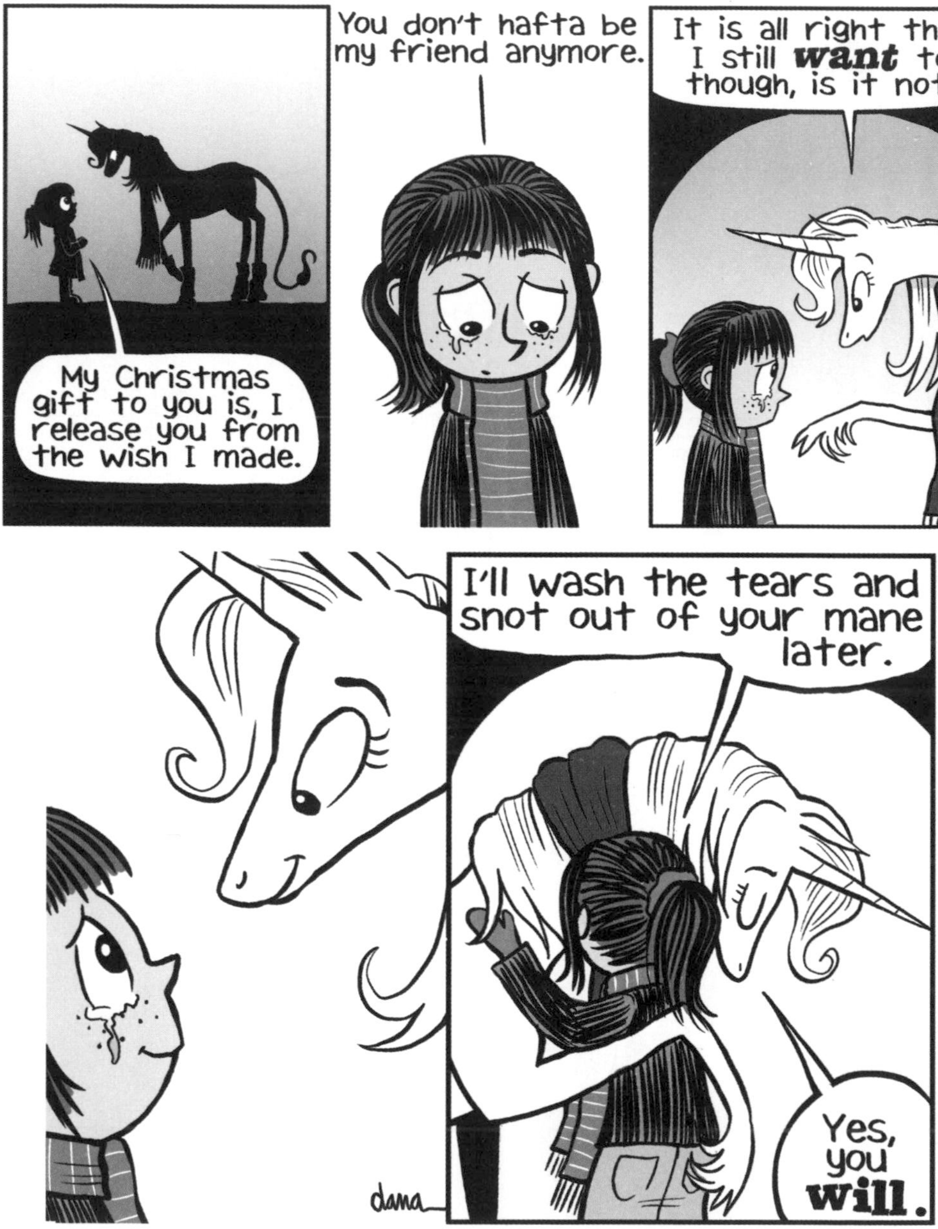
My Christmas gift to you is, I release you from the wish I made.
You don't hafta be my friend anymore.
It is all right that I still **want** to, though, is it not?
I'll wash the tears and snot out of your mane later.
Yes, you **will**.
dana

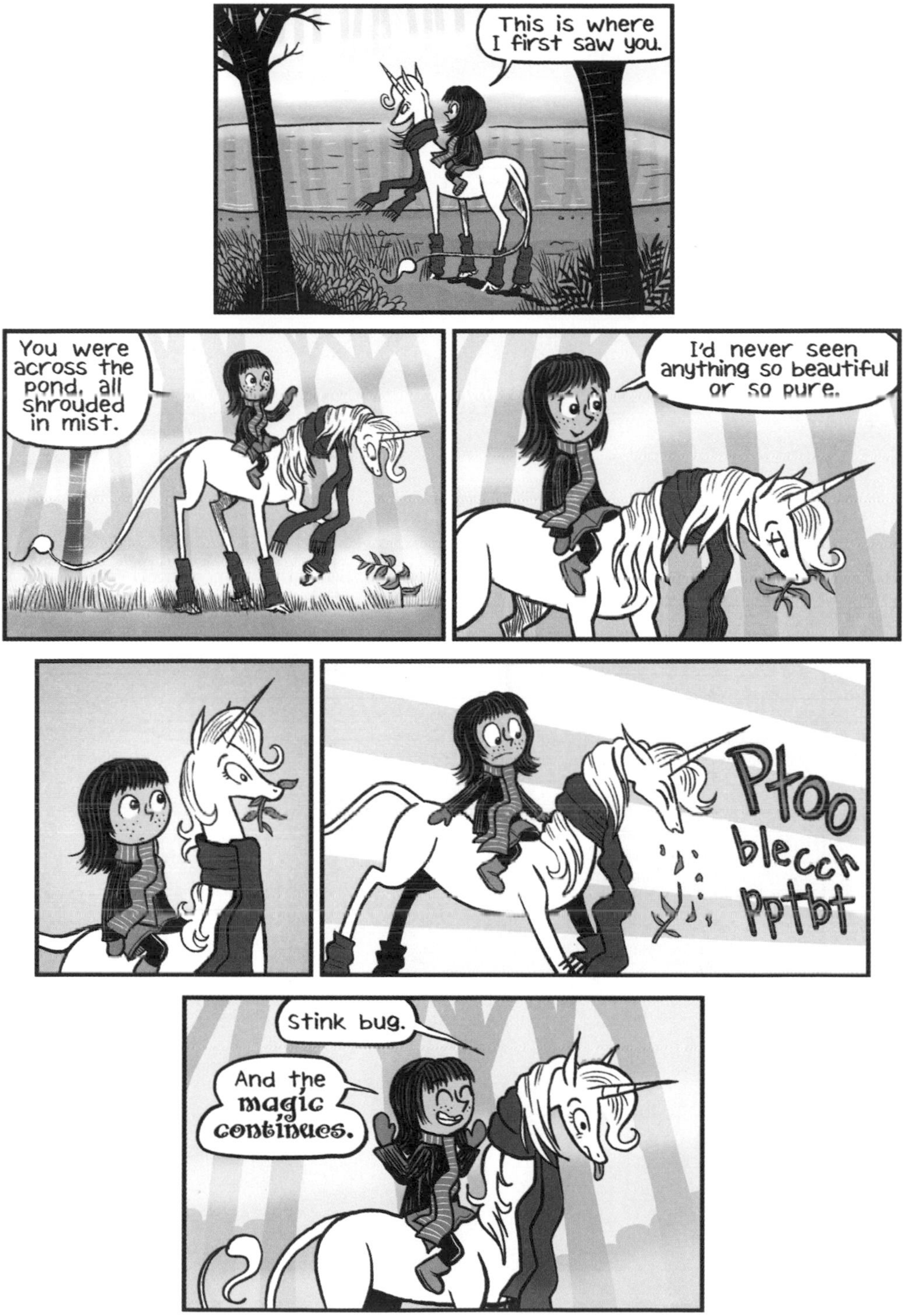
This is where I first saw you.
You were across the pond, all shrouded in mist.
I'd never seen anything so beautiful or so pure.
Ptoo
blecch
pptbt
Stink bug.
And the magic continues.

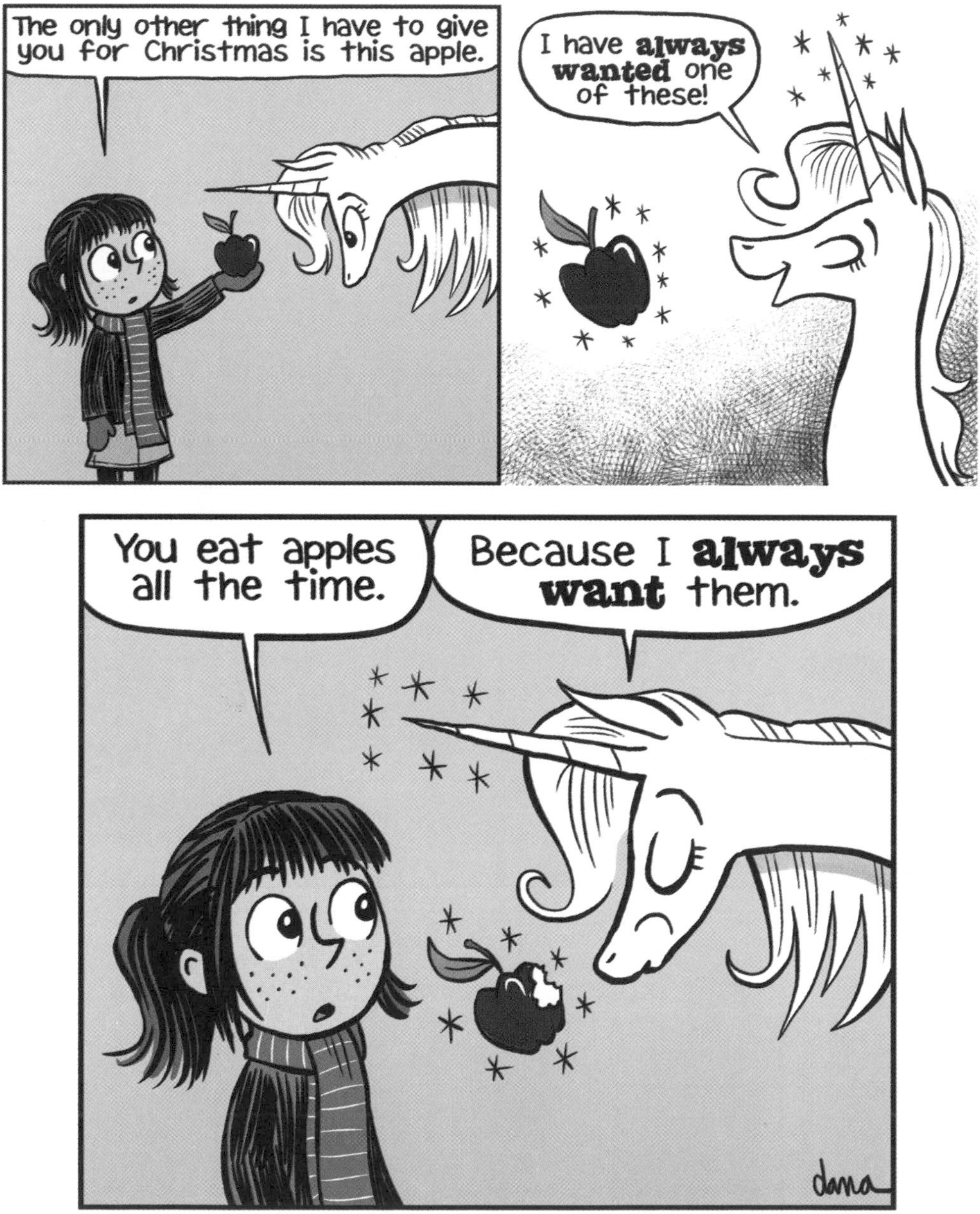

The only other thing I have to give you for Christmas is this apple.
I have **always wanted** one of these!
You eat apples all the time.
Because I **always want** them.
dana

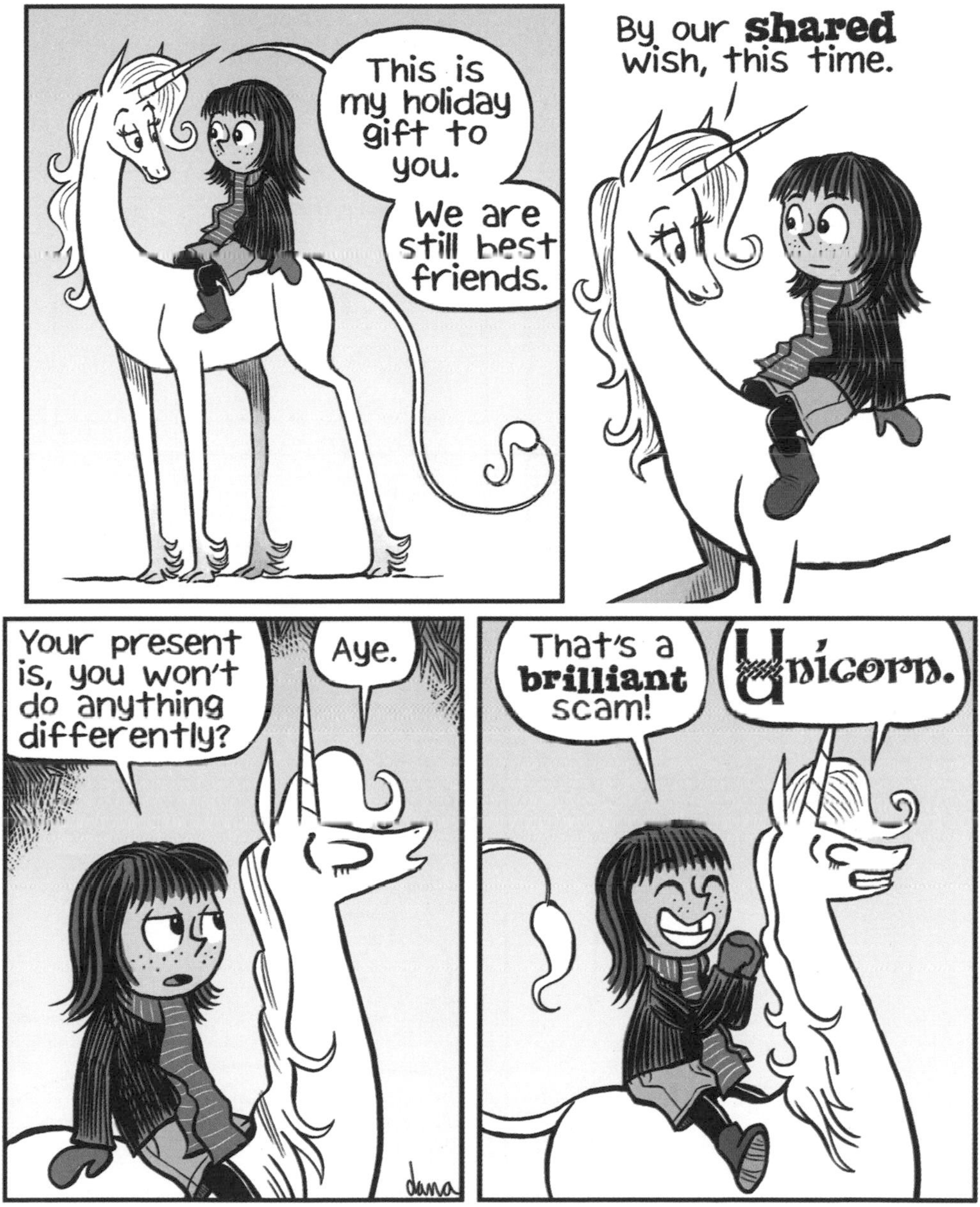
This is my holiday gift to you.
We are still best friends.
By our **shared** wish, this time.
Your present is, you won't do anything differently?
Aye.
That's a **brilliant** scam!
Unicorn.
dana

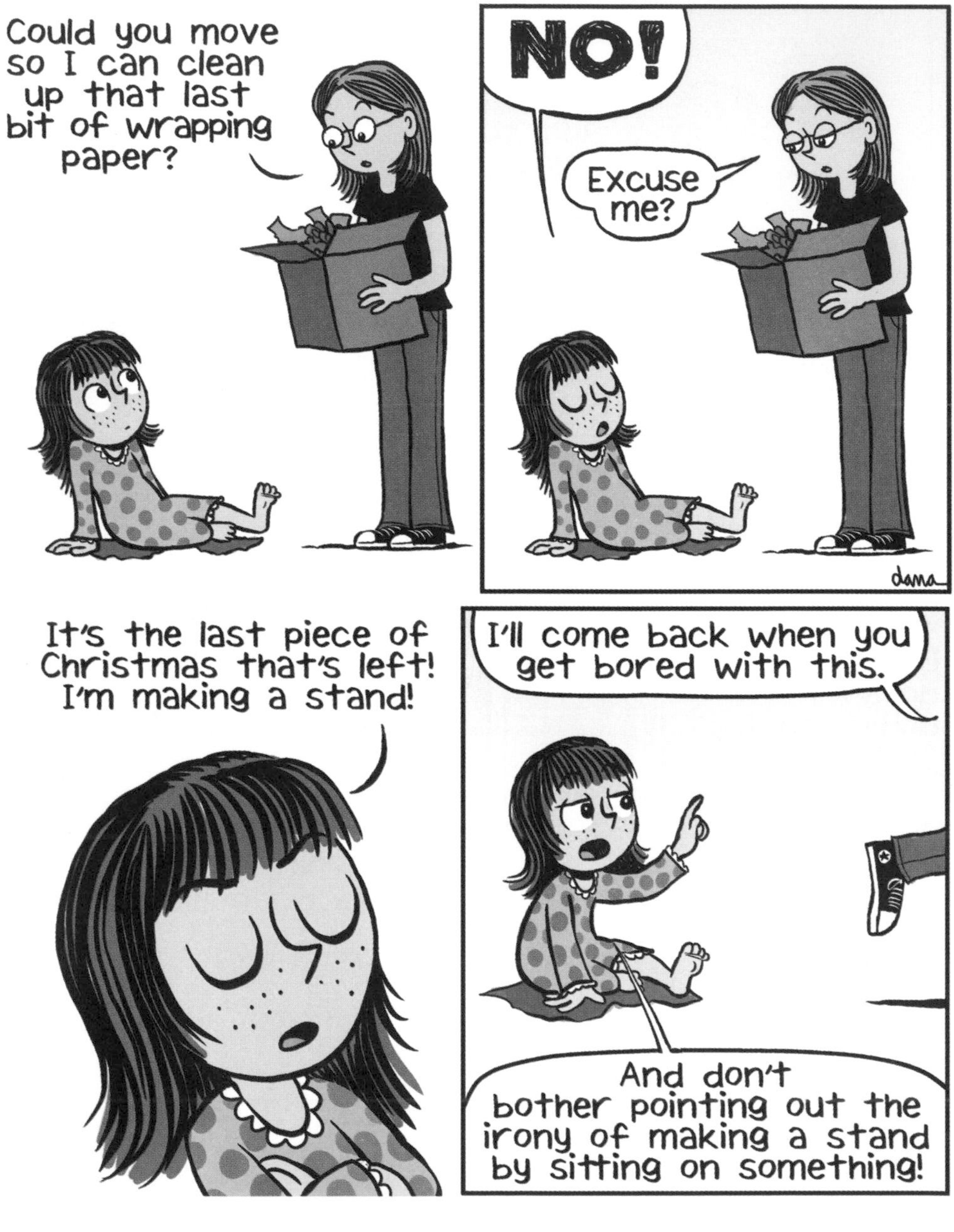
Could you move so I can clean up that last bit of wrapping paper?
NO!
Excuse me?
dana
It's the last piece of Christmas that's left! I'm making a stand!
I'll come back when you get bored with this.
And don't bother pointing out the irony of making a stand by sitting on something!

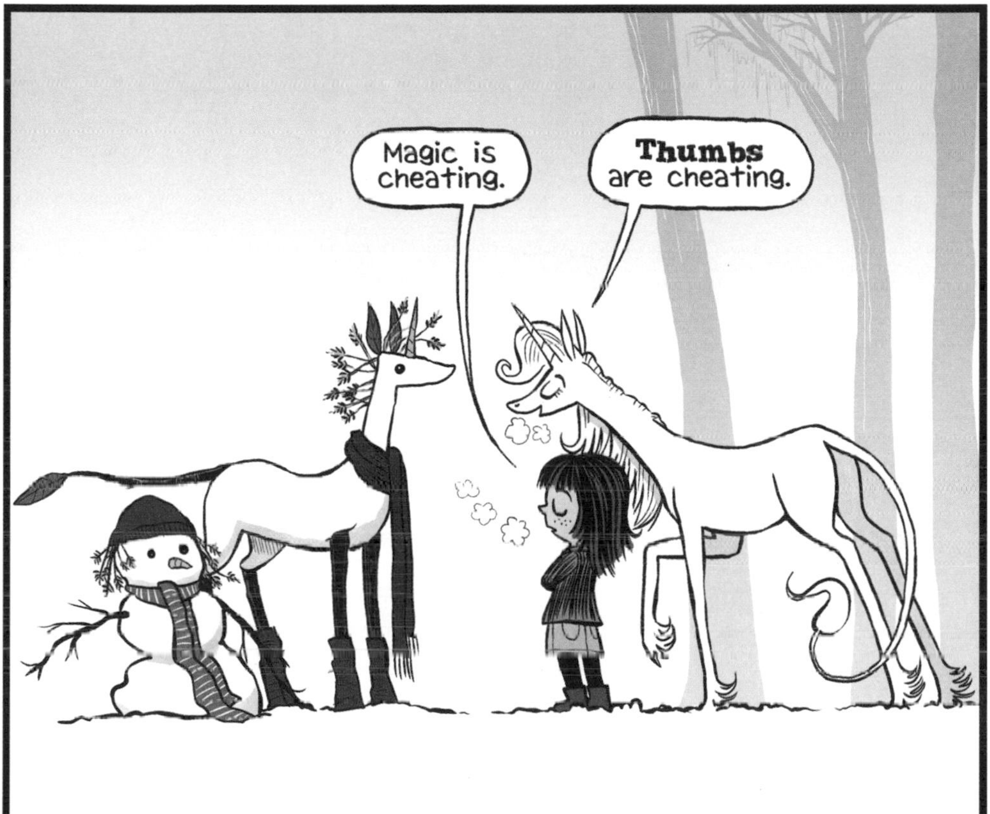
Magic is cheating.
Thumbs are cheating.
dana

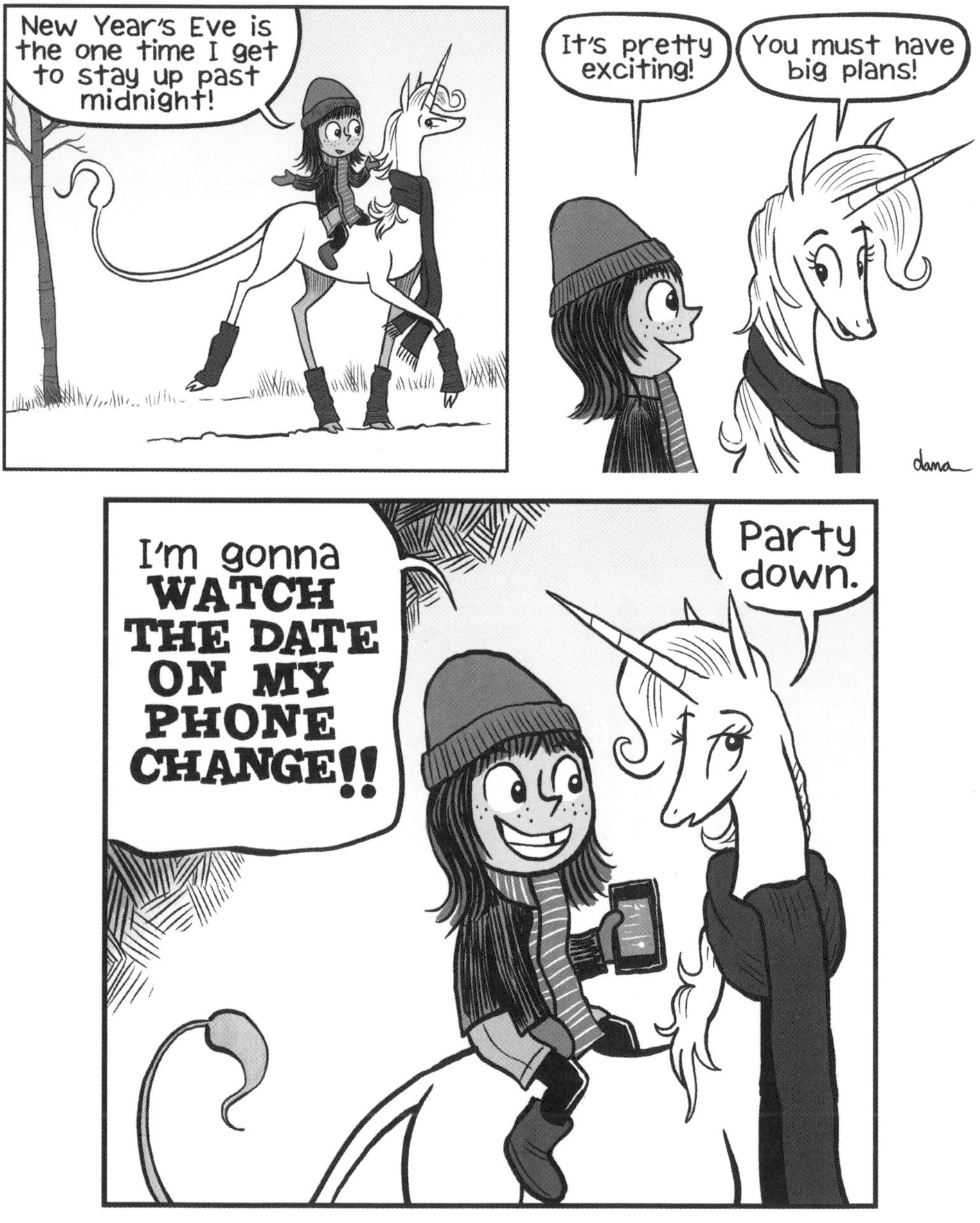
New Year's Eve is the one time I get to stay up past midnight!
It's pretty exciting!
You must have big plans!
dana
I'm gonna **WATCH THE DATE ON MY PHONE CHANGE!!**
Party down.

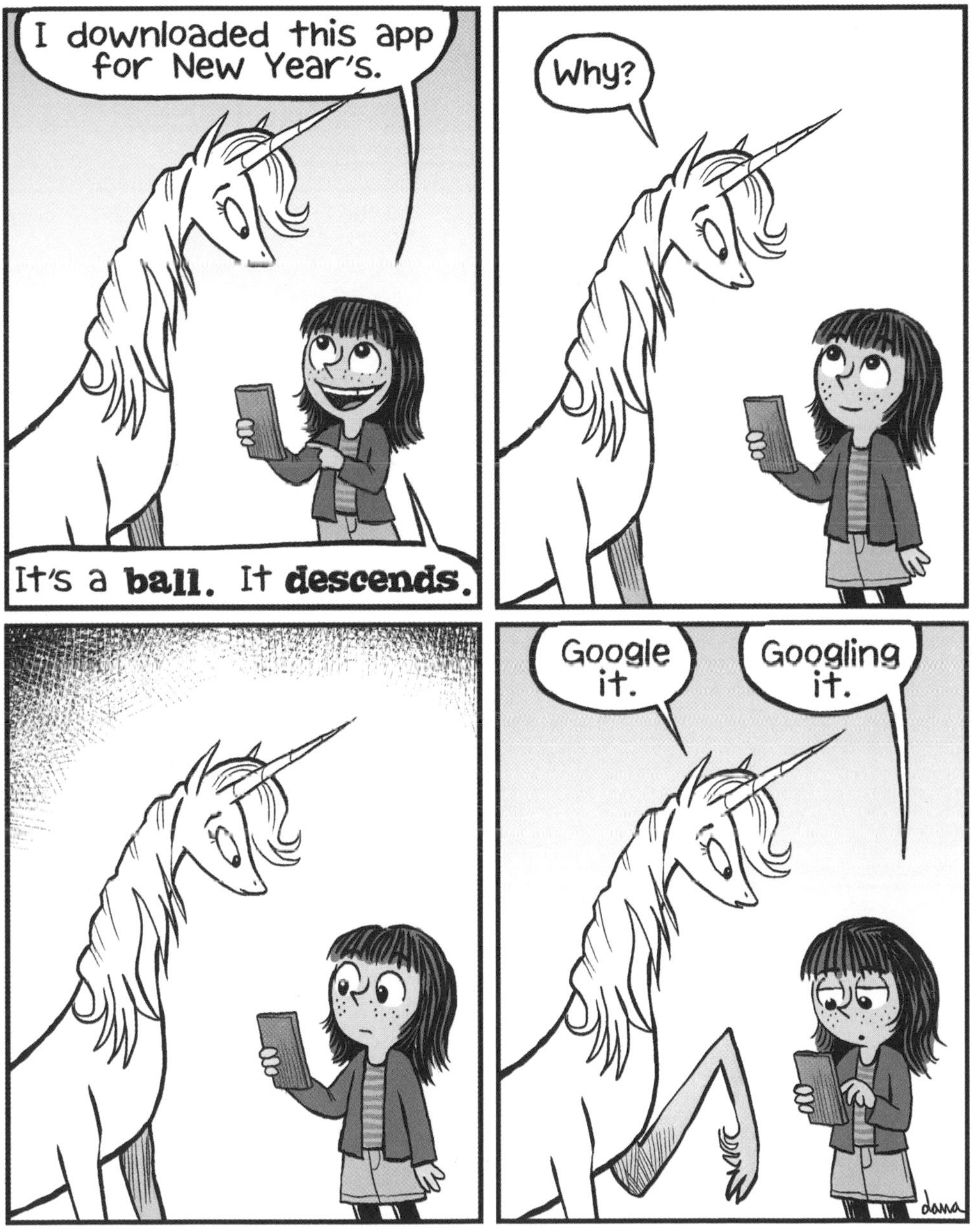
I downloaded this app for New Year's.
It's a **ball**. It **descends**.
Why?
Google it.
Googling it.
dana

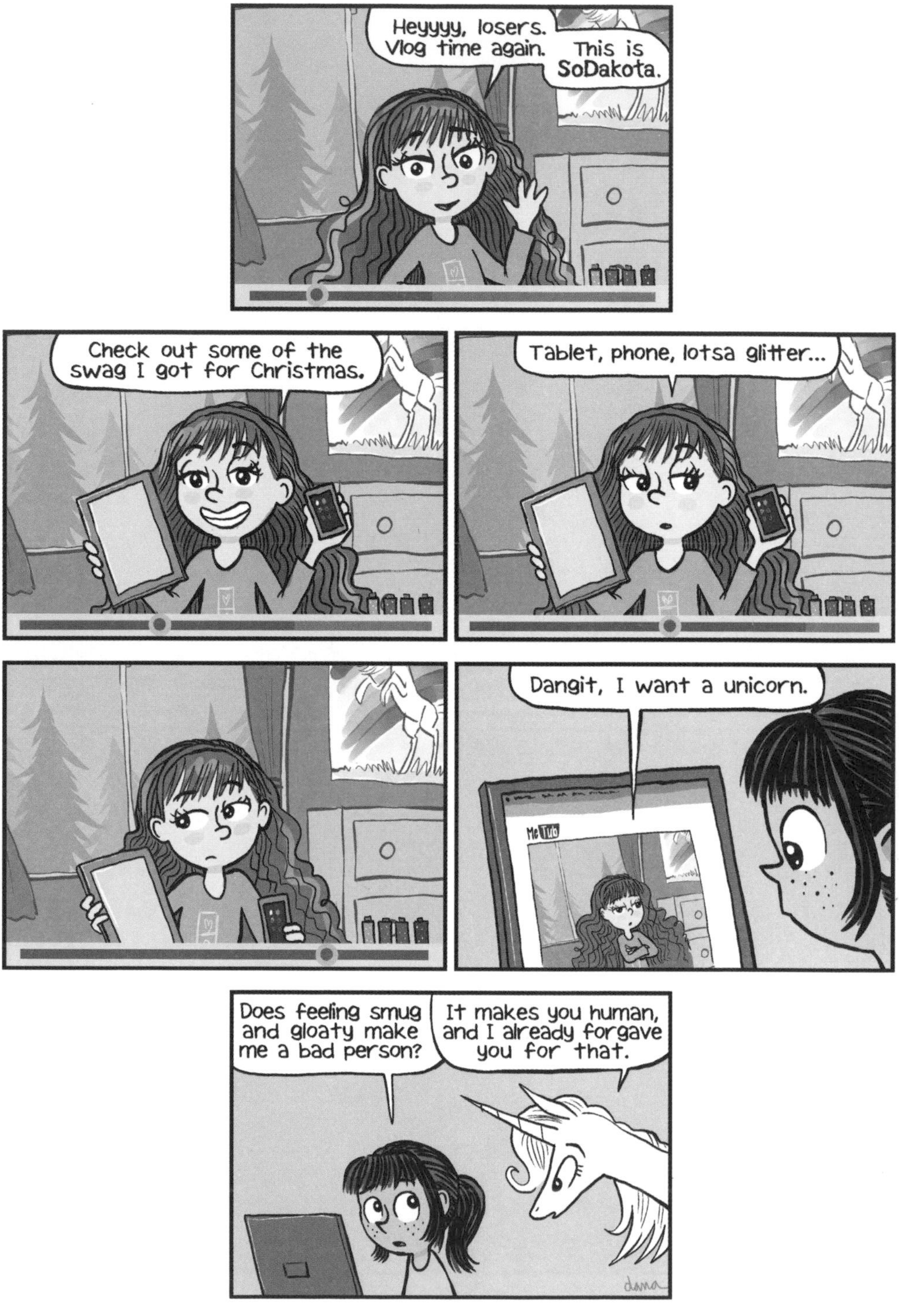
Heyyyy, losers. Vlog time again.
This is SoDakota.
Check out some of the swag I got for Christmas.
Tablet, phone, lotsa glitter...
Dangit, I want a unicorn.
MeTub
Does feeling smug and gloaty make me a bad person?
It makes you human, and I already forgave you for that.
dana

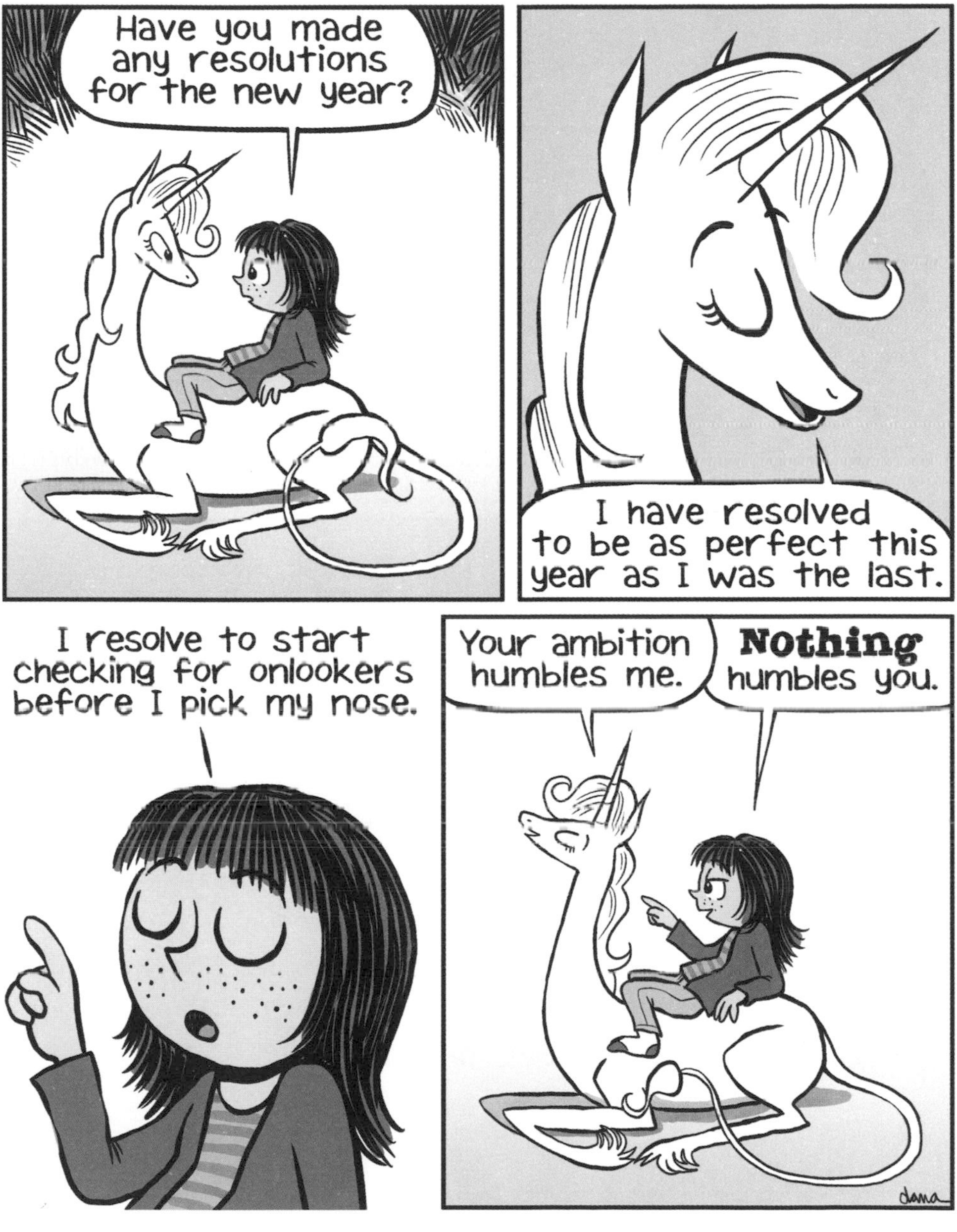
Have you made any resolutions for the new year?
I have resolved to be as perfect this year as I was the last.
I resolve to start checking for onlookers before I pick my nose.
Your ambition humbles me.
Nothing humbles you.
dana

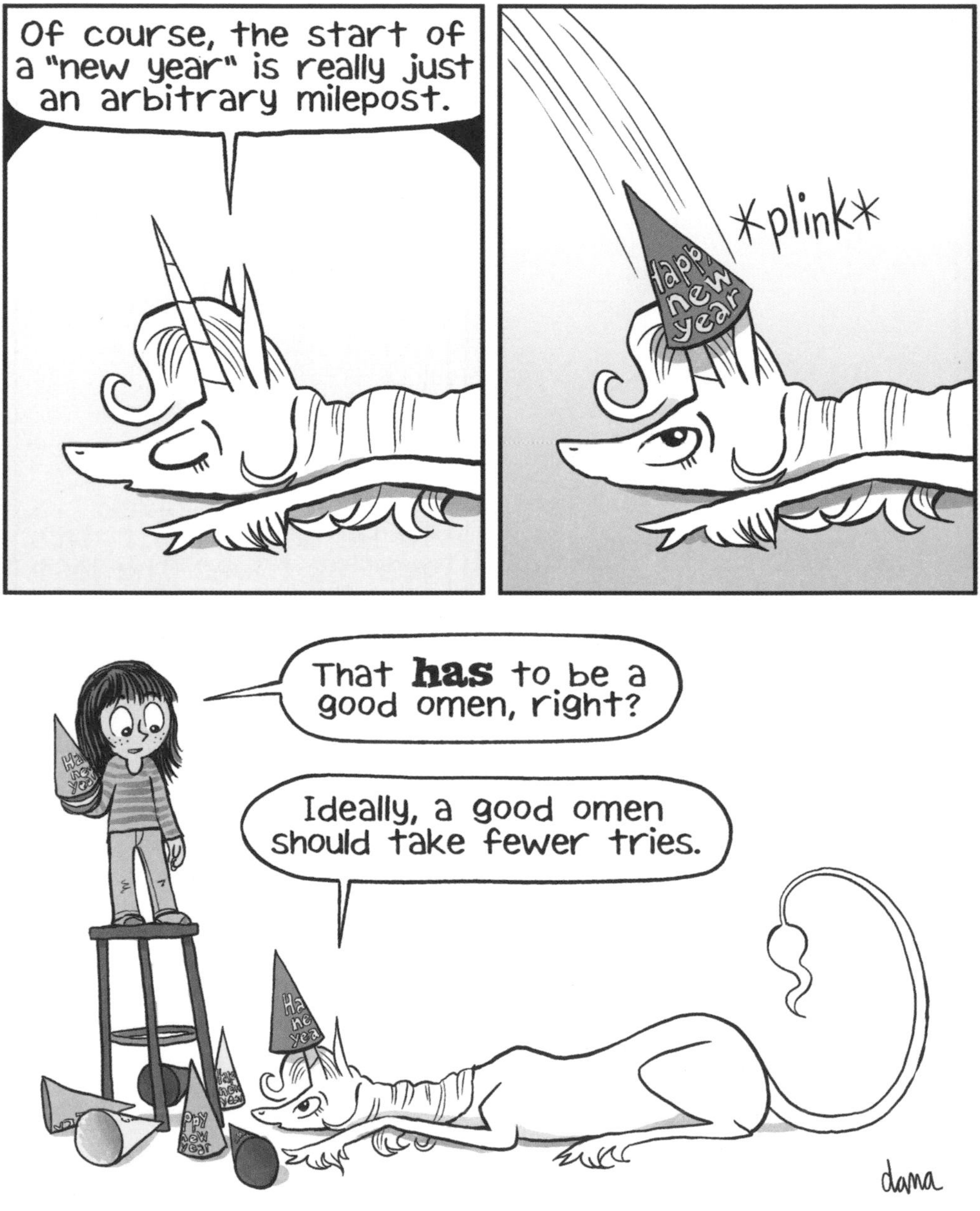
Of course, the start of a "new year" is really just an arbitrary milepost.
plink
Happy new year
That **has** to be a good omen, right?
Ideally, a good omen should take fewer tries.
dana

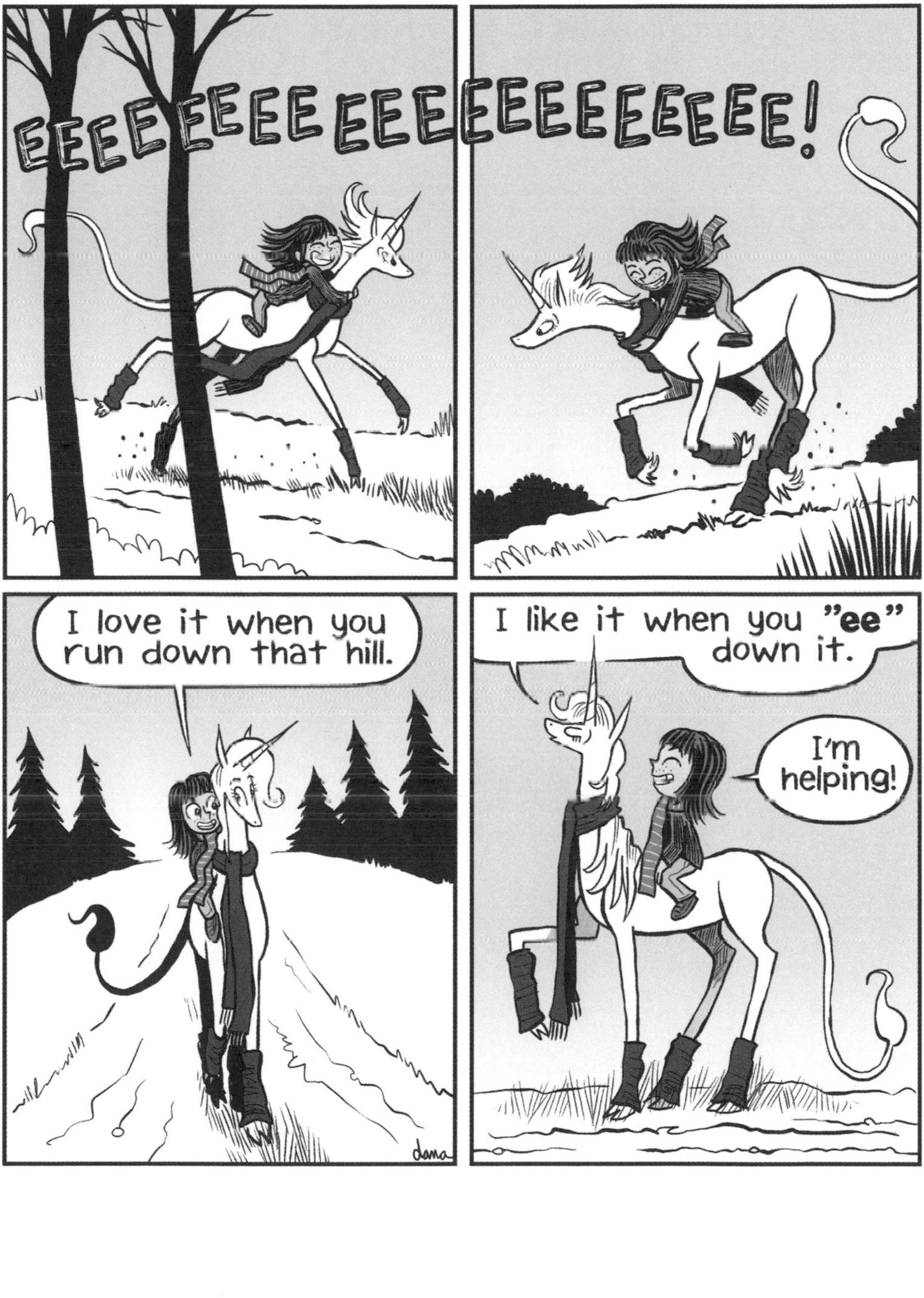
EEEEEEEEEEEEEEEEEEEEE!
I love it when you run down that hill.
I like it when you "ee" down it.
I'm helping!
dana

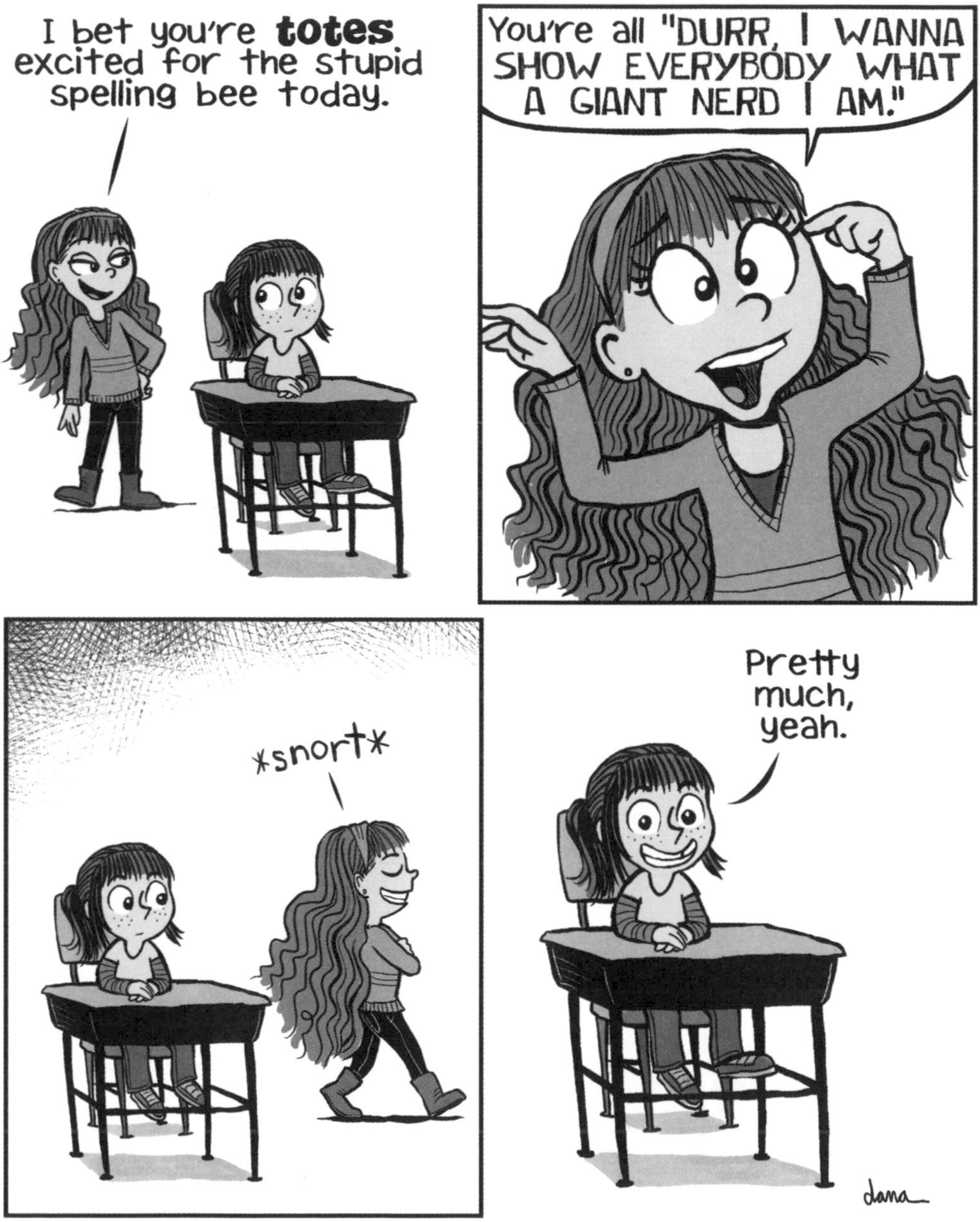
I bet you're **totes** excited for the stupid spelling bee today.
You're all "DURR, I WANNA SHOW EVERYBODY WHAT A GIANT NERD I AM."
snort
Pretty much, yeah.
dana

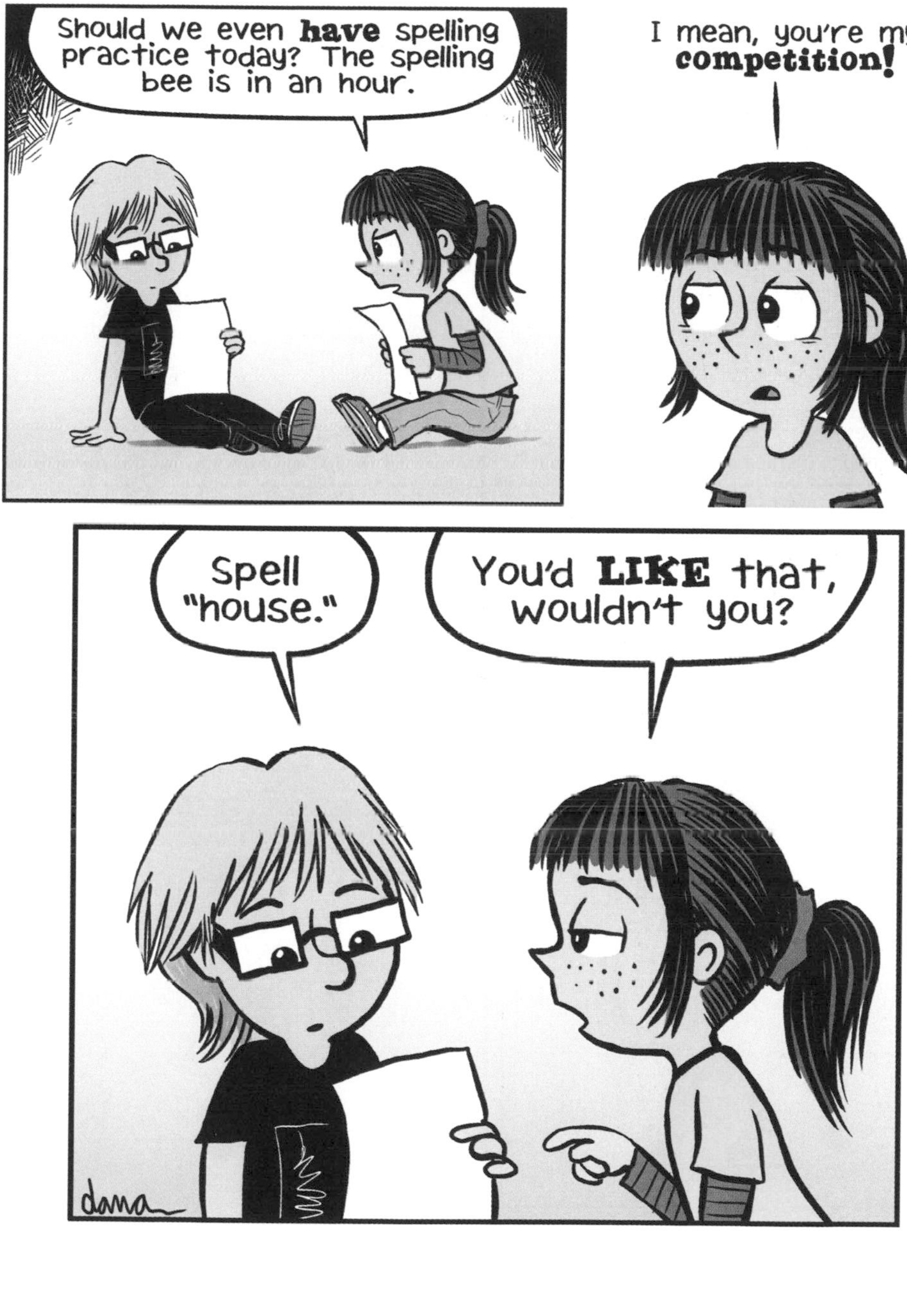
Should we even **have** spelling practice today? The spelling bee is in an hour.
I mean, you're my **competition!**
Spell "house."
You'd **LIKE** that, wouldn't you?
dana

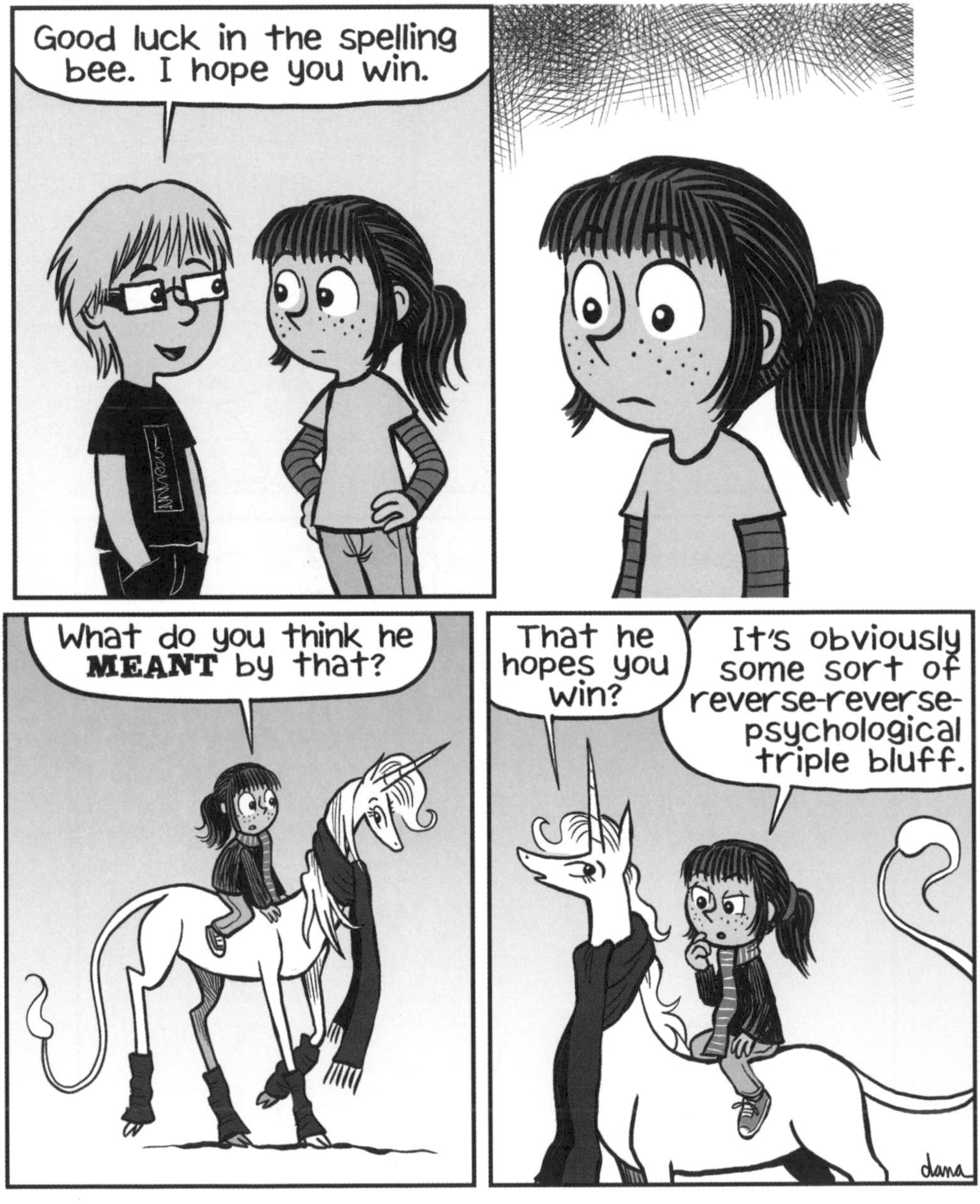
Good luck in the spelling bee. I hope you win.
What do you think he MEANT by that?
That he hopes you win?
It's obviously some sort of reverse-reverse-psychological triple bluff.
dana

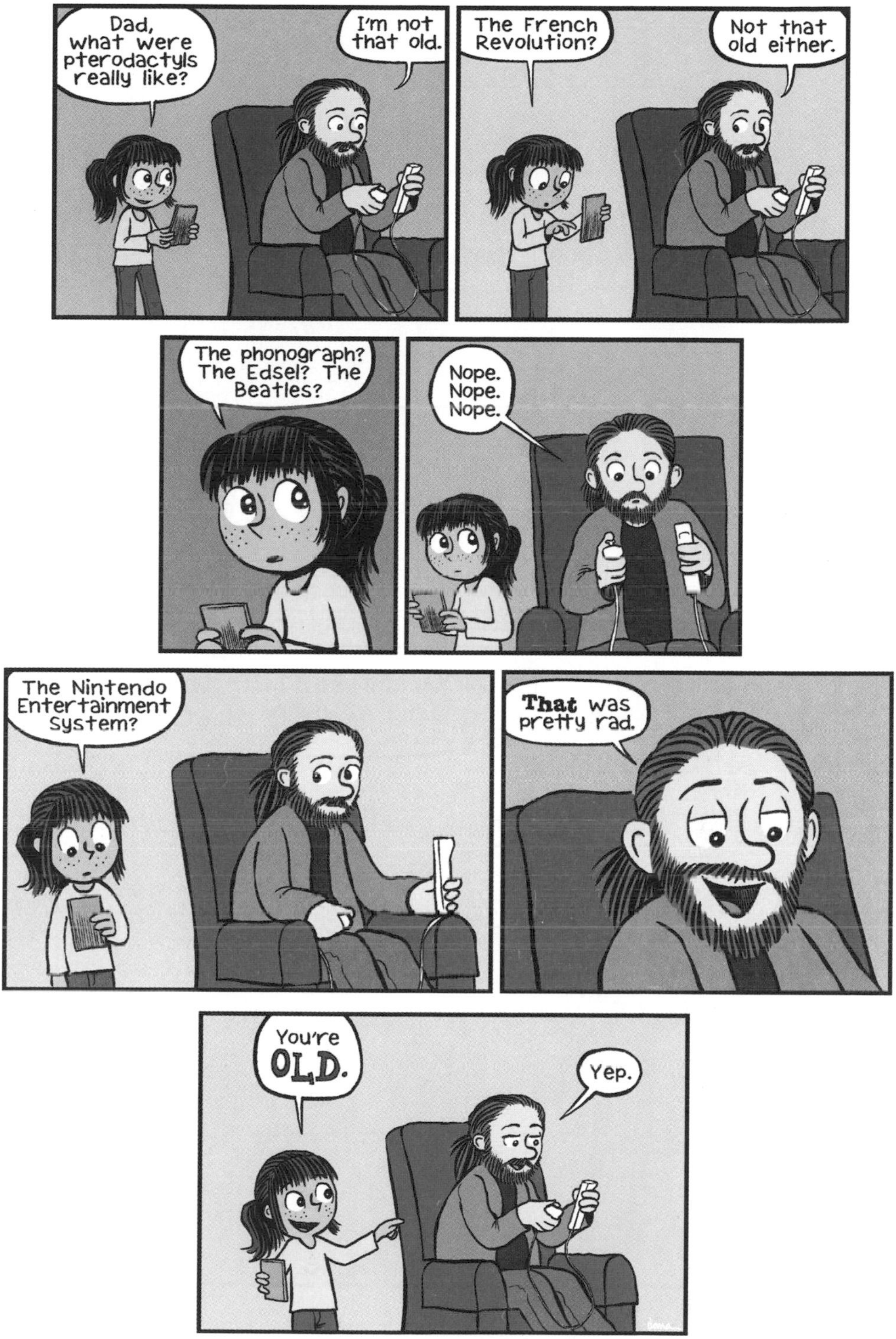
Dad, what were pterodactyls really like?
I'm not that old.
The French Revolution?
Not that old either.
The phonograph? The Edsel? The Beatles?
Nope. Nope. Nope.
The Nintendo Entertainment System?
That was pretty rad.
You're OLD.
Yep.

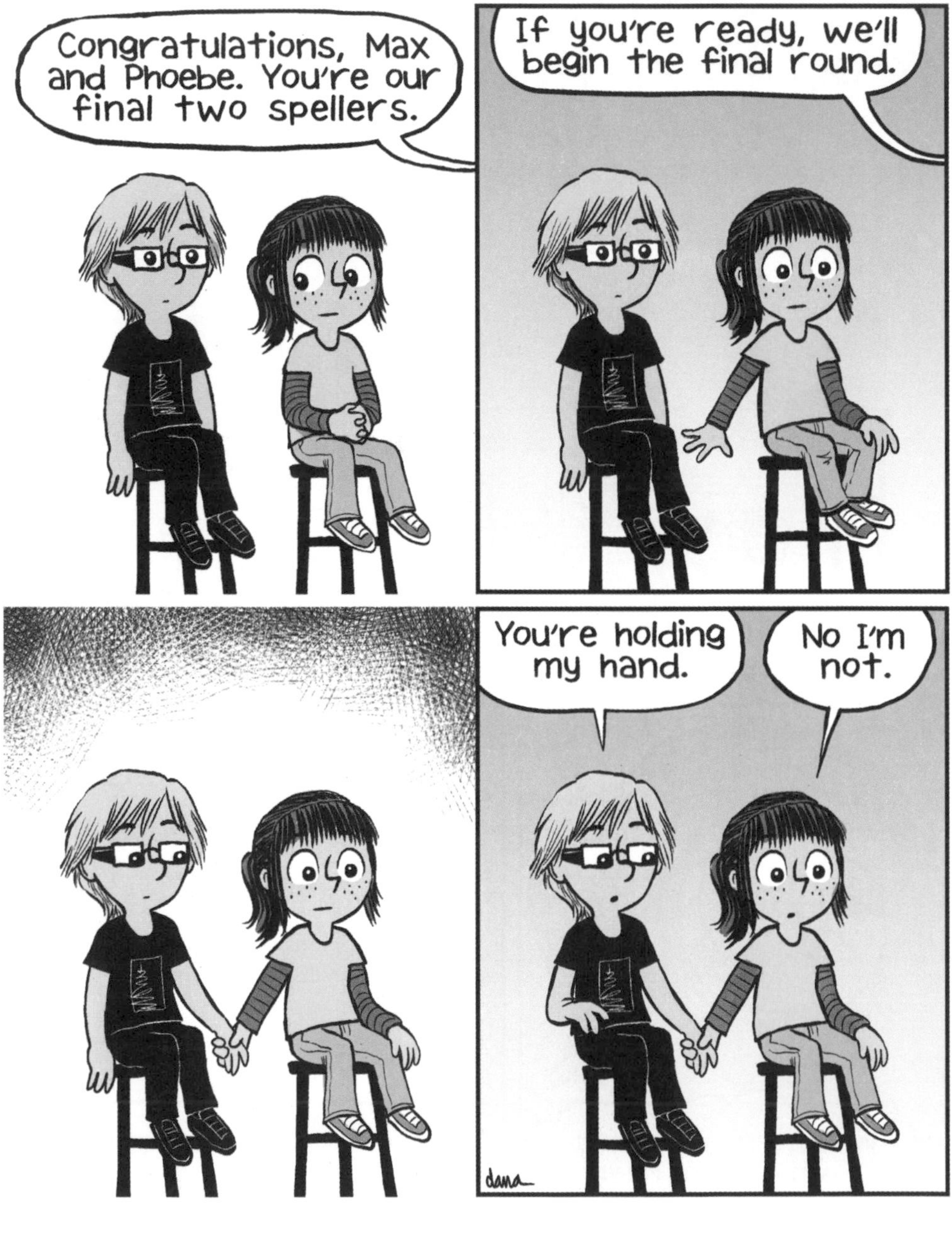
Congratulations, Max and Phoebe. You're our final two spellers.
If you're ready, we'll begin the final round.
You're holding my hand.
No I'm not.
dana

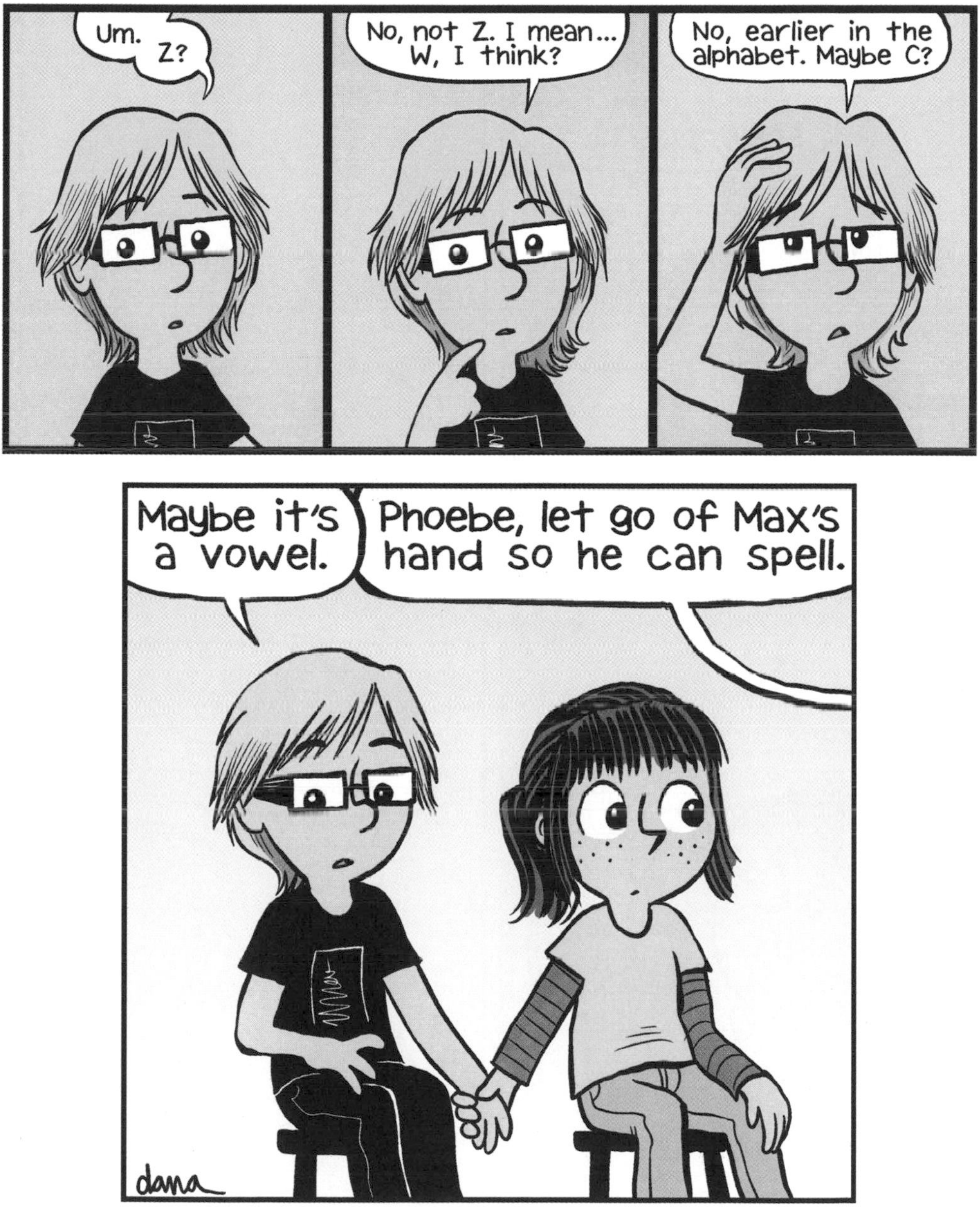
Um.
Z?
No, not Z. I mean...
W, I think?
No, earlier in the alphabet. Maybe C?
Maybe it's a vowel.
Phoebe, let go of Max's hand so he can spell.
dana

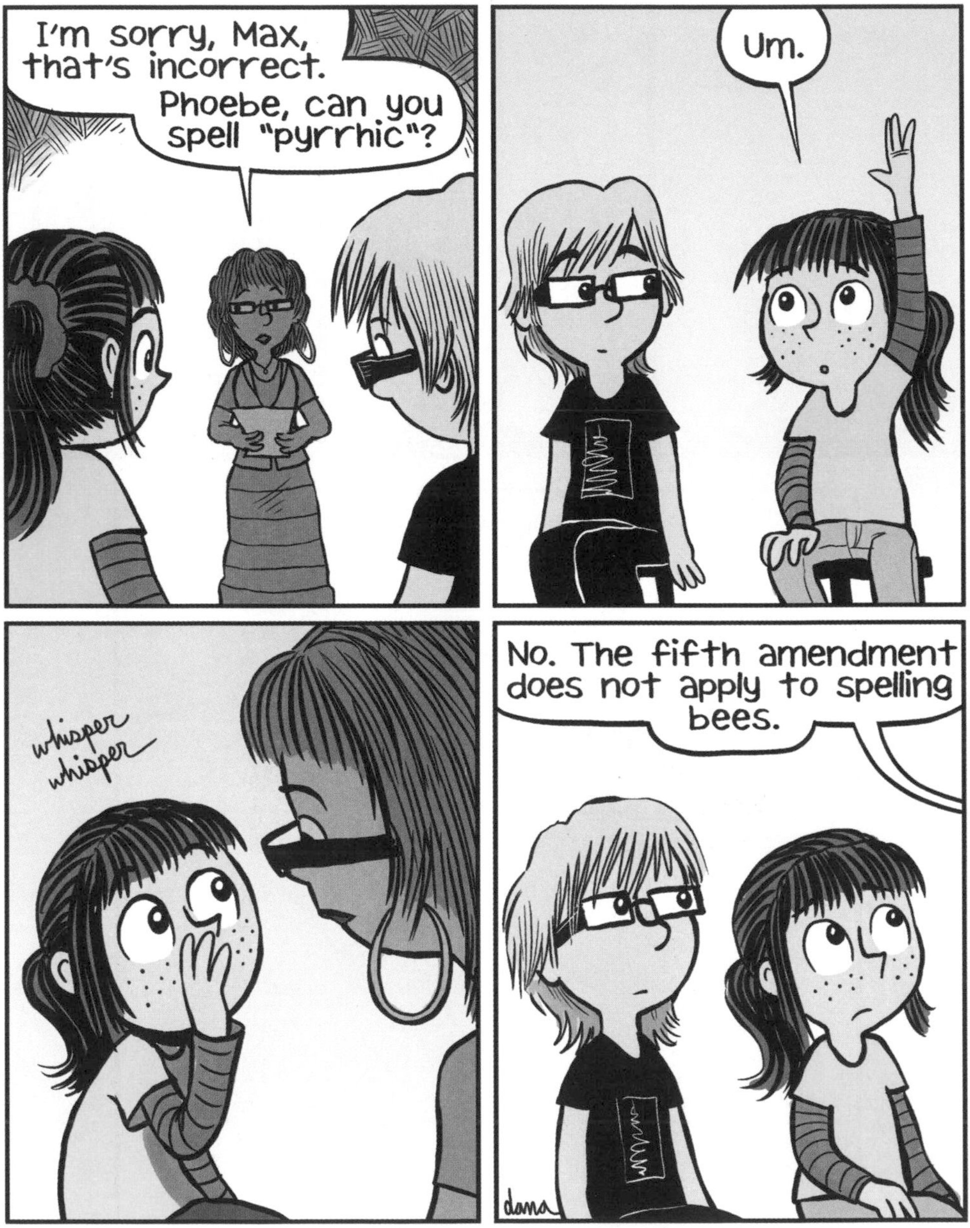
I'm sorry, Max, that's incorrect.
Phoebe, can you spell "pyrrhic"?
Um.
whisper whisper
No. The fifth amendment does not apply to spelling bees.
dana

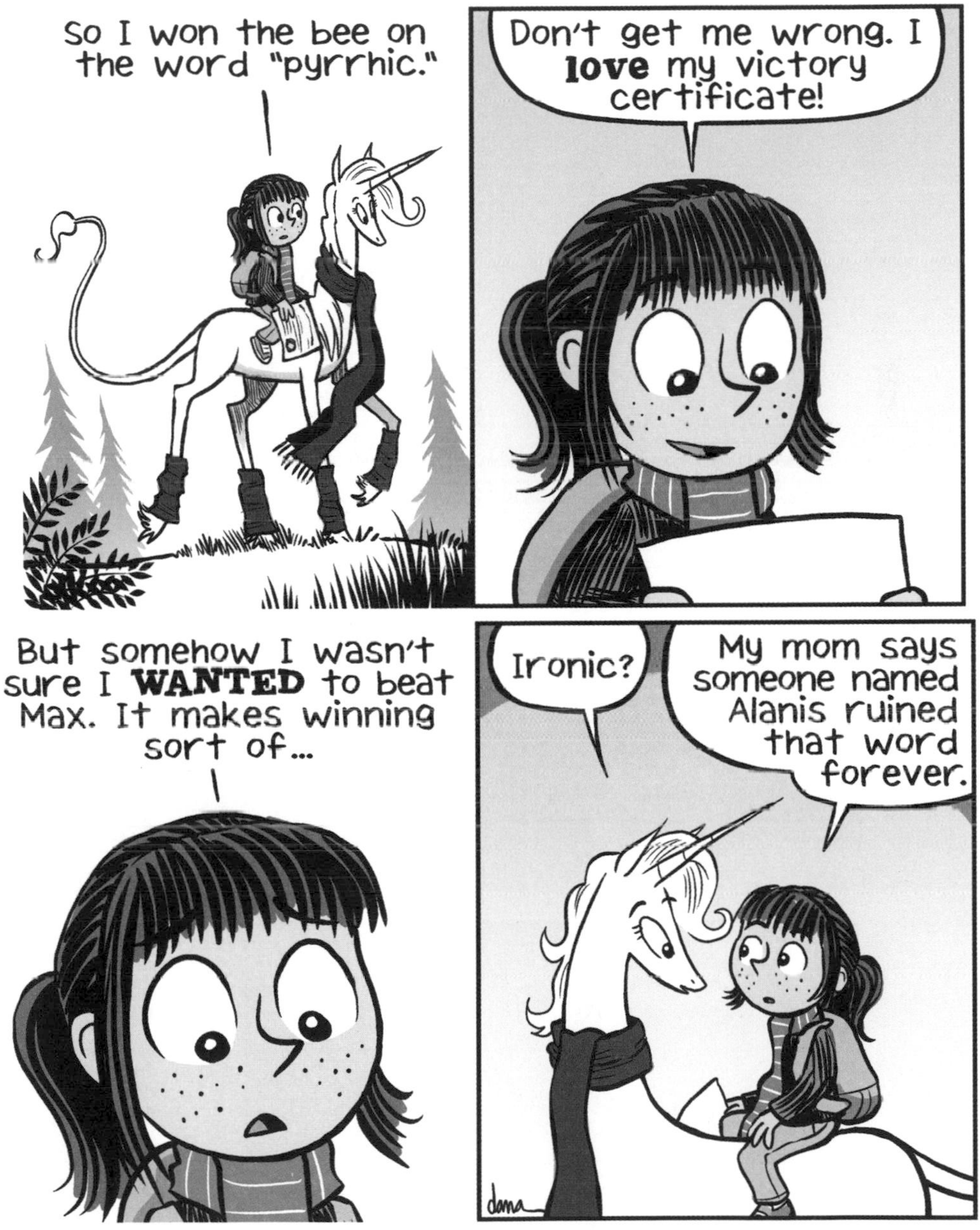
So I won the bee on the word "pyrrhic."
Don't get me wrong. I **love** my victory certificate!
But somehow I wasn't sure I **WANTED** to beat Max. It makes winning sort of...
Ironic?
My mom says someone named Alanis ruined that word forever.
dana

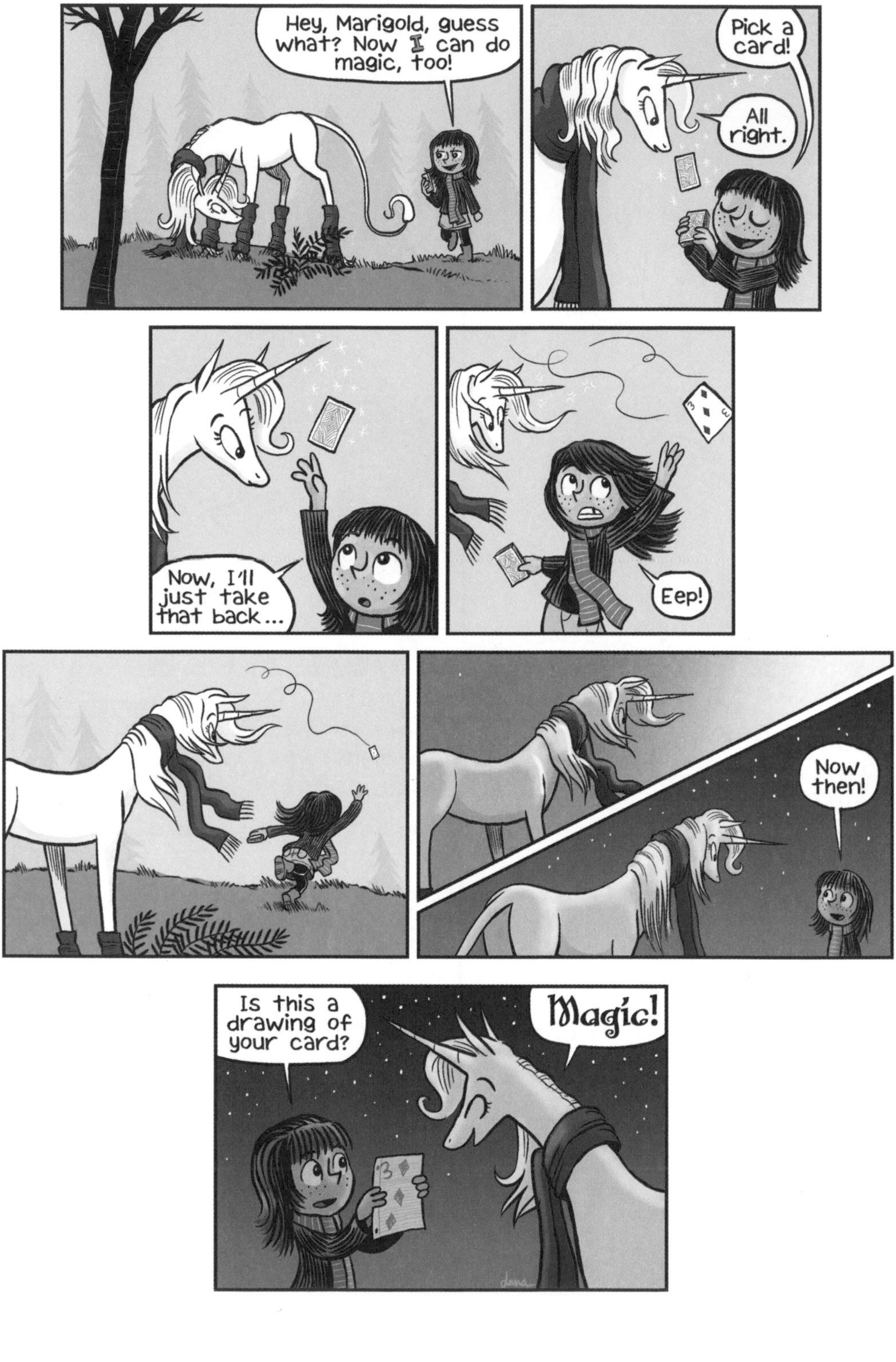
Hey, Marigold, guess what? Now I can do magic, too!
Pick a card!
All right.
Now, I'll just take that back...
Eep!
Now then!
Is this a drawing of your card?
Magic!

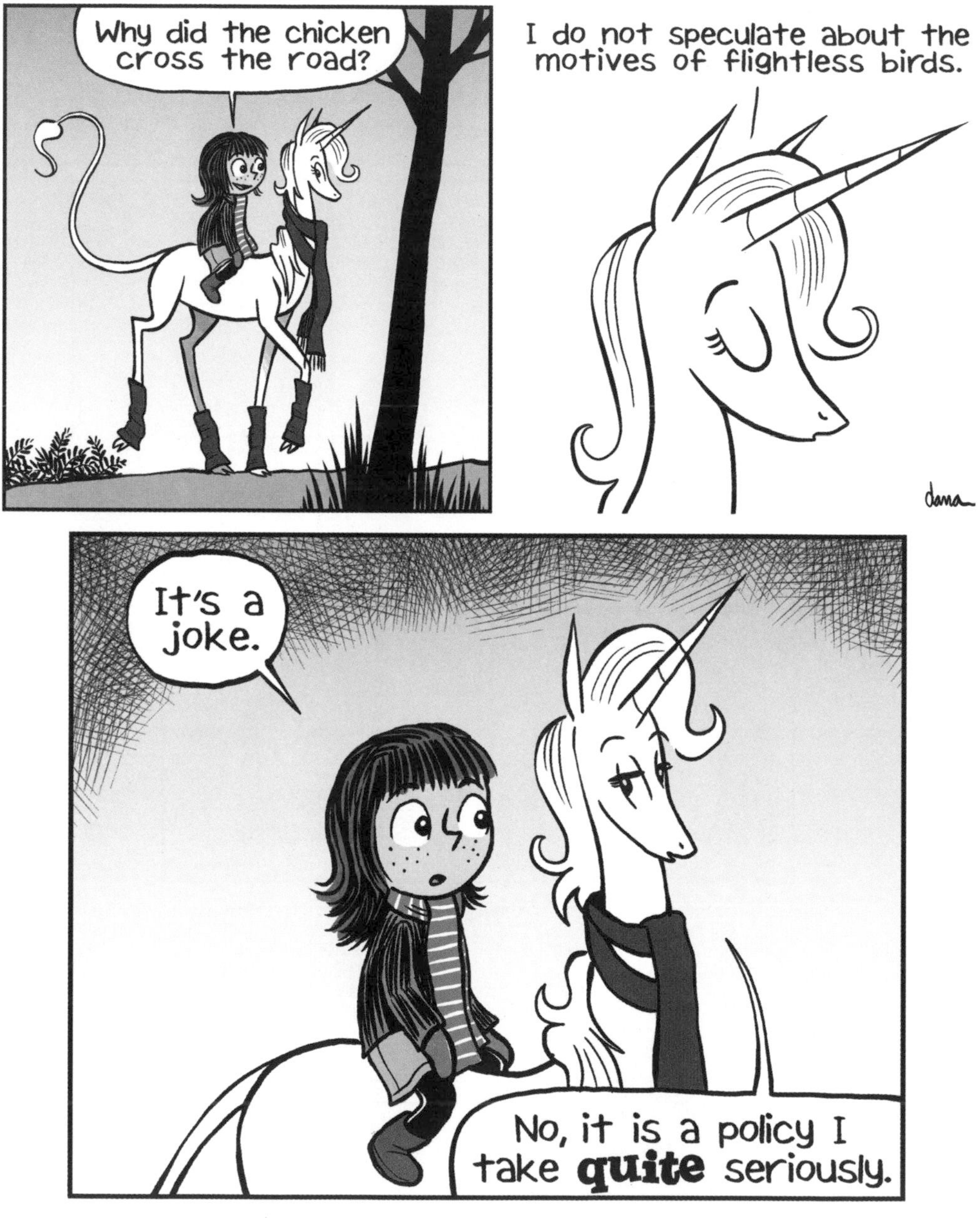
Why did the chicken cross the road?
I do not speculate about the motives of flightless birds.
dana
It's a joke.
No, it is a policy I take **quite** seriously.

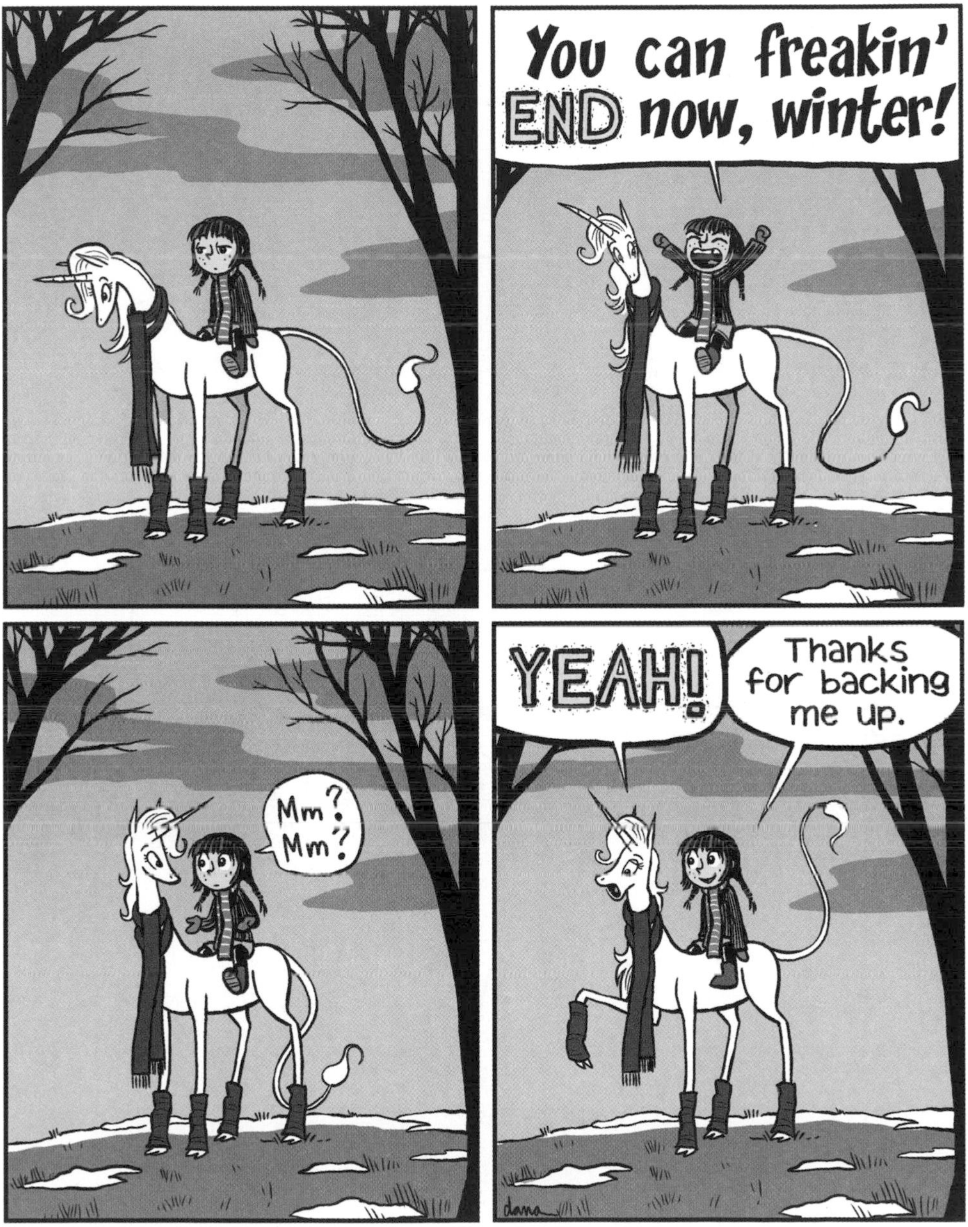
You can freakin' END now, winter!
Mm? Mm?
YEAH!
Thanks for backing me up.
dana

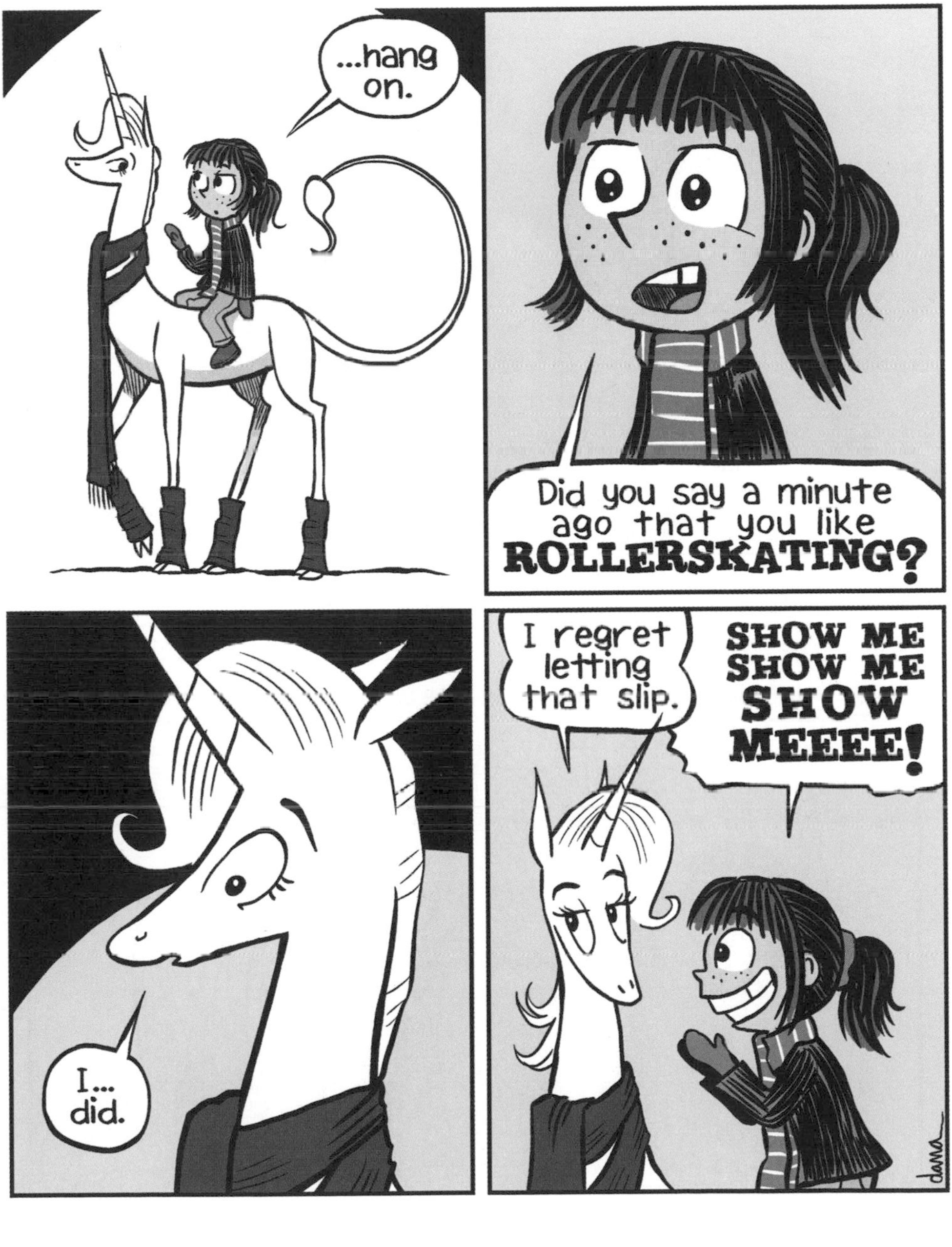
...hang on.
Did you say a minute ago that you like ROLLERSKATING?
I... did.
I regret letting that slip.
SHOW ME SHOW ME SHOW MEEEE!
dana

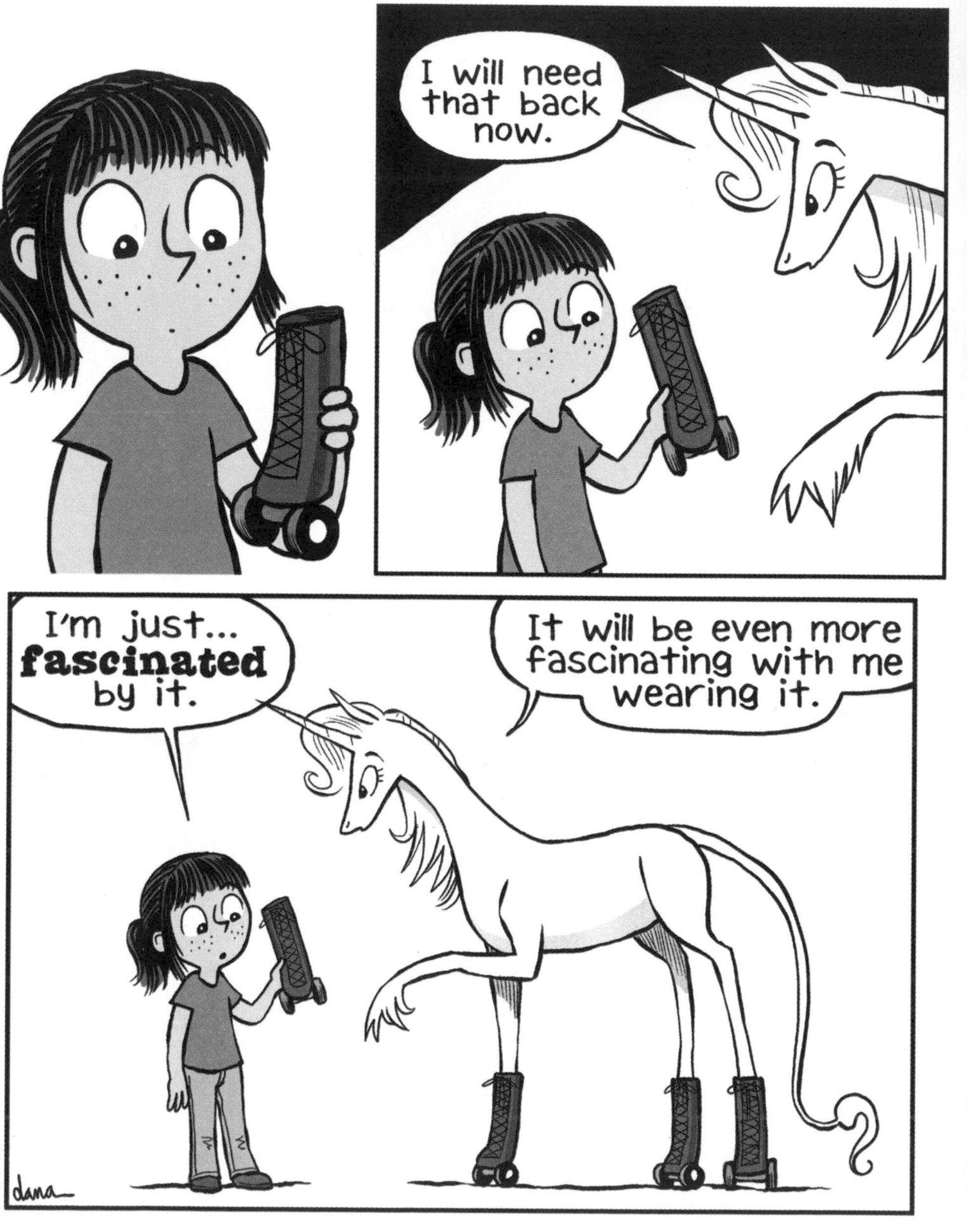
I will need that back now.
I'm just... **fascinated** by it.
It will be even more fascinating with me wearing it.
dana

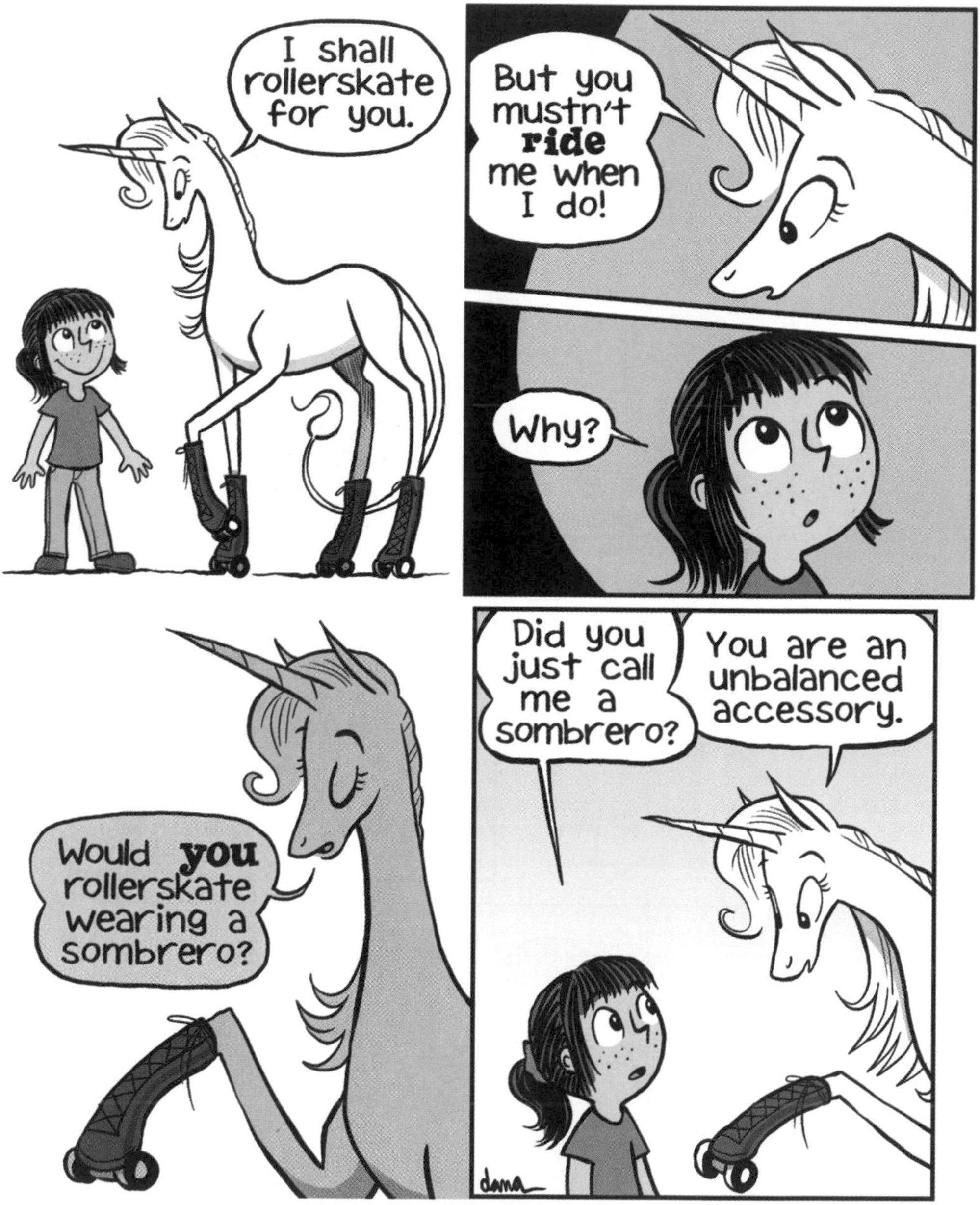

I shall rollerskate for you.
But you mustn't **ride** me when I do!
Why?
Would **you** rollerskate wearing a sombrero?
Did you just call me a sombrero?
You are an unbalanced accessory.
dana

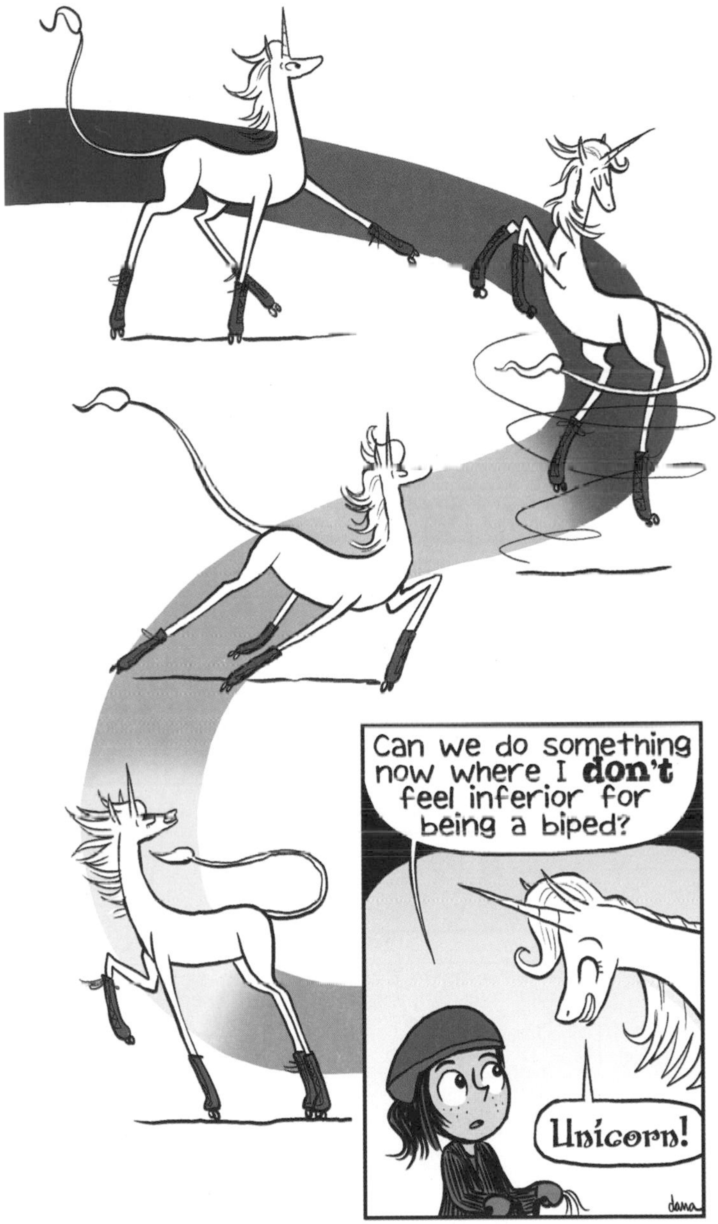
Can we do something now where I **don't** feel inferior for being a biped?
Unicorn!
dana

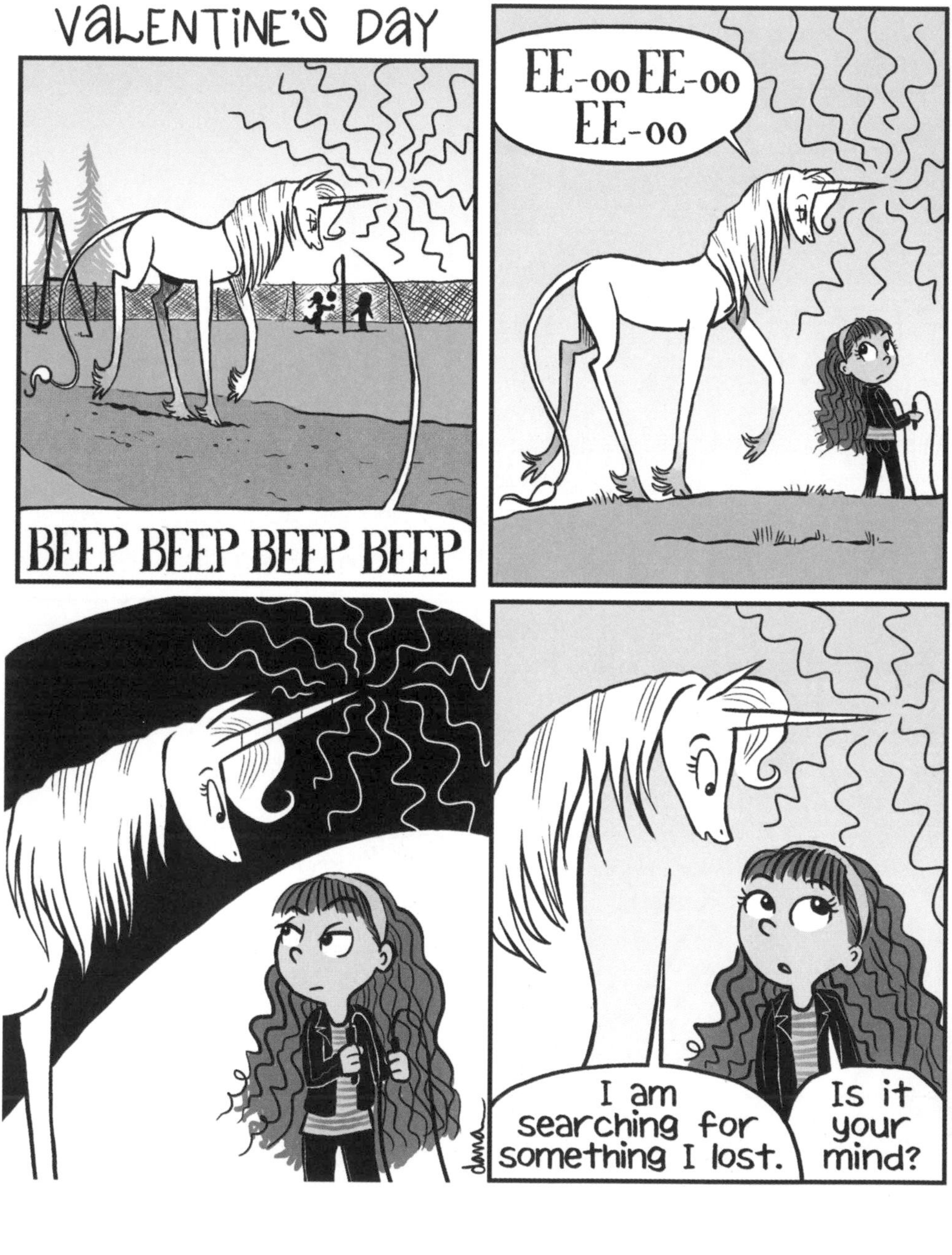
VALENTINE'S DAY
BEEP BEEP BEEP BEEP
EE-oo EE-oo EE-oo
I am searching for something I lost.
Is it your mind?
dana

Monday's mare is full of grace

Tuesday's mare has a big long face

Wednesday's horse is fond of pears

Thursday's horse can braid my hair

Friday's unicorn lands in a heap

Saturday's unicorn needs her sleep.

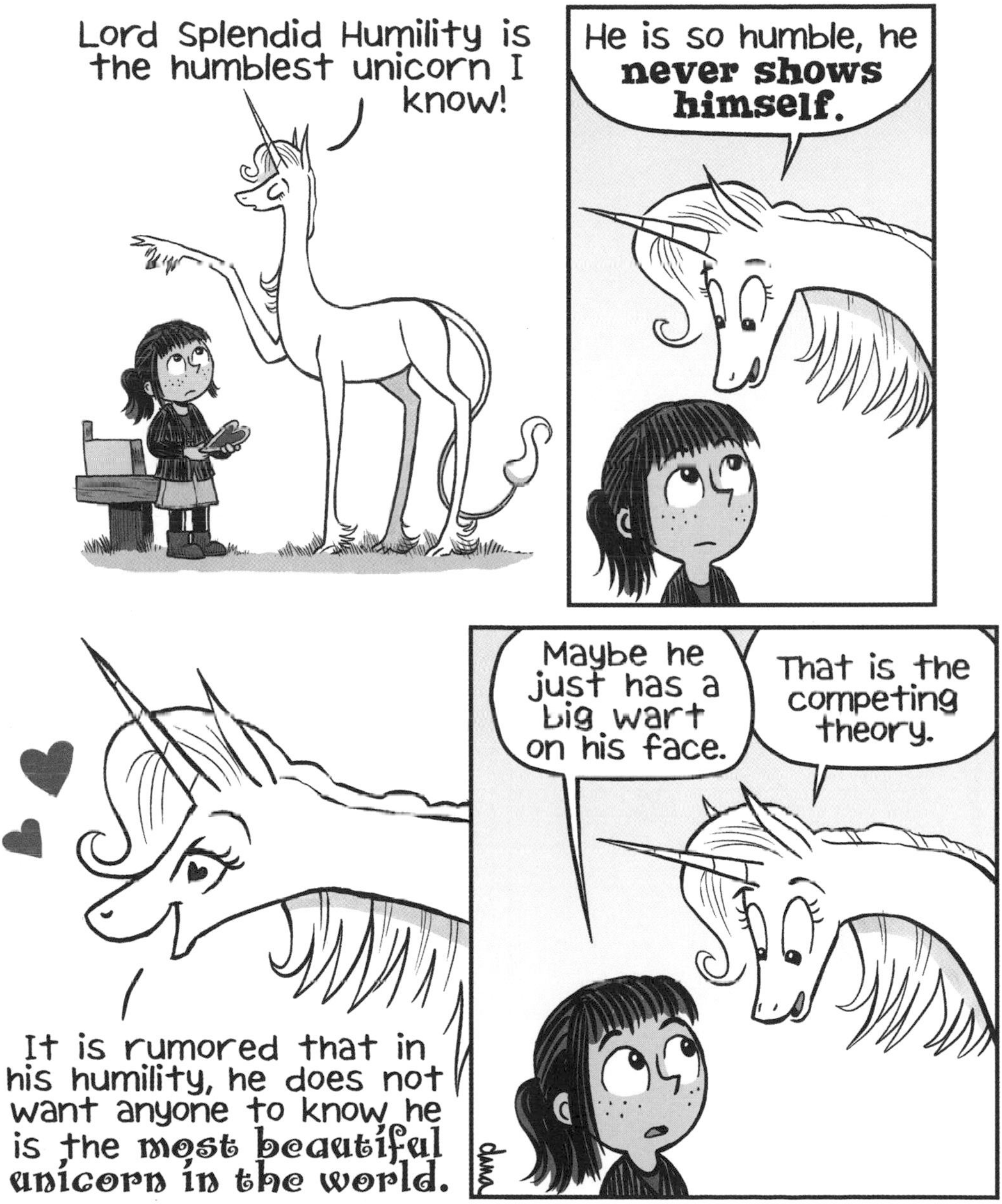

Lord Splendid Humility is the humblest unicorn I know!
He is so humble, he **never shows himself.**
It is rumored that in his humility, he does not want anyone to know he is the **most beautiful unicorn in the world.**
Maybe he just has a big wart on his face.
That is the competing theory.

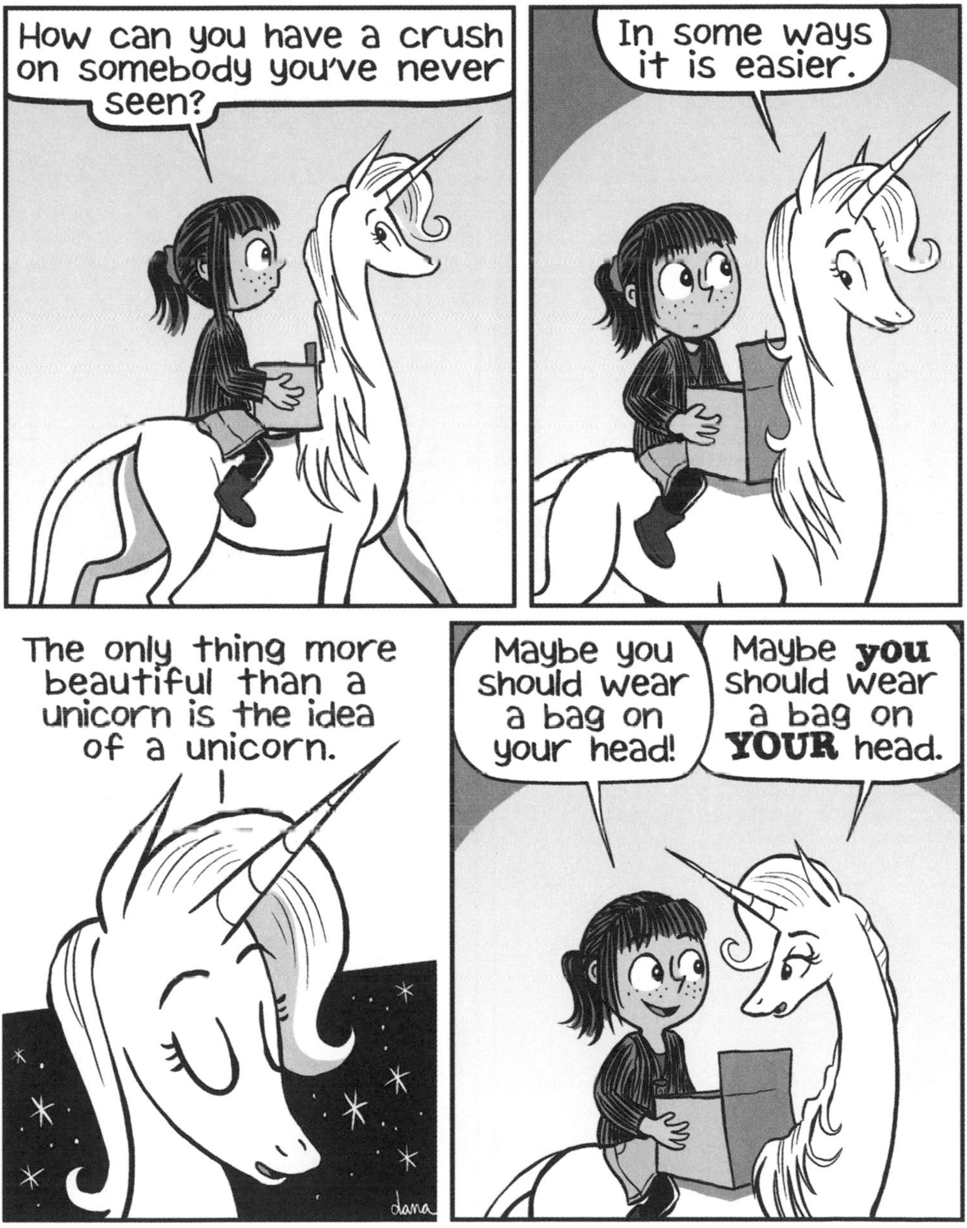
How can you have a crush on somebody you've never seen?
In some ways it is easier.
The only thing more beautiful than a unicorn is the idea of a unicorn.
Maybe you should wear a bag on your head!
Maybe **you** should wear a bag on **YOUR** head.
dana

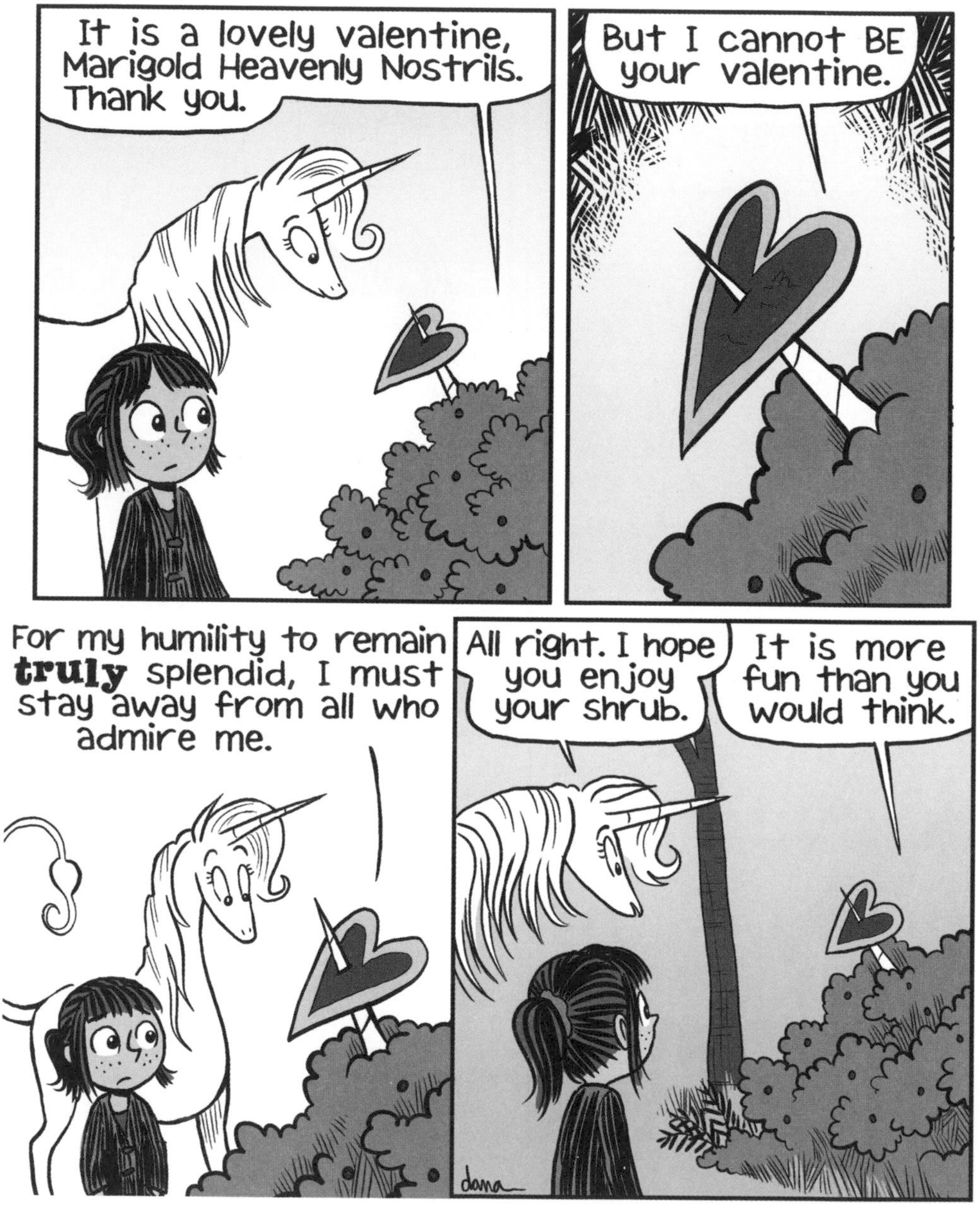

It is a lovely valentine, Marigold Heavenly Nostrils. Thank you.
But I cannot BE your valentine.
For my humility to remain **truly** splendid, I must stay away from all who admire me.
All right. I hope you enjoy your shrub.
It is more fun than you would think.
dana

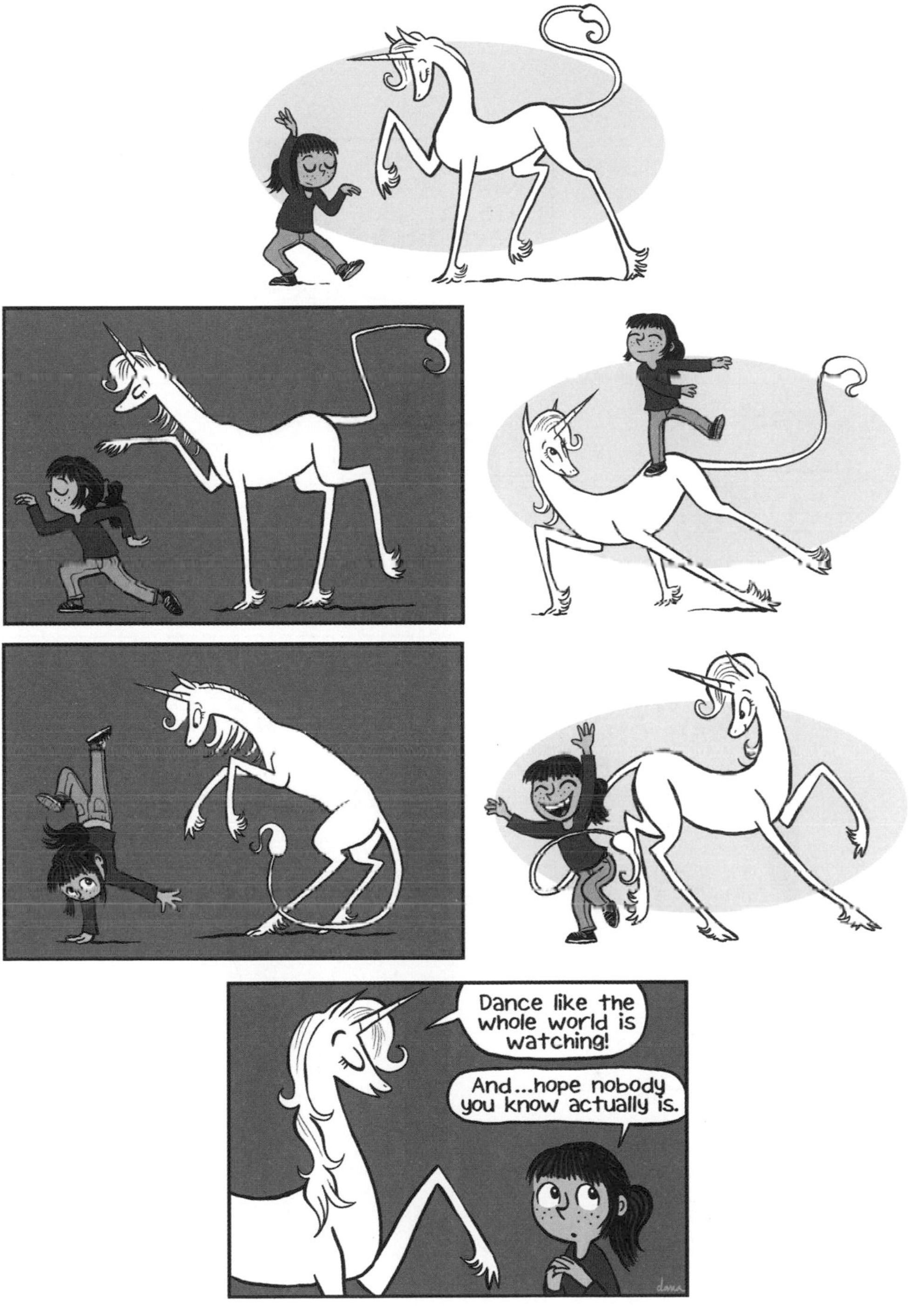
Dance like the whole world is watching!
And...hope nobody you know actually is.

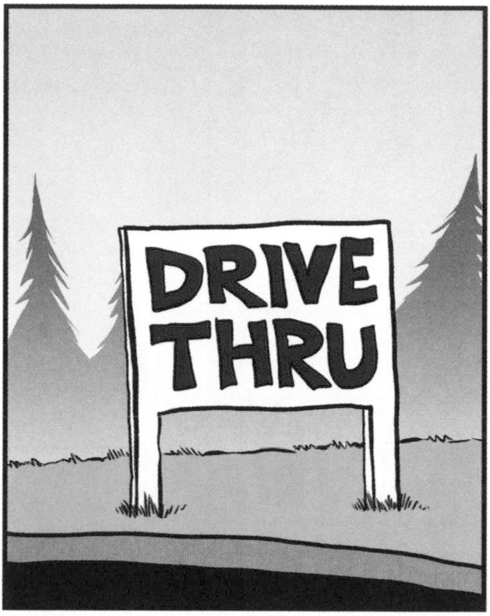
DRIVE
THRU

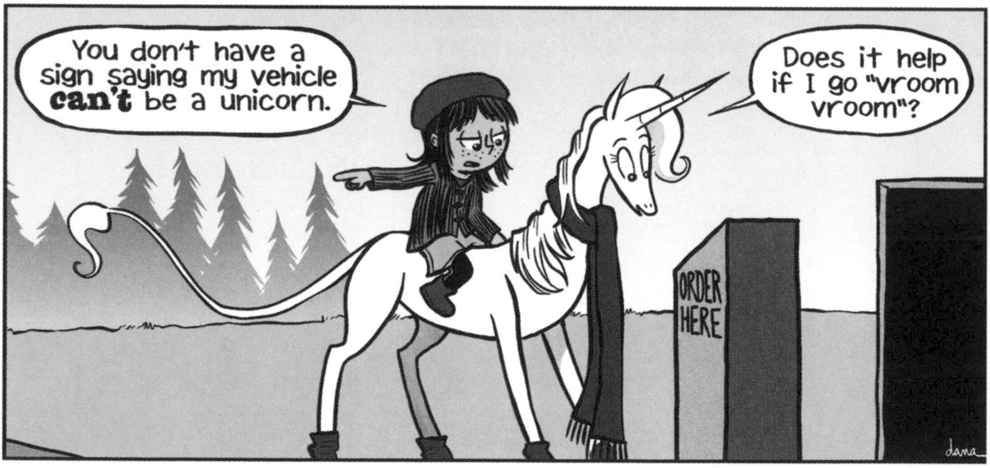
You don't have a sign saying my vehicle **can't** be a unicorn.
Does it help if I go "vroom vroom"?
ORDER HERE
dana

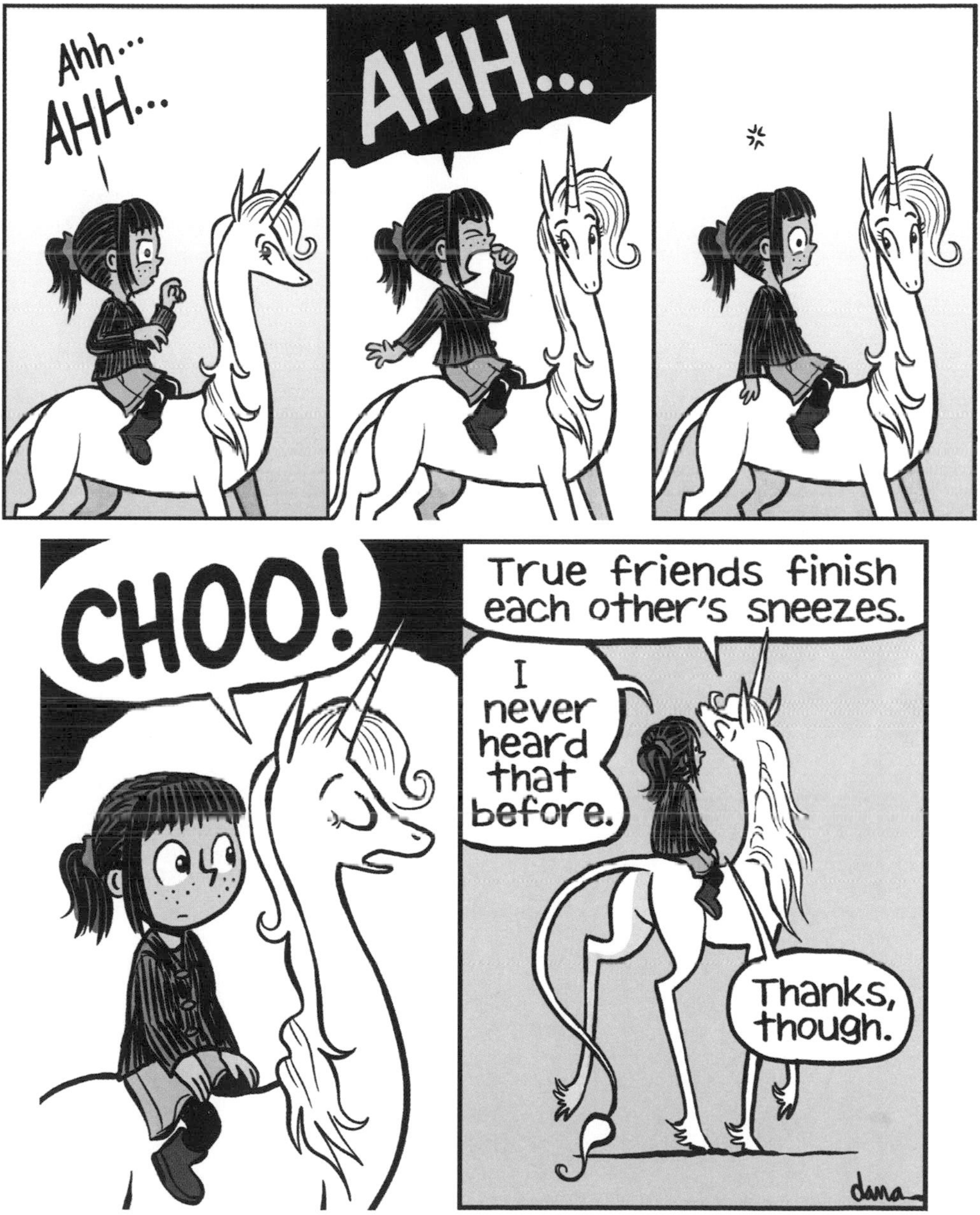
Ahh... AHH...
AHH...
CHOO!
True friends finish each other's sneezes.
I never heard that before.
Thanks, though.
dana

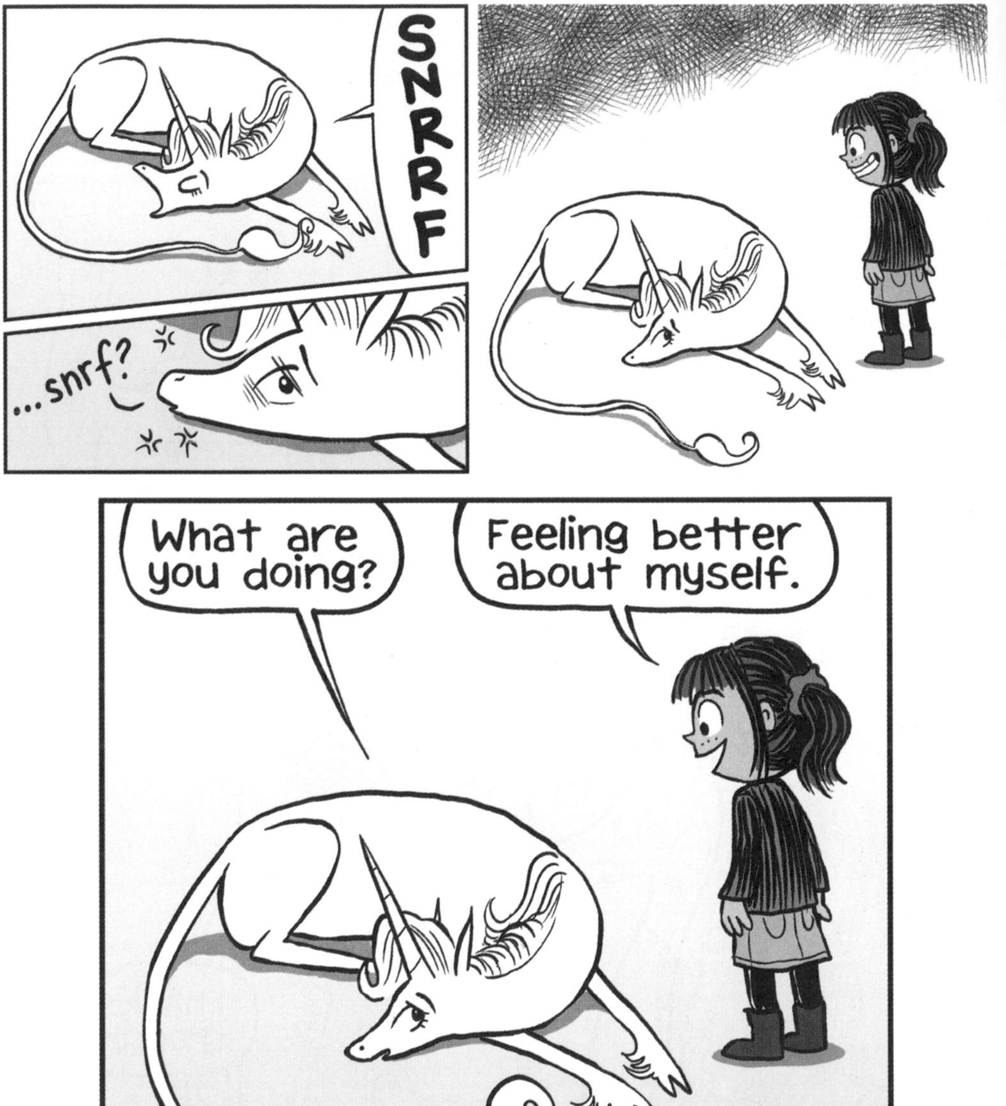
SNRRF
...snrf?
What are you doing?
Feeling better about myself.
dana

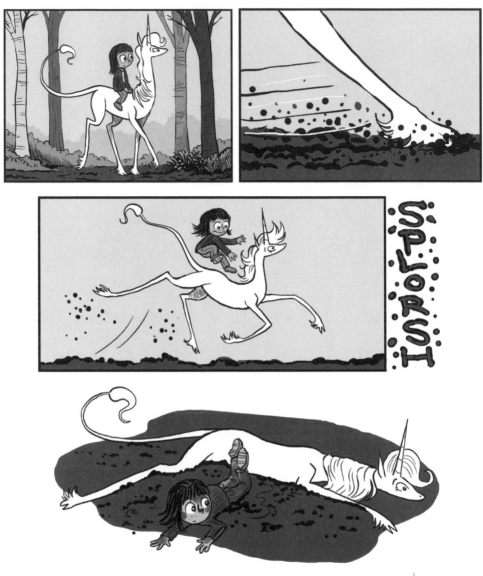

SPLORSH

Your coat is mud-resistant?

Only selectively.

Observe.

PHOEBE IS COOL

THAT'S almost better than **not** falling in a puddle.

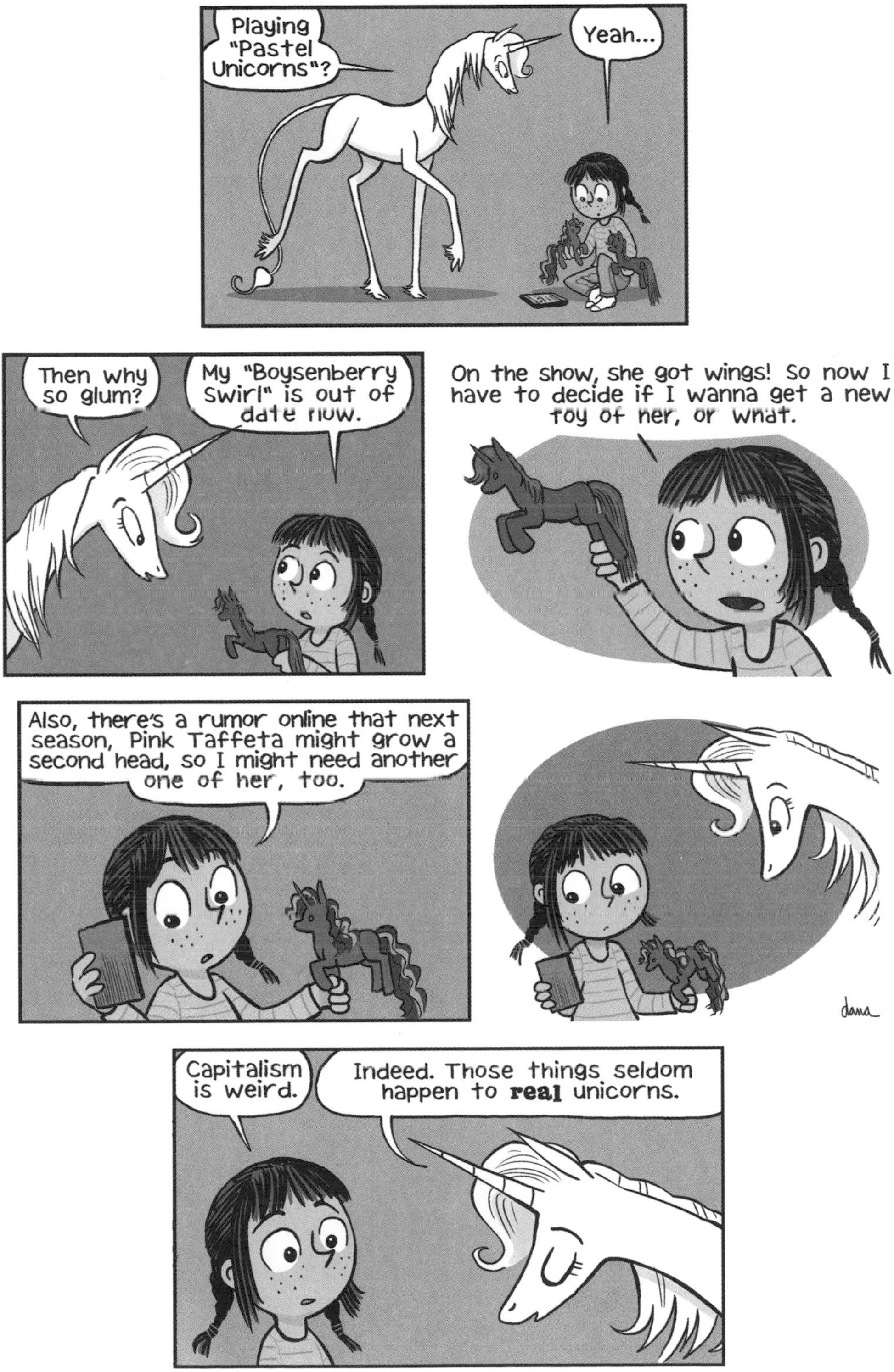
Playing "Pastel Unicorns"?
Yeah...
Then why so glum?
My "Boysenberry Swirl" is out of date now.
On the show, she got wings! So now I have to decide if I wanna get a new toy of her, or what.
Also, there's a rumor online that next season, Pink Taffeta might grow a second head, so I might need another one of her, too.
dana
Capitalism is weird.
Indeed. Those things seldom happen to **real** unicorns.

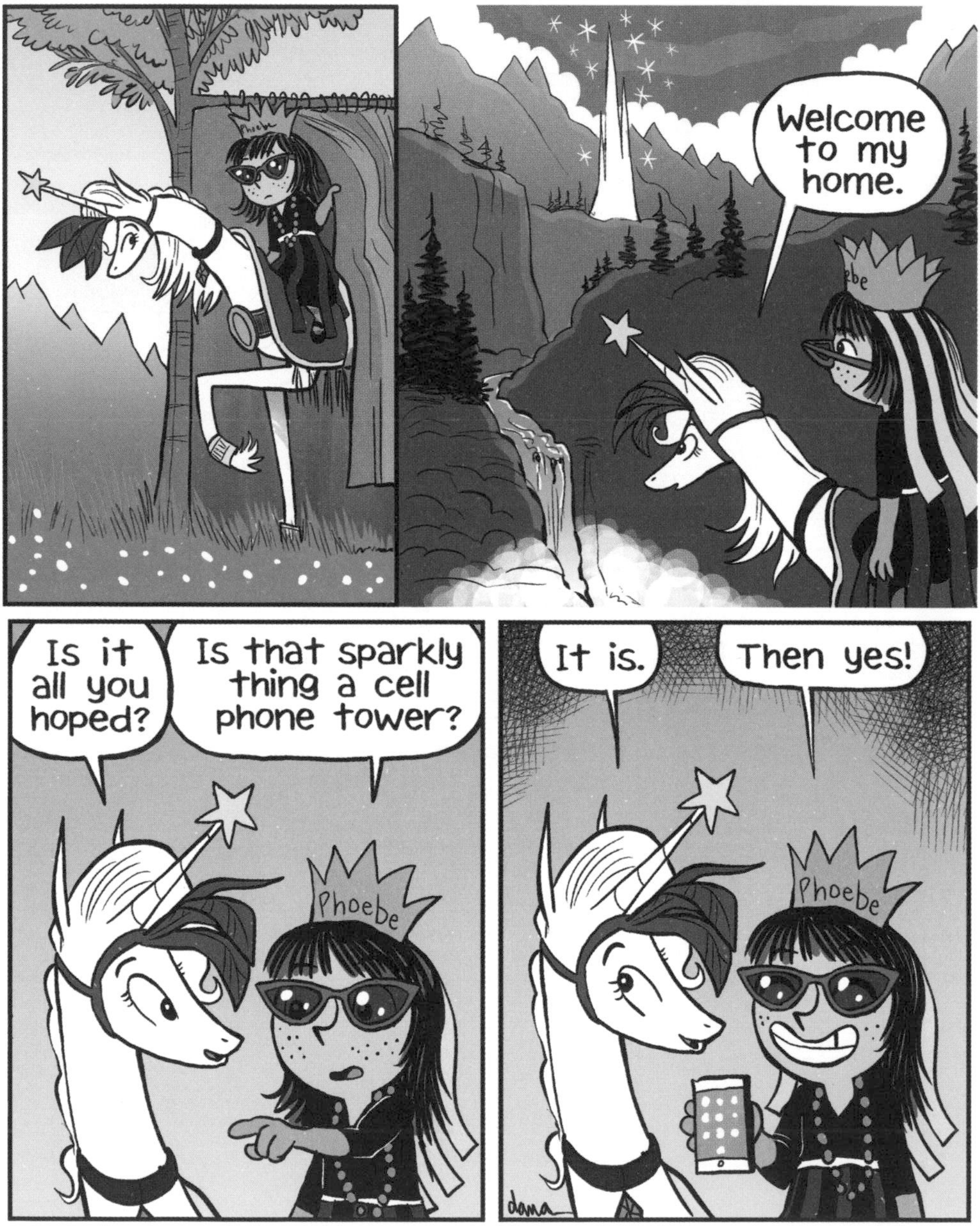
Phoebe
Welcome to my home.
ebe
Is it all you hoped?
Is that sparkly thing a cell phone tower?
Phoebe
It is.
Then yes!
Phoebe
dana

133

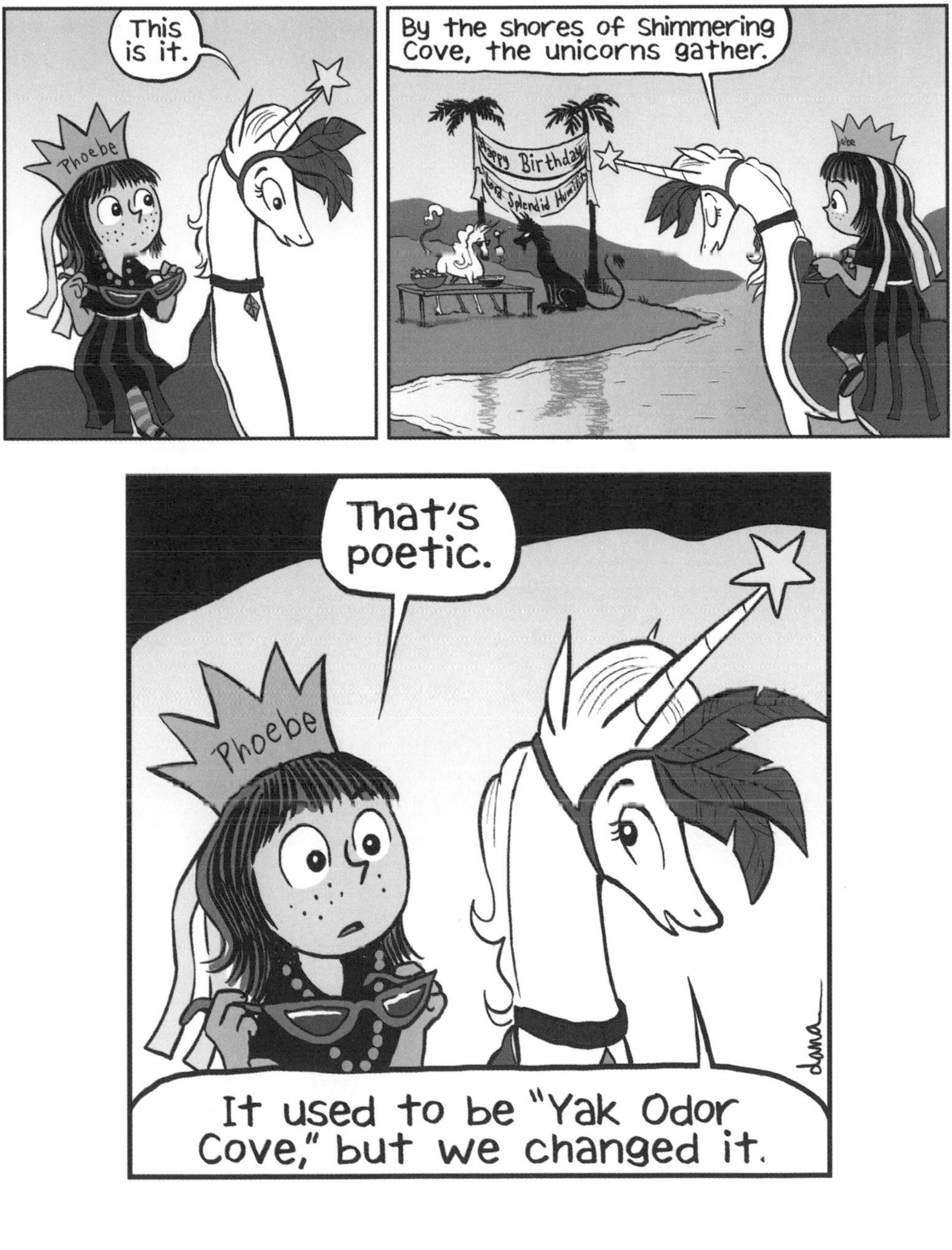
This is it.
Phoebe
By the shores of Shimmering Cove, the unicorns gather.
Happy Birthday
That's poetic.
Phoebe
It used to be "Yak Odor Cove," but we changed it.
dana

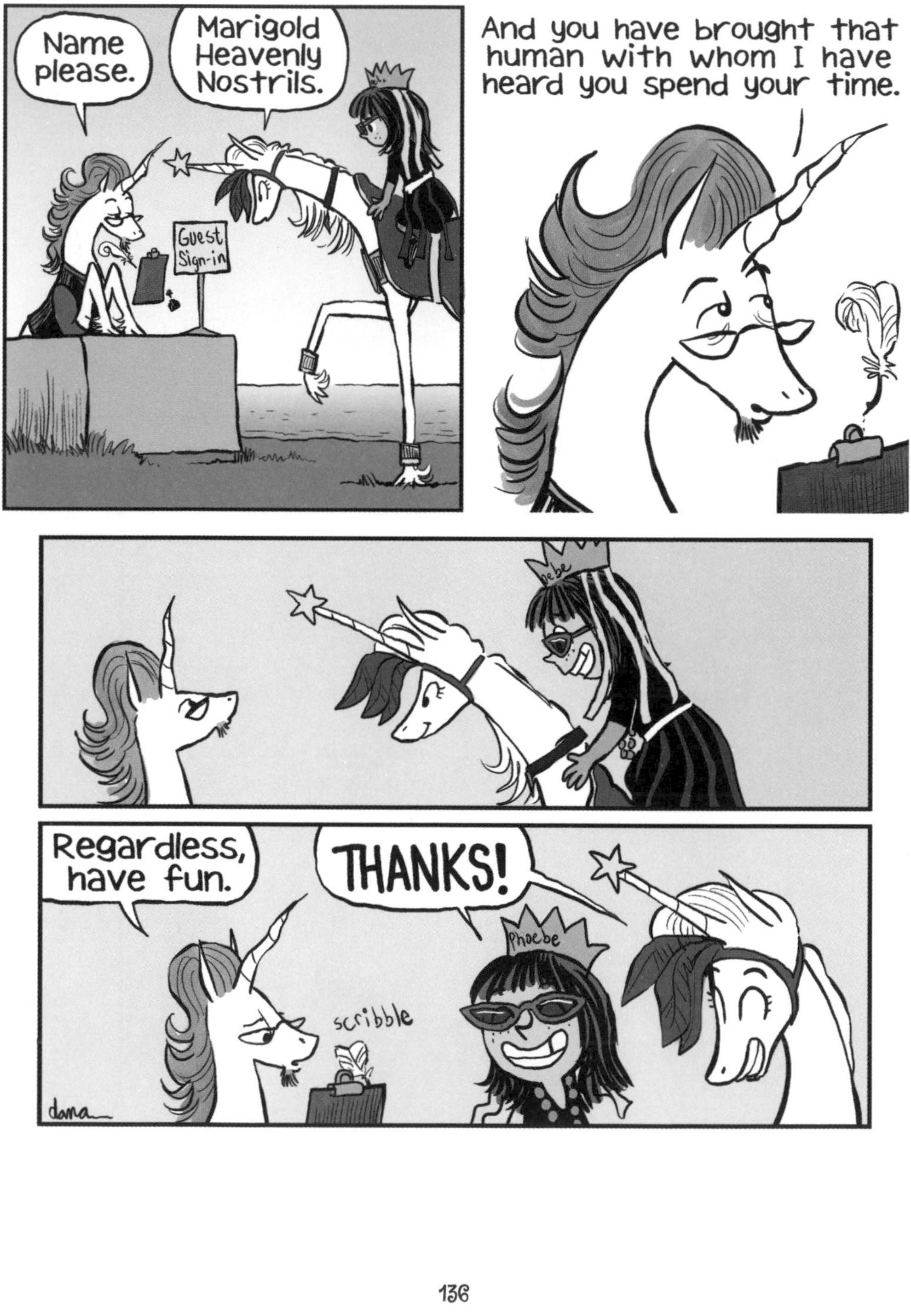
Name please.
Marigold Heavenly Nostrils.
Guest Sign-in
And you have brought that human with whom I have heard you spend your time.
Regardless, have fun.
THANKS!
Phoebe
scribble

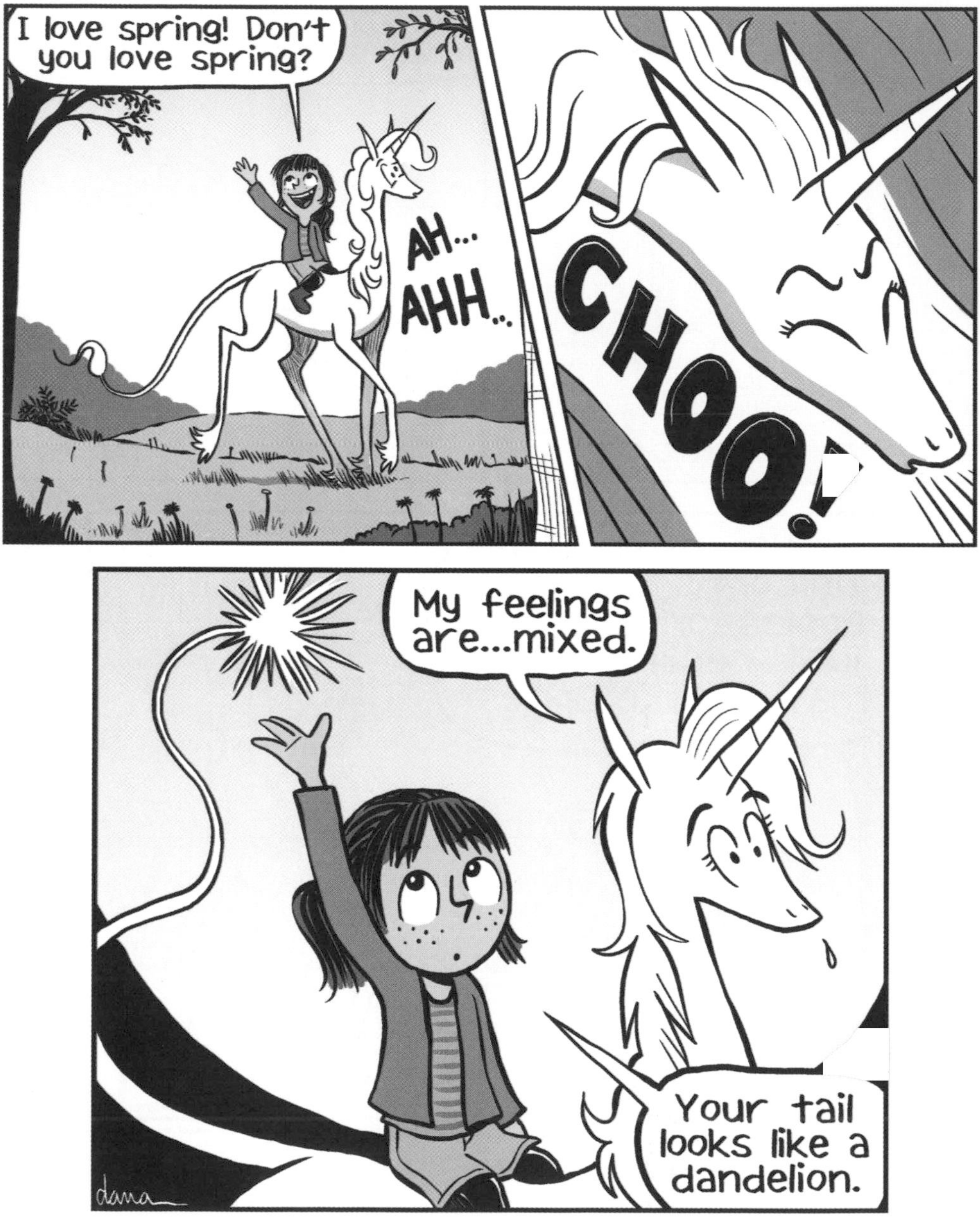
I love spring! Don't you love spring?
AH... AHH..
CHOO!
My feelings are...mixed.
Your tail looks like a dandelion.
dana

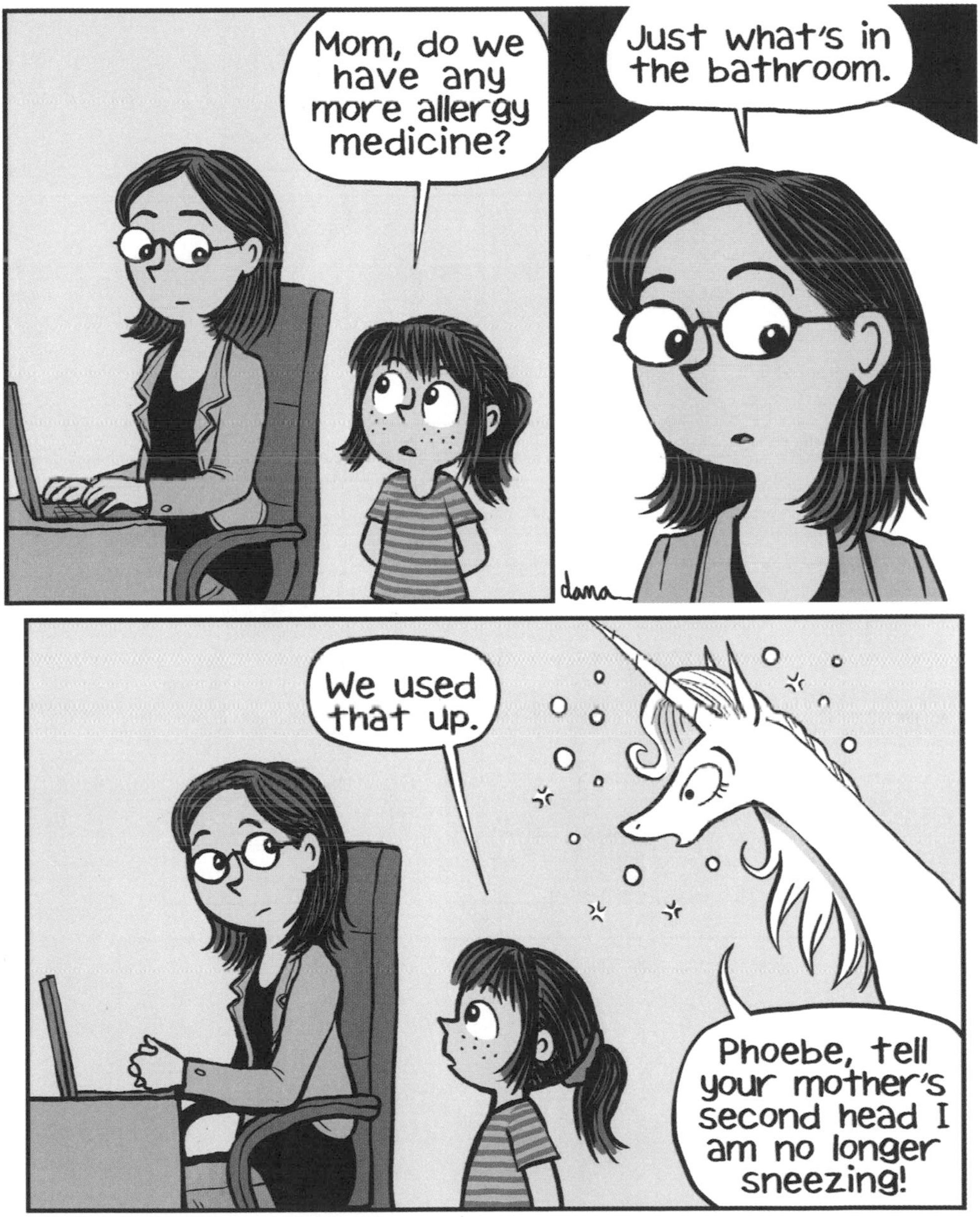
Mom, do we have any more allergy medicine?
Just what's in the bathroom.
dana
We used that up.
Phoebe, tell your mother's second head I am no longer sneezing!

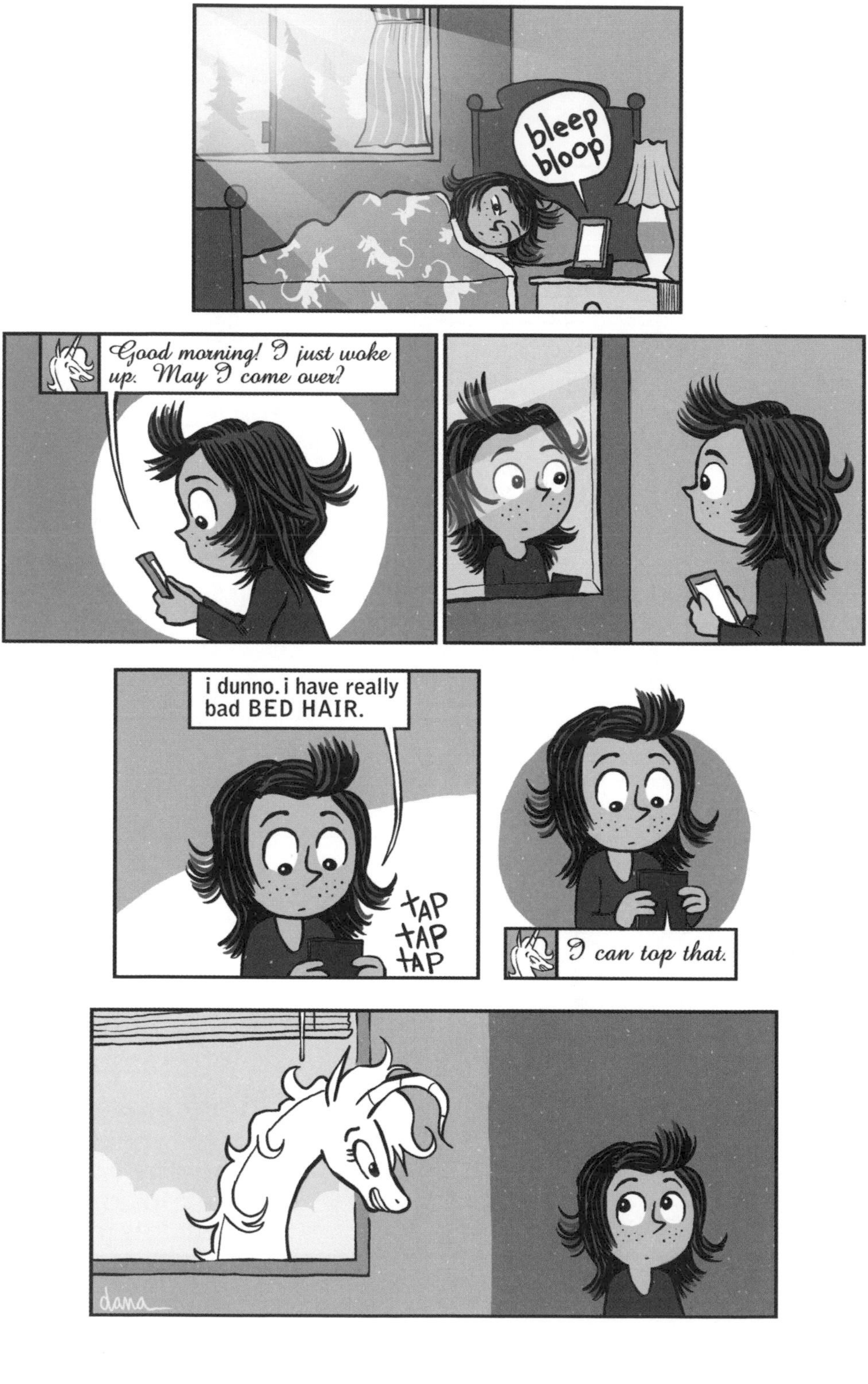
bleep bloop
Good morning! I just woke up. May I come over?
i dunno. i have really bad BED HAIR.
TAP TAP TAP
I can top that.
dana

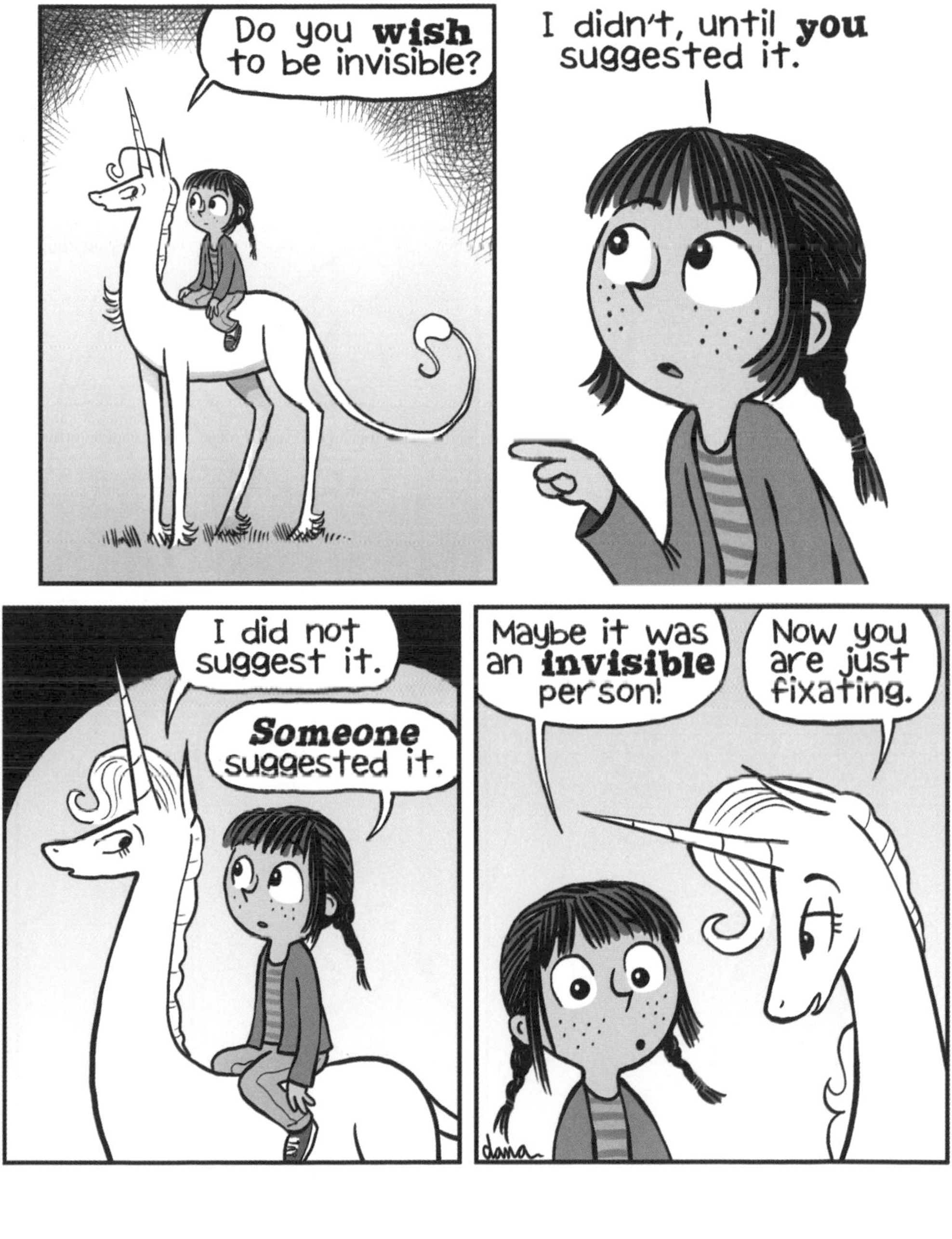
Do you **wish** to be invisible?
I didn't, until **you** suggested it.
I did not suggest it.
Someone suggested it.
Maybe it was an **invisible** person!
Now you are just fixating.
dana

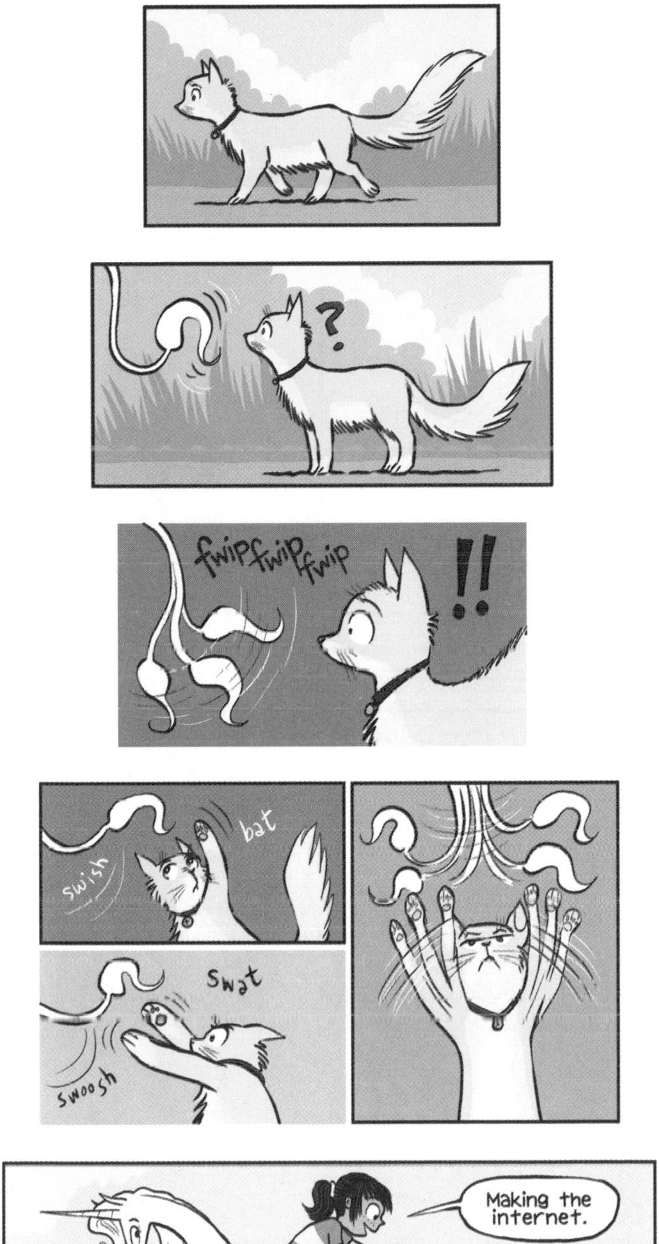
?
fwip fwip fwip
!!
swish
bat
swat
swoosh
What are you doing back there?
Making the internet.

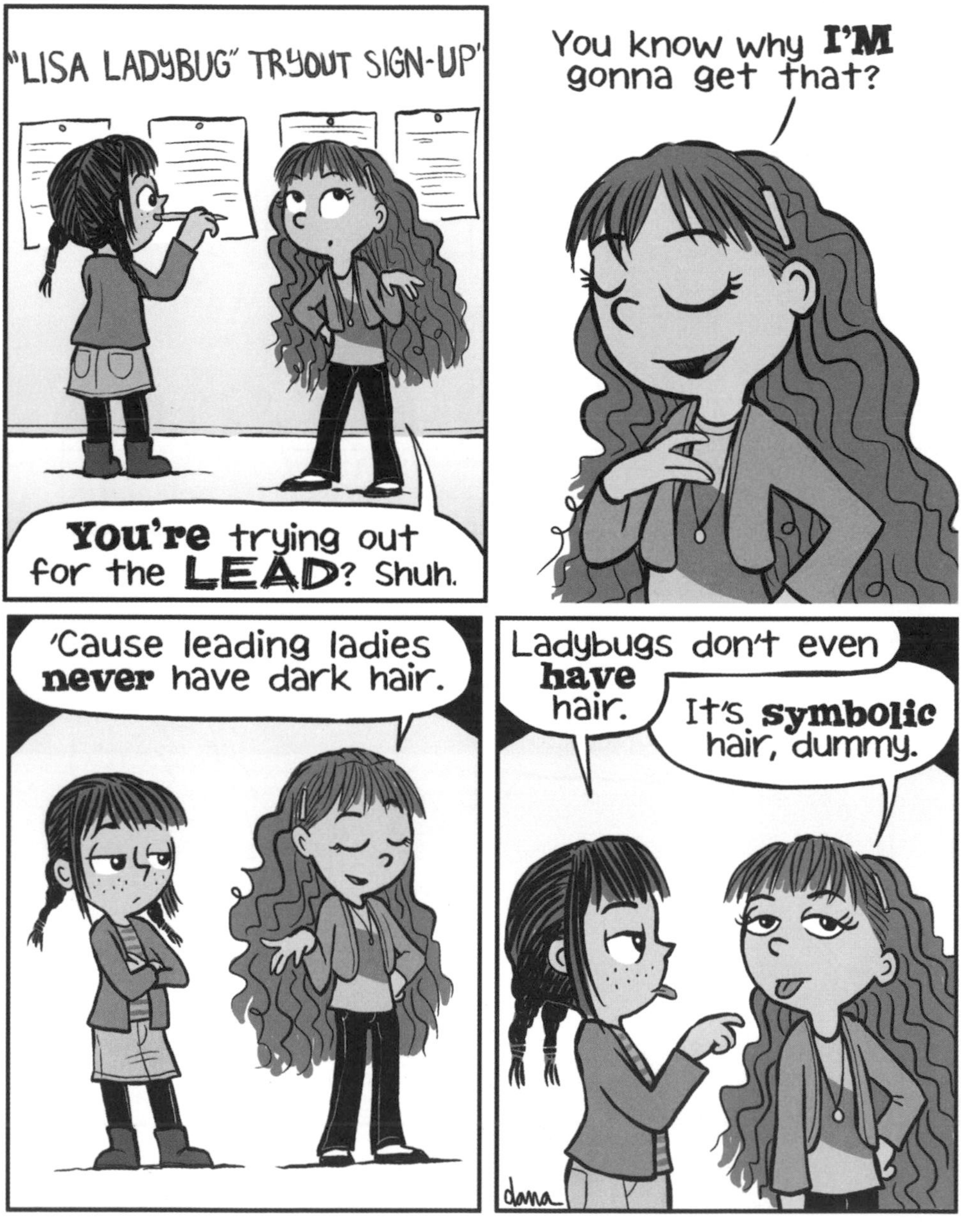
"LISA LADYBUG" TRYOUT SIGN-UP"
You're trying out for the **LEAD**? Shuh.
You know why **I'M** gonna get that?
'Cause leading ladies **never** have dark hair.
Ladybugs don't even **have** hair.
It's **symbolic** hair, dummy.
dana

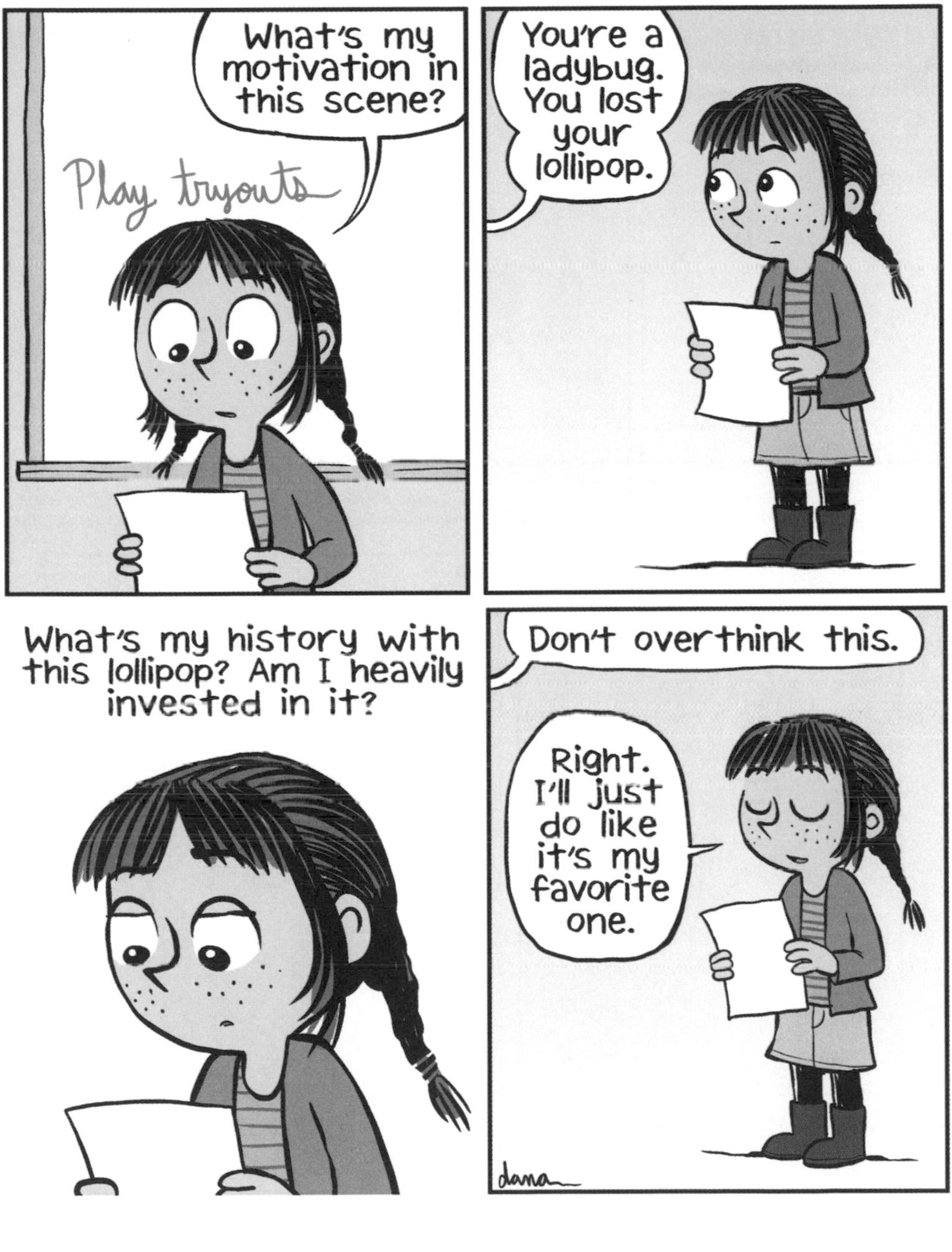
What's my motivation in this scene?
Play tryouts
You're a ladybug. You lost your lollipop.
What's my history with this lollipop? Am I heavily invested in it?
Don't overthink this.
Right. I'll just do like it's my favorite one.
dana

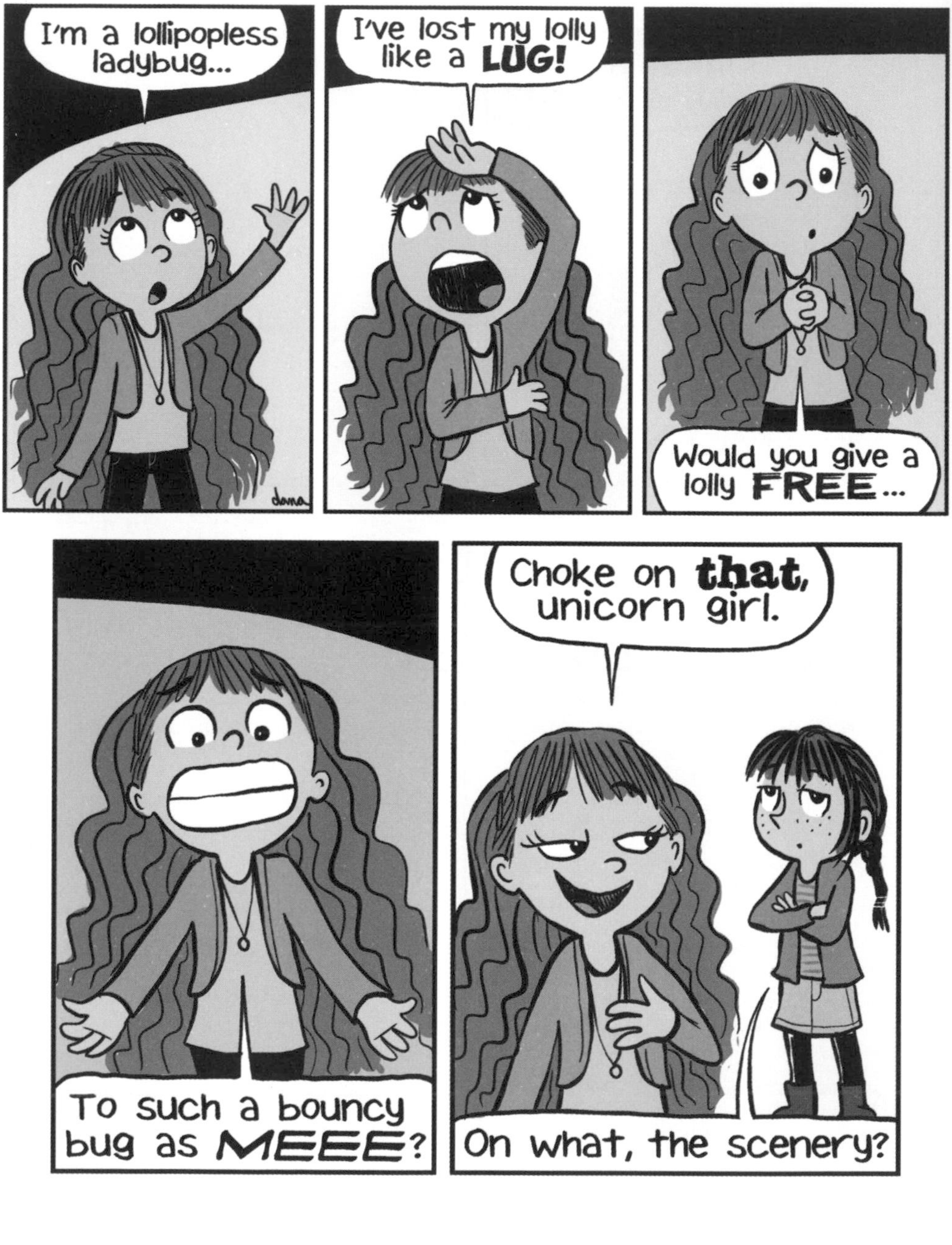
I'm a lollipopless ladybug...
I've lost my lolly like a LUG!
Would you give a lolly FREE...
To such a bouncy bug as MEEEE?
Choke on that, unicorn girl.
On what, the scenery?

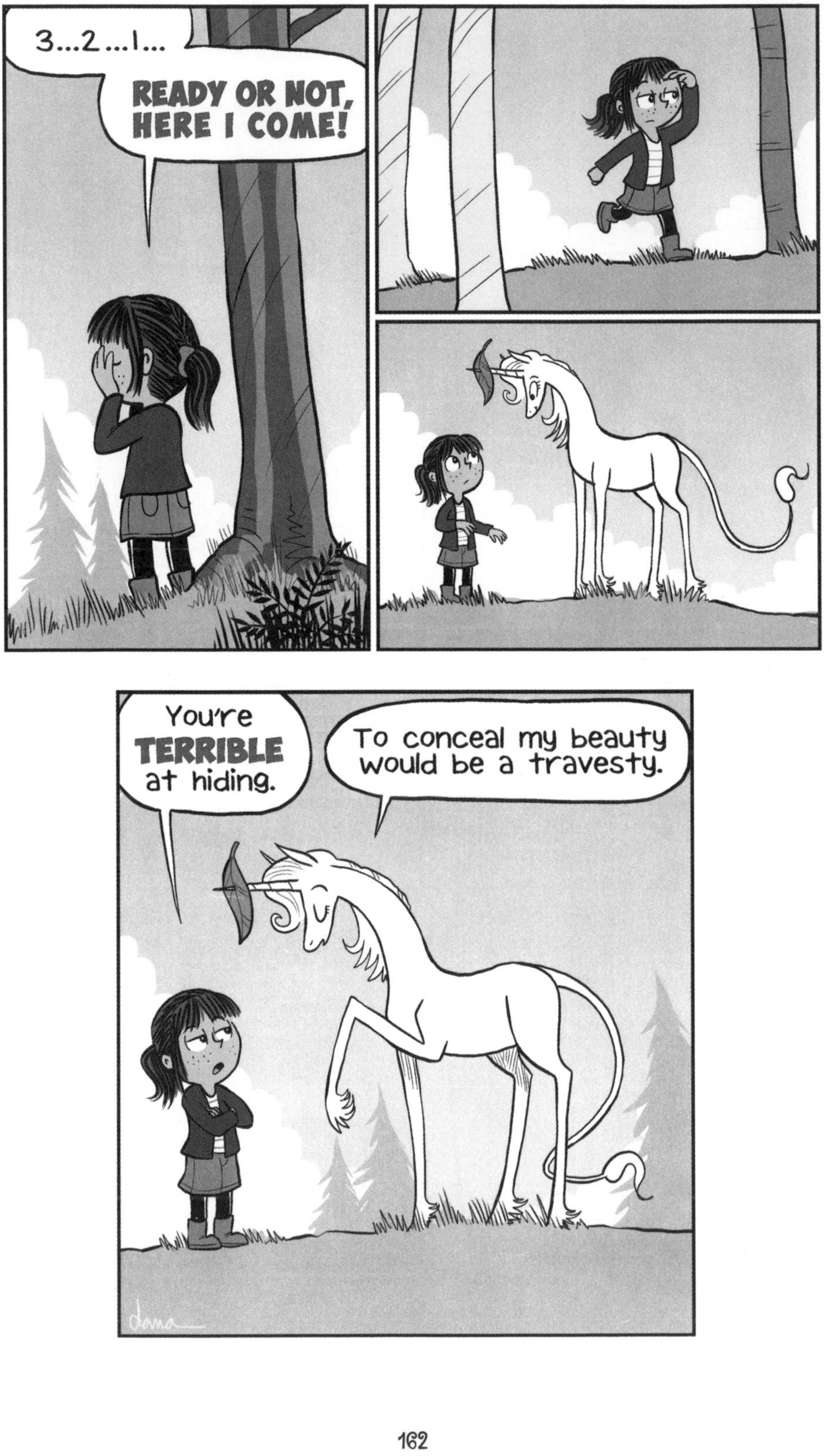
3...2...1...
READY OR NOT, HERE I COME!
You're TERRIBLE at hiding.
To conceal my beauty would be a travesty.
dana

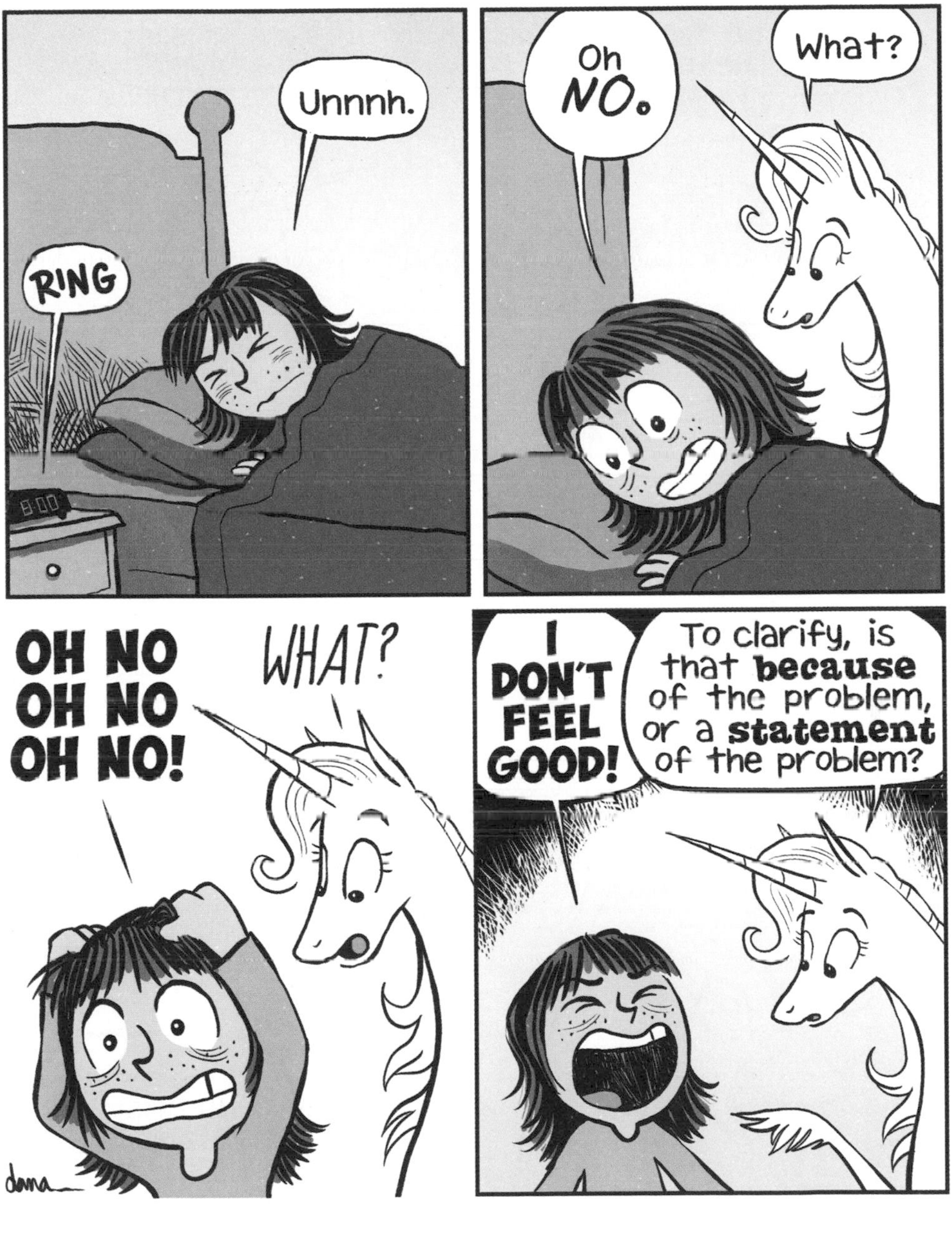
Unnnh.
RING
Oh NO.
What?
OH NO OH NO OH NO!
WHAT?
I DON'T FEEL GOOD!
To clarify, is that **because** of the problem, or a **statement** of the problem?

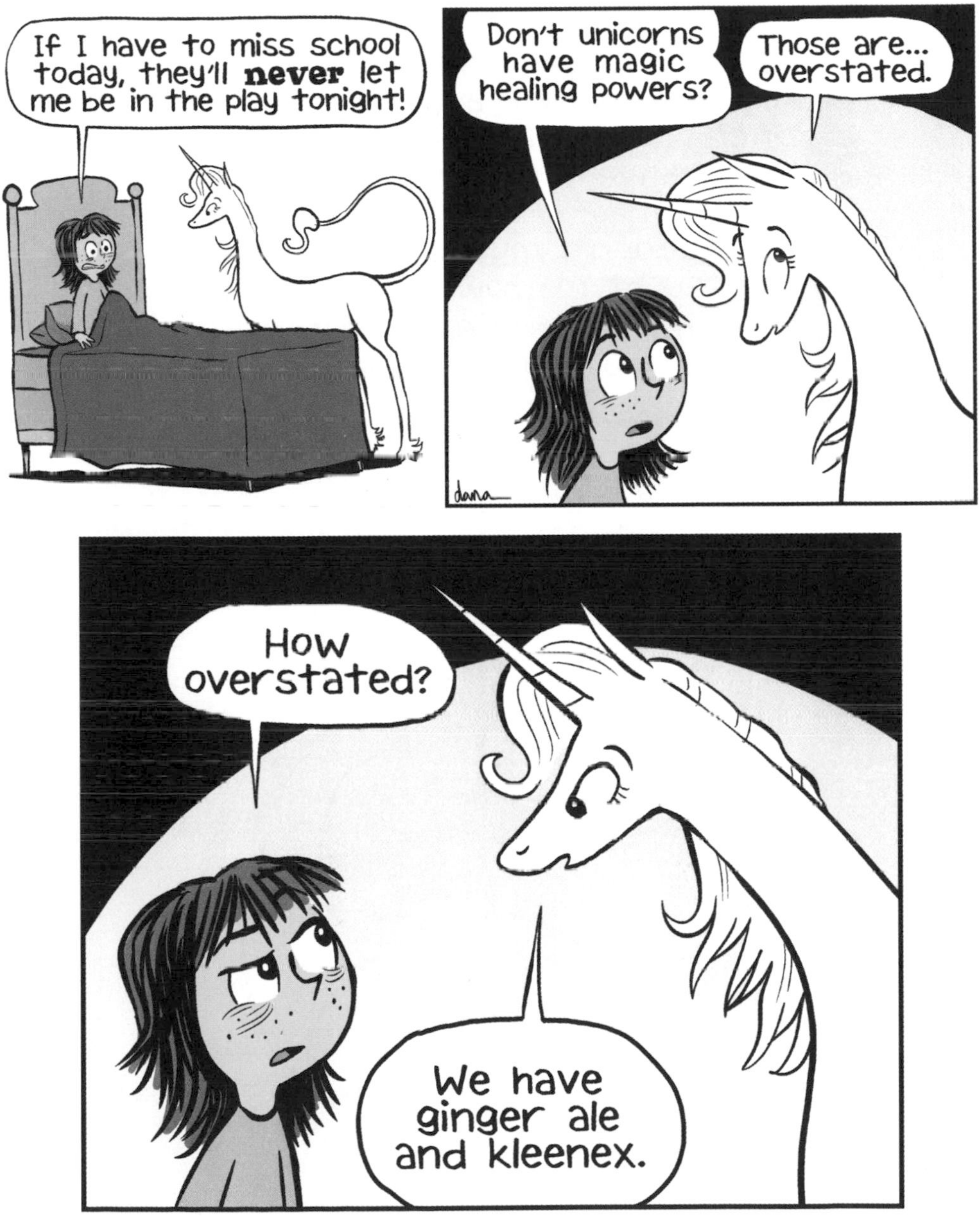
If I have to miss school today, they'll **never** let me be in the play tonight!
Don't unicorns have magic healing powers?
Those are... overstated.
dana
How overstated?
We have ginger ale and kleenex.

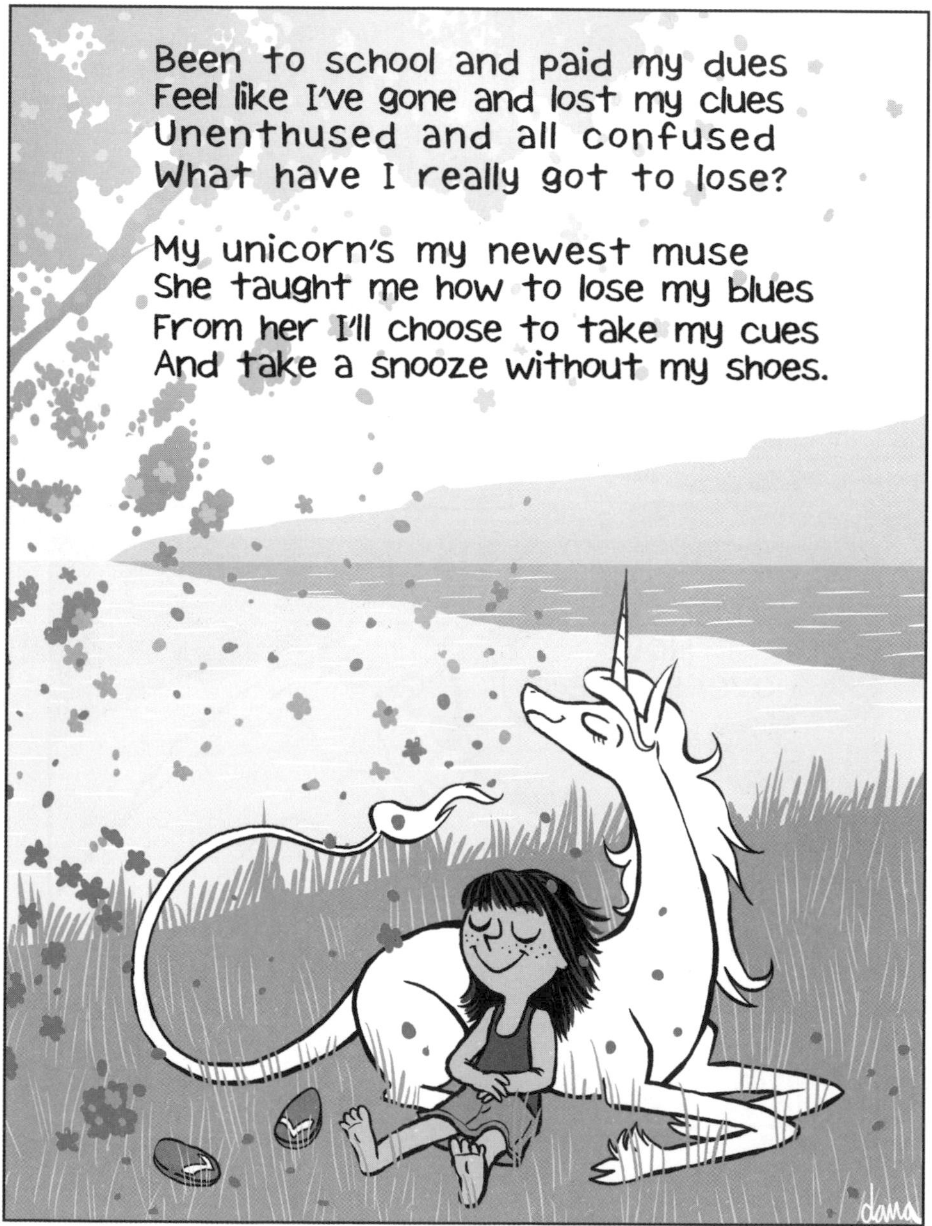
Been to school and paid my dues
Feel like I've gone and lost my clues
Unenthused and all confused
What have I really got to lose?

My unicorn's my newest muse
She taught me how to lose my blues
From her I'll choose to take my cues
And take a snooze without my shoes.
dana

with thanks to Ronnie Simonds

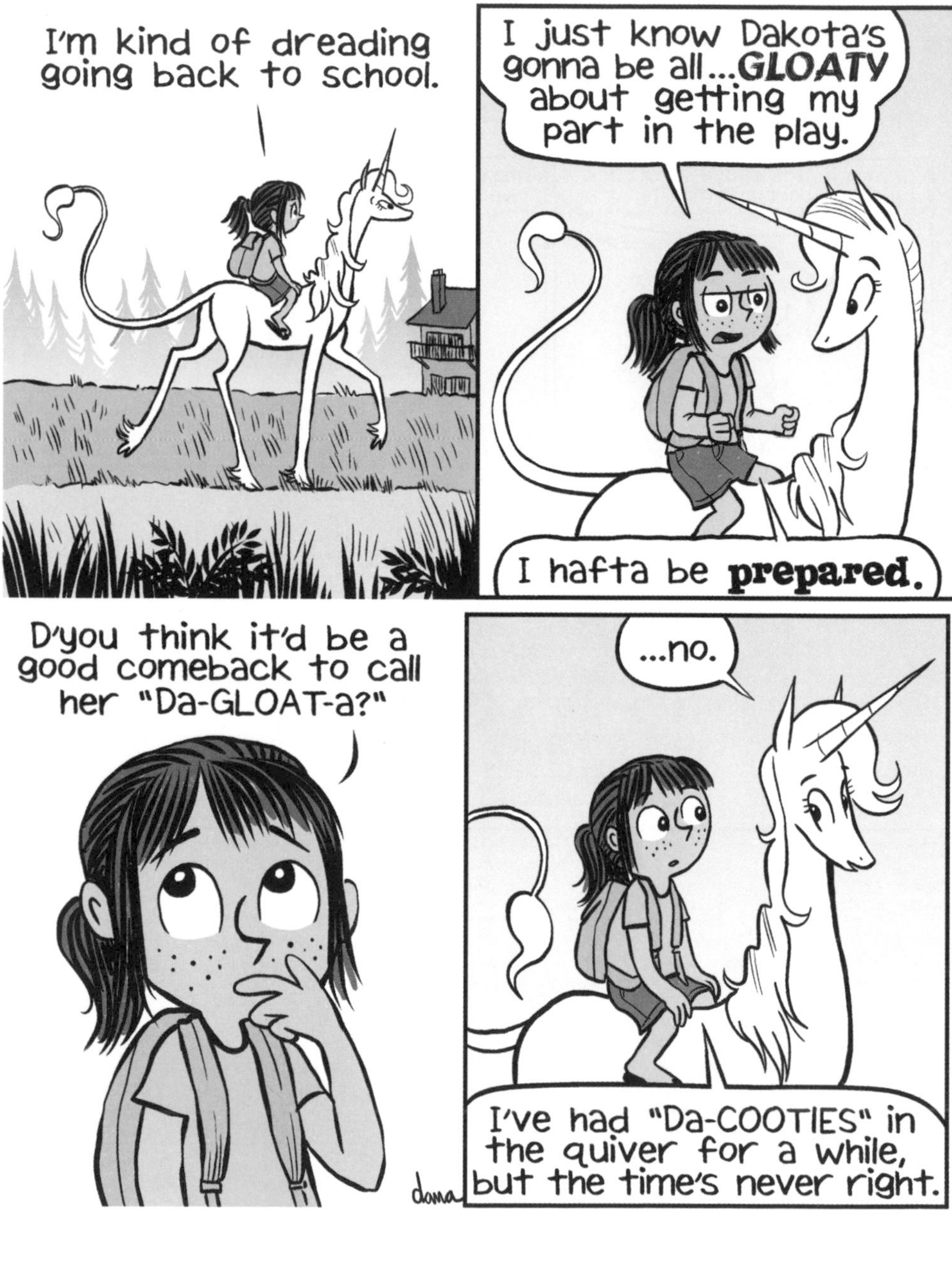
I'm kind of dreading going back to school.
I just know Dakota's gonna be all...GLOATY about getting my part in the play.
I hafta be prepared.
D'you think it'd be a good comeback to call her "Da-GLOAT-a?"
...no.
I've had "Da-COOTIES" in the quiver for a while, but the time's never right.
dana

193

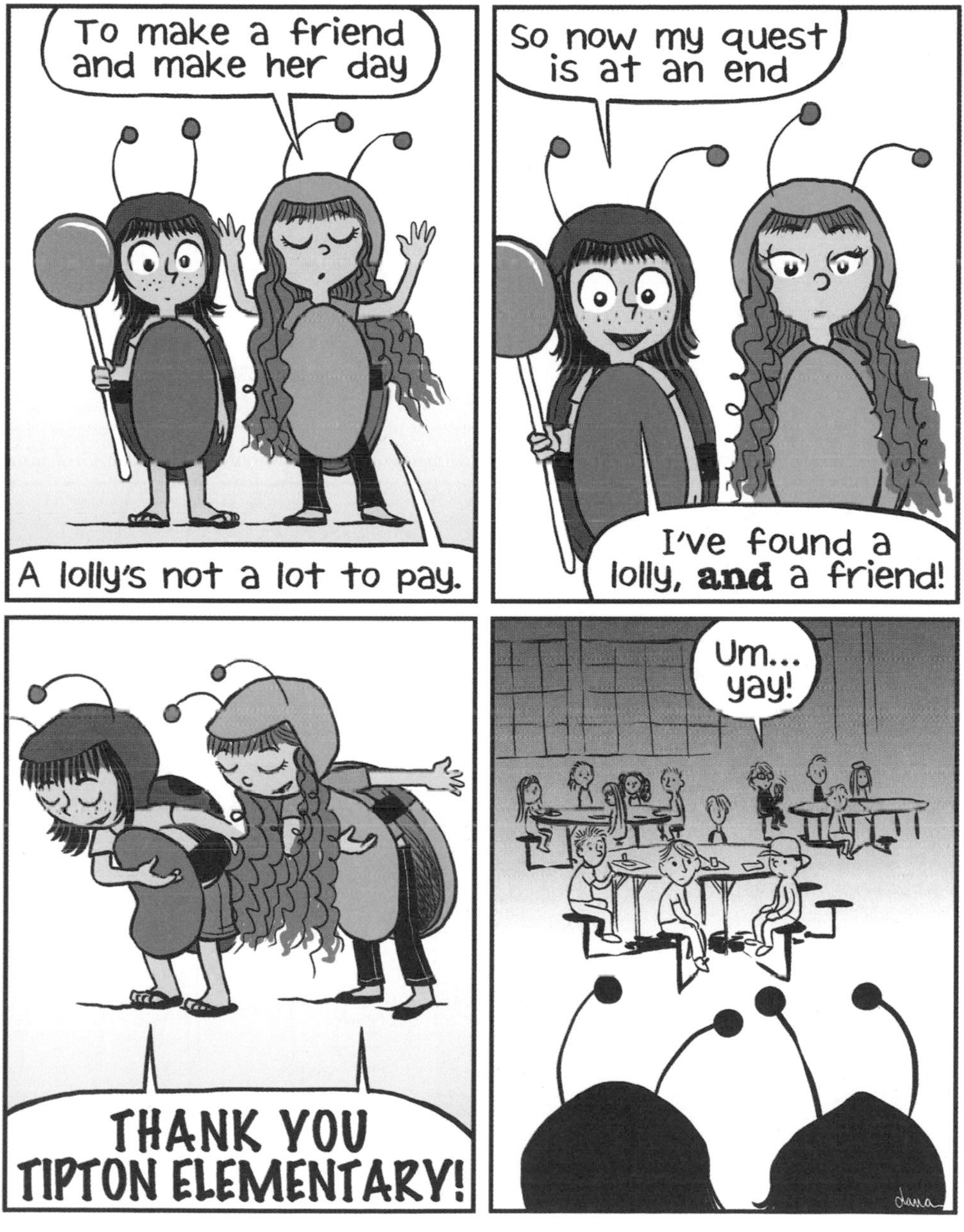
To make a friend and make her day
A lolly's not a lot to pay.
So now my quest is at an end
I've found a lolly, **and** a friend!
THANK YOU TIPTON ELEMENTARY!
Um... yay!
dana

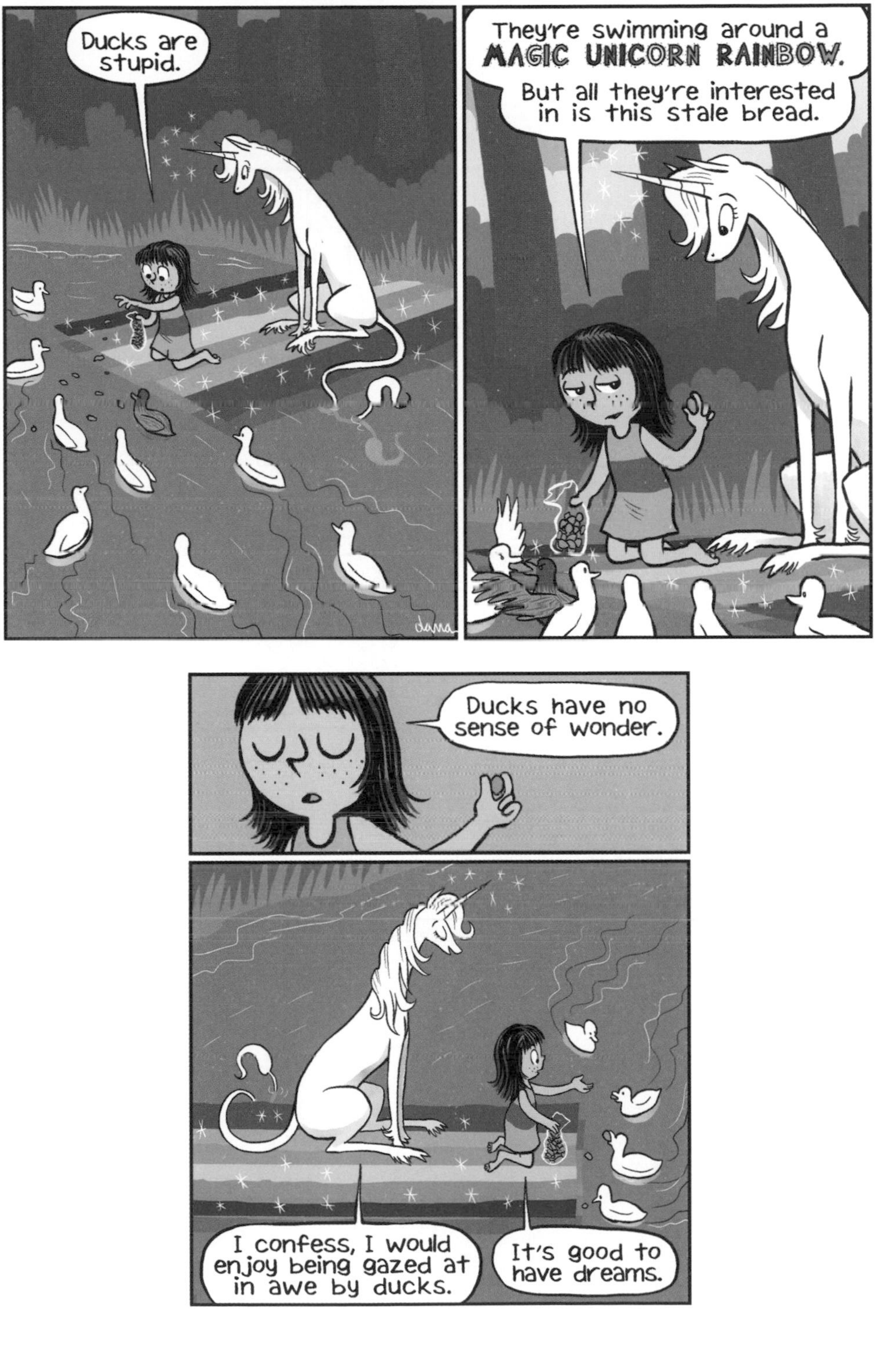
Ducks are stupid.
They're swimming around a MAGIC UNICORN RAINBOW.
But all they're interested in is this stale bread.
Ducks have no sense of wonder.
I confess, I would enjoy being gazed at in awe by ducks.
It's good to have dreams.

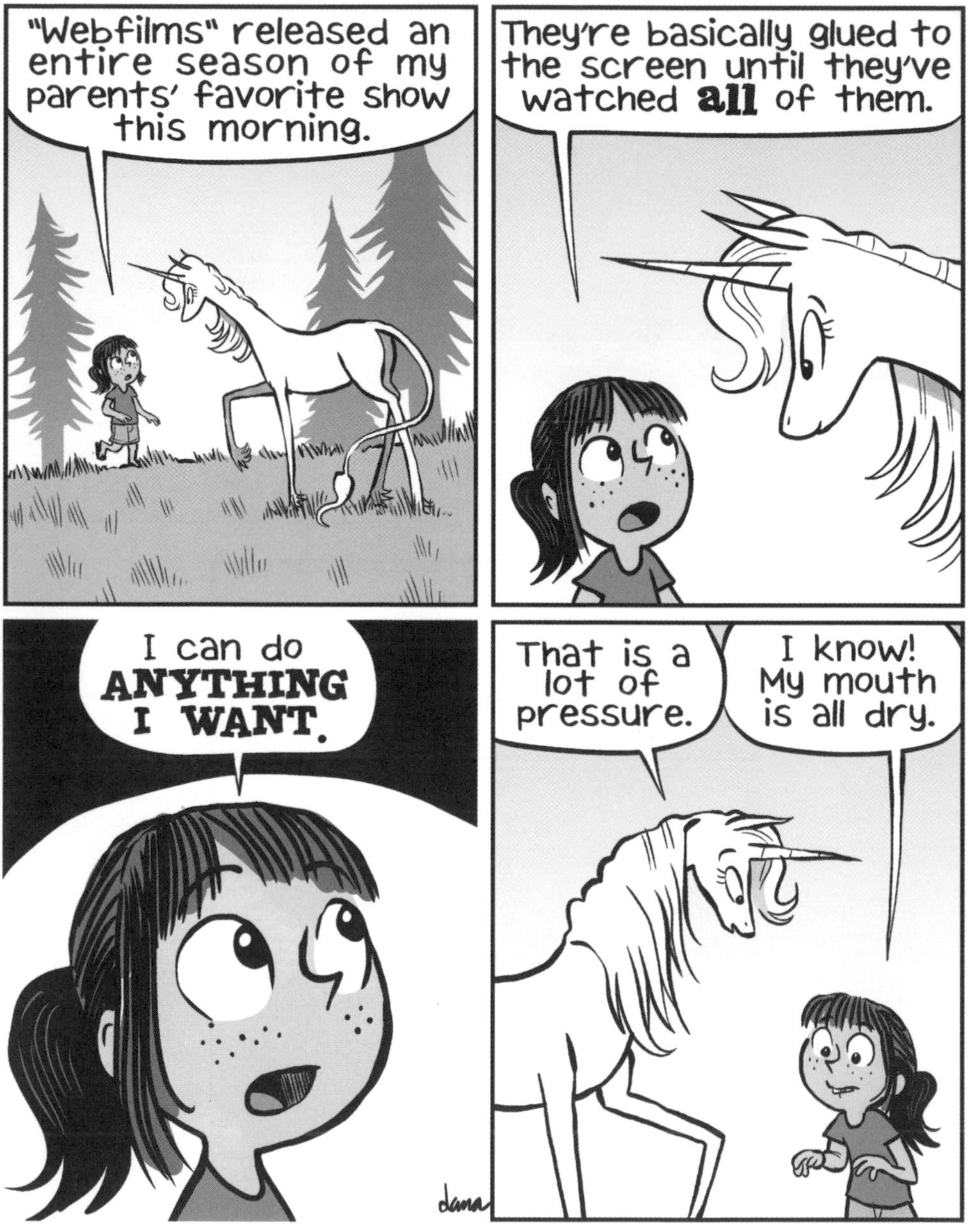
"Webfilms" released an entire season of my parents' favorite show this morning.
They're basically glued to the screen until they've watched **all** of them.
I can do **ANYTHING I WANT.**
That is a lot of pressure.
I know! My mouth is all dry.
dana

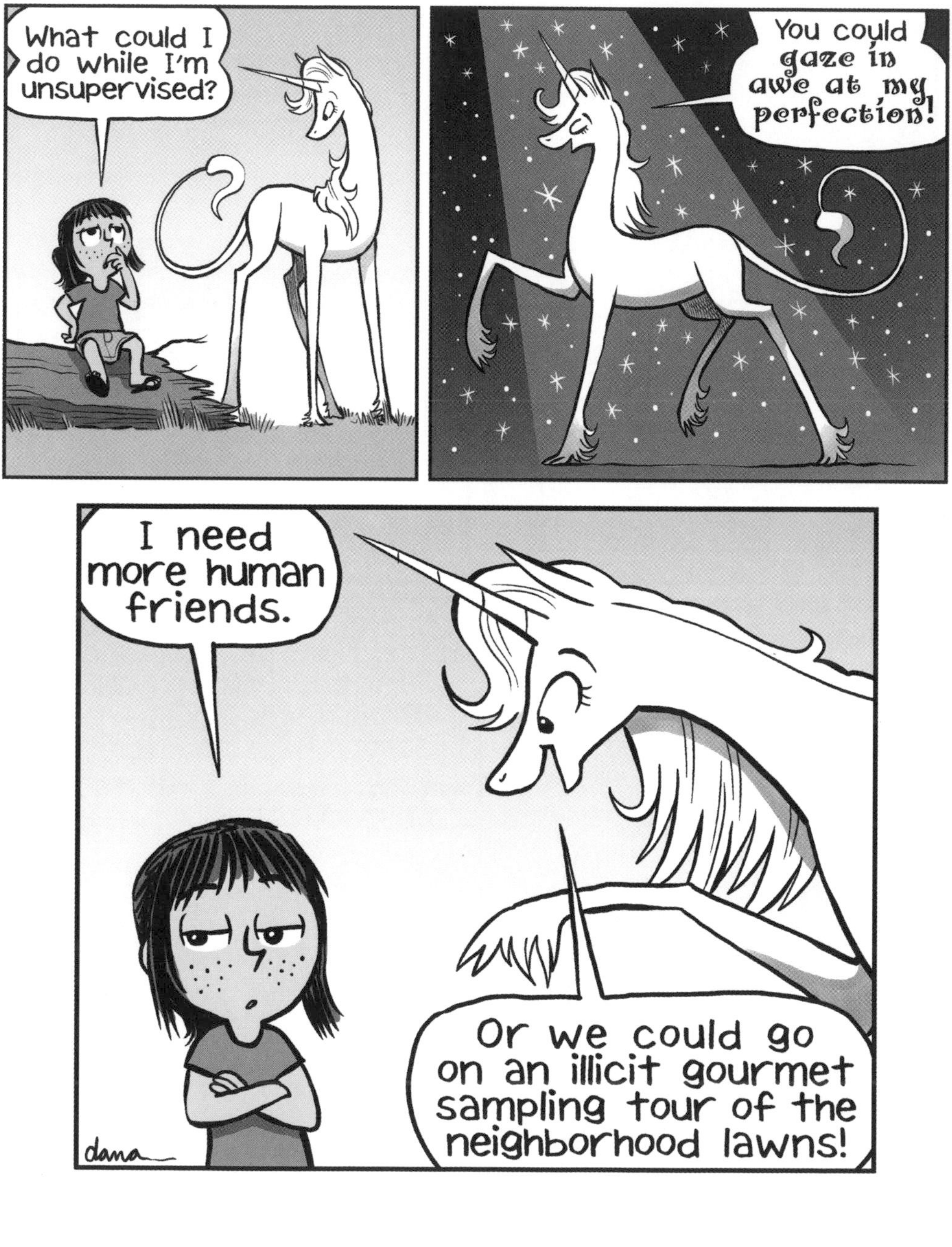
What could I do while I'm unsupervised?
You could gaze in awe at my perfection!
I need more human friends.
Or we could go on an illicit gourmet sampling tour of the neighborhood lawns!
dana

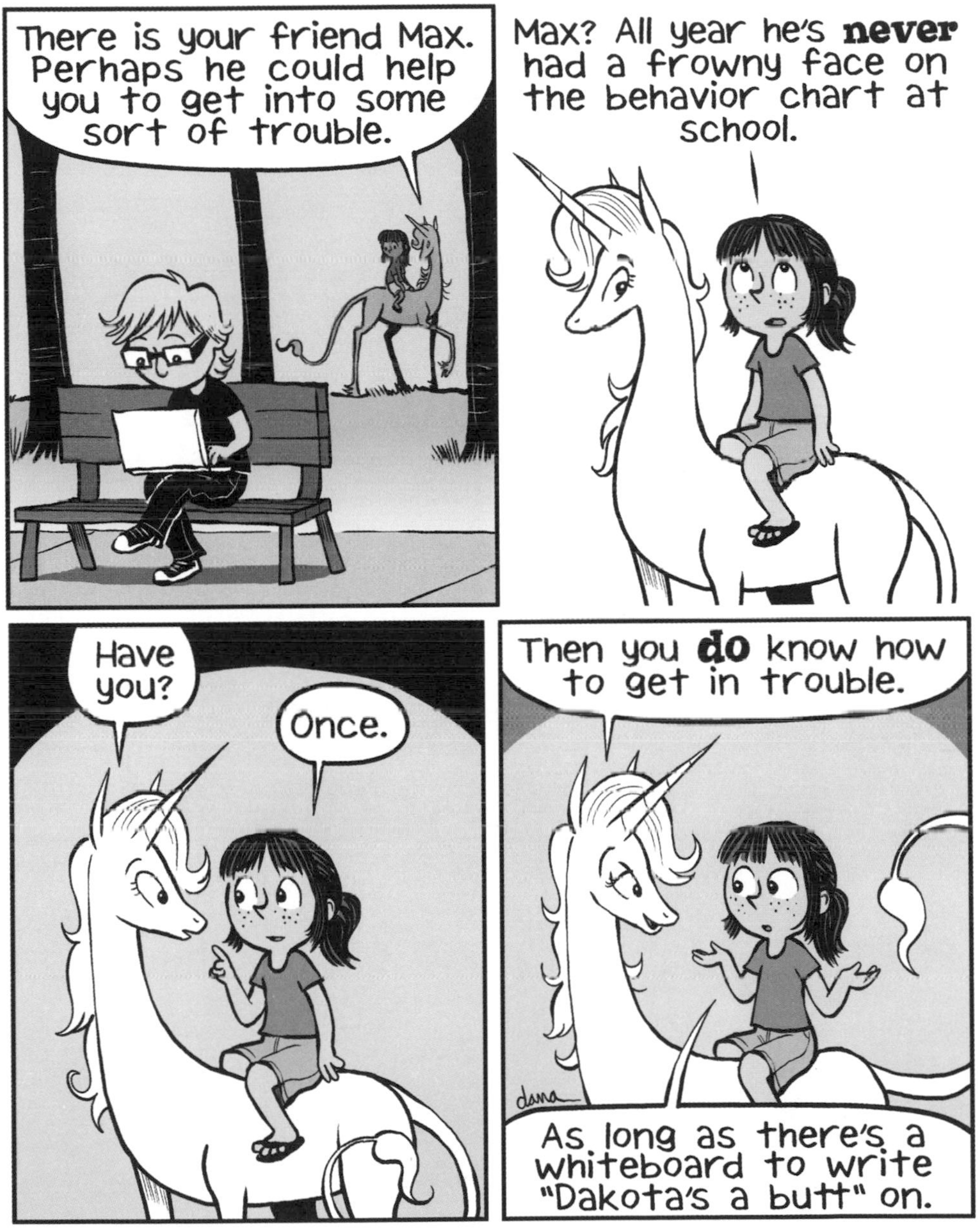
There is your friend Max. Perhaps he could help you to get into some sort of trouble.
Max? All year he's **never** had a frowny face on the behavior chart at school.
Have you?
Once.
Then you **do** know how to get in trouble.
As long as there's a whiteboard to write "Dakota's a butt" on.
dana

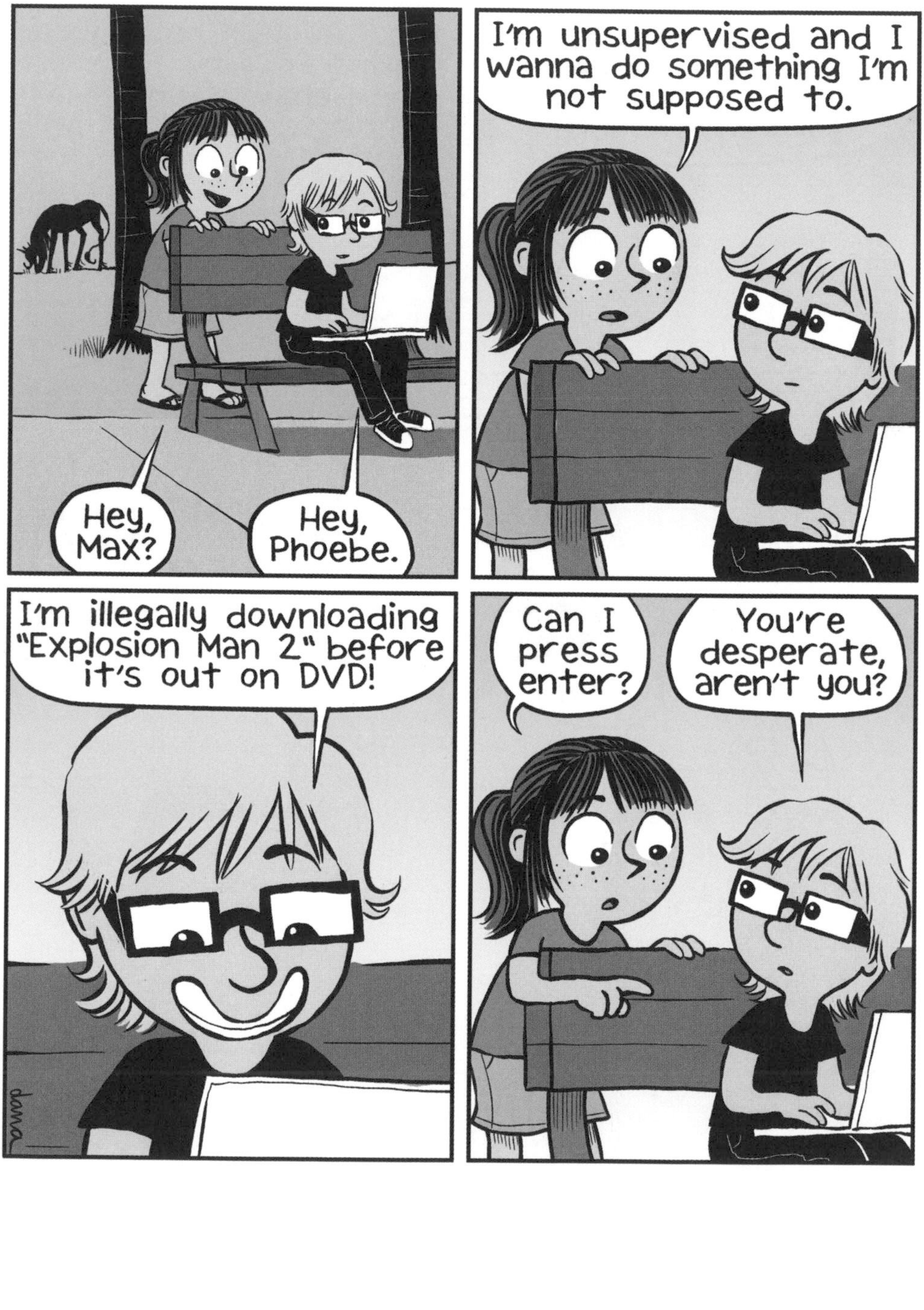
Hey, Max?
Hey, Phoebe.
I'm unsupervised and I wanna do something I'm not supposed to.
I'm illegally downloading "Explosion Man 2" before it's out on DVD!
Can I press enter?
You're desperate, aren't you?
dana

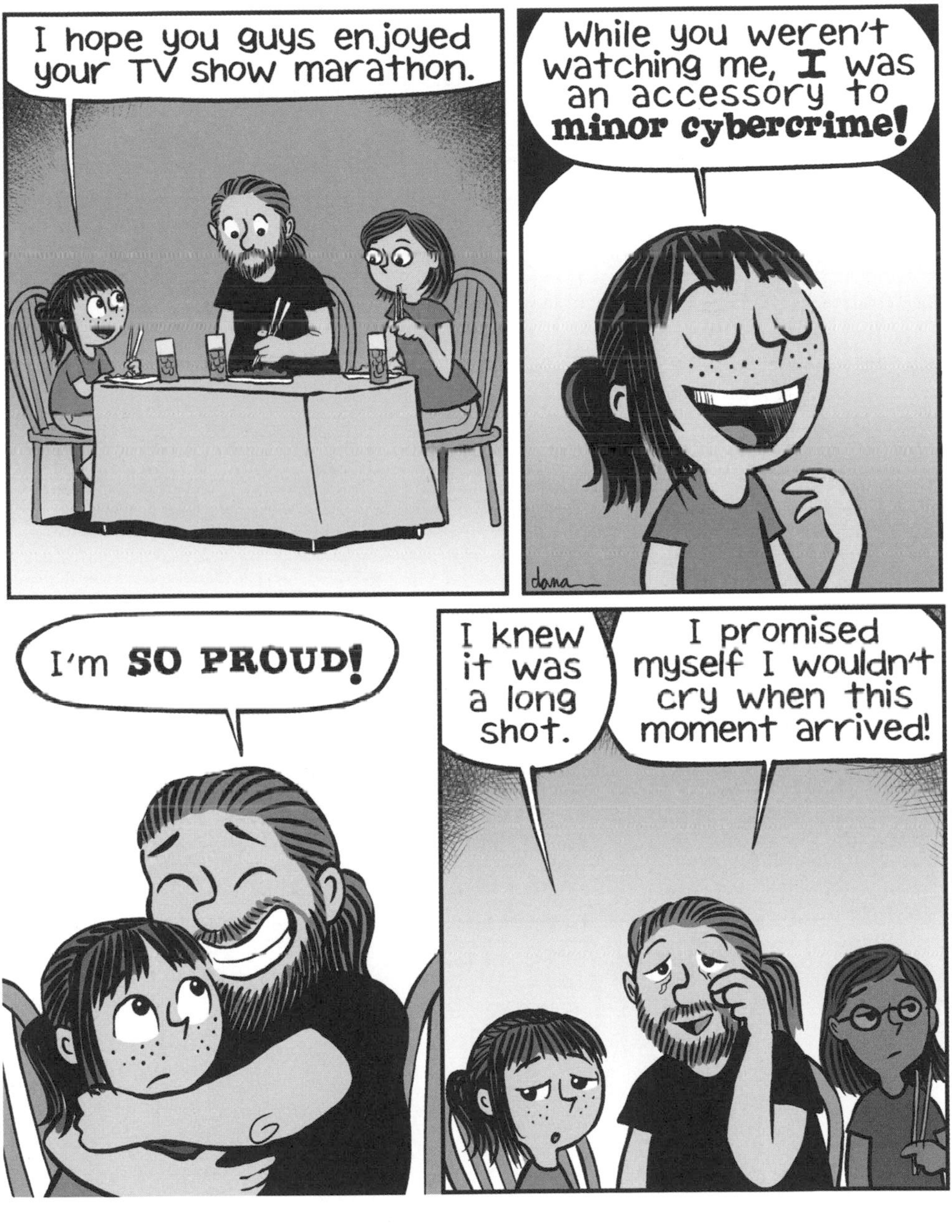
I hope you guys enjoyed your TV show marathon.
While you weren't watching me, **I** was an accessory to **minor cybercrime!**
dana
I'm **SO PROUD!**
I knew it was a long shot.
I promised myself I wouldn't cry when this moment arrived!

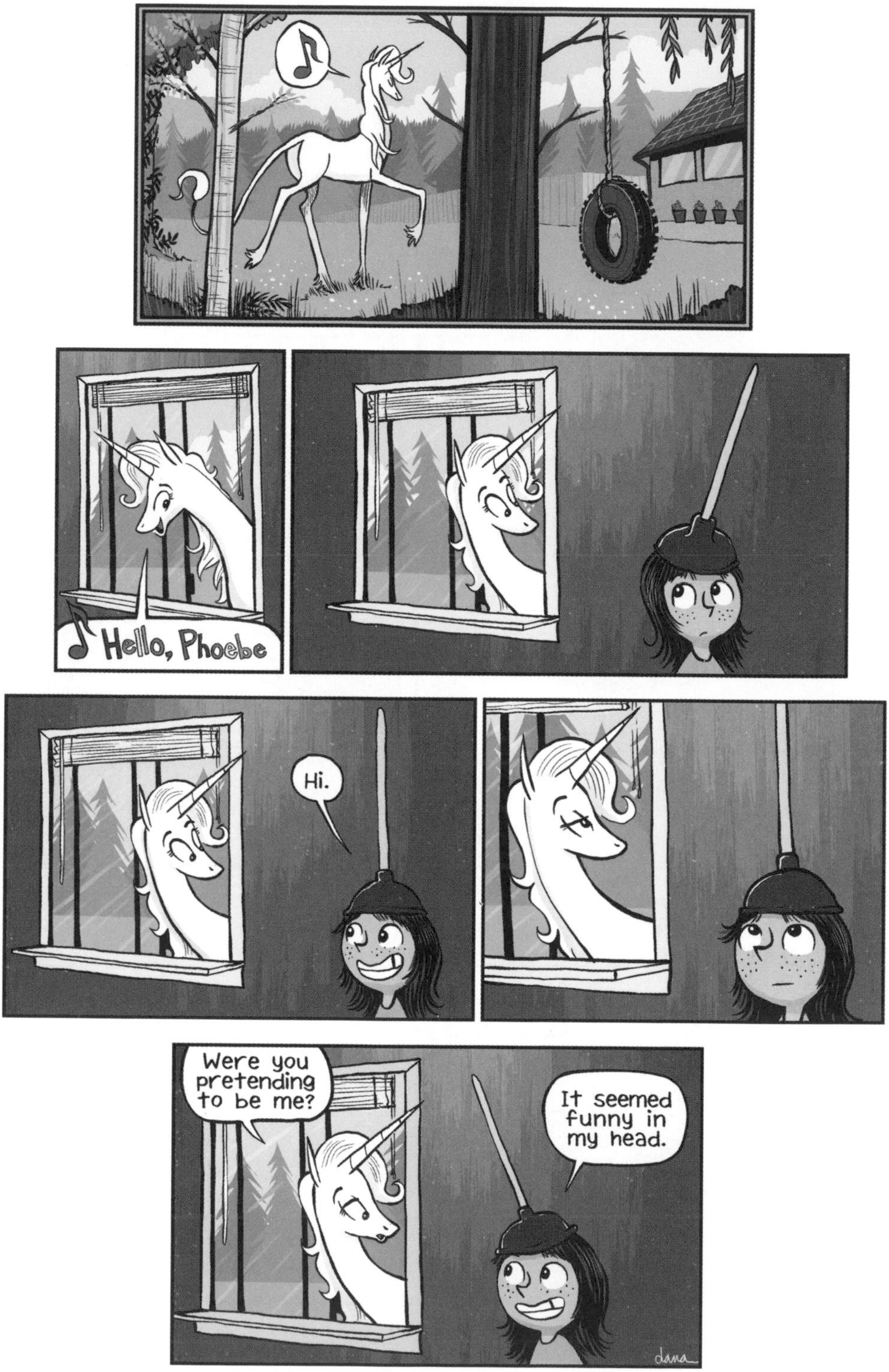
♪ Hello, Phoebe
Hi.
Were you pretending to be me?
It seemed funny in my head.
dana

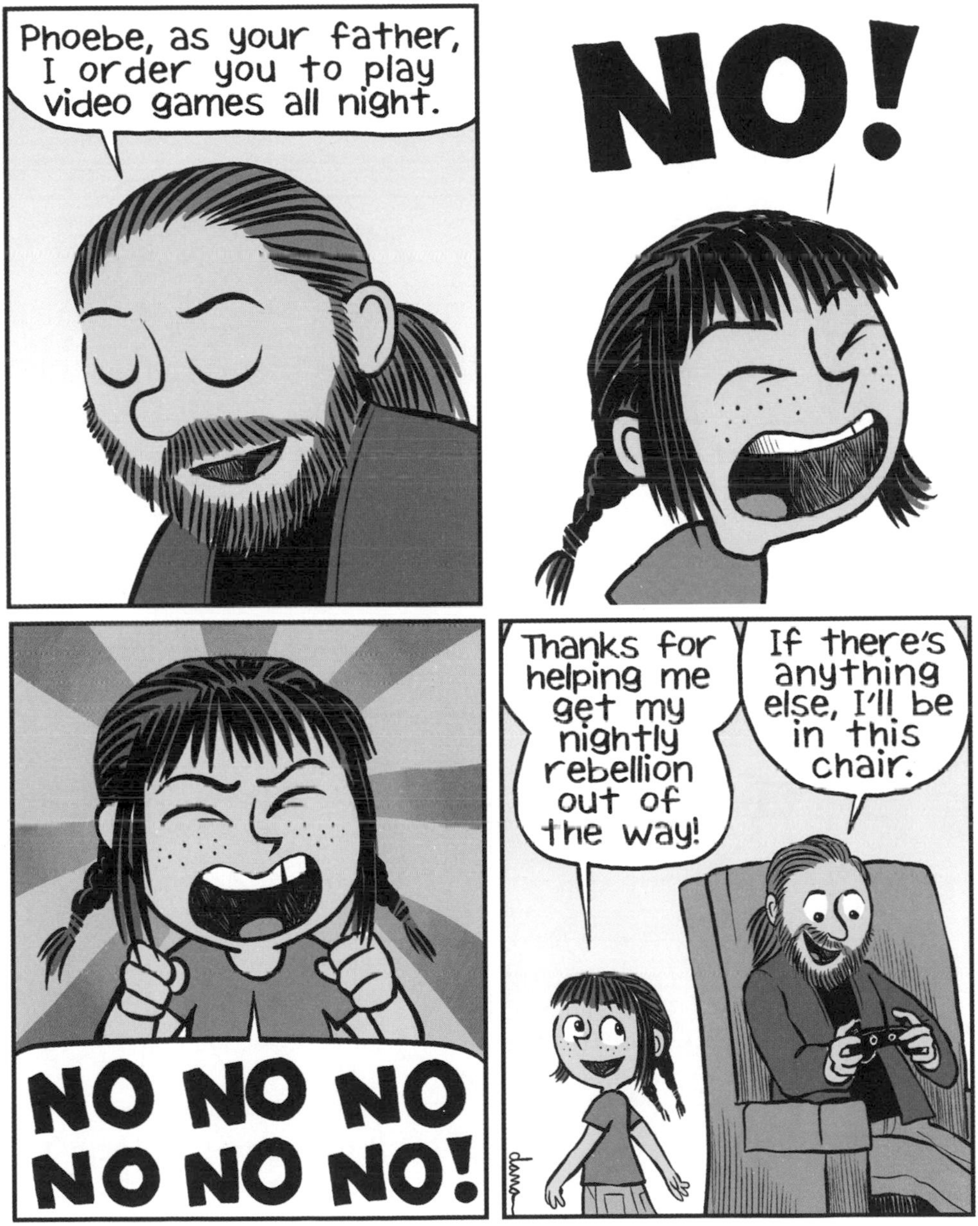
Phoebe, as your father, I order you to play video games all night.
NO!
NO NO NO NO NO NO!
Thanks for helping me get my nightly rebellion out of the way!
If there's anything else, I'll be in this chair.

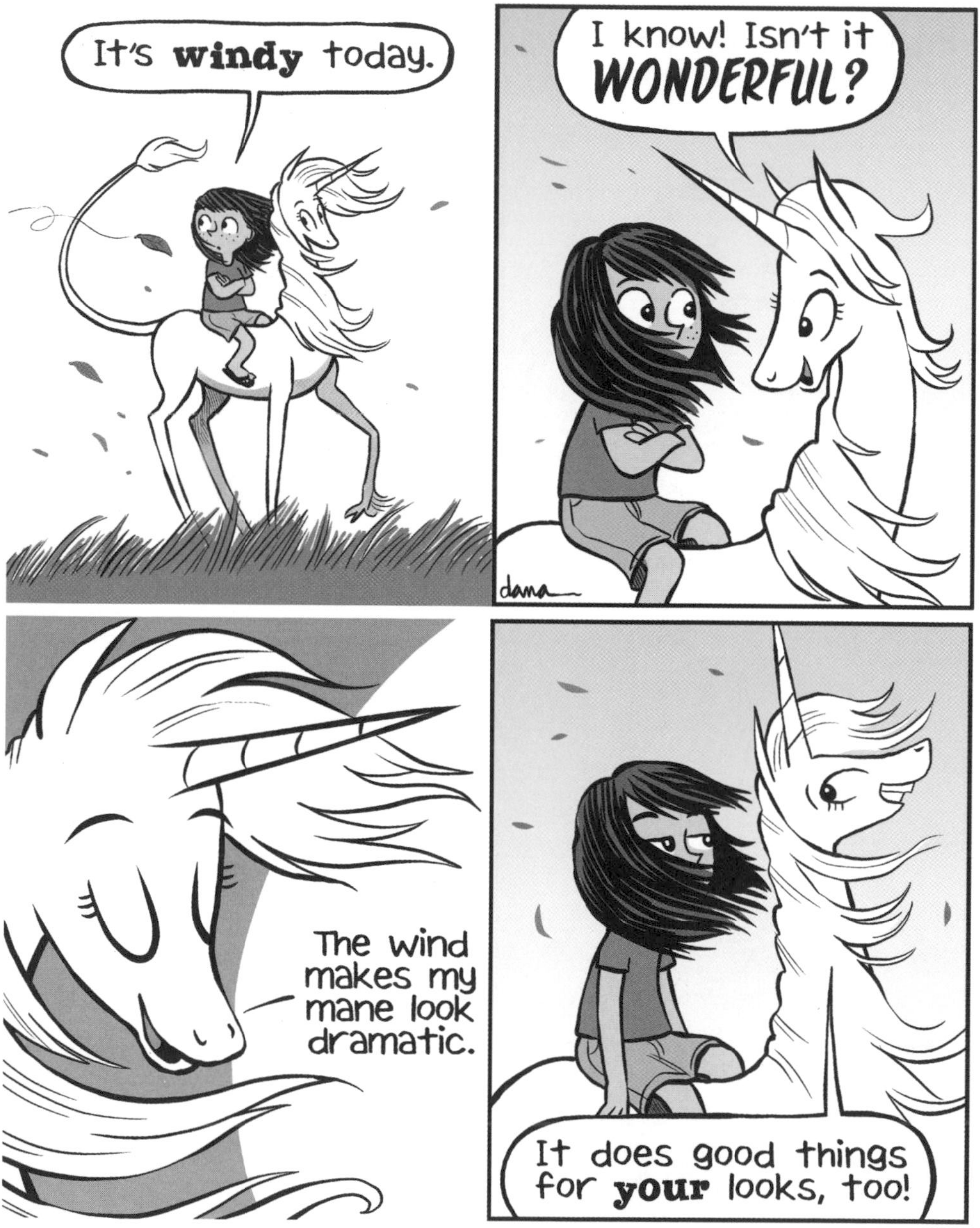
It's **windy** today.
I know! Isn't it **WONDERFUL?**
dana
The wind makes my mane look dramatic.
It does good things for **your** looks, too!

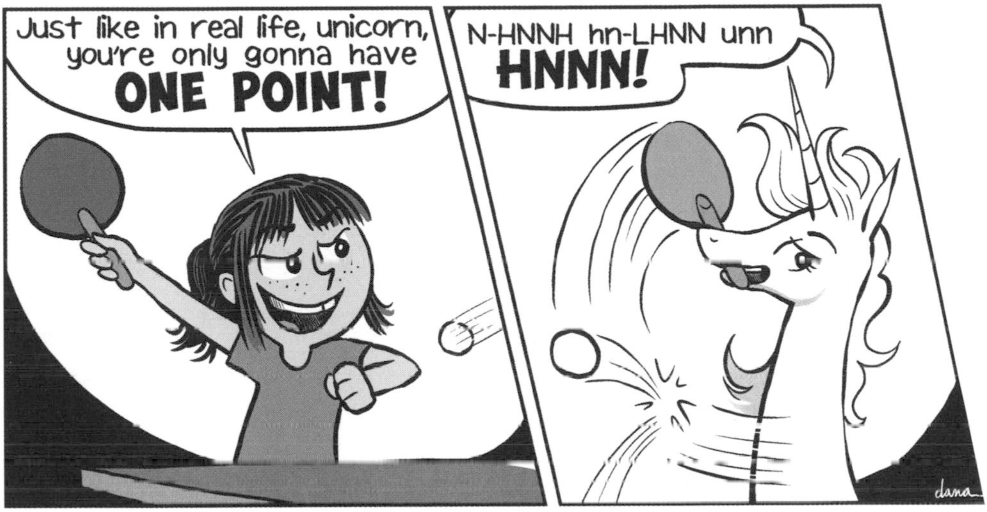
Just like in real life, unicorn, you're only gonna have ONE POINT!
N-HNNH hn-LHNN unn HNNN!
dana

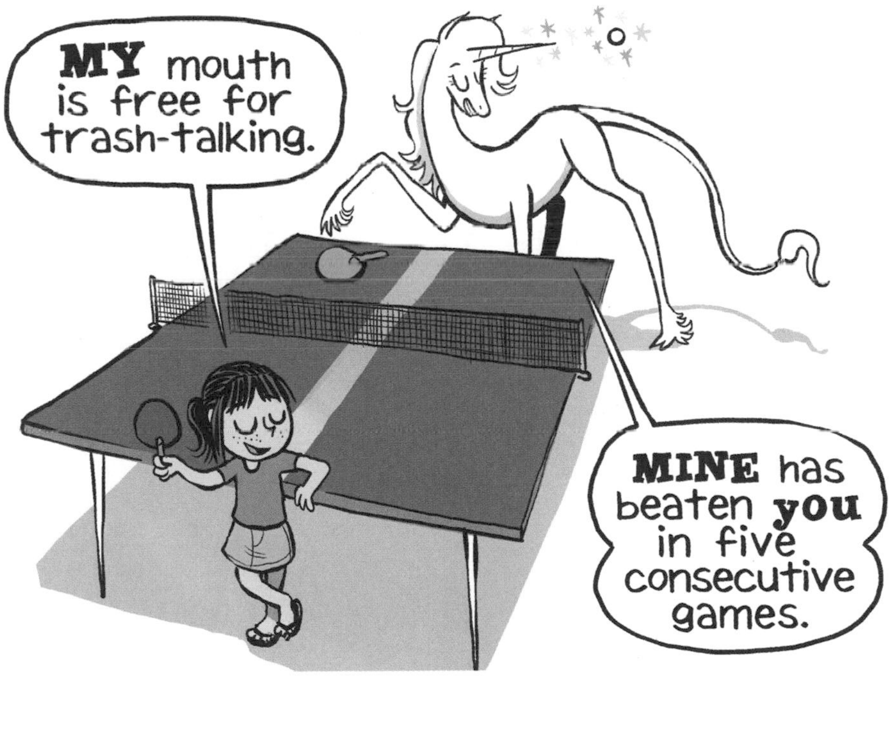
MY mouth is free for trash-talking.
MINE has beaten you in five consecutive games.

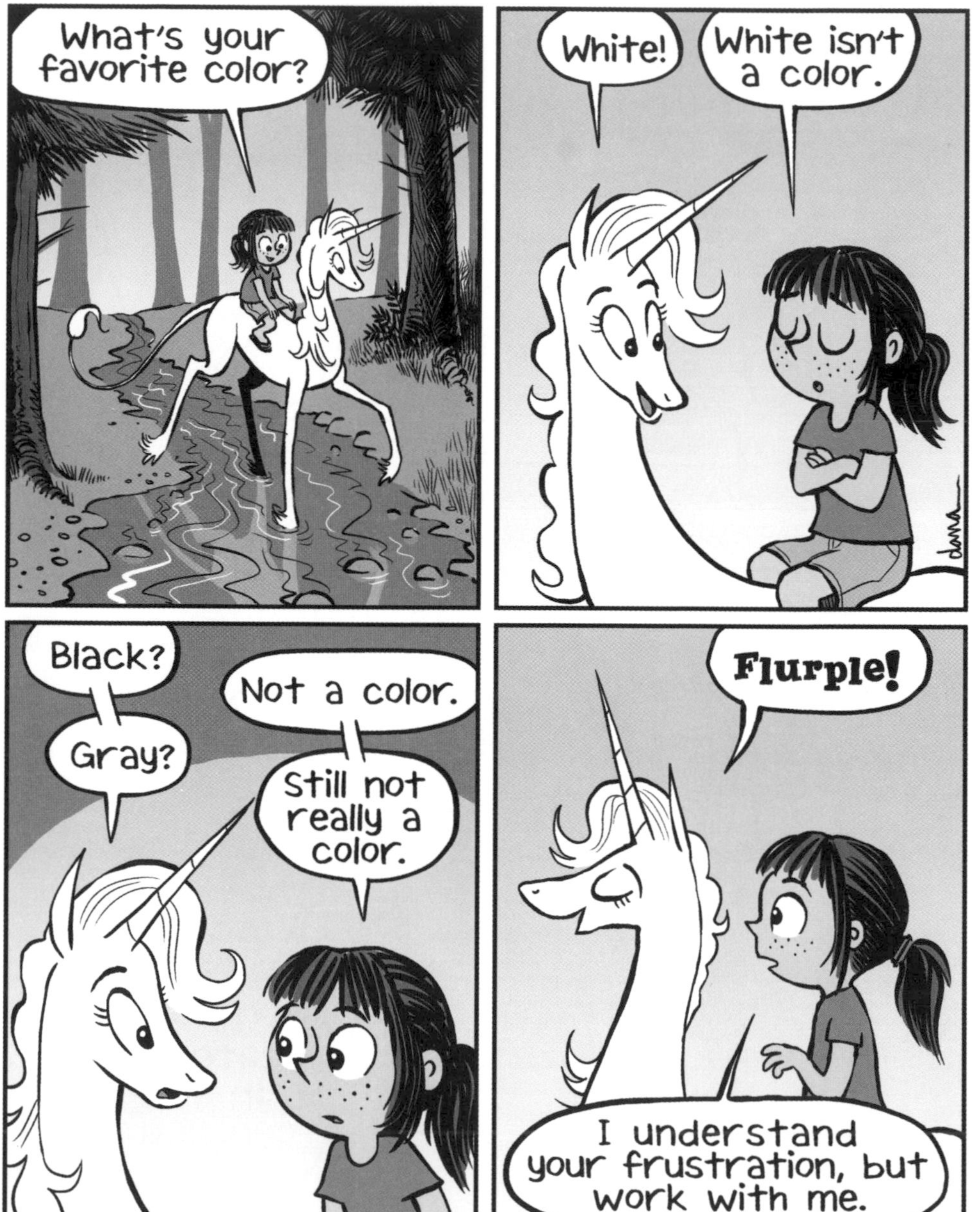
What's your favorite color?
White!
White isn't a color.
Black?
Gray?
Not a color.
Still not really a color.
Flurple!
I understand your frustration, but work with me.
dana

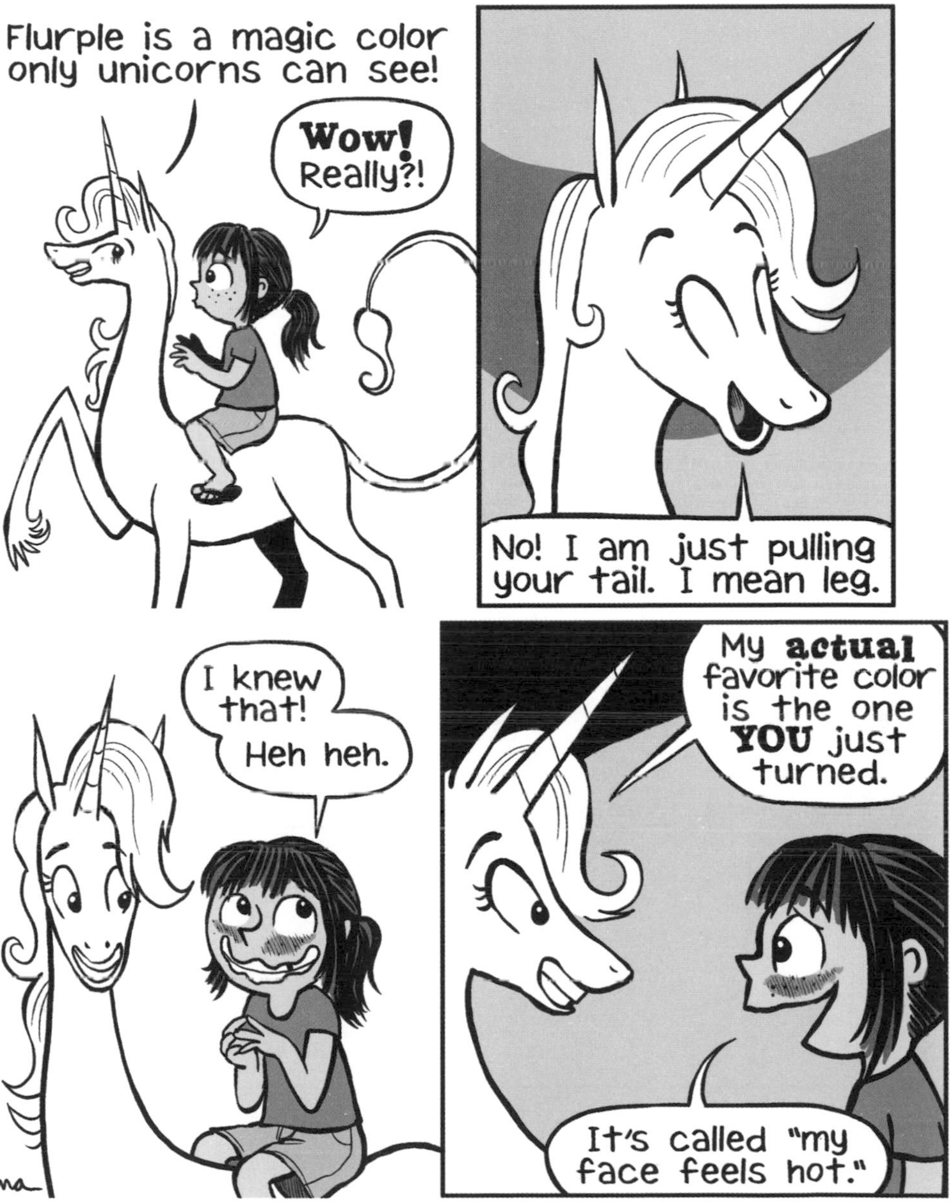
Flurple is a magic color only unicorns can see!
Wow! Really?!
No! I am just pulling your tail. I mean leg.
I knew that!
Heh heh.
My actual favorite color is the one YOU just turned.
It's called "my face feels hot."
dana

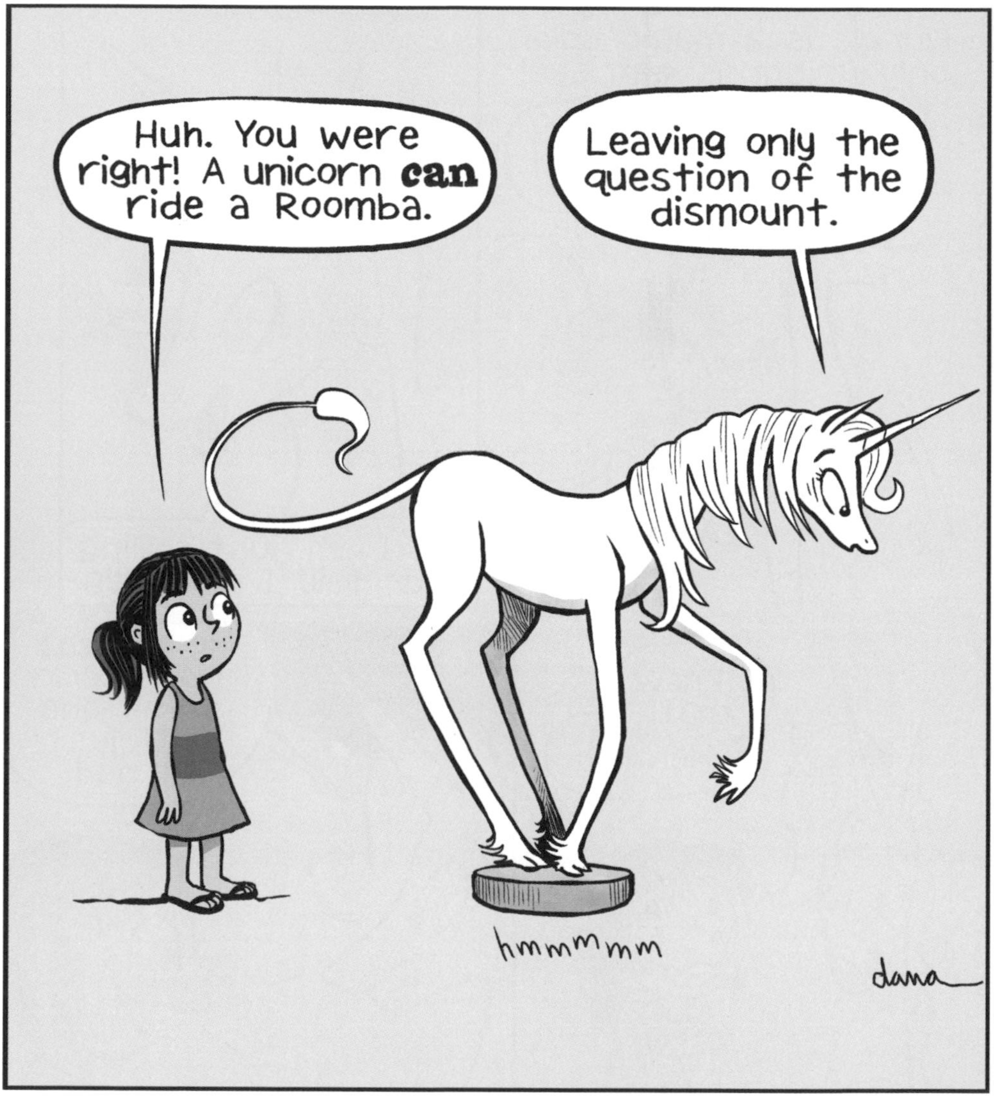
Huh. You were right! A unicorn **can** ride a Roomba.
Leaving only the question of the dismount.
hmmmmmm
dana

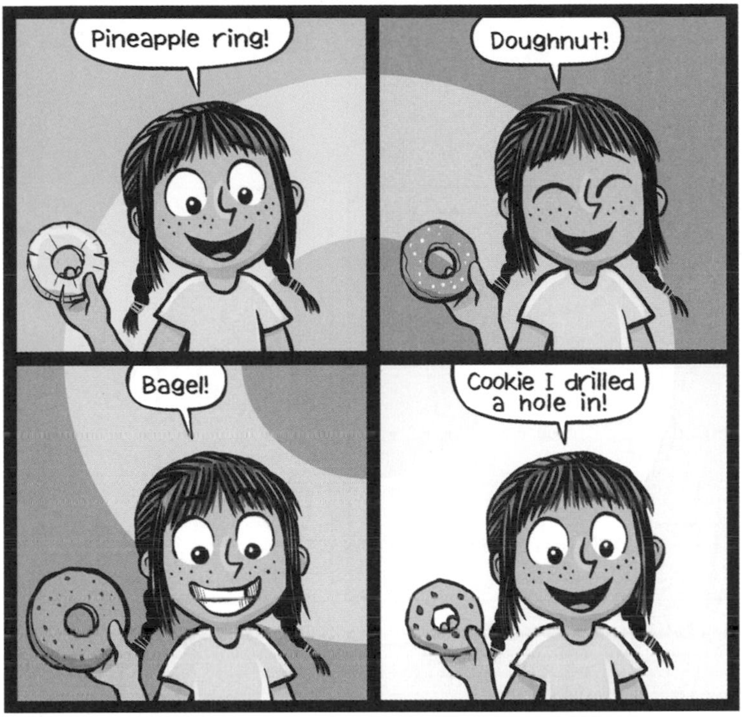
Pineapple ring!
Doughnut!
Bagel!
Cookie I drilled a hole in!

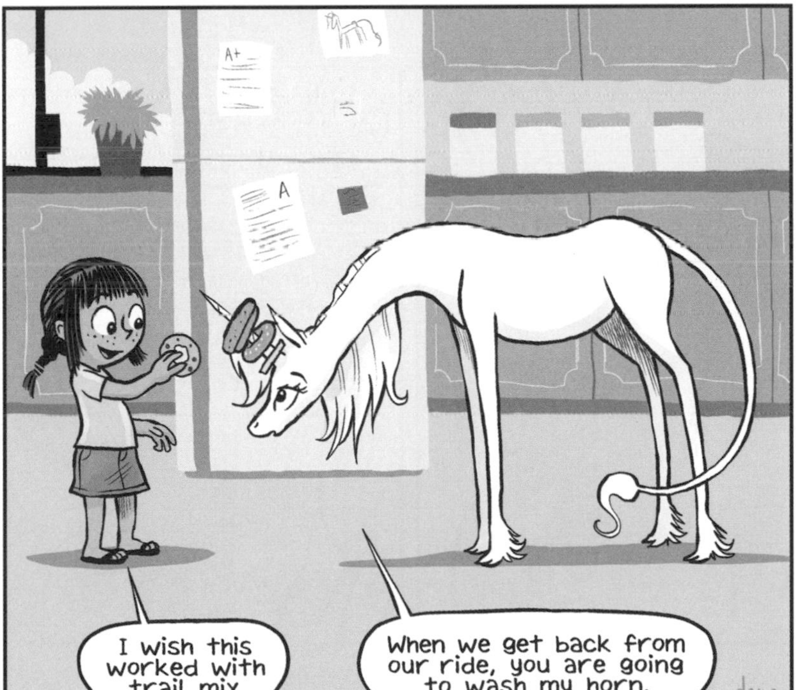
A+
A
I wish this worked with trail mix.
When we get back from our ride, you are going to wash my horn.
dana

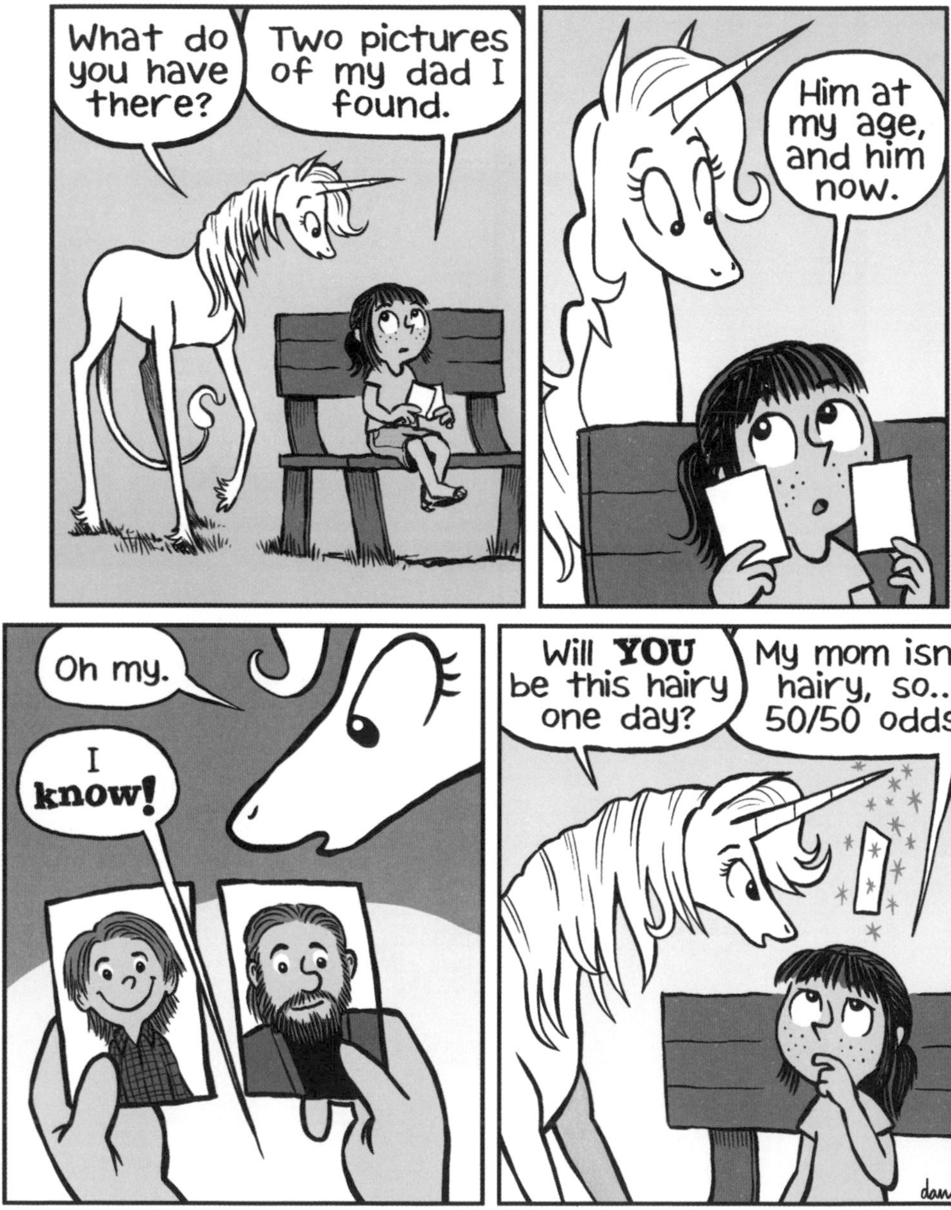
What do you have there?
Two pictures of my dad I found.
Him at my age, and him now.
Oh my.
I **know!**
Will **YOU** be this hairy one day?
My mom isn't hairy, so... 50/50 odds?
dana

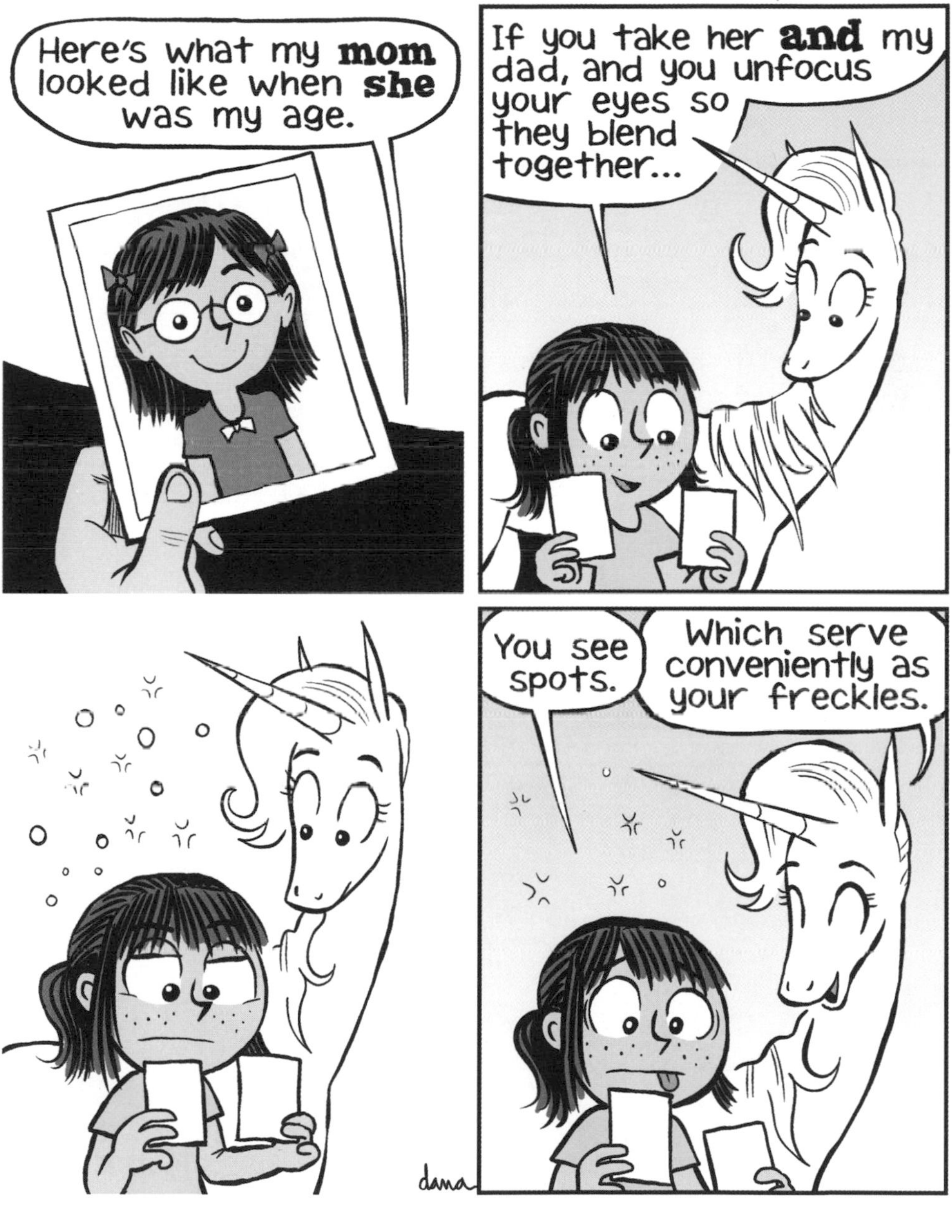
Here's what my **mom** looked like when **she** was my age.
If you take her **and** my dad, and you unfocus your eyes so they blend together...
You see spots.
Which serve conveniently as your freckles.
dana

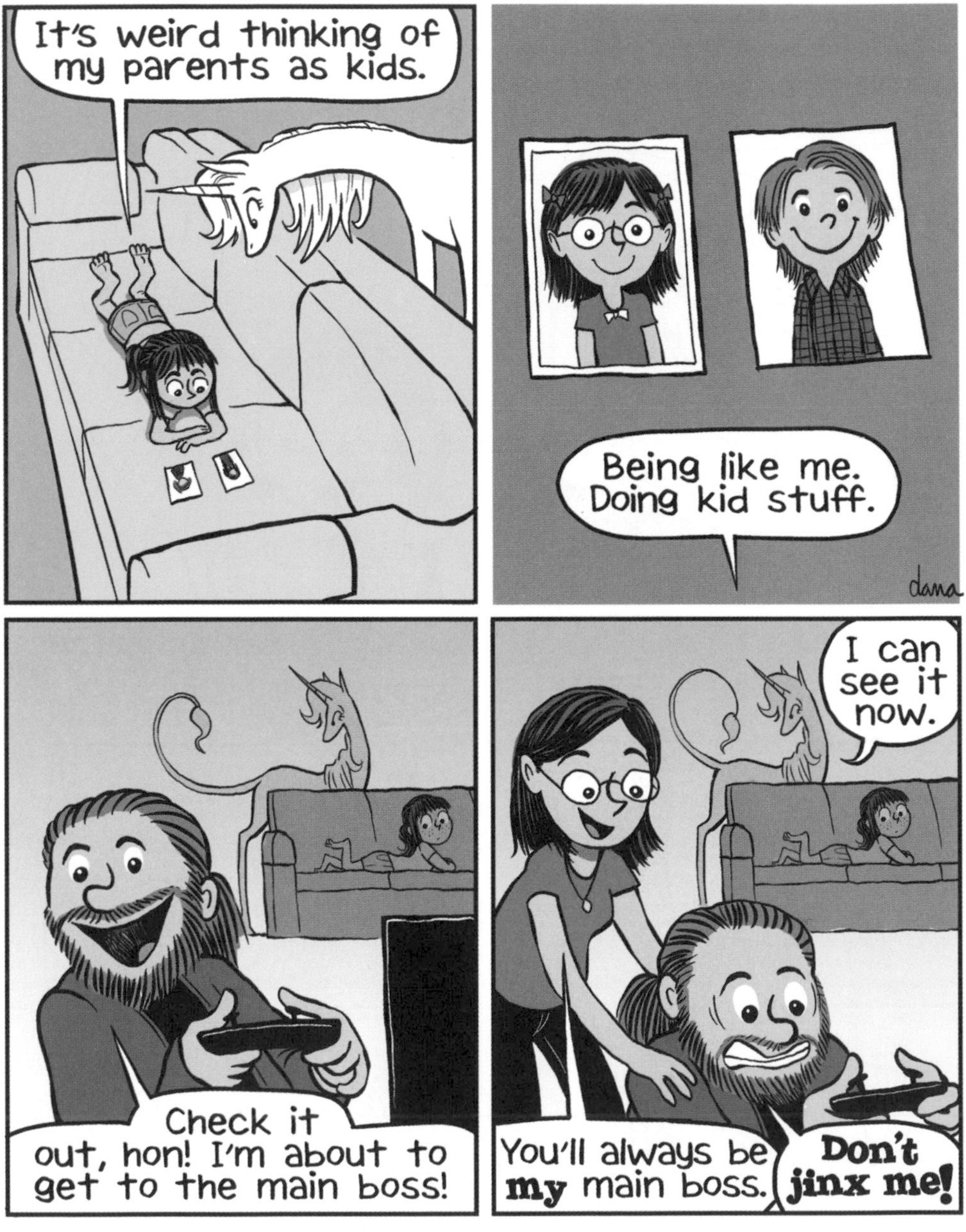
It's weird thinking of my parents as kids.
Being like me. Doing kid stuff.
dana
Check it out, hon! I'm about to get to the main boss!
I can see it now.
You'll always be **my** main boss.
Don't jinx me!

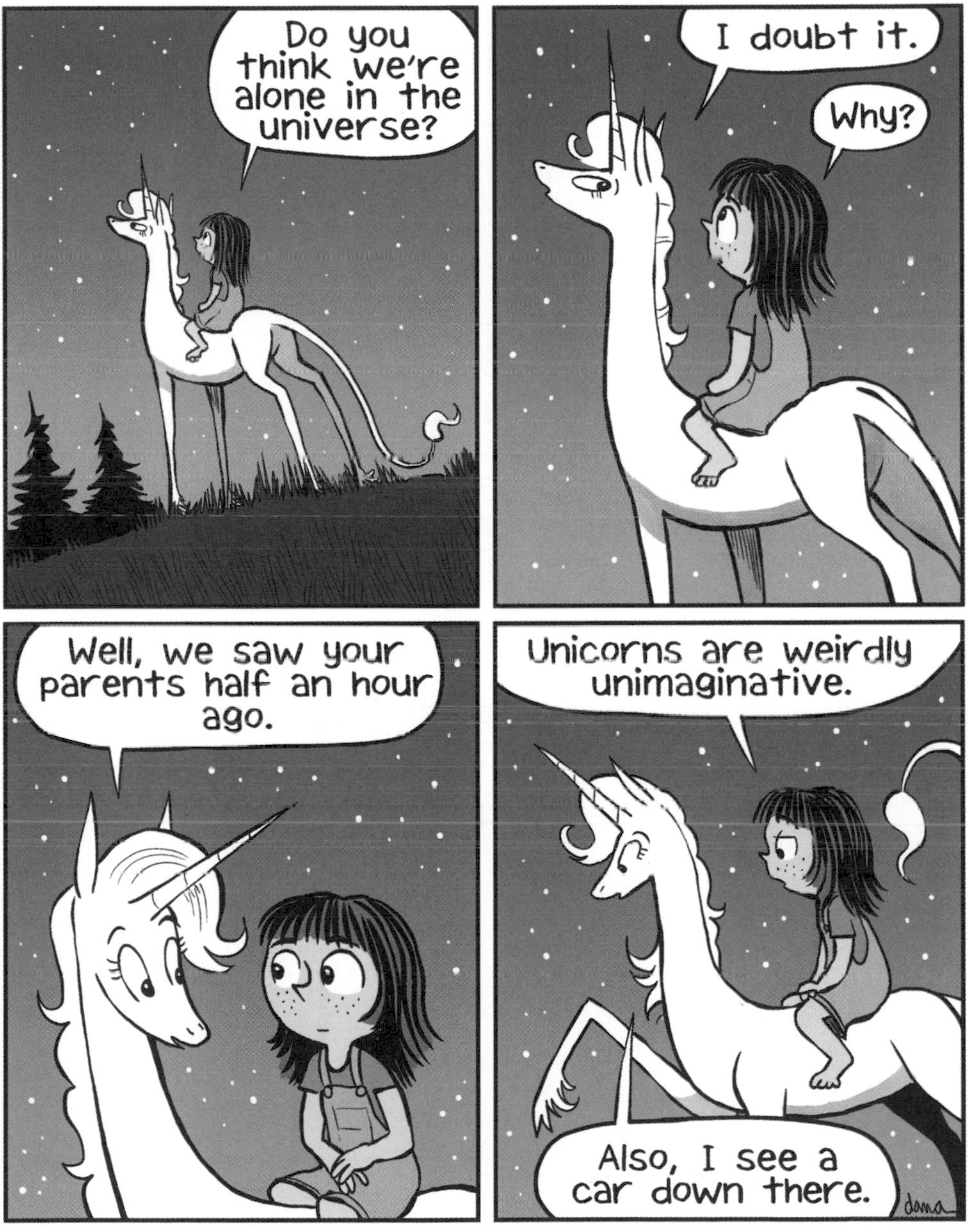
Do you think we're alone in the universe?
I doubt it.
Why?
Well, we saw your parents half an hour ago.
Unicorns are weirdly unimaginative.
Also, I see a car down there.
dana

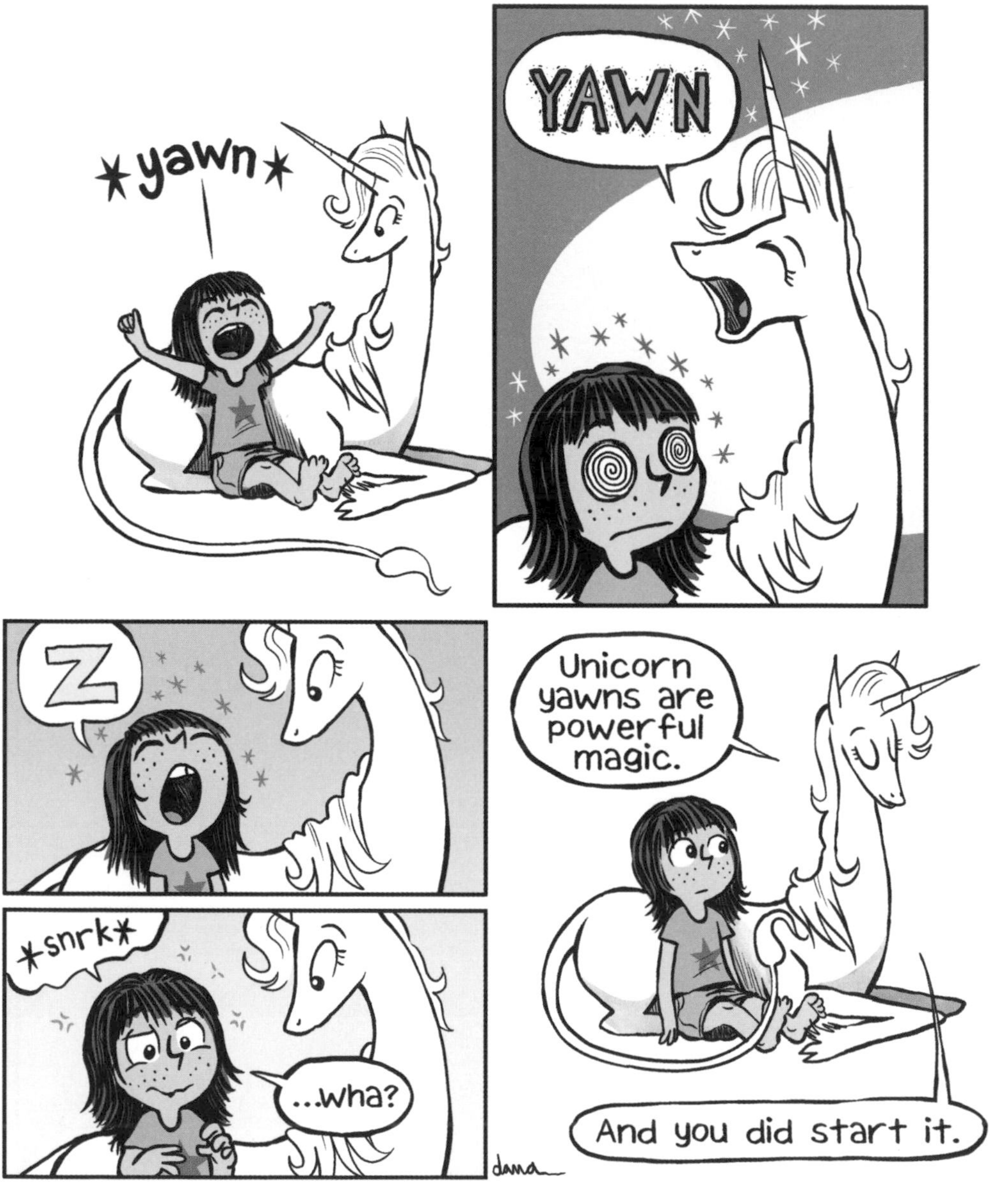
yawn
YAWN
Z
snrk
...wha?
Unicorn yawns are powerful magic.
And you did start it.
dana

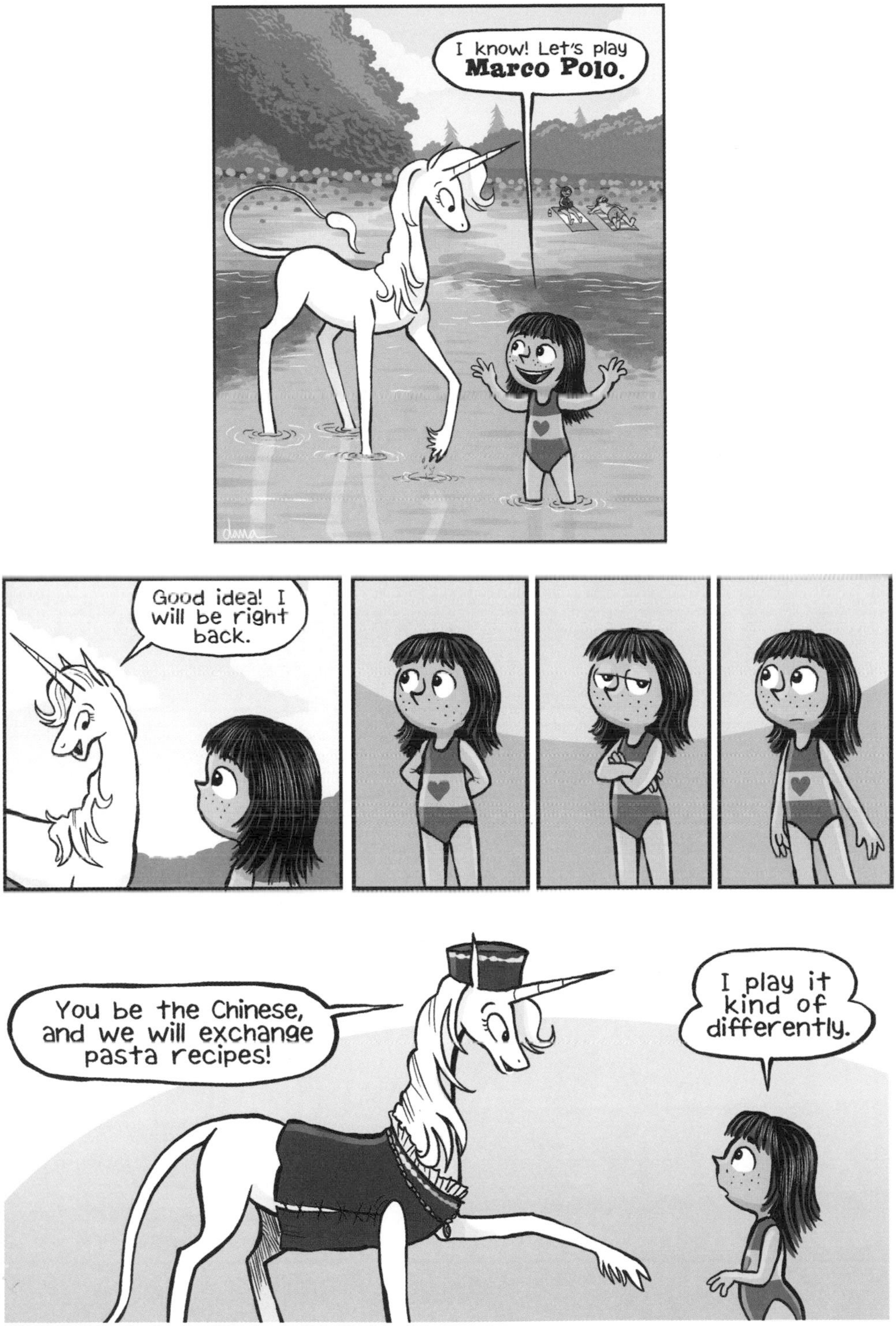
I know! Let's play **Marco Polo.**
Good idea! I will be right back.
You be the Chinese, and we will exchange pasta recipes!
I play it kind of differently.

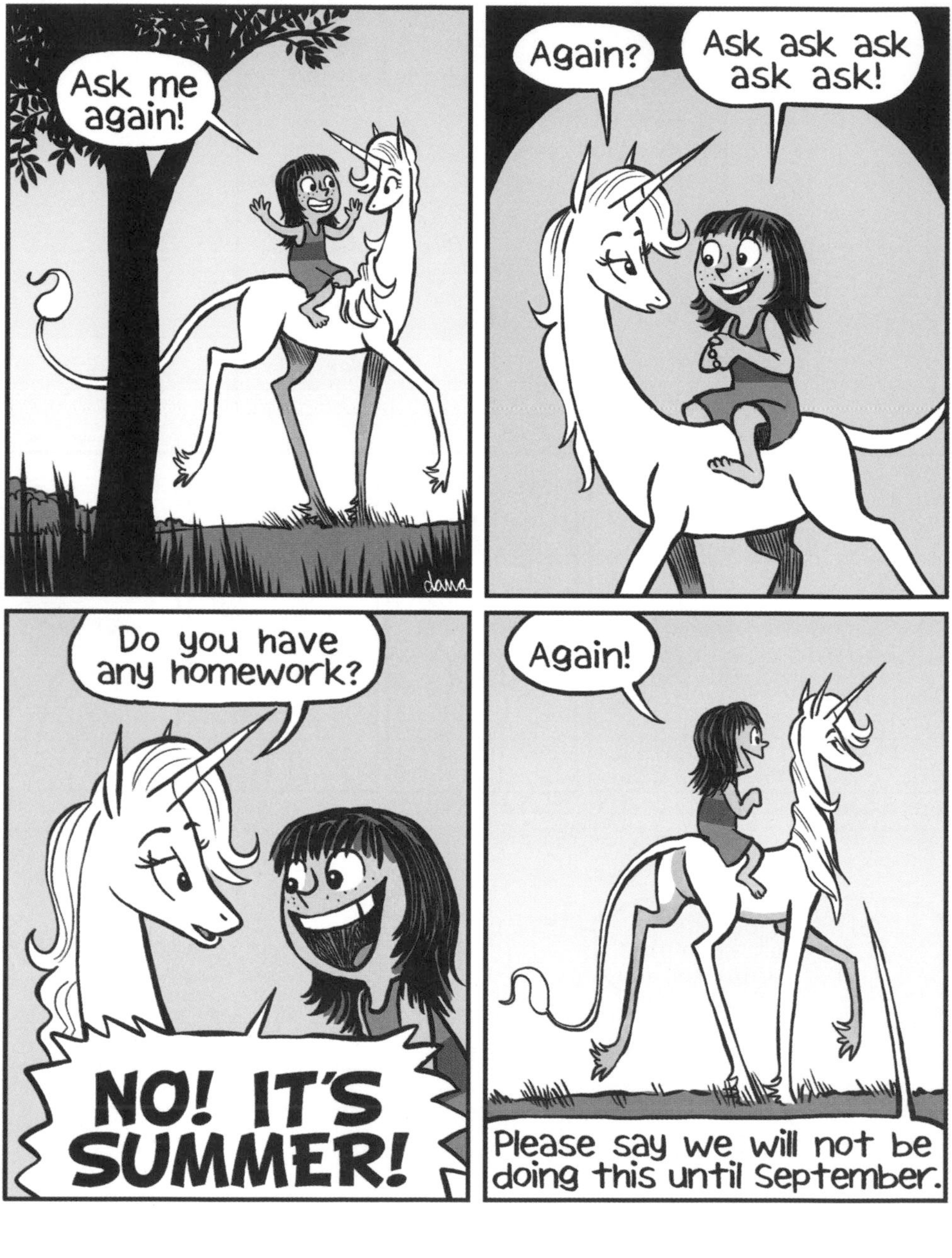
Ask me again!
dana
Again?
Ask ask ask ask ask!
Do you have any homework?
NO! IT'S SUMMER!
Again!
Please say we will not be doing this until September.

How to Draw Expressions

There are a lot of ways to draw expressions! There's really no single right way to draw any of them. But here's some of how I do it.

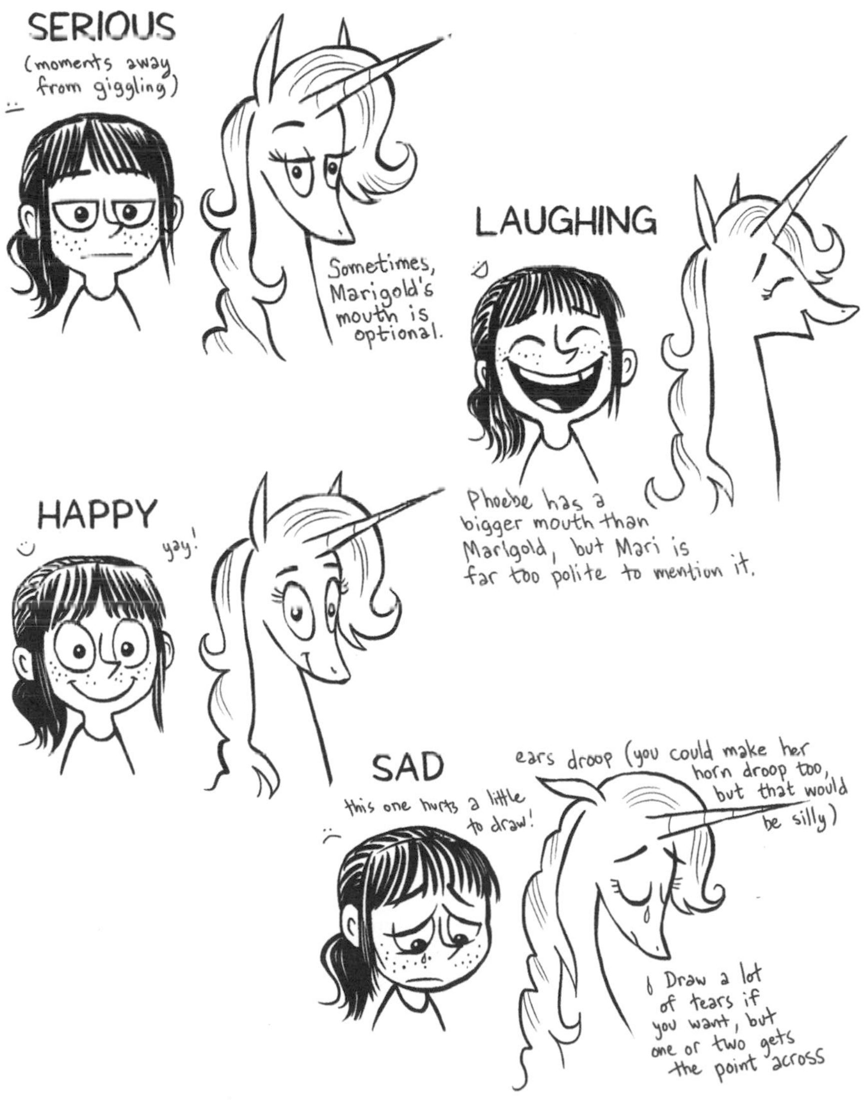
SERIOUS
(moments away from giggling)
Sometimes, Marigold's mouth is optional.
LAUGHING
Phoebe has a bigger mouth than Marigold, but Mari is far too polite to mention it.
HAPPY
yay!
SAD
this one hurts a little to draw!
ears droop (you could make her horn droop too, but that would be silly)
Draw a lot of tears if you want, but one or two gets the point across

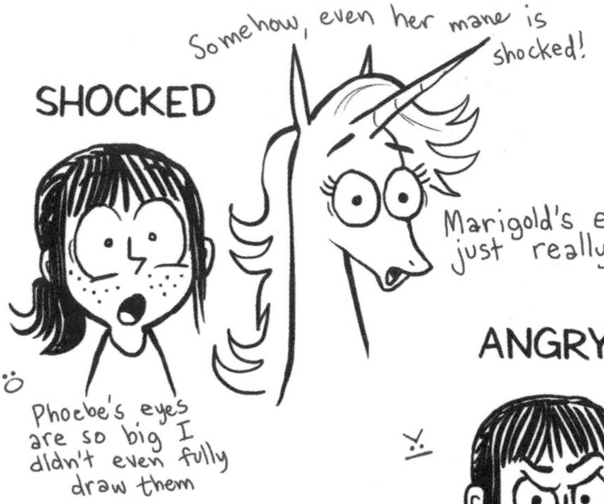
SHOCKED
Somehow, even her mane is shocked!
Marigold's eyes are just really round
ö
Phoebe's eyes are so big I didn't even fully draw them

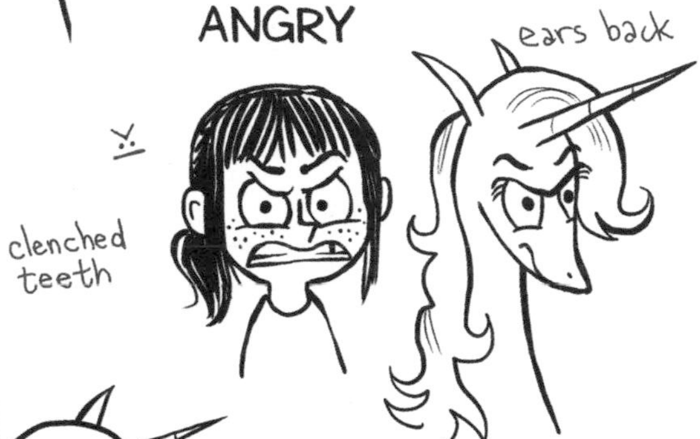
ANGRY
ears back
clenched teeth

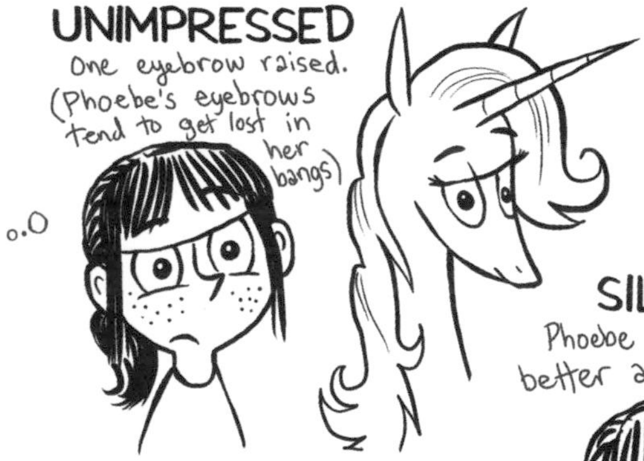
UNIMPRESSED
One eyebrow raised. (Phoebe's eyebrows tend to get lost in her bangs)
o.O

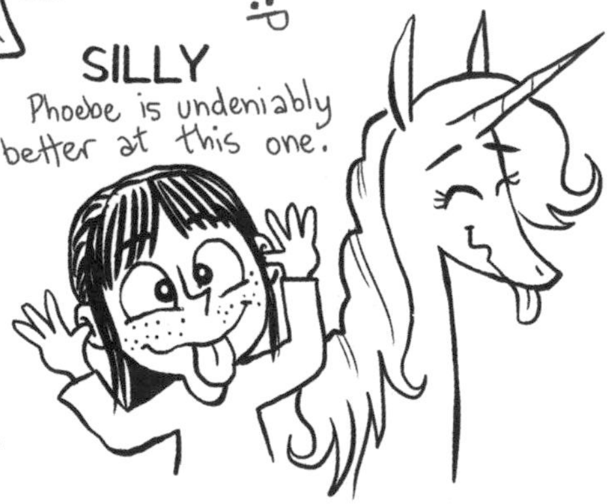
SILLY
Phoebe is undeniably better at this one.

Of course, you can (and should!) also just look at the expressions of people you know, too. Or just find a mirror!

(Fun fact: When I'm drawing facial expressions, I often make those expressions in real life, too, without really meaning to. Sometimes my husband looks at me and just starts giggling.)

Make Sparkly, Colorful Unicorn Poop Cookies!

Marigold is far too refined to ever use the word poop, but Phoebe knows delicious cookies when she tastes them! With an adult's help, make this sweet treat to enjoy with your friends.

INGREDIENTS: Store-bought refrigerated sugar cookie dough, four-pack of food colors, shiny sprinkles, edible glitter

INSTRUCTIONS:

1. Split the dough into four equal pieces and place each one in a separate bowl.
2. Add one food color to each bowl and stir to mix completely with the dough.
3. Refrigerate the bowls for 30 minutes.
4. Take a small piece of dough from each bowl. Roll each one on a counter or cutting board to make a rope-like shape. Then coil the four different colored pieces into a cookie shape until you've used all the dough.
5. Follow the directions on the cookie dough package to bake and cool.
6. Decorate with your favorite colors of sparkly sprinkles and edible glitter.

Makes about 24 cookies.

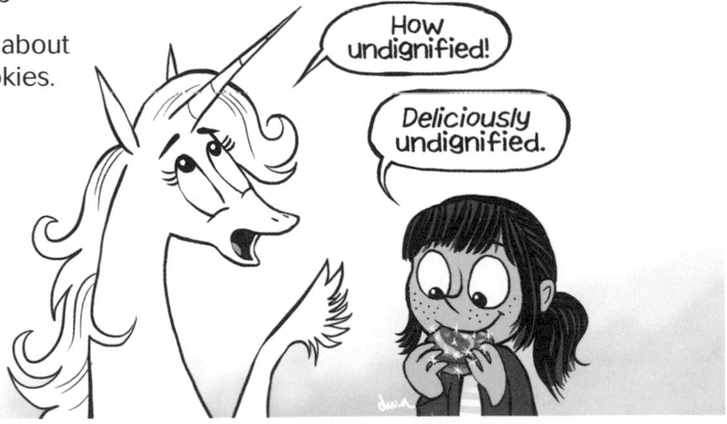
How undignified!
Deliciously undignified.

Make an Origami Figure of Marigold's Far-Removed Relative, the Happy Horse

First, make the Helmet Base.

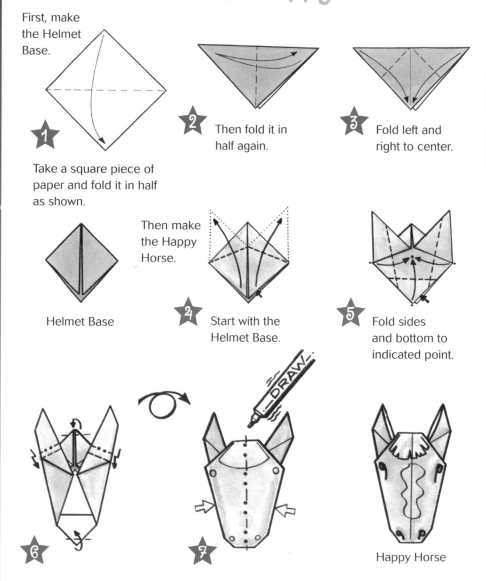

1 Take a square piece of paper and fold it in half as shown.

2 Then fold it in half again.

3 Fold left and right to center.

Helmet Base

Then make the Happy Horse.

4 Start with the Helmet Base.

5 Fold sides and bottom to indicated point.

DRAW

6

7

Happy Horse

Thanks to Jeff Cole, author of *Easy Origami Fold-a-Day Calendar 2015* (Accord Publishing, a division of Andrews McMeel Publishing) for the origami instructions.

Andrews McMeel Publishing
a division of Andrews McMeel Universal
1130 Walnut Street, Kansas City, Missouri 64106

www.andrewsmcmeel.com

19 20 21 22 23 SDB 14 13 12 11 10

ISBN: 978-1-4494-7076-0

Library of Congress Control Number: 2014921935

Made by:
Shenzhen Donnelley Printing Company Ltd.
Address and location of manufacturer:
No. 47, Wuhe Nan Road, Bantian Ind. Zone,
Shenzhen China, 518129
10th Printing—7/8/19

Look for these books!

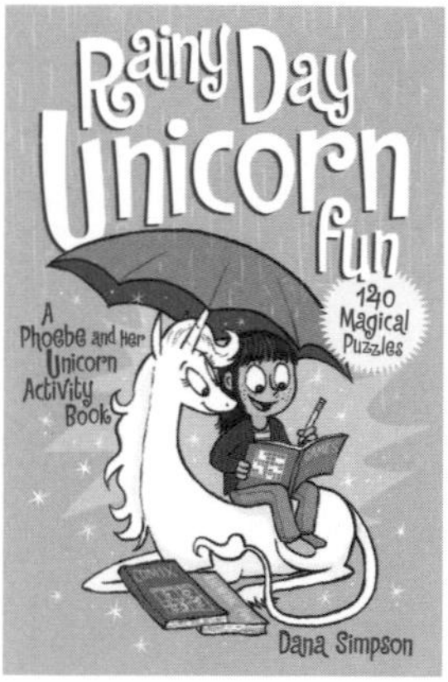
Rainy Day Unicorn fun
140 Magical Puzzles
A Phoebe and Her Unicorn Activity Book
Dana Simpson

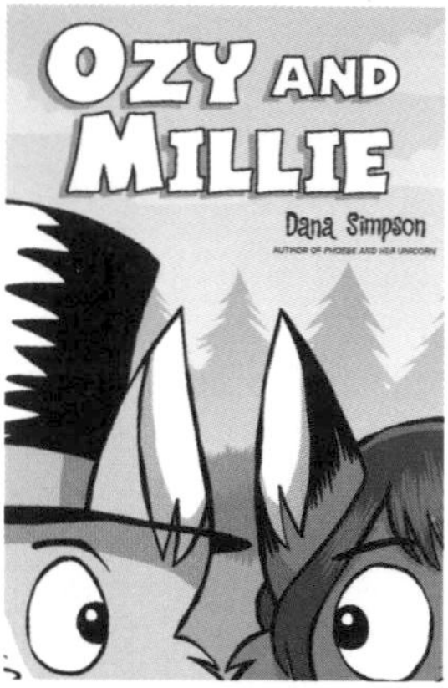
OZY AND MILLIE
Dana Simpson
AUTHOR OF PHOEBE AND HER UNICORN

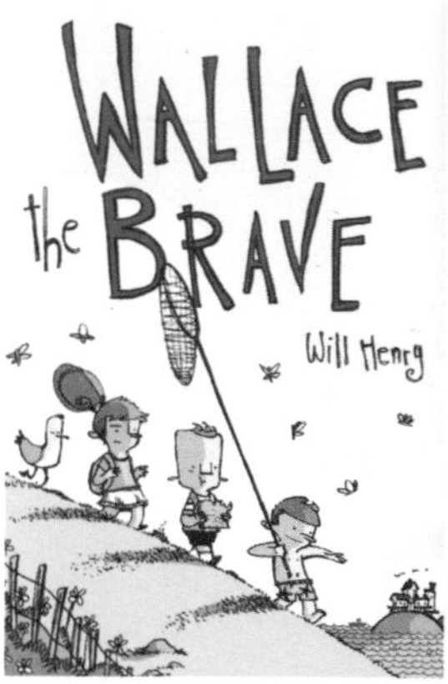
WALLACE the BRAVE
Will Henry

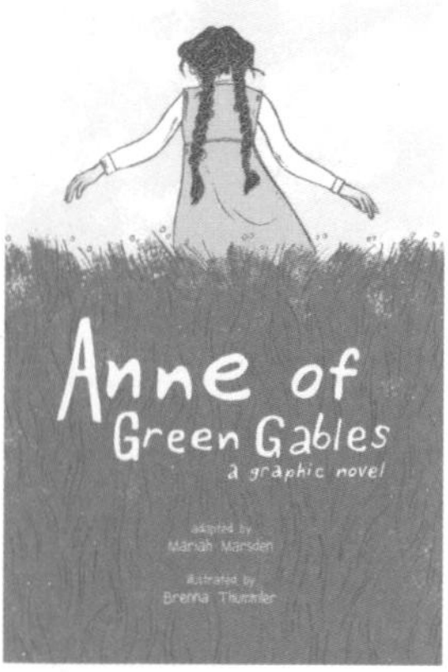
Anne of Green Gables
a graphic novel
adapted by Mariah Marsden
illustrated by Brenna Thummler

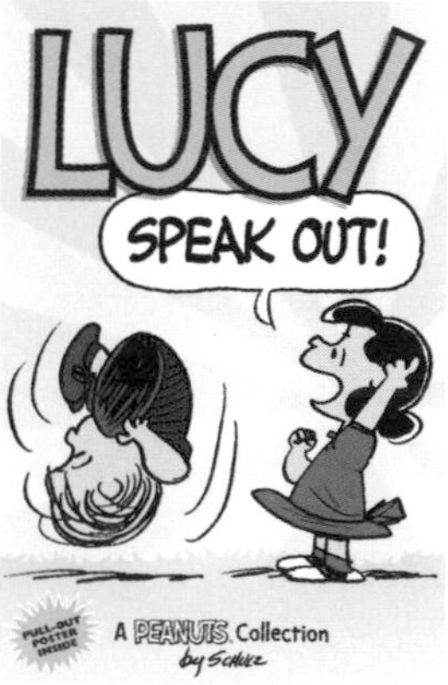
LUCY
SPEAK OUT!
PULL-OUT POSTER INSIDE
A PEANUTS Collection
by Schulz

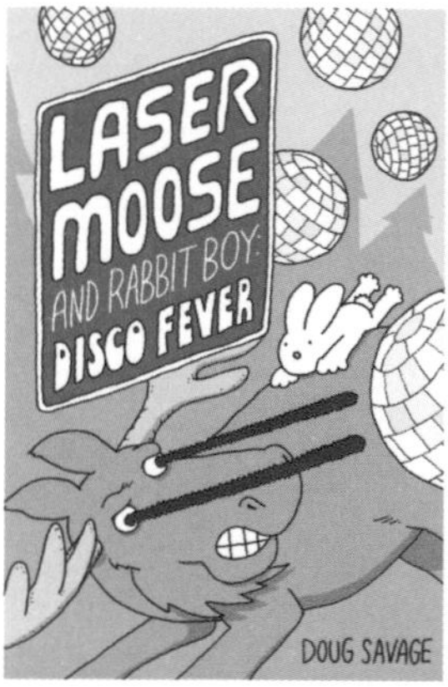
LASER MOOSE AND RABBIT BOY: DISCO FEVER
DOUG SAVAGE

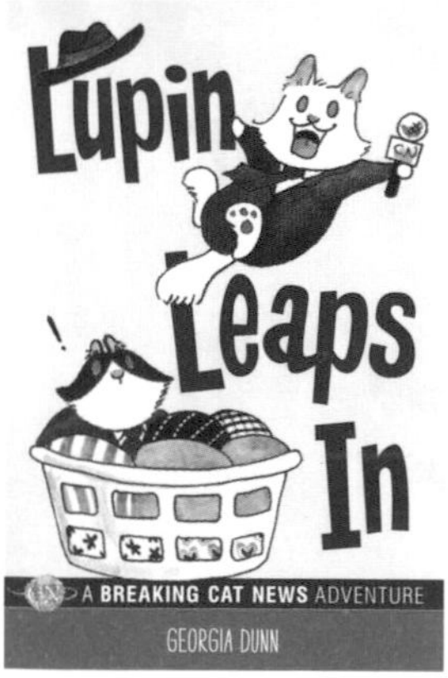
Lupin Leaps In
A BREAKING CAT NEWS ADVENTURE
GEORGIA DUNN

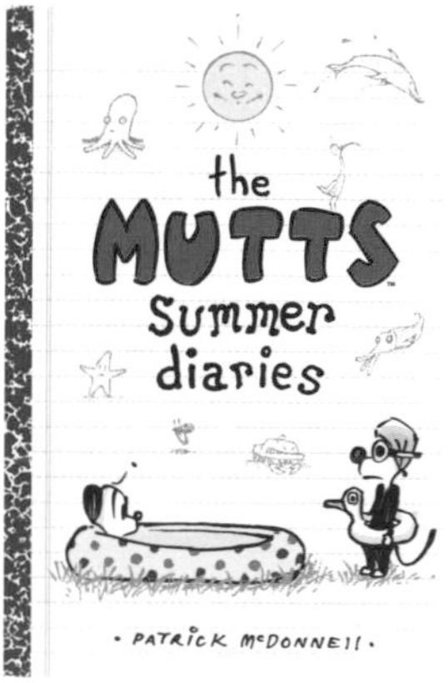
the MUTTS Summer diaries
PATRICK McDONNELL

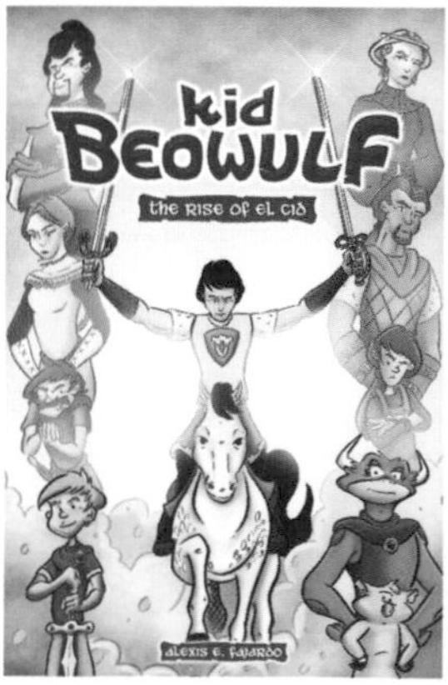
kid BEOWULF
the RISE of EL CID
ALEXIS E. FAJARDO